P9-EFI-614

"What counts for the reader is the ring of authenticity." —*San Francisco Chronicle*

DANIELLE STEEL

CROSSINGS

"Steel is one of the best." —*Los Angeles Times*

"A literary phenomenon . . . ambitious . . . prolific and not to be pigeonholed as one who produces a predictable kind of book."
—*The Detroit News*

"Steel has created characters who live powerful, tumultuous lives."
—*West Coast Review of Books*

"It's hard not to feel like a pawn in a 'mouse and cat' situation with Steel, she is so smooth and so deliberate with her plotting."
—*South Bend Tribune*

"There is a smooth reading style to her writings which makes it easy to forget the time and to keep flipping the pages."
—*The Pittsburgh Press*

Also by Danielle Steel:

KALEIDOSCOPE

FINE THINGS

WANDERLUST

SECRETS

FAMILY ALBUM

CHANGES

THURSTON HOUSE

CROSSINGS

ONCE IN A LIFETIME

A PERFECT STRANGER

REMEMBRANCE

PALOMINO

LOVE

THE RING

LOVING

TO LOVE AGAIN

SUMMER'S END

SEASON OF PASSION

THE PROMISE

NOW AND FOREVER

PASSION'S PROMISE

QUANTITY SALES

Most Dell Books are available at special quantity discounts when purchased in bulk by corporations, organizations, and special-interest groups. Custom imprinting or excerpting can also be done to fit special needs. For details write: Dell Publishing Co., Inc., 666 Fifth Avenue, New York, NY 10103. Attn.: Special Sales Dept.

INDIVIDUAL SALES

Are there any Dell Books you want but cannot find in your local stores? If so, you can order them directly from us. You can get any Dell book in print. Simply include the book's title, author, and ISBN number, if you have it, along with a check or money order (no cash can be accepted) for the full retail price plus $1.50 to cover shipping and handling. Mail to: Dell Readers Service, P.O. Box 5057, Des Plaines, IL 60017.

CROSSINGS

Danielle Steel

A DELL BOOK

Published by
Dell Publishing Co., Inc.
1 Dag Hammarskjold Plaza
New York, New York 10017

Copyright © 1982 by Danielle Steel

All rights reserved. No part of this book may be reproduced or transmitted in any form or by any means, electronic or mechanical, including photocopying, recording, or by any information storage and retrieval system, without the written permission of the Publisher, except where permitted by law. For information address: Delacorte Press, New York, New York.

Dell ® TM 681510, Dell Publishing Co., Inc.

ISBN: 0-440-11585-X

Reprinted by arrangement with Delacorte Press

Printed in the United States of America

One Previous Edition

November 1987

10 9 8 7 6 5 4 3 2 1

WFH

To John,
   Beyond words,
      beyond love,
         beyond anything. . . .

                    d.s.

"Strong people cannot be defeated. . . ."

CROSSINGS

Chapter 1

$\mathcal{T}$he house at 2129 Wyoming Avenue, NW, stood in all its substantial splendor, its gray stone facade handsomely carved and richly ornate, embellished with a large gold crest and adorned with the French flag, billowing softly in a breeze that had come up just that afternoon. It was perhaps the last breeze Washington, D.C., would feel for several months as the summer got under way. It was already June. June of 1939. And the last five years had gone all too quickly for Armand de Villiers, Ambassador of France.

He sat in his office, overlooking the elegant garden, absentmindedly staring at the fountain for a moment, and then dragged his attention back to the mountain of papers on his desk. Despite the rich scent of lilac in the air, there was work to do, too much of it. Especially now. He already knew that he would sit in his office until late that night, as he had for two months now, preparing to return to France. He had known the request to return was coming, and yet when he had been told in April, something inside him had ached for a moment. Even now, there were mixed emotions each time he thought of going home. He had felt the same way when he had left Vienna, London, and San Francisco before that, and other posts previously. But the bond was even stronger here. Armand had a way of establishing roots, of making friends, of falling in love with the places he was assigned to.

That made it difficult to move on. And yet this time he wasn't moving on, he was going home.

Home. It had been so long since he had lived there, and they needed him so badly now. There was tension all over Europe, things were changing everywhere. He often felt that he lived for the daily reports from Paris, which gave him some sense of what was going on. Washington seemed light-years removed from the problems that besieged Europe, from the fears that trembled in the heart of France. They had nothing to fear in this sacred country. But in Europe now, no one felt quite as sure.

Only a year before, everyone in France had been certain war was imminent, although now from what Armand heard, there were many who had buried their fears. But there was no hiding from the truth forever. He had said as much to Liane. When the civil war ended in Spain four months before, it became clear that the Germans were approaching, and their airfield just below Irún brought them within only miles of France. But even with that realization, Armand was aware that there were those who didn't want to see what was going on. In the past six months Paris had been infinitely more relaxed than before, on the surface at least. He had been aware of it himself when he had gone home for Easter, for secret meetings with the Bureau Central, when they told him that his assignment in Washington was at an end.

He had been invited to a constant round of glittering parties, in sharp contrast to the previous summer, before the Munich Accord with Hitler. There had been unbearable tension before that. But then, suddenly it was gone, and in its place was a kind of frenzied animation, and Paris was in her finest form. There were parties, balls, operas, art shows, and galas, as though by keeping busy, and continuing their laughter and their dancing, war would never come for the French. Armand had been annoyed at the frivolous gaiety he had seen among his friends at Easter, and yet he understood that it was their way of hiding from their fears. When he had returned, he and Liane had spoken about it.

"It's as though they're so frightened that they don't want to stop laughing, for fear that if they do, they will cry in terror and run and hide." But their laughter wouldn't stop the war from coming, wouldn't stop Hitler's slow, steady march across Europe. Armand sometimes feared that nothing would stop the man now. He saw Hitler as a terrifying demon, and although there were those in high places who agreed with him, there were others who thought that Armand had become too nervous in the long years of service to his country, and was becoming a frightened old man.

"Is that what living in the States has done to you, old boy?" his closest friend in Paris had teased him. He was from Bordeaux, where he and Armand had grown up together, and the director of three of the biggest banks in France. "Don't be foolish, Armand. Hitler would never touch us."

"The English don't agree with you, Bernard."

"They're all frightened old women too, and besides, they love to play at their war games. It excites them to think of getting into a row with Hitler. They have nothing else to do."

"What nonsense!" Armand had had to control his temper as he listened, but Bernard's wasn't the only voice he heard raised in derision at the English, and he had left Paris almost in a fury at the end of his two-week stay. He expected the Americans to be blind to the threat facing Europe, but he had expected to hear something different in his own country, and he hadn't heard enough. He had his own views on the subject, views of just how serious the threat was becoming, how dangerous Hitler was, and how rapidly disaster could befall them. Or perhaps, he thought on the way home, perhaps Bernard and the others were right. Perhaps he was too frightened, too worried about his country. In a way, going home again might be a good thing. It would bring him closer to the pulse of France.

Liane had taken the news well that they were leaving. She was used to packing up and moving on. And she had listened to his descriptions of the mood in Paris with concern. She was a wise, intelligent woman and had learned much from Armand over the years about the workings of international politics. Indeed, she had learned much from him, anxious to teach her his views, from the very beginning of their marriage. She had been so young and so hungry to learn everything about his career, the countries he was assigned to, the political implications of his many dealings. He smiled to himself as he thought back over the past ten years. She had been a hungry little sponge, soaking up every drop of information, gobbling every morsel, and she had learned well.

She had her own ideas now, and often she did not agree with him, or she was more adamant than he along the same vein. Their most furious battle had been only a few weeks before in late May, over the SS *St. Louis,* a ship carrying 937 Jews out of Hamburg, with Joseph Goebbels's blessing, and bound for Havana, where the refugees were refused entry, and where it would seem that they would perish as the boat languished outside the port. Others engaged in frantic efforts to find a home for the refugees, lest they be doomed to return to Hamburg and whatever fate might await them there. Liane herself had spoken to the President, drawing on her acquaintance with him, but to no avail. The Americans had refused to take them, and Armand had watched Liane collapse in tears as she realized all of her efforts, and those of countless others, had been in vain. There were messages from the ship, promising mass suicide rather than agreeing to return to the port from whence they had come. And at last, mercifully, France, England, Holland, and Belgium had agreed to take them, but still the battle between Armand and Liane had raged on. For the first time in her life she had been disappointed in her own country. Her fury knew no bounds. And although Armand sympathized with her, he insisted that there were reasons why Roosevelt had refused to take the refugees. It made her even angrier that Armand was willing to accept Roosevelt's decision. She felt betrayed by her own people. America was the land of rich and plenty, the home of the brave, land of the free. How could Armand excuse their failure to accept those people? It wasn't a matter of judgment, he attempted to explain to her, but of accepting that at times governments made harsh decisions. The important thing to acknowledge was that the refugees were safe. It had taken Liane days to calm down after that, and even then she had engaged in a lengthy and almost hostile discussion with the First Lady at a ladies' lunch. Mrs. Roosevelt had been sympathetic to Liane's anger. She too had been anguished over the fate of the passengers of the *St. Louis*, but she had been helpless to convince her husband to change his mind. The United States had to respect its quotas, and the 937 German-Jewish refugees exceeded the quota for the year. Mrs. Roosevelt reminded Liane again that all had ended well for the refugees. But nonetheless it was an event that had impressed Liane with the gravity of these people's plight in Europe, and suddenly she had gained a new understanding of what was happening far from the peaceful life of Washington diplomatic dinners. It made Liane anxious to return with Armand to France.

"You're not sorry to be leaving your country again, my love?" He had eyed her gently over a quiet dinner at home, after the incident of the *St. Louis* had finally died down.

She had shaken her head. "I want to know what's happening in Europe, Armand. Here, I feel so far away from everything." She had smiled at him then, loving him more than ever. They had shared an extraordinarily happy ten years. "Do you really think war will come soon?"

"Not for your country, my darling." He always reminded her that she was an American. He had always thought it important that she retain a sense of her own allegiance, so that she would not become totally swallowed up by his views and his ties to France. She was a separate entity, after all, and she had a right to her own allegiances and opinions, and thus far they had never interfered with his own. Now and then there was a raging battle, an outburst of disagreement between them, but it seemed to keep the relationship healthy and he didn't mind. He respected her views as much as his own, and he admired the zeal with which she stood up for what she believed in. She was a strong woman with an admirable mind. He had respected her from the moment he first knew her, in San Francisco, as a girl of just fifteen. She had been a magical child, with an almost ethereal golden beauty, and yet after years of living alone with her father, Harrison Crockett, she had gained a range of knowledge and wisdom unusual in such a young girl.

Armand could still remember the first time he had seen her, in a white linen summer dress and a big straw hat, wandering through the Consulate garden in San Francisco, saying nothing as she listened to the "grown-ups," and then turning to him, with a shy smile, to say something in flawless French about the roses. Her father had been so proud of her.

Armand smiled at the distant memory of her father. Harrison Crockett had been a most unusual man. Stern, and at the same time gentle, aristocratic, difficult, handsome, obsessed with his privacy and protecting his only child, and a brilliant success in shipping. He was a man who had done much with his life.

They had met shortly after arriving in San Francisco, at a deadly little dinner arranged by the previous consul before he left San Francisco for Beirut. Armand recalled that he knew Crockett had been invited, but was almost certain he wouldn't come. Most of the time Harrison Crockett hid behind the walls of his elegant brick fortress on Broadway, looking out over the bay. His brother, George, was far more inclined to go to parties, and was one of the most popular bachelors in San Francisco, not so much for his charm as for his connections and his brother's enormous success. But much to everyone's amazement Harrison had come to the dinner. He had spoken little and left early, but before he did, he had been very pleasant to Odile, Armand's wife. So much so, that she had insisted on inviting him and his daughter for tea. Harrison had spoken of the girl to Odile, and had been particularly proud of his daughter's mastery of the

French language, and with a proud smile, he had said that she was "a very remarkable girl," a comment they had both smiled at as Odile relayed it to Armand.

"At least he has one soft spot. He looks every bit as ruthless as they say he is."

But Odile had disagreed. "I think you're wrong, Armand. I think he's very lonely. And he's absolutely mad about the girl." Odile hadn't been far off the mark. Shortly after, they heard the story of how he had lost his wife, a beautiful girl of nineteen, whom he had worshiped. He had been too busy with his shipping empire before that, but apparently once he turned his mind to marriage, he had chosen well.

Arabella Dillingham Crockett had been brilliant as well as beautiful, and together she and Harrison had given some of the city's most devastating balls. She had floated through the mansion he'd built for her, looking like a fairy princess, wearing the rubies he brought her from the Orient, diamonds almost as large as eggs, and tiaras, made especially for her at Cartier, on her golden curls. Their first child was heralded with the same excitement as the Second Coming, but despite the accoucheur Harrison brought from England, and two midwives from the East, Arabella died in childbirth, leaving him widowed with an infant, a girl child in her image, whom he worshiped as he once had his wife. For the first ten years after his wife's death, he never left his house, except of course to go to his office. Crockett Shipping was one of the largest shipping lines in the States, with ships spread out all over the Orient, carrying cargo, as well as two extraordinarily handsome liners that carried passengers to Hawaii and Japan. In addition, Crockett had passenger ships in South America, and some that traveled profitably up and down the West Coast of the United States.

Harrison Crockett's only interests were his ships and his daughter. He saw a great deal of his brother, as they ran the empire together, but for a decade Harrison saw almost none of his old friends. Then at last he took Liane to Europe for a vacation, showing her all the wonders of Paris and Berlin and Rome and Venice, and when they returned at the end of the summer, he began to include his friends in his life again. Gone was the era of the grand parties in the mansion on Broadway, but he had come to realize how lonely his child was, and how badly she needed the company of other children, other people, and so Harrison slowly opened his doors again. What ensued were activities that centered only around his daughter: puppet shows, visits to the theater, and trips to Lake Tahoe, where he bought a handsome summer home. Harrison Crockett lived only to please and protect and cherish Liane Alexandra Arabella.

She was named after two dead grandmothers and her mother, three lost beauties, and somehow she managed to combine the charm and loveliness of all three. People marveled when they met her. Despite the sumptuous existence she led, there was no sign of it having affected her. She was simple, straightforward, quiet, and wise beyond her years, from spending so many years dining alone with her father, and sometimes her uncle, listening to them talk business and explain to her the business of shipping, and the politics of the countries into whose ports their ships sailed. In truth, she was happier with her father than she was with other children, and as she grew older she went everywhere with him, and eventually to the Consulate of France, on a spring day in 1922, to have tea.

The De Villierses fell in love with her at once, and what followed as a result was a bond between the De Villierses and Crocketts that flourished over the next three years. The four of them often took trips together. Armand and Odile went to stay at the handsome estate in Lake Tahoe, they traveled on one of his ships to Hawaii with Liane for a vacation, and eventually Odile even took Liane to France. Odile became for her almost a second mother, and it was a comfort to Harrison to see Liane so happy and so well guided by a woman he respected and liked. By then Liane was almost eighteen.

It was the following autumn, when Liane entered Mills

College, that Odile began to feel poorly, complaining of a constant backache, an inability to eat, frequent fevers, and finally a frightening cough that after several months refused to disappear. At first the doctors insisted that they could find nothing, and it was suggested quietly to Armand that Odile was simply homesick for her country, and he might consider sending her back to France. But vapors of that sort were unlike her, and he persisted in having her see doctors all over town. He wanted her to go to New York to see someone Harrison had recommended, but before the scheduled trip, it became obvious that she was far too sick to go. It was then that they finally discovered, in a brief and depressing operation, that Odile de Villiers was riddled with cancer. They closed her up and told Armand the news, which he shared the next day with Harrison Crockett as tears streamed down his face.

"I can't live without her, Harry. . . . I can't. . . ." Armand had stared at him in bereft horror as Harrison nodded slowly, tears in his own eyes. He remembered his own pain of eighteen years before only too well. And ironically, Armand was exactly the same age Harrison had been when he lost Arabella, he was forty-three years old.

But Armand and Odile had been married for twenty years, and the prospect of living on without her was almost more than he could bear. Unlike Harrison, they had no children. They had wanted two or three from the beginning, but Odile had never succeeded in getting pregnant, and they had resigned themselves long since to the absence of children in their lives. In fact, Armand had admitted to Odile once, he liked things better as they were. He didn't have to compete for her attention, and there had remained a honeymoon atmosphere between them for the past twenty years. And now, suddenly, their entire world was shattering around them.

Although at first Odile didn't know that she had cancer, and Armand fought valiantly to keep it from her, she very soon understood the truth and that the end was near. And at last, in March, she died as Armand held her in his arms.

Liane had come to see her that afternoon, carrying a bouquet of yellow roses. She sat by her bedside for hours, more for the comfort Odile gave her than any that she was able to give. Odile had exuded an aura of almost saintly resignation, and she was determined to leave Liane with her love and a last tender touch. As Liane had faltered for a moment in the doorway, fighting back the sobs that would come as soon as she left the house, Odile had looked at her with strength in her eyes for just a moment.

"Take care of Armand for me when I am gone, Liane. You've taken good care of your father." Odile had come to know him well, and knew that Liane had kept him from growing hardened or bitter. She had a gentle touch that softened every heart she came near. "Armand loves you," she had said, smiling, "and he will need you and your father when I am gone." She spoke of her death as if it were a trip she was taking. Liane had tried to deny to herself the truth about this beloved woman's condition. But there was no denying it to Odile. She wanted them all to face it, especially her husband, and then Liane. She wanted them to be prepared. Armand would try to avoid the truth by talking to her of trips to the seashore, to Biarritz, which they had loved when they were young, a cruise on a yacht along the coast of France perhaps the next summer, and another journey to Hawaii on one of the Crockett ships. But again and again she forced them all to face what was coming, what she knew, and what finally came that night after she had seen Liane for the last time.

Odile had insisted that she wanted to be buried where she was, and not sent back to France. She didn't want Armand making that dismal trip alone. Both of her parents were dead, as well as his. She left with no regrets, except that she had had no children who would care for Armand. She had put that trust in Liane.

The first months were a nightmare for Armand. He managed to carry on his work, but barely more than that. And

despite his loss, he was expected, to some extent, to entertain visiting dignitaries to San Francisco with small diplomatic dinners. It was Liane who did everything for him, as
she had for so long for her father. She carried a double responsibility then, despite the excellent staff at the Consulate
of France. It was Liane who oversaw everything for Armand.
That summer, her father scarcely saw her at Lake Tahoe,
and she refused the offer of a trip to France. She had a mission to attend to, a promise she had made, which she fully
intended to live up to—an awesome responsibility for a girl
of nineteen.

For a time Harrison wondered if there was something more
to her work and efforts, and yet after watching Liane more
closely for a time, he was certain there was not. And in a
way, he knew that what she did for Armand helped her cope
with her own sense of loss. She had been deeply stricken by
the death of Odile. Never having known her own mother,
there had always been a hunger in her soul for a woman she
could relate to, someone whom she could talk to in a way
she couldn't talk to her father, her uncle, or their friends.
As a child, there had been governesses and cooks and maids,
but few friends, and the women Harrison dallied with occasionally over the years never saw the inside of his home, or
met his child. He kept all of that far, far from Liane. So it
had been Odile who had filled that void, and then left it,
gaping open, a dull ache that never seemed to dim, except
when she was doing something for Armand. It was almost a
way of being with Odile again.

In a sense both Armand and Liane were in shock until the
end of the summer. Odile had been dead for six months by
then, and they both realized one September afternoon, as
they sat in the garden at the Consulate, looking at the roses
and speaking of Odile, that neither of them was crying as
they spoke of her. Armand even told a funny story at Odile's
expense and Liane laughed. They had survived it. They
would live through it, each one because of the other. Ar-

mand had reached out a hand and taken Liane's long, delicate fingers in his own and held them. The tears sparkled then in his eyes as he looked at her.

"Thank you, Liane."

"For what?" She tried to pretend she didn't know, but she did. He had done as much for her. "Don't be silly."

"I'm not. I'm very grateful to you."

"We've needed each other for the past six months." She said it openly and directly, her hand comfortable in his. "Life is going to be very different without her." It already was, for them both.

He nodded, thinking quietly to himself over the past six months. "It is."

Liane went up to Tahoe for two weeks then, before going back to college, and her father was relieved to see her. He still worried about her a great deal, and he was still concerned about her helping Armand constantly. He himself was only too aware that it was too much like her constant devotion to him. And Odile de Villiers had long since convinced Harrison that Liane needed other pastimes than caring for a lonely man. She was a young girl, and there was much that she should do. The year before, she had been scheduled to make her debut, but when Odile fell ill, she had refused.

Harrison brought it up to Liane again in Tahoe, saying that she had mourned for long enough and that the debutante parties would do her good. She insisted that they seemed silly to her, and wasteful somehow, all that money spent on dresses and parties and dances. Harrison stared at her in amazement. She was one of the richest young women in California, heiress to the Crockett Shipping lines, and it seemed extraordinary to him that the thought of the expense should even cross her mind.

In October, when she went back to Mills, she had less time to help Armand with his dinner parties, but he was on his feet again and fending well for himself, although he still felt Odile's absence sorely, as he confessed to Harrison when they had lunch together at his club.

"I won't lie to you, Armand." Harrison looked at him over a glass of Haut-Brion '27. "You'll feel it for a long time. Forever. But not in the same way you did at first. You'll feel it in a moment . . . a remembered word . . . something she wore . . . a perfume . . . But you won't wake up every morning, feeling as though there's a two hundred thousand pound weight on your chest, the way you did at first." He still remembered it all too clearly as he finished his wine and the waiter poured him a second glass. "Thank God, you'll never feel quite that agony again."

"I would have been lost without your daughter." Armand smiled a gentle smile. There was no way to repay the kindness, to let his friend know how much the child had helped him, or how dear she was to him.

"She loved you both dearly, Armand. And it helped her get over losing Odile." He was a wise and canny man, and he sensed something then, even before Armand did, but he said nothing. He had a feeling that neither of them knew how much they needed each other, with or without Odile. Something very powerful had grown between them in the past six months, almost as though they were connected, as though they anticipated each other's needs. He had noticed it when Armand came up to Tahoe for the weekend, but he had said nothing. He knew that his instincts would have frightened them both, especially Armand, who might feel that he had in some way betrayed Odile.

"Is Liane very excited about the parties?" Armand was amused at Harrison's excitement. He knew that Liane didn't really care a great deal. She was making her debut more to please her father, being well aware of what was expected, and dutiful above all. He liked that about her. She was not dutiful in a blind, stupid way, but because she cared about other people. It was important to her to do the right thing, because she knew how other people felt about it. She would have preferred not have come out at all, yet she knew that her father would have been bitterly disappointed, so she went along with it for him.

"To tell you the truth"—Harrison sighed and sat back in his seat—"I wouldn't admit it to her, but I think she's outgrown it." She suddenly seemed much more grown-up than nineteen. She had grown up a great deal in the past year, and she had been called upon to act and think as a woman for so long that it was difficult to imagine her with the giggling girls going to a grand ball for the first time.

And when the moment came, the truth of her father's words was more evident than ever. The others came out, blushing, nervous, frightened, excited to the point of being shrill, and when Liane sailed out slowly on her father's arm at her ball, she looked nothing less than regal in a white satin dress, her shimmering golden hair caught up in a little basket of woven pearls. She had the bearing of a young queen on her consort's arm, and her blue eyes danced with an inimitable fire as Armand watched her with a stirring in his soul.

The party Harrison gave for her was the most dazzling party of all. It was held at the Palace on Market Street, with chauffeured limousines pulling up directly to the inner court. Two orchestras had been hired to play all night, and the champagne had been sent from France. Liane wore a white velvet gown, trimmed with white ermine in delicate ropes all around the hem. The gown, like the champagne, had been sent from France.

"Tonight, my little friend, you look absolutely like a queen." Liane and Armand circled the room slowly in a waltz. He was there as Harrison's guest. Liane was escorted by the son of one of her father's oldest friends, but she found him stupid and boring and was pleased with the reprieve.

"I feel a little silly in this dress," she had said, grinning. For an instant she had looked fifteen again, and suddenly, with a quick shaft of pain, Armand had longed for Odile. He wanted her to see Liane too, to share the moment, drink the champagne . . . but the moment passed, and he turned his attention to Liane again.

"It's a pretty party, though, isn't it? Daddy went to so much trouble . . ." she said, but was thinking "so much expense." It always irked her a little, made her feel a little guilty, but he supported worthwhile causes too, and if it made him happy, then why not. "Have you enjoyed yourself, Armand?"

"Never more than at this exact moment." He smiled, at his most courtly, and she laughed at the chivalry, so unusual from him. Usually he treated her like a child, or at least a younger sister or a favorite niece.

"That doesn't even sound like you."

"Oh, doesn't it? And what exactly do you mean by that? Am I usually rude to you?"

"No, you usually tell me that I haven't given the butler the right set of fish forks from the safe . . . or the Limoges is too formal for lunch . . . or—"

"Stop! I can't bear it. Do I say all that to you?"

"Not lately, although I confess, I miss it. Are you getting on all right?"

"Not half as well lately. They don't even know which Limoges I mean, with you . . ." For a moment he wondered at what she had been saying. What she had been describing sounded like a marriage, but he couldn't have been like that with her . . . or could he? Was he so accustomed to Odile knowing all, that he had simply expected Liane to step into her shoes? How extraordinary of him, and how totally insensitive, but how much more extraordinary still that Liane had actually done all that she had for all those months. Suddenly it made him realize more than ever that he had missed her terribly since she had turned her attention back to school, not so much for the selection of the right Limoges, but because it had been so comforting to talk to her after a luncheon, or a dinner party, or in the morning, on the phone.

"A penny for your thoughts." She was teasing him a little, and his hand felt suddenly clumsy on her tiny waist.

"I was thinking that you were quite right. I have been very rude."

"Don't be ridiculous. I'll come back and help now, as soon as all this debutante nonsense is over with next week."

"Haven't you anything better to do?" He seemed surprised. As lovely as she was, there had to be a dozen suitors waiting in the wings. "No boyfriends, no great loves?"

"I think I'm immune."

"Now, that's an intriguing thought. A vaccination you've had, perhaps?" He teased and the music changed, but they stayed on the floor as Harrison Crockett watched. He was not displeased. "Tell me about this fascinating immunity of yours, Miss Crockett."

She sounded matter-of-fact as they danced. "I think I've lived alone with my father for too long. I know what men are like."

Armand laughed aloud. "Now, that's a shocking statement!"

"No, it's not." But she laughed too then. "I just meant that I know what it's like to run his house, pour his coffee in the morning, walk on tiptoe when he comes home from the office in a bad mood. It makes it difficult to take any of the young cubs seriously, they're so full of romance and ridiculous ideas. Half the time they have no idea what they're saying, they've never read a newspaper, they don't know the difference between Tibet and Timbuktu. And ten years from now, they'll come home from the office just as disagreeable as Daddy, and they'll snap at their wives over breakfast in just the same way. It's hard to listen to all that romantic gibberish and not laugh, that's all. I know what comes later." She smiled up at him in a matter-of-fact way.

"You're right, you've seen too much." And he was sorry really. He remembered all the romantic "gibberish" he had shared with Odile, when she was twenty-one and he was twenty-three. They had believed every word they'd said and it had carried them for a long time, through hard times and into rugged, ghastly countries, through disappointments and a war. In a way, because of her life with her father, Liane had lost an important piece of her youth. But undoubtedly, in time, someone would come along, perhaps someone not quite so young as the rest, and she would fall in love, and then the complaints over the morning coffee would be outweighed by what she felt, and she would be carried off on her own cloud of dreams.

"Now what are you thinking?"

"That one of these days you'll fall in love, and it'll change all that."

"Maybe." But she sounded both unconvinced and unconcerned. The dance ended and Armand escorted her back to her friends.

But something strange had happened between them during the weeks of her debut. When Armand saw her again, he looked at her differently than he had before. She seemed more womanly to him all of a sudden, and it didn't really make sense to him. But the rest of the girls at the parties had all been so girlish, such children. In comparison, Liane was so much more grown-up, so much more poised. He felt suddenly awkward with her, less comfortable than he had before. He had taken her for granted for a long time, assumed somehow that she was just a very charming child. But on her twentieth birthday she looked more mature than ever, in a mauve moiré gown that turned her hair to spun gold and turned her eyes to violet as she smiled at him.

Her birthday came just before the summer, and Armand was almost relieved when she went to Lake Tahoe for the summer months. She was no longer helping him at the Consulate, he was on his feet now, and he didn't want to take advantage of her. He saw Liane only when her father gave a dinner party, which was still very rare. And by sheer force of will Armand managed to stay away from Lake Tahoe until the end of the summer, when Harrison absolutely insisted that he come up for the Labor Day weekend, and when he saw her, he sensed instantly what Harrison had known for so long. He was deeply and passionately in love with the girl he had known since she was scarcely more than a child. It had been a year and a half since Odile died, and although he still missed her terribly, his thoughts were now invaded constantly by Liane. He found himself staring at her all through the weekend, and when they danced on a warm summer night, he led her back to the table quickly, as though he could not bear to be that close to her without pulling her deeper into his arms. And oblivious of what he felt, she cavorted near him on the beach, her long, sensuous limbs cast across a deck chair on the sand. She rattled on as she had in years past, and told him funny stories, and she was more enchanting than ever, but as the weekend drew to a close, she began to sense his mood and his eyes upon her, and she grew quieter, as though being drawn slowly into the same spell.

When they all returned to town, and Liane to college, Armand fought himself for several weeks and then finally, unable to bear it any longer, he called her and berated himself afterward for doing so. He had just called to say hello and see how she was, but she sounded strangely subdued when he called her, and he worried instantly that something might be wrong. Nothing was, she assured him in gentle tones, but she was feeling something she didn't quite understand and wasn't sure how to handle. She felt guilty toward Odile, and unable to talk to her father about the confusing emotions she felt. She was falling in love with Armand as desperately as he was falling in love with her. He was forty-five years old and she was not yet twenty-one, he was the widower of a woman she had loved and respected deeply, and she still remembered her parting words: "Take care of Armand for me . . . Liane . . . he will need you . . ." But he didn't need her that much anymore, and surely Odile had never meant for Liane to take care of him like that.

What ensued was an agonizing three months. Liane could barely keep her mind on her studies, and Armand thought he would go mad at his desk. They met again at a Christmas party given by her father, and by New Year's both of them had given up the fight. He took her to dinner one night, and afterward, in an agony of tension and emotion, he told her all that he was feeling, and was stunned when her emotions cascaded out with the same force as his. They began seeing each other weekly, on weekends, and kept to quiet haunts so as not to become the center of gossip around town, and at last Liane told her father, expecting some resistance, and possibly even fury, but what she got from him instead was delight and relief.

"I wondered when you two would finally realize what I've known for two years." He sat looking at her, beaming, as she stared.

"You knew? But how could you? I didn't . . . we didn't . . ."

"I'm just smarter than both of you, that's all." But he approved of the way they had proceeded. They had each felt out their emotions with caution and respect for the past. He knew that neither of them took the matter lightly, and he wasn't even bothered by the difference in their ages. Liane was an unusual young woman, and he couldn't imagine her happy with a man her own age. And to her, the twenty-four-year span between them mattered not at all, although Armand had expressed some concern about it in the beginning. Now he didn't give a care to something so minor as that. He adored her. He felt as though he had been born again, and he rapidly proposed marriage. On her twenty-first birthday they announced their engagement. Her father gave a lovely party, and life tasted like a dream, until two weeks later, when Armand received word that his term in San Francisco had come to an end. He was being moved on to Vienna as Ambassador. And like it or not, it was time to go. He and Liane discussed a precipitous marriage, but her father intervened. He wanted her to complete her final year in college, which meant waiting another full year until they could be married. Liane was crushed, but she was anxious not to disobey her father, and the two lovers agreed that they would survive the next year somehow, with visits when they could, and letters each day in between.

It was a difficult year for them both, but they managed, and on the fourteenth of June 1929, Armand de Villiers and Liane Crockett were married at old St. Mary's in San Francisco. Armand had left Vienna a month, for the "wedding of the year," as the San Francisco papers called it, and they both went back to Europe for a quick honeymoon in Venice, before returning to Vienna, where Liane would then be Ambassadress. And she stepped into those shoes with extraordinary ease. Armand tried to make everything easy for her, but she scarcely needed his help. After her years with her father, and the six months of helping Armand after Odile's death, she knew what to do.

Her father came to visit twice during their first six months there, unable to stay away. He had no business in Europe, but he longed for his daughter, and during his second visit she could no longer keep the news from him, although she had predicted accurately to Armand how he would react. She was having a baby the following summer, and her father responded with sheer terror, insisting privately to Armand that she had to be brought back to the States, had to have the best doctors, had to stay in bed, had to . . . He was haunted by memories of Liane's mother, and his agony when he had lost her. He was almost in tears when he went back to the States. And Liane had to write him daily to assure him that all was well. In May he arrived six weeks before the baby was due, and he almost drove them crazy with his worry, but Liane didn't have the heart to send him back to the States. When she went into labor, it was all Armand could do to subdue Harrison and to keep him busy, but fortunately the baby came quickly, a fat, angelic-looking girl with wisps of blond hair and round cheeks and a little rosebud mouth, born at 5:45 P.M. in a hospital in Vienna. When Harrison came to visit Liane three hours later, he found her eating dinner and laughing, as though she had spent the afternoon at the opera with her friends. He couldn't believe it, nor could Armand, who gazed at his wife as though she had wrought single-handedly the miracle of all time. He loved her more than life itself, and thanked God for this new life he had never even dreamed would be his. He was totally crazy about the baby, and when their second daughter was born two years later in London, he was just as excited all over again. This time they had convinced Liane's father that he could wait in San Francisco and that they would cable him the moment the baby was born, which they did. Their first child they had named Marie-Ange Odile de Villiers, which they had both thought about with great seriousness before doing. They both decided that it was what they wanted, and they knew that Odile would have been pleased. The second baby was named Elisabeth Liane Crockett de Villiers, which pleased Liane's father no end.

He came to London for the christening, and gazed at the baby with such rapture that Liane teased him afterward about it, but she also noticed on this trip that he didn't look well. He was sixty-eight years old, and had always been in good health, but he seemed older than his years now, and Liane was worried when she saw him off on the ship. She said something to Armand about it, but he had his hands full with a difficult diplomatic negotiation with the Austrians and the English, and afterward he felt guilty for not paying more attention. Harrison Crockett died of a heart attack on the ship on the way home.

Liane flew home to San Francisco without the children, and as she stood beside her father's casket she felt a loss she almost couldn't bear, and she knew that life would never be quite the same without him. Her Uncle George was already preparing to move into Harrison's house, and his shoes at Crockett Shipping, but her uncle was like a very dim star in the orbit of the bright planet that had been her father. She was glad that she didn't live in San Francisco and wouldn't have to see her uncle living in their house. She couldn't have borne watching the gruff, ornery old bachelor living her father's life and changing all the old ways. She left San Francisco within a week, with a feeling of grief that exceeded only what she had felt when Odile had died, and she was grateful to return home to Armand, to her babies, and to throw herself back into her life as Ambassadress at his side. From that moment on she always felt less of an allegiance to her own country. Her tie to the States had been her father, and now all of that was gone. She had the fortune her father had left her, but she would have much preferred to have her father living, and all that mattered to her now were her daughters and her husband and her life with them.

Two years after that they left London. Armand was reassigned as Ambassador to Washington. It was the first time in five years that Liane would be living back in the United States. It was an exciting time for them both, filled with the prospect of an important post for Armand and lots of responsibility for Liane, and the only thing that marred it was the fact that Liane lost a baby, this time a little boy, shortly after their arrival in the States. It had been a rough crossing, and she had had a hard time from the first. But aside from that, the years in Washington were a time they both remembered fondly, filled with spectacular dinners at the Embassy, glittering evenings amongst heads of state, nights at the White House, and acquaintances with important politicians who filled their lives with interesting events and fascinating friendships. It was a time they would miss now, and it seemed as though it were ending much too quickly. It was hard to believe that the Washington years had already come to a close. They would both miss their friends, as would their daughters. Marie-Ange and Elisabeth were respectively nine and seven now, and they had never known schools other than those in Washington. Armand had already made arrangements for them in Paris, and they both spoke perfect French, but still it would be a big change for them. And with a war possibly coming in Europe, God alone knew what would be in store. Armand had already discussed that possibility with Liane, and if anything happened, he planned to send the three of them back to the States. Liane could stay with her uncle in San Francisco, in her father's old house, and at least he would know that they were safe there. But for the moment, that didn't enter the picture. For the time being, as much as one could know that sort of thing, Armand knew that there would be peace in France, though of course there was no way of knowing for how long.

At present he had to ready the Embassy for his replacement, and he turned his attention back to the work on his desk, and it was almost ten o'clock when he looked up again. He stood up at his desk and stretched. He had been feeling so old lately, despite Liane's amorous protests, but at fifty-six he had led a very full life.

He locked the door to his office behind him, bidding good night to the two guards posted in the hall. And then he inserted his key in the lock of the private elevator at the rear that would take him to their apartments, and he stepped in with a tired smile and a sigh. It was always good to get home to Liane after a day's work, even after all these years. She was a wife any man would be lucky to even dream of having. She had been devoted and understanding and patient and humorous and loving for all of their ten years. As the elevator reached the fourth floor it ground to a halt, and he opened the door into the ornate marble hall that led to his study, their large paneled living room, and their dining room, and he could smell something delicious still being prepared in the kitchen beyond. And as he glanced up the marble staircase to the top floor, he saw her, still as lovely as she had been ten years before, her blond hair in a handsome pageboy on her shoulders, her blue eyes unlined, and her skin as fresh as it had been the first time he had seen her in his garden at fifteen. She was a rare beauty, and he cherished every moment with her, although these days the moments they shared were fewer than they had been in a long time, he was so damnably busy.

"Hello, my love." She slid her arms around his neck as

she reached the bottom of the stairs, nuzzling his neck in the way she had for the past ten years, and as it always did, the gesture warmed him to his very soul.

"How was your day, or shouldn't I ask?" He smiled down at her, proud of her, still proud that she was his. She was a beauty, and a rare, rare gem.

"I think I've almost finished packing. You won't recognize our bedroom when you come upstairs."

"Will you be in it?" His eyes danced as he looked at his wife, even after his long day.

"Of course."

"Then that's all I want to recognize. How are the girls?"

"They miss you." They hadn't seen their father in four days.

"We'll make up for lost time next week on the ship." He smiled at Liane. "Our reservations were reconfirmed today, and"—the smile widened—"I have quite a surprise for you, *chérie*. The gentleman who had reserved one of the four Grand Luxe suites has had to cancel, because his wife was taken ill. Which means . . ." He seemed almost to be waiting for a drumroll as Liane laughed and took his arm to escort him into the dining room. "It means that as a courtesy to this tired old returning Ambassador, we are being given one of the *Normandie*'s four most luxurious suites. Four bedrooms, a dining room of our own, if we wish to use it, which we won't. We'll be too busy enjoying the Grande Salle à Manger. But perhaps the children will enjoy having a dining room of their own and a living room with a baby grand piano. Our own promenade deck, my love, where we can sit at night, looking up at the stars . . ." His voice drifted off dreamily, as he was really looking forward to the crossing on the ship. For years now he had heard nothing but raves about the *Normandie*, and he had never been on it. Now it was an extra treat that he could give to his wife. No matter that she could have paid for all four of the Grand Luxe suites herself, he would never have let her. He had too much pride about that sort of thing, and he was happy to be able to spoil her a little, and happier still that they would have five days together, suspended between two worlds. At last he would be free of the final exhausting days at the Embassy in Washington, and he would not yet have been swallowed up by the work he was to do in France. "Isn't that good news?" His eyes danced.

"I can hardly wait." And then she giggled as she sat down at the enormous dining table set for two. "Since we have a piano in our cabin, should I practice the piano a little before we leave? I haven't played in years."

"Silly girl. Hmm"—he turned his attention to the odors emanating from the kitchen—"that smells awfully good."

"Thank you, sir. *Soupe de poisson* for my lord and master, *une omelette fines herbes, salade de cresson*, Camembert, Brie, and chocolate soufflé, if the cook hasn't fallen asleep."

"She must be ready to kill me with these hours I'm keeping."

"Never mind, my love." Liane smiled at him with a kiss in her eyes, and the maid came in with their soup.

"Did I tell you that we're dining at the White House tomorrow?"

"No." But Liane was used to surprise command social engagements. She had given dinner parties for as many as a hundred people with notice of only two days.

"They called today."

"Is the dinner for anyone important?" The soup was good, she liked their cozy dinners tête-à-tête, and like Armand, she wondered now how many moments like these they would have once they were back in France. They both suspected that he was going to be terribly busy, and she might not see much of him for a while. At least not at first.

Armand smiled at his wife. "Tomorrow night is for someone terribly important."

"Who?"

"Us. It's just a friendly little impromptu dinner for us before we leave." There had already been a formal farewell reception three weeks before. "Are the girls excited about the ship?"

Liane nodded. "Very."

"They can't possibly be as excited as I am. They call her the Ship of Light." And then he saw her smiling at him again. "Do you think me very foolish to be so excited about the trip?"

"No, I think you're very wonderful, and I love you."

He reached out and patted her hand then. "Liane . . . I am a very lucky man."

Chapter 2

*T*he long black Citroën that had been shipped over from Paris the year before drew up to the Pennsylvania Avenue entrance of the White House, and Liane stepped out. She was wearing a black satin dinner suit with broad shoulders and a narrow waist, and a white organdy blouse underneath the jacket, lined in the finest of white silk. Armand had bought her the suit at Jean Patou when he had gone to Paris at Easter, and it fit her perfectly. Patou had her measurements, and Armand always chose gifts for her that suited her to perfection, as this one did. She looked like a high-fashion model, with her long, slim figure and her perfectly smooth blond hair, as she stepped from the car. Armand emerged just behind her, wearing his dinner jacket. Tonight was an informal evening. None of the men would be wearing white tie.

There were two butlers and a maid waiting in the entry hall to greet them, to take any wraps the ladies might have brought and to direct them upstairs to the Roosevelts' private dining room. And of course there were presidential guards stationed in the hall.

It was a considerable honor to be entertained at the White House. Liane had been here several times to lunch quietly with Eleanor and a handful of other ladies, and she was particularly pleased to be dining here tonight. Upstairs on the second floor, in their living quarters, the President and his wife were waiting, she in a simple gray crepe de chine dress from Traina-Norell and a handsome rope of pearls. There was always something unassuming about the woman. No matter who had designed her clothes or the jewels that she wore, she looked as though she might have been wearing an old dress and a sweater, sensible shoes, and a warm smile. She was the kind of woman one would have wanted to come home from school to, as there would have always been a warm welcome waiting and a gentle smile.

"Hello, Liane." Eleanor saw her first and walked over quickly. The President was already engaged in animated conversation with the British Ambassador, Sir Ronald Lindsay, another old friend. "It's so nice to see you both." Her smile extended to Armand, who diligently kissed her hand and then looked into her eyes.

"We shall miss you most of all, madame."

"But not half as much as we shall miss you!" She spoke in a high-pitched, thready voice, which people made fun of often, and yet to those who knew her it had a comforting and familiar lilt. It was just another endearing aspect of Eleanor. It was difficult to find anyone who didn't love and respect her, and in the past five years Liane had been one of her most ardent fans, in spite of their recent heated exchanges over the SS *St. Louis.* Armand had already reminded Liane not to bring that up again tonight. She had heeded the warning in the car with an obedient nod and then a chuckle. "Am I as tactless as all that, my love?" "Never" had been the answer, but Armand had a fatherly way about him with his wife, and he often reminded her of things, as he would have the girls.

"How are the children?" Liane was quick to ask. The Roosevelts' grandchildren were always in and out of the White House.

"As naughty as ever. And the girls?"

"Excited, and wild. Every time I turn around they've unpacked their trunks to look for a favorite doll, or create some mischief." The two women laughed. With five children of her own, Eleanor was well versed in the ways of the very young.

"I don't envy you the task of packing up! It's bad enough for us in the summer when we go to Campobello. I don't think I could ever have managed getting them all the way to France. Surely one of my children would have leaped overboard on a dare, and we'd have had to stop the ship. I shudder at the thought, but Marie-Ange and Elisabeth are much better behaved. You should have a peaceful crossing."

"We hope so," Armand added, and then the threesome joined the others, the British Ambassador and his wife, Lady Lindsay, the Duponts of Delaware, the ever-present Harry Hopkins, a distant cousin of Eleanor's who was in Washington for two weeks, and Russell Thompson and his wife, Maryse, a couple that Liane and Armand enjoyed a great deal and saw often. He was an attorney, closely allied to the Roosevelt Administration, and she was from Paris, and a very lively girl.

Cocktails were served for half an hour, and then a butler announced that dinner was served in the President's dining room. As always at the dinners that Eleanor arranged, the food was exquisite, the menu superb. The table in the private dining room was set for eleven with a beautiful service of blue and gold Spode china, and heavy silver, on a cloth of very old and delicate lace. And there were large arrangements of blue and white iris, yellow roses, and white lilac set amongst long white candles in silver candelabra, and all around the room handsome murals of the American Revolution caught one's eye. It was a dinner Armand and Liane would long remember, as the President guided the conversation artfully between subjects of interest to all, often punctuated with an anecdote about something that had recently happened in Congress or the Senate. There was no talk of war during the entire meal. But inevitably, the subject came up over dessert. But by then everyone was sated and content, having eaten caviar, roast duck, a delicately smoked salmon, endive salad, and a rich array of cheeses from France.

The baked Alaska was almost a superfluous touch, but it was so delicate that hearing the men speak of war seemed less of an agony than it would have been earlier in the evening. But as usual the conversation became heated, with Roosevelt insisting, as he always did, that there was nothing to fear in Europe or the United States.

"But you can't mean that," the British Ambassador insisted, torn between the heavenly delights of the baked Alaska and the more pressing issues at the table. "For God's sake, man, even in your own country, you've been preparing for war. Look at the trade routes you've begun assigning to shipping, look at the industries that have been stepped up, primarily steel." The British knew only too well that Roosevelt was no fool, he knew what was coming, but he was determined not to admit it to his own people, or even here, amongst an assortment of close friends and international elite.

"There's no sin in being well prepared," Franklin insisted, "it's good for the country, but it doesn't carry with it implications of coming doom."

"Perhaps not for you . . ." The British Ambassador suddenly looked depressed. "You know what's happening over there as well as we do. Hitler is a madman. He knows it." He pointed to Armand, who nodded. In this group, his views were well known. "What are they saying in Paris this week?"

All eyes turned to Armand, and he seemed to weigh his words before speaking. "What I saw in April was very deceiving. Everyone is trying to pretend that the inevitable will never come. My only hope is that it won't come too soon." He looked gently at his wife. "I'll have to send Liane back if that happens. But more importantly than that"—his eyes left his wife and returned to the others—"a war in Europe now would be a tragedy for France, for all of us." He gazed sadly at the British Ambassador, and as their eyes met, both men knew that they saw all too clearly what was coming as Hitler pressed forward. It was a terrifying fate. But as silence fell over the table Eleanor quietly stood up, as a signal to the ladies that it was time to leave the gentlemen to their brandy and cigars. Coffee would be served to the ladies in an adjoining room.

Liane got up slowly, as she disliked this particular moment of any dinner. She felt always as though she were missing the most important conversations of all, once the men were alone to speak their minds on the important issues of the day, without tempering their words for the ladies. During the drive home she questioned Armand as to what she had missed.

"Nothing. It was the same talk one hears everywhere now. Fears and denials, Roosevelt standing his ground, the British certain of what they think will come. Thompson agreed with us, though. He told me quietly when we left the table that he's certain Roosevelt will be in the war before the year's out, if it comes. It would be good for the economy here, war always is." Liane looked shocked, but she knew enough about the truths of economics she had learned from her father to realize that what Armand was saying was true. "In any case, my little love, we shall be home soon enough to see for ourselves what's happening over there." He looked distracted during the rest of the drive home, he had a great deal on his mind, and Liane let her mind drift back to the warm embrace she had received from Eleanor when they left. "You must write to me, my dear. . . ."

"I shall," Liane had promised.

"Godspeed to you both." The peculiar voice had cracked, and her eyes were damp. She was fond of Liane, and well aware that before they met again, the welfare of both countries might be jeopardized in terrifying ways.

"And to you." The two women had hugged, and then Liane had slipped into the Citroën beside her husband for the short drive to the Embassy, which was still their home.

When they reached their front door, the chauffeur escorted them inside, and, as always, two guards waited, bid them good night, and then disappeared to their own quarters, where all appeared to be silent. The servants had all gone to bed, and it was long past the hours when the children would be up. But as they made their way toward their rooms, Liane smiled at her husband, tugged at his sleeve, and put a finger to her lips. She had heard a rapid shuffling and the click of a light.

"*Qu'est-ce qu'il y a?*" he whispered. He was less attuned than Liane to what she was hearing, but she swiftly opened the door to Marie-Ange's room with a broad smile.

"Good evening, ladies." She spoke in a normal voice, and Armand thought she was crazy, but then suddenly there was an eruption of giggles and scurrying feet. Both girls had been hiding in Marie-Ange's bed, and now they ran toward their parents with laughter and excitement.

"Did you bring us any cookies?"

"Of course not!" Armand still looked shocked. Liane knew her daughters better than anyone, and it always amused him how well she did so. He began to smile now too. "What are you doing up? And where is Mademoiselle?" Their nurse was supposed to see that they went to bed and stayed there. Mutiny against her was a difficult task, as they all knew, but now and then the girls succeeded, with enormous delight.

"She's sleeping. And it was so hot . . ." Elisabeth looked up at him with the wide blue eyes of her mother, and as always, something deep inside Armand melted as he looked at her and then picked her up in his powerful arms. He was a tall, well-built man, and even in his mid-fifties he had a physique and a strength that suggested youth. Only the lines in his face, and the full mane of well-combed white hair, indicated his years, but his daughters were oblivious of the fact that their father was so much older than their mother. All they cared about was that he was their papa, and they adored him, just as he adored them.

"You're very naughty to be up so late. What have you both been doing?" He knew that Marie-Ange would have started the revolution and Elisabeth was only too happy to follow. That much he knew of his daughters, and he was quite right. As he watched them Liane switched on the light, and what they saw was a sea of toys pulled out of the boxes and trunks where they had been packed. The room was filled with steamer trunks packed with the girls' dresses, coats, hats, and shoes. Liane always bought them in Paris.

"Oh, my God," Liane groaned. They had unpacked everything but their clothes. "What in heaven's name were you doing?"

"Looking for Marianne." Elisabeth said it in a saintly little voice and looked up at her mother with a smile bereft of front teeth.

"You knew I didn't pack her." Marianne was Elisabeth's favorite doll. "She's on the table in your room."

"She is?" But both girls began to giggle. They had just been having fun. And their father looked at them as though he would scold them, but he didn't have the heart to, they were too full of life and too much like their mother for him to ever really get very angry at them. And he had no reason to. Mademoiselle ruled them with an iron hand, and Liane was a marvelous mother. It allowed him to enjoy them without having to play the ogre. But nonetheless he admonished them now for a moment in French. He told them that they had to help their mother with the packing, not take everything apart. They had to get everything ready, he reminded them, because they were leaving for New York in two days.

"But we don't want to go to New York." Marie-Ange looked up seriously at her father, ever the spokesman for the team. "We want to stay here." Liane sat down on Marie-Ange's bed with a sigh, and Elisabeth climbed into her lap as Marie-Ange continued to negotiate with her father in French. "We like it here."

"But don't you want to come on the ship? They have a puppet theater, and a cinema, and a kennel for dogs." He had told her before, but now she wavered as he spoke of them again. "And we'll all be happy in Paris too."

"No, we won't." She shook her head, looking into her father's eyes. "Mademoiselle says there will be a war. We don't want to go to Paris if there's going to be a war."

"What's that?" Elisabeth whispered to her mother as she sat on her lap.

"It's when people fight. But nobody is going to be fighting in Paris. It will be just like it is here." Armand and Liane's eyes met over the heads of their girls, and Liane could see that Armand was going to have a serious talk with Mademoiselle in the morning. He didn't want the girls frightened with talk of war.

And then suddenly Elisabeth spoke up and broke the spell. "When Marie-Ange and I fight, is that a war?"

The others laughed, but Marie-Ange corrected her before her parents could. "No, stupid. A war is when people fight with guns." She turned to Armand. "Right, Papa?"

"Yes, but there hasn't been a war since long before you were both born, and we don't need to worry about that now. What you girls have to do is go to bed, and tomorrow help repack all these things you've taken out. *Au lit, mesdemoiselles!*" He attempted to sound stern, and although he almost convinced his daughters, he didn't even begin to convince his wife. He was putty in their hands. But he was also worried now that they would be frightened about a war in France.

Liane took Elisabeth back to her own room, and Armand tucked their eldest into her bed, and Liane and Armand met back in their own room five minutes later. Liane was still smiling at the mischief of the girls, but Armand was sitting on their bed, taking off his patent leather pumps, with a worried frown.

"What is that old fool doing frightening the girls with talk of a war?"

"She hears the same things we do." Liane sighed and began to unbutton the beautifully made black satin jacket from Patou. "But I'll speak to her in the morning about the girls."

"See that you do." The words were harsh, but the tone of

his voice was not as he watched his wife undress in her dressing room. There was always something more to say between them, some further reason why he couldn't tear himself away from her, even now, after an endless day and a long night. He watched the silky cream of her flesh appear as she took off the white organdy blouse, and he hastened quickly to his own dressing room to cast his dinner attire aside, and he returned only moments later in white silk pajamas and a navy-blue silk robe, his feet bare. She smiled at him from their bed, the lace of her pink silk nightgown peeking over the sheets as he turned off the light.

He slid into bed beside her and ran a hand gently up her arm until it reached the smooth satin of her neck, and then drifted down again to touch her breast. Liane smiled in the darkness and sought Armand's mouth with her lips. And there they met and held, in the darkness, their children forgotten, the nurse, the President, the war . . . and all they remembered as they peeled off each other's nightclothes was their hunger for each other, which only grew sharper over the years, instead of dimmer. As Armand's powerful hand touched her naked thigh, Liane moaned softly, parting her legs to welcome him to her, as she always did, and she smelled the muted spice of his cologne as he kissed her again and their flesh joined, and for the first time in a long time she found herself wanting another baby as he entered her gently at first and then with increasing passion, and as they kissed again with greater fervor, this time it was Armand who moaned softly in the night.

Chapter 3

The doorman at 875 Park Avenue stood stolidly at his post. The jacket of his uniform was of heavy wool, and the wing collar he wore cut into his neck. The cap with the gold braid sat on his head like a lead weight. It was eighty-seven degrees in New York in the second week of June, but he still had to stand at his post, cap on, jacket in place, bow tie straight, white gloves on, smiling pleasantly at the tenants as they came in and out. Mike, the doorman, had been on duty since seven o'clock that morning, and it was already six o'clock at night. The heat of the day had barely abated, and he had another hour to stand there before he could go home at last, in baggy pants, a short-sleeved shirt, comfortable old shoes, no tie, no hat. A blessed relief it would be, he thought to himself in his Irish brogue. And a beer he could be usin' too. As he stood there he envied the two men who manned the elevators. Lucky devils, at least they were inside.

"Good evening, Mike." He looked up from his heat-dimmed reverie to touch his fingers to his cap with mechanical precision, but this time to the greeting he added a friendly smile. There were those in the building he wouldn't bother to smile at, but this man was one he liked, Nicholas Burnham—Nick he had heard the man's friends call him. He always had a friendly word for Mike, a moment to stop and talk to him in the morning as he waited for his car to be brought around. They talked of politics and baseball, the latest strikes, the price of food, and the heat that had been shimmering off the streets of the city for the past two weeks. Somehow he always managed to give Mike the impression that he cared about him, that he gave a damn that the poor old man had to stand outside all day, hailing cabs and greeting ladies with French poodles, because he had seven children to support. It was as though Nick understood the irony of it all, and he cared. It was that that Mike liked about him. Nick Burnham had always struck him as a decent sort of man. "How did you survive the day?"

"Not bad, sir." It was not entirely true, as his feet, raw, hot, and swollen, were killing him, but suddenly they didn't seem so bad. "And you?"

"It was pretty hot downtown." Nick Burnham's office was on Wall Street, and Mike knew that he was big in steel, the most important young industrialist in the nation, *The New York Times* had called him once. And he was only thirty-eight years old. The difference in their stations in life and their incomes never bothered Mike. He accepted things like that, and Nick always gave him handsome tips and generous gifts at Christmas time. Besides, Mike knew that in some ways Nick didn't have an easy row to hoe. Not in this house anyway. As much as Mike liked Nick, he hated his wife, Hillary. A highfalutin, fancy bitch, she was. Never a kind word, never a smile, just a lot of fancy jewels and furs she'd soaked her husband for. When Mike saw them go out at night, more often than not she was saying something nasty to Nick, about one of the maids, or that he was late, or that she hated the people giving the party they were going to. A rotten little bitch she was, Mike always said, but a pretty one, not that that was enough. He wondered how Nick managed to stay such a pleasant man, married to a girl like that.

"I saw Master John today, with his new baseball bat." The two men exchanged a smile, and Nick broke into a big grin.

"You may hear the sound of breaking windows one of these days, my friend."

"Not to worry. I'll catch the ball if it sails down here."

"Thanks, Mike." He patted the old man's arm and disappeared inside the house as Mike smiled to himself. Forty-five minutes to go, and maybe tomorrow it won't be quite so hot. And if it is, well . . . that's the way things are. Two more men came in, and Mike touched his hat, thinking of Nick's son, John. He was a handsome little tyke, looked just like his old man, except that he had his mother's jet-black hair.

"I'm home!" Nick's voice rang out in the hall as it did every night, and as he put his straw hat on a table in the hall, he listened for familiar sounds, of John running down the hall to greet him perhaps. But tonight there were none. A maid in a black uniform and a white lace apron and cap came out of the pantry instead, and he smiled at her. "Good evening, Joan."

"Evening, sir. Mrs. Burnham is upstairs."

"And my son?"

"I believe he's in his room."

"Thank you." He nodded and walked down a long, thickly carpeted hall. The apartment had been entirely redone the year before, and everything was done in white and beige and cream. It managed to look both soothing and expensive at the same time, and had cost him an arm and a leg, particularly after the three decorators and two architects Hillary had hired and fired one by one, but the end result was one that he could live with and that he imagined had pleased her. It wasn't exactly the kind of place where one would expect to find a little boy, nor the kind of home where he could run his fingers along the wall or bounce a ball, but at least in the child's room, Nick had prevailed. There, everything was done in reds and blues, the furniture was comfortable old oak, the children's paintings on the wall were still a little overdone for Nick's taste, but at least he knew that these were rooms where John could have a little fun. There was a bedroom for his nurse, a large room for him, a little sitting room with a desk, which had been Nick's when he was a boy, and a large playroom filled with toys, where he could entertain his friends.

Nick knocked softly on the door of the hall that led to John's rooms, and instead of an answer, the door was instantly yanked open, and he found himself looking down into the smiling face of his only child. He swept him up in his arms with a happy smile, and a gurgle of laughter greeted his ears, as it did every night.

"You're crushing me, Dad!" But he didn't really seem to mind.

"Good. How's my favorite little boy?" He set him back on his feet, and John grinned up at him.

"I'm fine and my new bat is great."

"That's good. Break any windows yet?"

"Of course not." John looked offended as his father rumpled the blue-black hair. He was an interesting cross between Hillary and Nick, her creamy skin, Nick's green eyes, her hair. The two looked as entirely different as two people could, Hillary dark and small and delicate, Nick powerful and blond and strong, and yet the boy combined the best of both, or so everyone said. "Can I take my bat on the ship?"

"I'm not so sure about that, young man. Maybe if you promise to leave it in your trunk."

"But I have to take it, Dad! They don't have baseball bats in France."

"Probably not," Nick agreed. They were going over for a year, or six months, if things got too tense. Nick had so many contracts over there this year, that he had decided to run the Paris office himself, and leave his right-hand man in charge in New York. And of course he was taking Hillary and John. He wouldn't consider staying there for that long without them, and it was important that he go. At first Hillary had wailed and moaned and complained to him every day, but for the last month she had seemed resigned, and John had decided that it would be fun. They were putting him in an American school just off the Champs-Élysées, and Nick had rented them a handsome house on the Avenue

Foch. It belonged to a French count and his wife, who had moved to Switzerland the year before, during the panic before the Munich Accord, and now they were happy in Lausanne and in no hurry to return. It was a perfect arrangement for Nick, Hillary, and the boy.

"Want to come to dinner with me, Dad?" The nurse had just signaled John that it was time to go, and he turned hopeful eyes up to Nick.

"I think I'd better go upstairs to see your mom."

"Okay."

"I'll come down after you eat, and we can talk for a while. How's that?"

"That's good." John smiled at his father again and left with the nurse as Nick stood for a quiet moment in the room, looking at his old desk. His father had given it to him when he was twelve, and almost ready for boarding school, but he had given it to John long before that. And if he had his way, his son would never be sent away to school. He had hated his years away, feeling banished from his home. John would never know the agony of that, Nick had told himself long before besides, he was far too crazy about the boy to let him go.

He closed the door behind him then and walked back down the long beige hall until he reached the grand piano in the central hall, and then walked slowly up the carpeted stairs to their rooms.

As he approached the landing he saw that the door to their suite of rooms was ajar, and he could hear Hillary's voice beyond, calling shrilly to the maid, who ran in from Hillary's dressing room, carrying an armload of furs.

"Not those, dammit! For chrissake . . ." He could only see her from the back, her shining black hair hanging like silk to the shoulders of her white satin dressing gown, but he could see just from the way she was standing that she was annoyed. "You fool, I told you the sables, the mink coat, and the silver fox. . . ." She turned then and glanced at Nick, her dark eyes meeting his green ones for a long moment as everything stood still. He had told her often not to shout at the help, but it was something she had done all her life, and she had never adapted well to change. She was only twenty-eight years old, but she looked every inch a woman of the world, with her well-coiffed hair, her carefully made-up face, her long red nails, her stance, her style. Even in her dressing gown she was the epitome of chic. "Hello, Nick." The eyes and the words were cool, but she stood still as he approached, held up her cheek for him to kiss, and then turned her attention back to the maid. But this time she didn't raise her voice. "Would you please go back and get me the right furs." But even at that, her tone cut like a knife as Nick watched.

"You're awfully hard on that girl." It was a tone of gentle reproach, one she had heard ten thousand times before, and she didn't give a damn. He was always nice to everyone, except her, of course. He had ruined her life, but he'd got what he wanted out of it. Nick Burnham always got his way, but not with her. Not anymore, she told herself again and again. Once was enough. And she'd made him pay for it for the last nine years. If it hadn't been for Nick, she'd still be in Boston, maybe even married to that Spanish count who was so nuts about her the year she came out. . . . Countess . . . she liked the ring of that. . . . Countess. . . . "You look tired, Hil." He gently stroked her hair and looked into her eyes, but he met no answering warmth there.

"I am. How do you think everything in this house has got packed?" By the maids, he almost said, but he bit his tongue. He knew that in her mind she'd done it all. "Christ, I have to pack everything for you, for John, table linens, sheets, blankets, plates, your things . . ." Her voice grew high-pitched as she spoke, and he walked away and sat down on a Louis XV chaise longue.

"I can pack for myself, you know that. And I told you, the house in Paris has everything we need. You don't have to take your own bed linens and plates."

"Don't be an ass. God only knows who's slept in those

beds." And for an instant, just an instant, he almost said that they couldn't have been any worse than the people who had slept in hers. But he said nothing, he only watched as the nervous little maid returned, hopefully with the right furs this time: two sable coats, one mink, and the silver fox jacket she had received at Christmas, in a large handsome box, from God knew who. One thing was certain, it was not from Nick. The sables were, the mink, the chinchilla coat she was leaving behind, but the fox was an enigma, more or less, although he assumed it was from Ryan Halloway, the son of a bitch.

"What are you staring at?" Without intending them to, his eyes had strayed to the fox. They had fought about it several times before, and he did not intend to discuss it with her again. "Don't start that. I don't have to go to Paris, you know."

Oh, Christ, he thought to himself, not that. It had been such a long day, and he was so hot. He didn't want to fight with her today. "Do we really have to go through all this, Hil?"

"No, we don't. We could stay here, you know."

"No, we couldn't. I want to run my Paris office for the next year. I have important contracts over there, and you know it. So we're all going. Somehow, I've never thought of Paris as a rough place to live." But she did. For some reason, she was bound and determined to stay in New York. "Come on, Hil, you've always loved it over there."

"Sure, for a few weeks. Why the hell can't you fly back and forth?"

"Because I'll wind up never seeing you or John. For crissake." He stood up all at once, and the maid scurried out of the room. She knew the pattern of their fights. Eventually he blew his top and began to shout, and more often than not she threw something at him. "Can't we just let this thing lie? Can't you just accept that we're going? For chrissake, the ship is sailing in two days."

"So let it, or go by yourself." Her voice was like ice as she sat down on the bed, stroking the silver fox and looking up at him. "You don't need me over there."

"Is that right? Or is it that you'd like to get rid of me for a year, then you could run back and forth to Boston to visit that little son of a bitch." He knew how promiscuous she was, he had known for years. But he believed in preserving his marriage, for John's sake, for his own. His own parents had been divorced, and he had led a lonely, unhappy life as a child and had vowed never to do that to his own son. All he wanted was to be married and to stay that way, and he would, no matter what, no matter what Hillary did. But still the angry words slipped out more often than he wanted them to. "Aren't you ever afraid you'll get pregnant, Hil?" They both knew he meant by someone else.

"Apparently you've never heard of abortion . . . if what you say is true, of course, that I play around, which I do not. But babies are not exactly my thing, dear Nick, or don't you recall?" They always aimed their blows below the belt. They had for years.

"Oh, yes, I do." The muscles in his jaw tensed as he clenched one hand, but his voice was oddly soft. She had never forgiven him for what had happened nine years before. She had been the most beautiful debutante in Boston. He remembered well her raven hair in sharp contrast to the white gowns her parents had had sent from Paris. There were many men who wanted her. Her father was in his fifties when she was born, her mother thirty-nine, and they had long since given up hope of having a baby, when suddenly Hillary appeared. She had been spoiled from the beginning, adored by her father, pampered by her mother, grandparents, and nurse. She had had everything she wanted, and she intended to go on living that way forever, until suddenly, on the night of her debut, she saw Nick. He was tall, blond, and handsome, with one of Boston's prettiest girls on his arm. And everyone had whispered from the moment he walked in . . . Nick Burnham . . . Nick Burnham . . . a fortune in steel . . . sole heir of his father . . . At twenty-nine, he was one of the richest young men on Wall Street, handsome as hell, and single. Hillary had almost floated out of the arms of the man she was dancing with, and had gone to meet Nick. They were introduced by one of her father's friends, and she had done everything she could to sweep him off his feet. And with surprisingly little effort, she had succeeded. Nick had gone to Boston often after that, and then Newport the following summer, and it was there that it had happened. Hillary had wanted him to want her more than any other woman he had ever known, and she had given her virginity to him, because she thought she loved him, and because she wanted to own him.

What she hadn't counted on was that she would get pregnant, which she did the first time he made love to her. He was shocked at first, and Hillary was totally hysterical. She didn't want to have a child, she didn't want to get fat, have a baby . . . She had been so childlike as she cried in his arms that he had laughed at her. She said something about finding someone to help her get an abortion, but he wouldn't hear of it. She was an enchanting woman-child, and the idea of a baby pleased him to no end, after the initial shock had passed. He spoke to her father without telling him about the baby, asked for Hillary's hand, and informed Hillary that they were getting married, which they did before the summer ended. It was a lovely wedding in Newport, and Hillary looked like a fairy queen in the white lace dress that her mother had worn at her own wedding. But beneath the happy smiles, she hid a sinking heart. She wanted Nick, but she didn't want to have a baby. She hated every moment of their early days of marriage, despite his constant cosseting and spoiling, because she knew he had married her because of the baby, and she didn't want competition from the child.

When the time approached, Nick did everything he could for her—bought her extravagant gifts, helped her set up the nursery, promised that he would be there to hold her hand—but she sank into a terrible depression in her ninth month, which the doctor felt contributed to a lengthy and nightmarish labor. It was an event that almost cost Hillary her life, and the baby's, and she never forgave Nick for the agony she went through. The depression persisted for six months after the birth of the child, and for a long time Nick thought that he was the only one who would ever love Johnny, but finally Hillary began to come around.

Or so he thought, and then the following winter, she had gone back to Boston for Christmas, without the baby, and visited friends. Suddenly she seemed to be taking forever to come home, and he realized that she was staying there to go to all the parties that her friends gave, and she was pretending to herself and others that she wasn't married, and she was just a debutante again, and she was having a grand time. A month after Hillary had left for Boston, Nick went up to get her, and insisted that she come home. A grand row had ensued between them, and she had even begged her father to let her stay there. She didn't want to be married, to live in New York, to take care of a baby, but this time her father was shocked. She had chosen to marry Nick, and he was a good husband to her. She had a responsibility to go back and at least try to work out the marriage, and she had a responsibility to the child as well, but she returned to New York with the cheer of a prisoner facing execution, feeling betrayed by all, and hating Nick the most, because he represented everything she didn't want in life, which was growing up. Her father had spoken to Nick before they left. He blamed himself for his daughter's behavior. He knew that she had been spoiled as a child, but he never realized that she would expect that as a way of life forever, shirking responsibilities on all fronts and hurting her husband and child. But Nick assured him that in time, and with patience, Hillary would grow into her new role. And at the time, he believed it, and he exercised as much patience as he had promised her father he would, but it was to no avail. She continued to take no interest in the baby, and the following summer she went to Newport, this time taking Johnny and the nurse, to avoid any further comment. She stayed there for the entire summer, and when Nick went up to see her, he became aware that she was having an affair. She turned twenty-one that summer, and was having a hot romance with the brother of one of her friends. He had just graduated from Yale and thought that he was very racy, sleeping with Hillary Burnham, which he told half the town, until Nick paid him a visit, and the boy went back to Boston with his tail between his legs and the tongue-lashing Nick had given him still ringing in his ears. But the real problem in it all was Hillary. Nick took her back to New York again, and attempted to shape her up in earnest, but in the next few years she bounced back and forth between Newport, Boston, and New York like a yo-yo, having affairs whenever she thought she might not get caught, including this last one. She had gotten involved with Ryan Halloway while Nick was in Paris. It didn't mean a thing to her, and Nick knew it, but it was her way of telling Nick repeatedly that she wasn't really married, never would be, that he couldn't own her, that she was free forever, free of him, and their son, and her father, who had died three years after she had married Nick. Her mother had long since given up all hope of having some influence upon her, and eventually so had Nick. She was what she was, a striking, very pretty woman, with a bright mind, which she wasted, and a sense of humor that still amused him, on the rare occasions when they talked. Most of the time they just fought now, or he ignored her. He had thought once or twice of divorcing her, and knew that he would have no trouble doing that, but if he did, she would get custody of Johnny. The courts were almost always favorable to the mother, unless she was a prostitute by profession, or hooked on dope. So in order to keep his son, Nick had to live under the same roof with Hillary, for better or worse, as long as he could stand it, and there were times when he thought he truly could not.

He had had some faint hope that by taking her to Paris, it would distract her, and she might behave herself for a while over there. But the trip was not off to an auspicious beginning. He knew that the affair with Ryan had ended after Christmas, but he also suspected that she was working on something new. She always got particularly edgy when something new was starting, like a racehorse fretting at being penned in. He knew that there was nothing he could do to stop her. As long as she kept her affairs reasonably secret, he was resigned to living with her, and in recent years she had grown a little warmer toward their son. No matter, Nick saw to it that Johnny had warm, loving nurses, and he had a father who adored him, which was more than Nick had had at the same age. But he would never agree to give up Johnny, to divorce and live a life that would rob him of the child he loved. Johnny was the center of his existence, and if that meant putting up with Hillary and her infidelities and her temper, then it was a price he was willing to pay.

He watched her now as she sat down at her dressing table, ran a comb through the silky hair, and watched him in the mirror, and then, as though to annoy him doubly, she took a long swig of the Scotch and water that was in a glass on her dressing table. And suddenly he realized that beneath her white satin dressing gown she wore a black silk dress.

"Going somewhere, Hil?" His voice was even, his eyes like bright-green rocks.

She hesitated only for a moment, the Thoroughbred in her flaring her nostrils. He could almost see her feet prancing as she readied for another race. "As a matter of fact, yes. There's a party tonight at the Boyntons."

"Funny"—he smiled ironically, he knew her too well now—"I didn't see the invitation."

"I forgot to show it to you."

"No matter." He started to leave the room, and she turned in her seat, speaking softly.

"Do you want to come, Nick?"

He turned and looked at her. There probably *was* a party at the Boyntons. But he very seldom went to parties. When he did, she invariably wound up in a corner, flirting with someone new or even an old friend. "No, thanks. I brought some work home."

She turned her back to him again. "Don't say I didn't ask you."

"I won't." He stood in the doorway, watching her sip her drink again. "Give them my best, and try to come home early." She nodded. "And Hil . . ." He hesitated.

"Yes, Nick?"

He decided to go ahead and say it. "Try not to leave New York in flames when you go. And whatever you're up to, kiddo, remember, we set sail in two days. And one way or the other, you're coming with me."

"What does that mean?" She stood up and turned to face him.

"It means that whether you leave some bleeding heart behind or not, you're coming. You're my wife, however much you may want to forget that."

"I never do." There was bitterness in her voice as she said it. She hated being married to him, more so because he had been so nice to her. It made her feel guilty toward him, and she didn't want to feel guilty. She wanted to be free.

"Have a good time." He closed the door softly behind him and went downstairs to see his son. And as soon as he had left the room, Hillary dropped the dressing gown from her shoulders, revealing the little black silk halter dress she had bought at Bergdorf Goodman. She clipped diamond earrings into place and looked in the mirror. She knew she would see Philip Markham at the party, and she wondered as she finished the Scotch and water how Nick always knew. Nothing had happened with Phil yet, but he was leaving for Paris in August, and who knew what would happen then . . . who knew. . . .

Chapter 4

The vast, splendidly designed ship lay in her berth at Pier 88 on the Hudson River, and every inch of her looked the part of the elegant queen. As Armand stood for a moment outside the limousine, he glanced upward at the three graceful smokestacks silhouetted against the sky. She weighed eighty thousand tons, and yet was the swiftest, most sophisticated vessel on any sea. To look at her took your breath away, and there was an inevitable moment of reverent silence as one perused her beauty. She was still more beautiful under full steam, and yet even here, at rest in her berth, she was undeniably a queen.

"Papa! Papa! I want to see." Elisabeth catapulted out of the Citroën first, and stood beside her father for a moment, her small hand clasped firmly in his. "Is that it?"

"No." Armand smiled down at his youngest daughter. "It is *she*. *La belle Normandie, mon trésor*. You will never see another ship like this one, little one. No matter what they build in years to come, there will never be another *Normandie*." It was a sentiment already echoed by many. In the seven years since she had been launched, she had been traveled by the great and elite, the rich, the spoiled, the elegant, lovers of beauty and of the sea, and there was not a soul among them who did not agree. The *Normandie* was an extraordinary vessel, and totally unique, the most beautiful, most elegant, swiftest. A floating island of luxury in every imaginable way.

Armand turned as he sensed his wife standing beside him. For a moment he had forgotten all of them. If he had allowed himself to, he might have cried. There was something about the *Normandie* that swelled the heart and made one particularly proud of France. What an accomplishment this ship was. What pride one had to feel just sensing the labor of love that had gone into her, from stem to stern, and hull to sky. She was a veritable beauty.

Liane sensed Armand's emotions and silently agreed as she watched her husband's face, and when he turned to her, she smiled.

"You look like a proud papa all over again," Liane teased in a gentle voice as he laughed.

But he nodded agreement, without shame. "What a victory for France."

By then Marie-Ange had joined her sister, and the two girls were hopping up and down with glee. "Can we go on board now, Papa? Can we? Can we?"

Liane took them each by the hand, and Armand busied himself giving orders to the porter and the chauffeur, and five minutes later they passed through the enormous archway marked COMPAGNIE GÉNÉRALE TRANSATLANTIQUE, and stepped into an elevator that took them to an elevated section of the quay. There were three separate entrances for the 1,972 passengers who would come aboard, discreetly separate and labeled PREMIÈRE CLASSE, TOURISTE, and CABINE. *"Première classe"* was first of course, and there would be 864 passengers entering through that archway before the ship sailed that afternoon. And when Armand, Liane, and the girls stepped onto the *Normandie*'s deck, it was shortly after noon. They had left Washington at 5:00 A.M., by train, and reached New York half an hour before. They had been met by a limousine from the Consulate in New York and whisked directly to Pier 88, on West 50th Street.

"Bonjour, monsieur, madame." The uniformed officer

smiled down at the two impeccably dressed little girls in matching pale-blue organdy dresses with white gloves and straw hats and shining black patent leather shoes. *"Mesdemoiselles, bienvenue à bord."* He looked pleasantly at Armand then. The young officer loved his job, and in the years that he had been assigned to checking passengers on board, he had met Thomas Mann, Stokowski, Giraudoux, Saint-Exupéry, movie stars such as Douglas Fairbanks, heads of states, giants of the literary world, cardinals and sinners, and crowned heads from almost every European country. It was exciting just waiting for them to say their names, if one did not recognize them at first glance, which, more often than not, he did. *"Monsieur?"*

"De Villiers," Armand said quietly.

"Ambassadeur?" the young man inquired, and Armand confirmed it with a silent nod.

"Ah, bien sûr." Of course. He noted as he glanced at his passenger list again that the De Villierses would be occupying one of the ship's four most luxurious suites. He had no way of knowing that it was a courtesy of the "Transat," as the CGT was called, and he was impressed to realize that the ambassador and his family would be occupying the Grand Luxe suite Trouville. "We will show you to your cabin at once." He signaled to a steward who materialized at his side and immediately took Liane's small carrying bag. The rest of their trunks had been sent ahead several days before, and what they had brought with them on the train would meet them in their stateroom only moments after they reached it themselves. The service on the *Normandie* was supreme.

The Trouville suite was on the promenade deck, and it was one of two suites available on that deck, with a promenade of its own, looking out over the handsome open air space of the Café-Grill. There were benches and lamps, and the stairways and railings formed a graceful design as Armand glanced down from their private terrace. Inside, there were four large elegant bedrooms, one for Liane and himself, one for each of the girls, and one for their nurse as well.

There were additional rooms available on the same deck for extra servants they might have brought along. One of these was needed for Armand's male assistant, Jacques Perrier, who was traveling on the ship as well, so that Armand could continue his work. But the rest of the "studios" would not be used by them, and would be kept locked. The only other inhabitants of this rarefied upper deck would be the family in the Deauville suite, which was identical to the Trouville in its grandeur and expense, but in no way similar to the De Villierses' suite of rooms. Each first-class cabin on the ship was done in an entirely different decor, with no repetitions from suite to suite. Down to the last detail, each single room was totally unique. And as Armand and Liane looked around their suite, their eyes met, and Liane began to laugh. It was so outrageously extravagant, so elegant, so beautiful, that she felt as excited as their girls.

"*Alors, ma chérie.*" He smiled at her as the steward left them in the main foyer, standing beside the promised baby grand piano. "*Qu'en penses-tu?*" What do you think? What could she think? It was a miraculous place to spend five days, five weeks . . . five months . . . five years. . . . One would like to stay aboard the *Normandie* forever. And she could see in her husband's eyes that he thought so too.

"It's incredible." All around them, on their way aboard, they had noticed the lavish art deco motif, the rich woods, handsome sculptures, enormous glass panels everywhere. It was beyond being a floating hotel, but more like a floating city of perfection, where absolutely nothing was out of sync, and everything one saw was a caress to the eye. She sat down on a dark-green velvet couch and giggled at Armand. "Are you sure I'm not dreaming? You won't wake me up, and we'll be back in Washington?"

"No, my love." He sat down beside his wife. "It's all true."

"But this suite, Armand, I cringe to think what it must cost!"

"I told you, they upgraded us from the deluxe rooms I had reserved." He looked victorious again as he smiled at his wife. It pleased him to make her happy, and it was obvious that she was as overwhelmed as he. In her years of traveling with her father, she had seen great luxury, but this was something more, something totally remarkable and unique. Just to be on the *Normandie*, for a moment, one felt like a part of history. It was easy to believe that there would never again be a ship quite like this, and that people would be talking about it for years and years. "Would you like a drink, Liane?" He opened double wood-paneled doors to reveal an enormous well-stocked bar, and Liane stared at it and then him.

"Good God! You could float the ship on all of that!" But as she spoke he opened a bottle of Dom Pérignon champagne. He poured her a glass and held it out, turning to pour one for himself as well, and then while standing looking at his beautiful wife, he raised his glass, his eyes on hers, and toasted her. "To two of the world's most beautiful ladies . . . *La Normandie . . . et ma femme.*" The ship, and his wife. Liane looked happy as she took a sip of the sparkling wine, and then she came to stand beside him. It felt like a honeymoon again, and she had to remind herself that the girls were in the next room.

"Shall we take a walk and look around?" Armand asked.

"Do you think the girls will be all right?"

He looked at her in amusement and then laughed. "Here? I think they'll manage." And Mademoiselle was already helping them to unpack their toys and dolls, as the trunks had been waiting in their rooms.

"I know exactly what I want to see."

"And what is that?" He watched her run a comb through her long blond hair, and felt a pang of lust for her. He had been so busy in recent weeks, he had scarcely seen her. It seemed as though they never had time to be together. But hopefully, on the ship, they would have time to stroll, wandering from deck to deck, and to chat as they had enjoyed doing so much for the past ten years. He felt lonely when he didn't have enough time to talk to her. But on this trip, he had promised himself, he and Jacques Perrier would only work from nine to noon, and the rest of the time he would be free. The trip was of course a rare opportunity for Perrier as well. A young man of about Liane's own age, he would normally have traveled back to France on a lesser ship, and in second class. But this time, as a reward for his five years of devoted work, Armand had intervened on his behalf, a special discount was obtained, and it was possible for him to make the crossing on the *Normandie* with them. Liane had been pleased for Jacques at the news, but now she hoped that he would find his own pursuits. Like Armand, she was hungry for them to have some time alone together. And she knew that the girls would have plenty to do, with the swimming pool, the children's recreation rooms, the kennels, where they could visit the traveling dogs, the puppet theater, and the cinema. There was lots for them to do, and, hopefully, for Jacques too. Liane asked Armand as they left the suite if he thought Jacques might already be on board.

"He'll find us after we sail, I'm sure." He had spent two days in New York on his own, seeing some friends, and was undoubtedly having some sort of party in his room. "Now, what is it that you're so anxious to see, Liane?"

"Everything!" Her eyes shone like a little girl's. "I want to see the bar with the varnished pigskin walls, the winter garden . . . the main salon . . ." She smiled up at her husband then. "I even want to see the gentleman's *fumoir*. It looks incredible in the brochure." She had done her homework well, and Armand was amused.

"I don't think you'll get in to see the gentleman's smoking room, my love." His eyes took her in again in the pretty red silk suit. It was difficult to believe that they had been married for ten years. She didn't look a moment over nineteen. From his vantage point of twenty-four more years, she always looked somewhat like a child. And now, as she strolled along on his arm, they made an extremely handsome pair as they wandered down to the boat deck, to the forward promenade, from where they could see New York in the heat of the bright June day. But here, on the ship, there was a slight breeze. They went back indoors a few moments later and down to the promenade deck, where they took a quick tour of the first-class lounge and glanced into the theater, and Liane spoke to him about the pool.

"It has a terraced shelf for the girls, so they'll be safe."

"Those two little fish?" Armand smiled down at his wife. "They would be safe in any pool."

"I still feel better knowing there's a protected area of the pool for them. Do you suppose it's open now?" She wanted to see everything at once.

"I suspect they keep it closed until the ship sets sail." The *Normandie* was famous for its rather elaborate farewell parties, and undoubtedly it would have occurred to some to visit the pool with a bottle or two of champagne. They never would have got the visitors off the ship in that case. It was difficult enough as it was. Everywhere, they could see people visiting the ship, glancing into staterooms, peeking into elegant lounges and suites.

Once past the theater, they wandered on to the library, a handsome, serious-looking room, and it was just past it that Liane discovered the winter garden she'd read about, and she almost gasped as they stepped inside. There was a tropical jungle of greenery everywhere, marble fountains delicately splashing water, and tall glass cages filled with exotic birds, and there was an open-air sensation due to the fact that they had reached the forward of the ship. Liane thought it was the most exotic room she had ever seen and she turned to her husband with a look of happy disbelief. It seemed more than ever like a dream.

"It's even prettier than the photographs in the brochure." In fact, the whole ship was. Even from these first glimpses, there were treasures everywhere, touches that could not be portrayed adequately in a photograph or sketch, and could barely even be described. It was all like an exquisite fairyland, filled with extraordinarily handsome, interesting-looking people in a setting more spectacular than Versailles or

Fontainebleau. They both agreed that they had never seen anything anywhere to rival it, and as they made their way back to the other end of the ship, to the sun deck, where they would live for the next week, other voices echoed their thoughts in whispered tones: "Extraordinary . . . *extraordinaire* . . . *un miracle* . . . *incroyable* . . . incredible . . . remarkable . . . she's every inch a queen." People constantly compared her to other ships, yet there was no comparison to be made. She stood alone. The *Normandie*. A solitary work of art. A crown of jewels in France's fleet.

"Shall we see if Jacques is here, Liane?" They were walking past the studios, approaching their rooms, and for just an instant Liane felt her heart give a tiny tug. She didn't want to see Jacques yet, didn't want to see him here at all. She wanted Armand to herself, to share the voyage with only him. She was almost sorry they had brought the girls. It would have been so wonderful to have had the next five days alone with him.

"If you like, Armand." Ever obedient, she knew how much Armand needed Jacques. Yet it would have been nicer if they hadn't had to do any work on board. But such was the existence Armand led. Responsibilities above all. They stopped and knocked, but with relief, Liane noted that there was no response. A steward approached them at once.

"You're looking for M. Perrier, Ambassadeur?"

"I am."

"He is in the Café-Grill with friends. Would you like me to show you the way?"

"No, no, it's quite all right." Armand smiled pleasantly at the man. "There'll be plenty of time after we set sail." At least he knew the young man was on board. He had felt sure he would be by now, but he had wanted to be absolutely sure. There were still some very important memos they had to get out, in preparation for Armand's arrival in France. "Thank you very much."

"Not at all. I'll be your chief steward for the trip. Jean-Yves Herrick." He pronounced it *Err-eek,* and Armand had known from his accent that he was from Bretagne. "I believe you'll find a message from Captain Thoreux in your suite."

"Thank you again." Armand followed Liane inside, and beside an enormous handsome basket of flowers on the piano and two baskets of fruit from their Washington friends, there was indeed a letter from Captain Thoreux, inviting them to watch the ship set sail from the bridge, a rare privilege granted to few, and Liane was pleased.

"Do you suppose he'd let us bring our camera?"

"I don't see why not. Do you want to check on the girls before we go?" But when she did, she found that they had disappeared. Mademoiselle had left the De Villierses a note, informing them that the girls wanted to see the kennels and the tennis court on the upper sun deck, and Liane knew that they would be safe with Mademoiselle. There was lots for all of them to explore, and she followed Armand now, back in the direction they had come. The bridge, they discovered, was on the sun deck at the front of the ship, and directly over the winter garden that had so enchanted Liane a little while before.

Two officers quietly stood guard outside the wheelhouse, keeping the curious from getting inside, and Armand handed them the note Captain Thoreux had sent, and they were rapidly ushered inside to meet him themselves. He was a wiry, white-haired man with deep creases around deep-set blue eyes, and he kissed Liane's hand and then shook Armand's, welcoming them aboard his ship as they sang its praise.

"We're all very proud of her." He beamed. The *Normandie* had just won the Blue Riband again, for speed records across the Atlantic, but she was equally remarkable for her beauty as well, as they all knew.

"She's even more beautiful than we dreamed. An extraordinary ship." Armand looked around at the perfectly regimented order of the bridge. It looked like the insides of a Swiss clock. Everything was immaculate, hushed, in perfect order. Charts were spread out on a large table, the view from here was superb, and there was an elevated platform where the captain and his first officer stood, ruling the movements of the ship, which Armand had heard for several years were also the smoothest of all ships afloat. There had been some talk of unpleasant vibrations at first, but even that problem had been overcome in the *Normandie*'s early days. And because of the remarkable design of her hull, it was also said that she had almost no wake. She was in every possible aspect beyond even her designer's and builder's dreams.

From a quiet corner, where they would not get in the way, Armand and Liane watched the ship get under way, pulling out slowly from Pier 88, assisted by tugs until she left the port, and then turning slowly east, pointing her nose toward France, until at last the port of New York slowly disappeared, and they were at sea. Armand was once again impressed by the swiftness of the ship's maneuvers and the smooth workings of Captain Thoreux's team.

"We hope that you will both have a very pleasant journey." Thoreux smiled again at Liane. "And it would be my great honor if you would join me for dinner tonight. We have some very interesting people on the ship. We always do." He was too proud of his ship not to boast a bit, but he had every right to do so, and Armand accepted the invitation with pleasure, wondering who else was on board, and who they would meet at the captain's table. He hoped that Liane might have a little fun, make some friends, and find some people to keep her amused while he worked with Jacques. They thanked the captain again and returned to the Trouville suite.

It was by then three in the afternoon, and Armand suggested that they order some sandwiches and tea in their room. They had a pantry of their own, and the dining room they'd noted before would be useful at times like this, and as Liane stretched out on the large, comfortable blue-satin-covered bed, he read her the menu and she grinned.

"You won't be able to roll me off the ship in France if I eat all that."

"You can afford to add a pound or two." She had a tendency to be too thin, but he had to admit he liked her that way: long, elegant, and lean. It always gave her the look of a young colt, especially when she played games with the girls on their lawn. There was ever something youthful about Liane, especially now as she peeled off the red silk suit, to reveal tiny cascades of satin and lace. He slowly put the menu aside, and with another thought in mind he approached, but just then their doorbell rang. He hesitated for a moment and Liane sighed.

"I'll be right back." But before she heard his voice, she knew. It was Jacques Perrier, ever devoted to the task at hand. His earnest horn-rimmed, spectacled face, his dark suits, his briefcase always chock-full. Liane knew him only too well. The honeymoon with Armand would end before it ever began, with Jacques Perrier's help. She heard them now, conferring in the living room, and a moment later Armand came back to her.

"Is he gone?" Liane sat up on the bed, her garter belt and stockings and brassiere still in place on her lissome frame.

"No . . . I'm sorry, Liane . . . there were some cables that apparently came in just before we left. . . . I have to . . . just a moment . . ." He faltered for a moment, trying to read her eyes. But she only smiled at him.

"It's all right. I understand. Will you work here?"

"No, I thought we'd go to his room. You order something to eat. I'll be back in half an hour." He came to kiss her quickly on the lips and then was gone, his mind filled with his duties for France, and she glanced at the menu again. But she was not hungry for food, she was hungry for Armand, for more of his time, and there was never enough. She lay down on her bed and then relaxed, listening to the soft murmuring of the ship until she fell asleep, dreaming of Armand and a beach somewhere in the South of France. She was trying to get to him, but she couldn't get past a guard who insisted that she couldn't get through. And the guard wore the face of Jacques Perrier. She slept like that for two hours, while Marie-Ange and Elisabeth escorted their governess to the swimming pool.

In the Deauville Suite, Hillary Burnham stood staring at the wood-paneled bar with an air of exasperation. There were gallons of champagne, but she couldn't find the Scotch. "Goddamn lousy bar. Stinking French, all they ever think of is their bloody wine." She slammed the door and turned to stare at Nick, her black eyes shining like shimmering black onyx, her hair like black silk over a spectacularly beautiful dress of white crepe de chine. She had thrown the hat to match on a chair when she walked into the living room of the suite, scarcely noticing the decor, or acknowledging the beauty of her surroundings. All she did was tell her maid to start unpacking her clothes and iron the black satin skirt with the raspberry satin top that she was going to wear that night.

"Don't you want to take a look around before you have a drink, Hil?" Nick was watching her as she stalked away from the bar with a shake of her head, and she reminded him, as she had a long time before, of a petulant, desperately unhappy child. He never quite understood why she was that way. One could tell oneself that she had been spoiled when she was young, that marriage chafed her more than it did most, that she was disappointed in her life, but it was still hard to understand why. Underneath the sharp tongue, and the harsh words, there was still a beautiful girl who could still turn his knees to mush. It saddened him that he could never inspire the same in her. For a mad moment or two he had told himself that she might be different on the ship, that away from her friends and her fast life, she might once again become the girl he had first met, but it had been a foolish thought and he knew that now. There had been several clandestine phone calls made from her dressing room the night before, and at eleven o'clock she had gone out for a couple of hours. He didn't ask her where she'd gone. It didn't really matter now. They were leaving for a year, and whatever it was, he knew that she would be leaving it behind. "Would you like some champagne?" His voice was polite now, but less warm than it had been before.

"No, thanks. I think I'll go have a look at the bar." She glanced at a map of the ship and saw that there was one just beneath where they were, and she ran her lipstick quickly across her lips before heading for the door. Johnny was out on their private deck with his nurse, excitedly watching the skyline of New York as they pulled out of port, and for a moment Nick felt torn, and then made a rapid decision to follow his wife. This was a good place not to fall into old ways, and he wanted to keep an eye on her. Whatever she had done in New York, he was not going to let her do it for the next year. The American community in Paris was not overly large, and he didn't want her creating any scandals there. And if she was going to be as restless as she had been for the last nine years, then he was going to just have to tag along. "Where are you going?" She looked back at him over her shoulder, with a look of surprise.

"I thought I'd join you at the bar." He kept his voice even and their eyes met and held. "Do you mind?"

"Not at all." They spoke to each other like strangers, and a moment later he followed her down the hall. She descended to the Grillroom on the boat deck, where the buffet ran all day and all night, and the walls were of the varnished pigskin that had so intrigued Liane. It was an enormous airy-looking room that looked out on the first-class promenade, where many of the passengers had gathered as the ship set sail. And now, in couples and small groups, they wandered into the grill, their faces animated, their voices filled with chatter and laughter, excited about the trip. Only Hillary and Nick seemed to sit in total silence, or so he felt as he watched the people come in and sit at tables. He felt odd not saying anything to his wife, but then he realized that they scarcely knew each other anymore. She was almost a stranger to him. All he knew about her was that she went to parties constantly, bought new clothes, and disappeared to Newport and Boston whenever she could. It was more than a little odd to be sitting here together, and he wondered suddenly, as she ordered a Scotch and water, if she felt trapped, being there with him. He couldn't even imagine what to say. What do you say to a woman who has been avoiding you for almost nine years? "Hi, how's your life? Where have you been for the past decade? . . . Hello, my name is . . ." He began to smile to himself at the absurdity of what he was feeling, and when he looked up, he saw her eyeing him with a mixture of curiosity and suspicion.

"What's funny, Nick?"

He was about to say something pacifying and vague, but then he decided not to. "We are, I guess. I was trying to remember the last time we sat at a table like this, all by ourselves, with no place to go, nowhere to rush off to. It's funny, that's all. I was wondering what to say to you." It was so easy to send her into a rage and he really didn't want to. He almost hoped that they could make friends again. Maybe the year in Paris would do them good. Maybe without her little circle in Boston to run off to she'd make an effort. He smiled again at the thought and covered one of her long, beautiful hands with his, feeling beneath his fingers the ten-carat diamond he had bought her. He had bought her a lot of jewelry at first, but she rarely seemed as pleased to receive it as he was to give it, and in recent years his gifts to her had stopped. He knew though that there had been gifts from others, like the fox jacket the winter before, and a large emerald brooch she had worn often, as though to flaunt it at him . . . a ruby ring . . . He forced his mind back from his thoughts. They would do no one any good now. He looked into the big black eyes and smiled at her. "Hello, Hillary. It's nice to see you here."

"Is it?" The anger seemed to fade, replaced by something sad. "I don't know why it should be, Nick. I haven't been much of a wife." There was no apology in her voice, only a tinge of bitterness in the statement.

"We've become strangers in the last few years, Hil, but it doesn't have to be that way forever."

"It's already been that way forever, Nick. I'm all grown up and someone you barely know, and to tell you the truth, most of the time I can't even remember who you are. I have these distant memories of the parties we went to long ago, of how handsome you were, and how exciting, and I look at you, and you look the same. . . ." Her eyes grew too bright and she looked away. "But you're not."

"Have I changed that much in all these years?" He looked sad too. These were words they should have said long before, and never had, and suddenly here they were in a bar on a ship that had just set sail, beginning to open up their hearts. "Am I so different now, Hil?"

She nodded, her eyes bright with tears, and then she looked up at him again. "Yes, you're my husband." She said it as though it were a terrible word, and he could see the old restlessness in the way she moved her shoulders and suddenly moved back from the table in her seat, as though to escape him.

"Is that such a bad thing?"

"I think—" She almost choked on the words, but for once she decided to go ahead and say it. He might as well know how she felt. Why not? "I think for me it is. I don't think I was ever meant to be married, Nick." This time it was said in a voice of confession, the bitterness was gone, and she looked like a beautiful young debutante again, the debutante he had "raped," in her words once, and got pregnant, and "kidnapped" from her home, and "forced" into marriage. She had rewritten the screenplay long since, and she believed what she said. There was no point arguing with her, or reminding her that she had wanted to go to bed with him, that it was as much her fault as his that she had got pregnant, and that he had tried to make the best of it with her, but she had never even wanted to try. "I feel . . . I feel so trapped being married . . . as though I'm a bird that can't fly, but can only flap its wings, hobbling around the ground, going nowhere, being made fun of by its friends. It makes—" She hesitated for a moment and then went on. "It makes me feel ugly . . . like I'm not what I used to be anymore."

"You're even more beautiful than you were." He said it, looking into her eyes, and taking in the creamy skin, the silky hair, the delicate shoulders, and graceful arms. There was nothing ugly about Hillary Burnham, except at times the way she behaved, but he didn't say that now. "You've grown up to be an exceptionally beautiful woman. But that's not surprising. You were always an exceptionally beautiful girl."

"But I'm not a girl anymore, Nick. I'm not even a woman." She paused as though groping for words. "You don't know what it's like for a woman to be married. It's like you become someone's possession, their *thing*, no one sees you as yourself anymore." It was something he had never thought of, and it sounded a little crazy to him now. Was that what she had been fighting all these years? Was that what all the affairs were all about? Her fight to make herself separate, to be someone and something on her own? It was a novel thought to him.

"I don't think of you as a possession. I think of you as my wife."

"What does that mean?" For the first time in half an hour there was anger in her voice again, and she signaled for another Scotch as a waiter drifted by. "My wife. It sounds like 'my chair, my table, my car.' My wife. So what? Who am I when I'm with you? I'm Mrs. Nicholas Burnham. I don't even have a name of my own, for chrissake. Johnny's mother . . . it's like being someone's dog. I want to be *me. Hillary!*"

"Just Hillary?" He looked at her with a sad smile.

"Just Hillary." She looked back at him for a long time and took a sip of her drink.

"Is that who you are to your friends, Hil?"

"Some of them. At least the people I know don't give a damn about who you are. I'm sick to death of hearing about Nick Burnham—Nick Burnham this . . . Nick Burnham that . . . Oh, you must be Mrs. Nicholas Burnham . . . Nick Burnham's wife . . . Nick Burnham . . . Nick Burnham . . . Nick Burnham!!" She raised her voice as he shushed her.

"Don't tell me to shut up, damn it. You don't know what it's like." It felt good to confront him. That was something new in their totally separate lives. Now perhaps he could understand what lay behind her ferocious independence. But the funny thing was that it was precisely that that had drawn her to him originally and he knew it. She had liked the fact that he was Nicholas Burnham, with all the weight that carried with it. "And I'll tell you something else. No one in Boston gives a damn about who you are, Nick." That wasn't entirely true and they both knew it, but it made her feel better to say it. "I have my own friends there, and they knew me before I married you." He had never realized that that was so desperately important to her. He wondered suddenly if there was some way he could ease the burden of this anger she felt. And just as the thought entered his mind a steward approached them.

"Mr. Burnham?"

"Yes?" He thought instantly of Johnny. That he had got hurt somewhere on the ship, and they had come to find him.

"You have a message from the captain." Nick glanced at Hillary and saw her eyes blaze, and he suddenly knew something more, that she hadn't told him in the past hour over drinks. She was jealous of him.

"Thank you." He accepted the gold-banded envelope with a nod, and the steward disappeared as Nick took out the single engraved sheet with the formal wording. "Captain Thoreux . . . requests the pleasure of your company at dinner . . . in the Grande Salle à Manger at nine o'clock this evening." It was what was referred to as the Second Sitting, and the most elegant of the two, the first one being at seven.

"What's that all about? Are they already kissing your ass, Nick?" She had finished the second drink, and her eyes were too bright, but not with tears now.

"Shhh, Hil, please." He looked around to see if anyone had heard her. The idea that anyone kissed his ass embarrassed him. But there was no escaping the fact that he was a very important man, and it was inevitable that he would be pursued. He wore his mantle of importance well, albeit at times almost too humbly, which made it all the more insane that his wife resented who he was. He was the last human being on earth to cram it down her throat. But she had heard it all too often. "The captain is inviting us to dinner."

"Why? Do they want you to buy the boat? I hear this tub is called France's floating debt."

"If she is, she's a beauty and well worth it." He had learned long since not to respond directly to her questions when she was in that kind of mood, it only made her more angry. "The invitation is for nine o'clock. Do you want to have something to eat now?" It was only four-thirty. "We could have something here or go into the Grand Salon for tea."

"I'm not hungry." He watched her eye the waiter for another drink, but he shook his head and the waiter disappeared.

"Don't treat me like a child, Nick." She almost hissed the words at him. All her life people had done that, her mother, her father, her governess, Nick. The only people who didn't were people like Ryan Halloway and Philip Markham. They treated her like a woman. "I'm all grown up now, and if I want another drink, I'll have one."

"If you drink too much, it'll make you seasick."

For once she didn't argue with him, but took out her gold Cartier compact with the diamond clasp as he signed the check for their drinks, and put on a bright red slash of lipstick. She was one of those women who, with very little effort, could turn the heads of an entire room, and she came damn close to it as they walked outside to the promenade for some air. New York was already long gone now. The *Normandie* was going thirty knots, and scarcely leaving any wake behind her.

They stood there side by side at the rail, in silence for a time, and he thought over what he had learned about his wife during the past hour of conversation. He had never before realized how much she resented being his wife, or at least not for those reasons. She wanted to be her own woman, and not belong to any man. Maybe she was right, he wondered, maybe she shouldn't be married. But it was too late for those thoughts now. He would never let her go. He would never give up Johnny. He glanced down at her where they stood and for an instant wanted to put an arm around her, but he sensed instinctively that it wouldn't be the right thing to do, and instead he sighed softly in the wind as other couples strolled past them. He longed for that kind of friendship and ease with his wife, but they had never had that between them. They had had sex and passion and magic and teasing, in the beginning anyway, but they had never had the quiet that grows between two people who are comfortable with each other. In a way, he questioned if they had ever really shared love, or only their bodies.

"What are you thinking about, Nick?" It was an odd question from her, and he turned to look down at her with a slow smile.

"Us. What we have, what we don't." Dangerous words, but he was feeling a little daring. The wind was whipping his face, and he felt oddly free here. It was the kind of magic they talked about on ships, feeling as though one were in a separate world. The rules of one's normal life, so carefully adhered to, no longer seemed to apply here.

"What do we have, Nick?"

"Sometimes I'm not sure anymore." He sighed and leaned down against the rail. "I know what we had at the beginning."

"The beginning wasn't real."

"The beginning never is. But ours was as real as most. I loved you very much, Hil."

"And now?" Her eyes dug deep into his.

"I still love you." Why? he asked himself. Why? Maybe it was because of Johnny.

"In spite of all I've done to you?" She was honest about her sins, some of the time at least. And like him, she felt especially free now, especially after the two Scotches.

"Yes."

"You're a brave man." The words were open and honest, but she didn't tell him that she loved him. To do so would have been to strip herself bare, to admit that she belonged to him, and she would no longer do that. She tossed her hair in the wind then and looked out to sea as he watched her. Without looking at him, she spoke. It was as though she didn't want him to see into her soul, or maybe she didn't want to hurt him any more than she already had. "What am I supposed to wear to this dinner tonight?"

"Whatever you want." He sounded suddenly tired and sad. The moment had passed, but he had wanted to ask her if she loved him. Maybe it didn't matter anymore. Maybe she was right. They were married. She was his. He owned her. But he knew that in her case, thinking that he owned her was a delusion. "The men wear white tie. I guess you should wear something pretty formal."

She knew that in that case the raspberry and black satin outfit wouldn't do, and as they wandered back to their cabin on the sun deck, she mentally meandered over what she had brought in her trunks and settled on a delicate mauve satin gown.

When they reached the Deauville suite, Nick glanced into their son's room, but he still hadn't returned from his tour around the ship with his nurse, and Nick was suddenly sorry that he hadn't taken him himself. But as he returned from Johnny's room, he saw Hillary looking at him. She had taken off the white crepe de chine dress and was standing there in a white satin slip and stocking feet, looking more beautiful than ever. She was the kind of woman one wanted to ravage until she screamed. He hadn't thought of her that way when she was eighteen. But he thought of her that way now. Often.

"Good God, you should see the look on your face!" Hillary began to laugh her deep, throaty laugh as Nick approached her. "You look positively wicked, Nick Burnham!" But she didn't seem to mind it. She stood there, the strap of her slip falling off her shoulder, and he saw that she wore no bra, and every inch of her seemed to taunt him.

"Then don't stand around looking like that, Hil, unless you want to get into serious trouble."

"And what kind of trouble is that?" He stood directly in front of her, and could feel the warmth from her tantalizing body. But this time he didn't play with words with her, he crushed his lips down on hers, never wondering if she would reject him. You never knew with Hil, it depended on the importance of her lover at the current moment. But there was no lover now. She was on a ship, miles from shore, lost between two worlds, and she stretched her arms up to her husband, and without further ado he swept her up in his arms, walked into their bedroom, and slammed the door with one foot before depositing her on the bed and tearing the white satin slip from her body. What it revealed was a white satin of a different kind, and his mouth drank in the cream of her flesh, like a man dying of hunger. She gave herself with a passion dimly remembered from the past, spiced now with the knowledge of years she had acquired since he met her. But he asked no questions now, he thought of nothing but his rampant desire for her, which seemed to know no bounds as their bodies plunged on the peaceful ship and his body covered hers and at last they lay spent. He watched her afterward as she slept, and knew the truth of her words of an hour before. She was his wife. There was no doubt about that. But he would never own her. No man would. Hillary owned herself, always had, always would. She was always just out of reach, and as he watched her lying peacefully in his arms, he knew with a bittersweet sorrow that he had always wanted the impossible. She was like a rare jungle beast one longed to tame. And the truth was, she was right, secretly he did want to own her.

Chapter 5

To a woman, the ladies who entered the Grande Salle à Manger that night, sauntering slowly down the stairs as people watched, would have made any man proud. Their hair and makeup were done to perfection, they were impeccably turned out by the maids they had brought along, and most of their gowns had been designed in Paris. The jewels competed only with the brilliant lights in the room, equal to the brilliance of one hundred and thirty-five thousand candles and reflected in the endless walls of hammered glass sixty feet longer than the Hall of Mirrors at Versailles. The room, three decks high, seemed filled to the rafters with ruby taffetas and sapphire velvets and emerald satins, and here and there a gown of gold. Liane herself looked exquisite in a black strapless taffeta dress she had bought at Balenciaga. It cascaded behind her in a sea of ruffles. But it was when Hillary Burnham came down the stairs that everyone seemed to stare at her clinging Grecian gown of the palest mauve satin. It molded to her exquisite form in a way that made everyone hold their breath, including the captain. Around her neck she was wearing pearls the size of very large marbles. But it wasn't the rope of pearls that caught the eye, but the raven-black hair, the creamy skin, the brilliant black eyes, and her body as it swayed slowly down the stairs to the captain's table.

The captain's table was just in front of the enormous bronze statue representing peace, which stood tall among the diners, her head held high, though not as high as Hillary's as she reached the table, with Nick just behind her, impeccable in white tie and tails, with mother-of-pearl studs in his starched shirtfront, diamonds circling them and at their center. But it was the diamonds at Hillary's ears, peeking from behind the shaft of black satin hair, which set off the dancing lights in her eyes.

"Good evening, Captain." Her voice was deep and husky, and in spite of their best efforts, everyone lost the thread of their conversations at the table. Captain Thoreux stood up, bowed in well-executed, almost military fashion, and bent to kiss her hand.

"*Madame . . . bonsoir.*" He stood to face her again and introduced her to the group. "Mme. Nicholas Burnham," and then he introduced Nick. The group at the captain's table was considerably older than were they, except for Liane. But most were of the captain and Armand's generation. Their wives were elegant and well dressed but slightly overstuffed, and heavily bejeweled, as though if they counterbalanced their portly shapes with an equal quantity of jewels, one might not notice their excess weight. But no one looked at them once Hillary arrived. The men's eyes were riveted to Hillary and her gown, which seemed to flow over her like water, straight across her shoulders in the front, and then down to a point just below her waist in back, revealing the delicious flesh every man who saw her longed to touch.

"Good evening, everyone." She made no effort to remember their names, and awarded a second glance only to Armand, looking extremely handsome tonight, wearing his decorations with his white tie. She made no effort to talk to Liane, although they sat across the table from each other, but Nick seemed to make a special effort to make up for her, chatting pleasantly with two older women on either side, and an elderly man who turned out to be an English lord. Liane noticed that Nick glanced frequently at his wife, not so much as an affectionate sign, as Armand had done two or three times since the dinner began, but rather as though he were checking up on her. She saw him appearing not to strain to hear what Hillary said, but she had the feeling that Nick Burnham did not trust his wife, and between the *plateau de fromages* and the soufflé Grand Marnier, she began to suspect why. Hillary was speaking to the elderly Italian prince on her left, and had just told him that she always found Rome extremely dull. But as though to keep him intrigued, she smiled pleasantly as she made the slight, and then looked past him again to cast an eye at Armand. "I understand you're an ambassador." She glanced then at Liane, and it was obvious that she was wondering if Liane was his daughter or his wife. "You're traveling with your family?"

"I am. My wife and daughters. Your husband tells me that you have a son on board. Perhaps we can get the children together sometime to play." Hillary nodded, but she seemed annoyed. It looked somehow as though children's games were not precisely what she had in mind. There was a predatory quality about her tonight, a woman looking for easy prey, and with a face and body like that, Liane thought to herself, it couldn't be very hard to find. She was amused at Armand's polite rebuff. She never worried about him, the only one she ever lost him to was Jacques Perrier. As it turned out, they had worked all afternoon, and he had come back to the Trouville suite just in time to bathe and get dressed, a circumstance Liane was accustomed to, although she had hoped to see more of him on the ship.

"Perhaps," she had threatened him as she ran his bath and handed him a kir, "I shall have to throw Jacques overboard." Armand had laughed, grateful for an understanding wife. But he had not seen her earlier on their private deck, staring out to sea, with a look of sorrow on her face. She longed for the days of long ago, when he was a less important man, and there hadn't been a constant flow of memos and cables and reports to occupy his mind, and he had had more time for her. He so seldom did now.

She wondered then what Nick Burnham was like. He

seemed a pleasant man, but he offered very little of himself. He was polite, well-bred, he seemed to take in the entire scene with quiet eyes, but one knew him no better when dessert was served than one had known him when he had first sat down. She wondered if perhaps he adopted such a bland facade to counteract his more than startling wife. Liane had a feeling that she was out to shock. It was not that her dress was inappropriate, but it was designed obviously to catch the eye and keep it there. One thing was certain, Hillary Burnham was not shy.

Nicholas was observing his wife through new eyes tonight. He had watched her from the moment they introduced her as his wife, to see how she would react, following her confessions to him that afternoon in the bar. Insanely he hoped that something in her would soften, but she was no different than before. The moment the captain said the fateful words "Mme. Nicholas Burnham," she was out to prove something to them all. It almost made Nick sorry for her to see her chafe at the bonds she so ardently resented. But there was nothing he could do to help her. Even a kindly look from him annoyed her and she rapidly turned her attention to Armand, with a come-hither look in her eyes. But the ambassador appeared not to notice.

"This isn't Boston or New York, Hil," Nick whispered later as the entire group headed toward the Grand Salon. "If you give yourself a bad name here, it'll stick with you for the next five days." He was referring to her unsuccessful attempt at flirtation with Armand, the captain, and two of the other diners.

"Who gives a damn? They're a bunch of old bores."

"Are they? I rather thought you liked the ambassador." It was his first truly cutting remark of the trip, but he was tired suddenly of her games. Even when he tried to understand her, inevitably she angered him or hurt him. And she was also straining obviously at the bit, and it worried him. He was never quite sure what she would do or say. "Do yourself a big favor while you're on board."

"What's that?"

"Behave yourself."

She turned to face him then, stopping dead in her tracks with a wicked smile. "But why? Because I'm your wife?"

"Don't start that crap again. As it so happens, that's exactly who you are. There are almost a thousand important, influential people on this ship, and if you don't watch your ass, my dear, every one of them is going to know just what you are." His anger was full-blown now. He could do nothing to stop it and no longer cared to.

"And what's that?" She was almost laughing at him now, totally oblivious of his concern. And he had been about to answer her with two simple words: "A whore," but the captain was at their sides again in the magnificent room, and Hillary turned to him with a charming smile. "Will there be dancing tonight?"

"Of course, my dear." The captain, like the other officers aboard the ship, had seen droves of Hillarys over the years, some older than she, some not. Lovely, spoiled, bored with their lives ashore, tired of marriages and husbands who had faded from their lives long years before, but they had seen few quite as beautiful as this. She stood beside their table in the Grand Salon now, and even in the splendor of the room, she was aware of every pair of male eyes on her. There were glowing crystal fountains filled with light, windows twenty-two feet high, and murals etched in glass, covered with ships, and an orchestra had already begun to play, but Hillary was the finest attraction of all. She had wilted not one bit from the feast in the dining room. If anything, she seemed more effervescent than the endless flow of French champagne. "In fact"—the captain smiled at Nick—"may I have your permission, sir, to ask Madame for the first dance?"

"Of course." Nick smiled pleasantly his assent and watched them as they walked away. The orchestra was playing a low French waltz, and Hillary's body moved with extraordinary grace as the captain guided her expertly around the floor, and other couples joined them, among them Armand and Liane.

"Well, my love, have you fallen head over heels for the siren from New York?" Liane smiled at him as they danced.

"I have not. I am far more impressed by the beauty from the West Coast. Do you suppose I have a chance with her?" He brought her fingers to his lips and kissed them, keeping his eyes on hers. "Are you having fun, *chérie*?"

"I am." She smiled happily as she looked around the room. She was never happier than when she was in Armand's arms. "She's quite something, though, isn't she?" She was still intrigued with Hillary, and Armand looked over his wife's head with a peaceful glance.

"The *Normandie*? Ah, yes, she is."

"Now, stop it." Liane laughed. "I know you hate to gossip, but I can't resist. You know exactly who I mean. I mean the Burnham woman. She's the most beautiful thing I've ever seen."

"Indeed." He nodded, a smiling sage. "Beauty and the Beast are rolled into one. I don't envy him. But I think he knows exactly what he's got on his hands. He watches her every move."

"And she knows it, and she doesn't give a damn."

"I wouldn't say that." Armand shook his head. "I think she does it to annoy him. One could murder a woman like that."

"Maybe he's madly in love with her." Liane enjoyed the thought of a passionate romance.

"I think not. If one looks deep into his eyes, he's not a happy man. Do you know who he is, Liane?"

"More or less. I've heard his name. He's in steel, isn't he?"

Armand laughed. "He isn't 'in' steel. He *is* steel. A few years ago he was the youngest, most important industrialist in the States. His father died when he was quite young, and left him not only a fortune that almost defies the imagination, but an empire to run as well. He has proven himself admirably. I believe he's crossing over now because he has some very important steel contracts with France. And today, he is truly the master of his industry."

"At least he's on our side."

"Not all the time." Liane's eyes raised to Armand's. "He has contracts with the Germans too. And that, my love, is how an empire is run. Without a heart at times, but always with a firm hand and quick mind. It's too bad he can't exercise the same power over his wife."

Liane slowly digested this as the dance came to an end. She was more than a little shocked to realize that Burnham was selling steel to Hitler as well as to France. To her that seemed a betrayal of all that she believed in, and she was surprised at Armand's easy acceptance that business was business, but he was more familiar than she with the world of international politics, and dealings and compromises were the norm for him.

"Does that shock you about Burnham, Liane?" He looked down at her pensive expression and she nodded.

"It does."

"Those are the ways of the world, my love."

"That's not how you do business, Armand." She was so idealistic that it touched him. She had so much faith in him and his integrity, and that meant a great deal to him.

"I don't sell steel, my little love. I deal in the honor and well-being of France on foreign shores. That is by no means the same thing."

"The principles should be the same. What's right is right."

"It's not always as simple as that. And according to what they say, he's a very decent man." It was the impression Liane had of him, but now she was not as sure. For a moment she wondered if that was the problem with his wife, perhaps she didn't respect him. But she realized almost as soon as the thought came that that had nothing to do with the way Hillary behaved. She was selfish and unpleasant and spoiled, and she probably always had been. There was a sharp edge to her that nothing veiled, and her beauty was outweighed by the evil that lurked within her. "I wouldn't, however, say that his wife is a decent girl."

"Hardly that." Liane smiled.

"There are very few men as lucky as I." He bent to whisper in her ear and then escorted her off the floor. She danced with the captain then, the Italian prince, and her husband again, and then they excused themselves and returned to the Trouville suite, and she was happy to be alone with Armand at last. She yawned as she took off the lovely black dress. Armand was in his dressing room, and when he returned, he found her already in bed and waiting for him, and his own words echoed in his own head again. There were few men in the world as lucky as he, and when he came to bed, Liane proved it to him again, and they fell asleep in each other's arms.

It was a very different scene from the one in the Deauville suite, where Hillary was, as usual, making trouble. Nick had forced her to come back to the suite. She had found someone more interesting to dance with at last, from another group, and Nick had accused her of being rude. And in the end, after watching her cavort for too long, he thanked the captain for a lovely time and excused himself with his wife, to return to their suite.

"Who the hell do you think you are?"

"The person you hate most, my dear. Your husband, the man who holds the end of the gilded chain you wear." He had smiled at her to quell the fury he felt, but she had gone into their room and slammed the door, and tonight it was Nick who sought refuge in the bottle of Scotch. And as he drank he found himself thinking of Armand and Liane. He thought they made a handsome pair, and he admired the grace and poise with which Liane moved and behaved. She was an impressive woman in her quiet way, and her subtle glow hadn't gone unnoticed, even in the shadow of Hillary's far more gaudy light. He was tired of her games, he decided with his fourth glass of straight Scotch. More tired than she knew. More tired than he himself was willing to admit most of the time. If he would have allowed himself to feel the pain, it would have been too much to bear. In the end he put the bottle away, and at three o'clock that morning he went to bed, grateful that Hillary had taken a sleeping pill and was already asleep.

Chapter 6

The sea air was having the effect that it always did. The next day on the ship, everyone seemed to wake earlier than they were used to, having slept better than they had in years, and with appetites that brought the stewards to their rooms with heavily laden trays. And Armand sat in their private dining room with the girls and Mademoiselle, while Liane bathed. The girls were already anxious to get out and move about the ship.

"And what are you going to do today?" He smiled at the girls over a breakfast of kippered herring and shad roe, and Marie-Ange made a face as she watched him eat. "Would you like a taste?" he teased, and she vehemently shook her head.

"No, thank you, Papa. We're going swimming with Mademoiselle. Will you come?"

"I'm going to do a little work with M. Perrier this morning, but perhaps your mother will."

"What will your mother do?" Liane appeared in their dining room, wearing a white cashmere dress, her long blond hair pulled back in a neat bun, and white suede shoes. She looked as fresh as an English rose, and Armand admired her again, wishing suddenly that he had lingered in bed long enough for them to make love. "Good morning, girls." She kissed them both, greeted Mademoiselle, and then stopped to kiss Armand on the top of his head.

"You look lovely, my dear." It was obvious that he was sincere, and she smiled at him.

"At this hour of the day?" She looked surprised and pleased. He always noticed what she wore and how she looked and she could see in his eyes when he was especially taken with her. As he had a moment before, she wished now that Armand had stayed awhile in their room. But he had been quick to hurry out of bed. He had a great deal of work to do, and he had promised her that he would finish before lunch. "Anyway, what was it that you were volunteering my services for?"

"A swim with the girls. How does that sound to you?"

"Like a fine idea." She smiled at Marie-Ange and Elisabeth. "I'd like a little time to shop, and maybe walk a bit. But we'll still have plenty of time to swim." She smiled at the girls and poured herself a cup of tea, glancing at Armand. "You know, if I don't walk off some of this food, I'm going to weigh two hundred pounds when we reach Le Havre." She looked at his enormous meal and helped herself to a piece of toast.

"I don't think there's any real danger of that." He accepted a final cup of tea from his wife and looked at his watch. And almost as though the signal had been prearranged, they heard their doorbell ring and it was Jacques Perrier, with the eternal briefcase in his hand. Mademoiselle had let him in, and he greeted Liane solemnly and then Armand.

Bonjour, Madame . . . Monsieur l'Ambassadeur . . . Tout le monde a bien dormi?" He inquired how they had slept, and he sat down with a mournful look. He was, as always, anxious to get to work, and Armand stood up with a sigh.

"I'm afraid, ladies, that duty calls." He smiled into his assistant's eyes and went into the bedroom to get his own briefcase. He emerged a moment later with a sober look and his official face. "We're off." He waved to the girls as they left, and suggested to Perrier on their way out that they go to the gentleman's *fumoir* on the promenade deck, two decks below. There weren't liable to be too many men there now, and they could get their work done in peace amidst the morocco leather settees and easy chairs in the enormous room without interruption. Perrier was quick to agree. He had spent the evening there himself the night before, having no particular interest in the dancing in the Grand Salon. Instead he had chosen to read his memos in the *fumoir*, and prepare for the next day's work. He had stopped at the adjoining Café-Grill on the way back to his room and had had a brandy and a late-night snack, and then he had gone to bed at midnight, before Liane and Armand had returned to their suite.

"Did you sleep well, Perrier?" Armand inquired as they descended the grandiose staircase in the smoking room. There were no women there. It was entirely reserved for men, and was meant to remind them of their clubs, but it was far more sumptuous than any club, with walls covered with gold bas-relief of Egyptian sporting scenes, and two-deck-high ceilings, which were characteristic of almost all the *Normandie*'s gathering rooms. Armand selected a quiet corner with two large leather chairs and a desk and put aside the newspaper published on the ship. They had enough to do.

"I slept very well, thank you, sir."

Armand looked around before opening the folders he had brought. "This is quite a ship, Perrier, isn't it?"

"Indeed, sir, she is." Even he, with his lack of interest in frivolity, had been impressed since the moment he came aboard. There seemed to be startling beauty everywhere, breathtaking design, the finest that their country could produce, from boiserie to sculpture to delicately carved glass, the eye took it all in and the senses soared, even here in the smoking room. "Well, shall we get to work?"

"Yes, sir." The familiar folders came out, and they worked quietly for hours, Perrier making careful notes and putting each folder aside as the matter was resolved. And by ten thirty they had begun to warm up. It was then that Armand noticed Nick Burnham come in. He was wearing a blazer and white slacks and a tie, which pronounced him an alumnus of Yale. He chose a quiet spot across the room, picked up the newspaper of the ship, and began to read, but he glanced at his watch once or twice, and Armand assumed correctly that he was meeting someone there. He wondered if he too had brought an assistant along. He knew that there were many businessmen who did, yet somehow Nick didn't seem quite the type. He seemed more the sort of man who would leave his business at the office at the end of a day, and concentrate on other things. He didn't have the driven qualities of many of his colleagues in the business world. Just then another man came in and looked around. Nick Burnham stood as soon as the newcomer came in. The man then strode across the room, with an almost military gait, and shook hands firmly with Nick and sat down. He ordered a drink from one of the fleet of waiters standing by, and the two men sat down and leaned toward each other in quiet conversation for a time, and Armand guessed that there was business being done. Nick nodded his head frequently and made several brief notes, and the older man he was talking to looked pleased when at last he sat back in his chair, nodding slowly as he looked at Nick and lit a cigar. Whatever it was that they had discussed, it had gone well. At last the second man stood up, they shook hands, and the man crossed the room again, exiting this time through the Café-Grill, as Nick watched, his lips pursed, his eyes following the man's every step until he was gone. Then Nick took out his notes again and when Armand glanced up, he was intrigued by the look on Nick's face. During his entire conversation with the other man he had seemed interested but casual, his body relaxed, his face intent, but not nearly as intent as he looked now, going over his notes. Perhaps he was more driven than he seemed.

Armand realized again what an important man Nick was, and that undoubtedly the deal being discussed in the smoking room was one that involved staggering sums. Yet the man had about him an apparently easy, relaxed manner. As

Armand watched him now, he sensed that the casual ease was only a front, an air he had given himself long since to put those he dealt with falsely at ease. There was nothing relaxed about him now, and Armand could almost sense the wheels turning at full speed in Nick's head. He thought him a most intriguing man, and hoped that before the trip ended they would have time to talk. He caught Nick's eye as he left the room, and Burnham smiled pleasantly at him. He had liked the way Armand had handled Hillary's misbehavior the previous night. He had made it politely obvious that he was impervious to her charms, and Nick was relieved. He didn't particularly want to have to deal with one of her affairs in the close quarters of first class on the ship, and he sensed that Armand was a decent man. They sensed that about each other, and there was a kind of silent camaraderie as Nick smiled and then Armand went back to his work.

Nick went out on deck on the first-class promenade for a breath of air, and when he glanced up, he saw Liane on the terrace of the Trouville suite, her face turned toward the wind. He stood there watching her for a long moment. There was a lovely grace to the woman. She looked like an ivory sculpture in her white cashmere, and he remembered again how quiet and poised she had been the night before. But then he saw her daughters come onto the terrace to claim her attention and a moment later she followed them inside, not having noticed him standing there.

Liane walked the girls around the shops before they went to the pool, and they bought a present for Armand. Liane chose an Hermès tie, and Marie-Ange absolutely insisted that they buy him a little bronze model of the ship on a marble stand. He could put it on his desk in Paris, they said, and Liane agreed to let them buy the treasure for their father. They left it in their suite before going on to the pool with their mother and Mademoiselle.

The pool itself was an extraordinary sight. The enameled sandstones and bright mosaics were designed in intricate patterns everywhere, and the pool was over seventy feet long.

Even filled with the happy swimmers who cavorted in the deep end, it didn't seem crowded, and the girls were almost squealing with delight as Liane led them to the terraced shallow end. She had changed into a navy-blue knit swimsuit with a white belt, and she tucked her hair into a white cap before diving into the deep end of the water. She swam with long, skilled strokes back to the girls as they splashed about in their red bathing suits, beginning to make friends. There was a little boy in a red tank suit much like theirs, and Elisabeth had just learned that his name was John. When John looked up at Liane, she noticed his eyes were a brilliant emerald-green, in sharp contrast to his fair skin and almost jet-black hair. She had the feeling that she had seen him somewhere before. There was something familiar about his eyes, and his smile.

Liane then went for a swim, and as she swam she noticed that groups had begun to form, people were calling each other by their first names, and like the children, they had begun to make friends. But she saw no one she knew. With Armand so busy with Jacques Perrier, they had socialized less than most, and when she was alone, she felt a little strange about leaving their rooms. She took the air on their private promenade, or went on quiet walks, or as now, she did something with the girls. But she was not one of those women to hang around, chatting with the other women in shops, or picking up people over tea in the Grand Salon.

They swam for well over an hour, and then at last Liane urged them from the pool. She took them back to the suite to change for lunch, and escorted them to the children's dining room, decorated by Laurent de Brunhoff with Babars painted on the walls, holding each other's tails. The girls had fallen in love with it the night before, when they'd eaten there with Mademoiselle. And as Liane left she saw the little boy from the pool come in with his nurse. She smiled down at him and he waved at the girls, and then she returned to her suite to change. She had only ten minutes left to dress for lunch and she wondered if Armand would be back soon, but as she sat down on the couch to wait in a beige wool suit from Chanel, a steward rang the bell and handed her a note. Armand and Jacques had not yet finished their work, and he preferred to stick with it until they had, so he could at least spend the afternoon with her. For just a moment as she read his distinctive scrawl, she felt her heart sink, but she smiled at the steward anyway and went downstairs to the Grande Salle à Manger to eat alone.

She was seated at a table for eight, and two of the couples had opted not to dine. The other couple was from New Orleans, a pleasant older pair who made easy conversation about the ship. Liane noticed that the wife wore a diamond ring the size of a sugar cube, and she didn't have a great deal to say. The husband was in oil, he said. They had lived in Texas for years, and Oklahoma before that, but in their twilight years they had moved to New Orleans. She and Armand had been there once. She spoke to them for as long as she could, but they all fell silent over dessert. And before the coffee came they excused themselves to go and take a nap, and Liane sat alone, looking over the dining room and the animated tables everywhere. She felt lonely for Armand, wishing that he would finish his work. And after eating some fresh fruit and a cup of tea, she stood up and walked outside, where she almost immediately ran into Nick Burnham with his son, and then she realized where she had seen the boy before. He was the child she and the girls had met at the pool, and then again in the dining room. He looked very much like Nick, which was why he had looked so familiar to her. She smiled at the child and then at Nick, before talking to the boy.

"How was your lunch?"

"Very good." He beamed, he looked happy holding on to his father's hand, happier than he had looked before. "We're going to the puppet show."

"Would you like to come?" Nick smiled, and Liane hesitated. She wanted to wait in the suite for Armand, but she could leave him a note and take the girls, and when he came, she could always leave them there. Mademoiselle could pick them up when the show was over.

"Yes, I would. I'll go back and get my girls and meet you there." She wondered briefly, as she hurried back to the Trouville, where Hillary Burnham was, but she didn't look the type to spend much time with her son, Liane assessed, and she was quite right. In their suite she found Marie-Ange and Elisabeth playing a game in their rooms. Mademoiselle wanted them to take a nap, but Liane rescued them and left a note for Armand. "Gone to the puppet show with the girls. Meet us there. Love, L." And then the three of them ran off to the children's playroom on the same deck. There was a carousel, and a Punch and Judy show about to begin. She spotted Nick and John sitting in a row of empty seats, waiting for them. Liane and the girls sat down just as the lights began to dim, and the next hour flew by as the children laughed and screamed and answered the questions they were asked by Punch, and applauded heartily when the show came to an end.

"That was fun." John looked up at Nick with a broad grin. "Now can we go on the carousel?" It had just been turned on and stewardesses were assisting the children to climb up, as a row of waitresses prepared generous portions of ice cream. The *Normandie* was like a fairyland for grown-ups, and the children as well. As grandiose as the rest of the ship was for the adults, this was every bit as wonderful for the smaller folk. Elisabeth and Marie-Ange disappeared rapidly from their mother's side and selected horses on either side of their new friend, and all three of them waved happily as the carousel began to turn.

"I just don't believe this place." Nick smiled at Liane. "I think I like their playrooms better than ours."

Liane laughed. "I think I do too." For a moment they stood there watching the children giggling and talking on the carousel. "We saw your son this morning in the swimming pool, and I thought I knew him from somewhere." She smiled at Nick. "Except for his hair, he looks just like you."

"And the girls are the image of you." In truth, Liane thought Elisabeth looked more like Armand, but they both had her blond hair. Armand's hair had once been as dark as little John's, but it had been white now for years, but one could see that his coloring had not been fair, unlike Nick, who seemed almost Viking-like with his broad shoulders and green eyes and blond hair. "This is going to be a fun trip for them." Liane nodded, lost for a moment in her own thoughts, wondering if it would also be a fun trip for herself and Nick. She was beginning to feel that she had scarcely seen Armand since the trip began, and she hadn't seen Hillary with Nick for lunch. She wondered to herself what a woman like that did for fun. She looked like the kind of woman who had fun only when surrounded by men, wearing slinky gowns and covered with jewels and furs. It was hard to imagine her sitting by the pool, or reading a book on deck, or playing tennis. And as though he had read her thoughts, Nick turned to her again. "Have you played any tennis yet?"

"No. I'm afraid I'm not very good."

"Neither am I, but if you have time for a match sometime, I'd love to play. I saw the ambassador hard at work today in the smoking room, and if he wouldn't object, I'd enjoy a game of tennis very much." There seemed to be no ulterior motive in his voice, and Liane suspected that he was a lonely man.

"Does Mrs. Burnham play?" There was no catch in her voice, but he wondered if it was a reproach.

"No, she doesn't. She played a lot in Newport as a girl, but she hated it." And then, "You're from San Francisco, aren't you?"

She was surprised that he knew, and he read it in her face and answered with his easy smile. "Someone mentioned your maiden name last night. Crockett, wasn't it?" She nodded again. "My father used to do business with yours." That was easy to believe; her father had had huge steel contracts for his ships. "We have an office out there, it's a beautiful town, but I always seem to end up on this side of the world."

She smiled at him, amused. "Paris isn't so bad."

"I guess not." He grinned. Neither was the *Normandie*, nor any of the other places he stayed. It was just too bad Hillary didn't feel that way, but she had her own reasons for wanting never to leave home. "Is your husband being stationed back in France?"

"For now anyway. He hasn't lived there in years, I guess they thought it was time to bring him back for a while."

"Where were you before the States?"

"London, and Vienna before that."

"That's another of my favorite towns. I hope to have a chance to visit there on my way back from Berlin sometime." He said it candidly, as though he had nothing to hide, and Liane looked shocked.

"Will you be living in Berlin?"

"No. Paris. But I have some business there." His eyes examined hers carefully, to see what reaction lay there. But he knew from the way she had stiffened just from the word *Berlin*. "My business, Mrs. de Villiers, is selling steel. Not always to my favorite people, I'm afraid." It was very much what Armand had said, but she didn't approve and it showed.

"The time will come eventually for all of us to choose sides."

"Yes." He nodded in agreement with her. "It will. But not for a while, or so I'm told. And in the meantime I have contracts to live up to, not only with France."

"Do you sell to the English too?"

"I did. They've made other arrangements now."

"Perhaps they didn't approve of your business dealings in Berlin." And then suddenly as she said the words she blushed, sensing that she had gone too far. "I'm terribly sorry . . . I didn't mean . . . I shouldn't have said . . ."

But again Nick Burnham smiled his peaceful smile. She hadn't offended him, and he respected her for speaking her mind. "Perhaps you're right, and don't apologize for what you said. You were right with what you said at first, the time will come for all of us to choose sides. I'm just trying not to let my personal views affect my work for now. I can't afford to play those kind of games. I have a steel business to run, but I sympathize with what you feel." He looked very gently down at her, and she was doubly embarrassed for what she had said. He was a very easy, personable man. And there was something more to him as well, an openness, an honesty, a lack of pretense or show. There was something very solid and strong about the man. She could see it even in the gentle way he spoke to his son when the children returned. He was the kind of man one felt that one could turn to at any time, and one always knew that he would be there, rock solid, a good man to be with in a storm.

She turned then and saw Armand, looking for her from the door. She waved and he approached, and she saw that he looked almost as tired as he did at home.

"How was the Punch and Judy show?" He kissed her gently on the cheek, watched the girls, who were back on the carousel with John, and then noticed Nick Burnham approach. The two men exchanged a brief hello and a shake of hands.

"Did you get your work done, Ambassador?"

"More or less, at least for today." He smiled at his wife. "Were you very lonely at lunch, Liane?"

"Very. But Mr. Burnham was kind enough to invite us to join him here. The girls met his son this morning at the pool, and they've become fast friends." She smiled up at Armand again, oblivious of all eyes but his. "Where's Jacques? Did you push him overboard?"

"Would that I could. But that briefcase of his would never sink, it would simply follow me to Le Havre like a shark, and devour me the instant I set foot on shore." Liane and Nick Burnham laughed, and they chatted on for a few moments about the ship. There was a play scheduled in the theater that night, it had been a big hit in Paris the winter before, and Liane and Armand were looking forward to it. "Would you and Mrs. Burnham care to join us for that?"

"I'm afraid my wife doesn't speak French." Nick smiled regretfully at his new friends. "But we might join you for drinks afterward." Liane and Armand said that they thought that might be an excellent idea, but when they left the theater at eight o'clock that night, they didn't see the Burnhams in the Grand Salon, and Liane talked Armand into going back to her favorite room, the winter garden beneath the bridge. They sat there for several hours, drinking champagne and looking out into the night. And as they sat between the aquariums filled with rare fish and cages filled with exotic birds, Armand admitted that he was relieved the Burnhams hadn't come. The task of keeping Hillary at bay hadn't held much appeal, although he liked Nick, and Liane agreed.

"He asked me to play tennis sometime while you work. Would you mind?" She turned her deep-blue eyes to him.

"Not at all. I feel guilty enough as it is, leaving you with nothing to do."

"On this ship?" Liane laughed. "I would be ashamed to admit it if I could find nothing to do here."

"Are you having a good time, then?"

"A very good time, my love." She leaned toward him and spoke in a whisper. "Especially right now."

"Good." At last they wandered back to the Café-Grill, and then out onto the promenade, and then they ascended to their private deck and into their rooms. It was almost two o'clock by then, and Liane was half asleep.

"Are you working tomorrow morning again?"

"I have to, I'm afraid. Why don't you play tennis with that chap. I'm sure there's no harm in it." Liane agreed. Nick wasn't the kind of man to make passes at someone's wife, and he had his hands full enough as it was. Liane and Armand settled comfortably in their bed, and he had had every intention of making love to her, but before either of them could pursue the thought, he was snoring softly and she was sound asleep.

Chapter 7

"Where are you off to at this hour?" Nick was drinking coffee in their private dining room, and John and his nurse were playing on the deck, when Hillary appeared in a pair of white slacks and a red silk shirt, cut like a man's. It set off her dark shiny hair, and the creamy color of her skin. She had disappeared also the day before, having explained to Nick that she had gone for a massage at the pool, and then a facial in the beauty shop. The treatment had taken almost all day.

"I thought I'd take a walk." She glanced at him and her eyes were cold.

"Don't you want something to eat?"

"No, thanks. I thought I might go for a swim in a while. I'll eat after that."

"Okay. Where shall I meet you for lunch?"

She hesitated, but not for long. They were on the trip together, after all, she had to make some effort for him. "How about the Café-Grill?"

"Don't you want to eat in the main dining room?"

"The people at our table bore me to tears." So much so that the night before, she had excused herself before the dessert and it had taken him two hours to find her afterward. She had gone down to the tourist decks, for a look around, and declared it a hell of a lot more fun when she returned. But he had told her that he didn't think she ought to go down there. "Why not?" She had looked both surprised and annoyed, and he had explained that if nothing else, the jewels she wore made it unsafe, and she had only laughed at him. "Are you afraid the peasants will hold me up?" He hadn't answered and she had only laughed again, but she seemed much more docile than she had that afternoon, except when he suggested drinks with the De Villierses. She had declared them both prissy bores, and had gone back to her room for another bottle of champagne. He noticed that she was drinking a lot on the trip, but she had drunk a lot in New York too. He just didn't see as much of her there, and it was easy to notice the bottles decreasing rapidly in their private bar. She seemed to do most of her heavy drinking in their room.

"Hil . . ." He started to say something as she left. "Do you want company today?" He felt somehow as though he ought to be with her. He had promised himself that things were going to be different on this trip. But they weren't yet. They couldn't be. She never let him near her, and now she shook her head again.

"No, thanks. I want to have another massage before lunch."

"The massages must be great." There was suspicion in his voice again, and he berated himself silently for what he thought. It was crazy to distrust your own wife to that extent, yet she had cuckolded him so often before that now he suspected her at every turn.

"They are."

"See you at lunch." She nodded and closed the door, without saying good-bye to their son. John came in a few minutes afterward and looked around.

"Did Mom go out?"

"Yes. She went to get a massage at the pool, like yesterday."

John looked up at his father with confused eyes and shook his head. "She doesn't even know where the pool is. I wanted to show it to her and she said she had something else to do." Nick nodded, pretending almost not to hear, but he had already heard too much. And he knew that she was at it again. But where? And with whom? In tourist class? In cabin? With a purser on another deck? He couldn't chase her everywhere. He was going to confront her at lunch, but now he forced his mind back to his son.

"Do you want to go look at the dogs?"

"Sure." The little boy beamed and they went upstairs to the upper sun deck, to see the dozen or so French poodles being exercised there. There was also a Saint Bernard, a Great Dane, two small ugly pugs, and a Pekingese, and John petted each of them in turn as his father looked out to sea, lost in his own thoughts. He was thinking of Hillary again, and wondering where in hell she was. For an instant he wanted to scour the ship and turn it upside down, but what was the point. He had fought this battle for nine years, and he had long since lost. He knew it well. Even on the ship she was the same as she was in Boston or New York. She was rotten to the core and had always been, the only thing he thanked her for was their son. He turned his eyes back to John and smiled. He was holding one of the funny, snortling little pugs.

"Dad, when we get to Paris, can I have a dog?"

"Maybe, we'll have to see what the house is like."

"Could I really maybe?" John's eyes almost popped out of his head and his father laughed.

"We'll see. Why don't you put your friend down for now, and I'll take you to the playroom to find your other friends."

"Okay. But can we come back?"

"Sure." And as they left, Nick glimpsed the tennis courts and remembered his invitation to Liane the day before. Her husband hadn't seemed to object, and he would enjoy a game or two to burn off steam. It was either that or throw something at the wall in his suite. He had to find something to do to calm his nerves between now and one. He was almost sorry that he had not yet met a man with whom to play. But Hillary was right about one thing at least, the group at their table in the Grande Salle à Manger was extremely dull. There were not too many young people on the ship, it was a very expensive journey, and most who made it in first class had long since "arrived." There were important journalists and authors, attorneys and bankers, musicians and conductors, but all of them had reached a certain stature in life, not unlike Armand. And few of them were as young as Nick, possibly none of them, except the ambassador's wife, Liane, and his own. He was used to being the youngest man around, but for a moment he regretted it. He would have liked to have had a male friend his own age along just then.

He escorted his son downstairs to the playroom, where he spotted Armand and Liane's girls, and then after a moment's hesitation he decided to take a walk on the promenade outside the Grill, and he saw Liane there, sitting on a bench with a book, her head bent and her blond hair flying in the wind.

He hesitated before he approached, but in the end he decided to anyway. "Hello." She looked up in surprise and then smiled as she saw him. She was wearing a pink cashmere sweater set and gray slacks, and a double strand of pearls. This was acceptable only as morning dress, for a walk on the promenade, but she had no other plans. "Am I disturbing you?" He stood, with his hands in his pockets, braced against the wind, in white flannel slacks and blazer once again, but today he wore a bright red bow tie.

"Not at all." She closed her book and slid over on the bench.

"Is the ambassador already at work?"

"Of course." She smiled. "His assistant arrives every day at nine o'clock, with one of those big hooks they used to use in vaudeville, and whether Armand has finished his breakfast or not, Jacques drags him off." Nick grinned at the image she conjured up.

"I saw him yesterday. I must admit, he doesn't look like much fun."

"He isn't, but he'll make a good ambassador one day."

And then she smiled again. "Thank God Armand was never like that."

"Where did you two meet?" It was a little bit impertinent to ask, but he was intrigued by them. It was obvious that they had a special bond, a deeply woven tie of love, despite the span of years that separated them, and the fact that Armand obviously worked very hard. But she seemed to understand and sympathize, and wait ever patiently for him. He wondered how one found a woman like that. Perhaps by being not quite so impetuously taken with a young debutante of eighteen. And yet Nick knew, from the age of their oldest child, that Liane must have married young as well. She couldn't have been more than thirty now, he thought. In fact, she was thirty-two, but she had always been mature well beyond her years, woman enough to marry—unlike Nick's wife, the spoiled child bride.

"We met in San Francisco when I was very young."

"You still are."

"Oh, no." She laughed. "I was fifteen then, and . . . ." She hesitated for a moment, but one said things to people on ships that one would not say at other times. She fell prey to that magic now, and turned to him with wide-open blue eyes. "Armand was married to someone else, a woman I loved very much. My mother died when I was born, and Odile, Armand's wife, was like a mother to me. He was the consul general in San Francisco then."

"Did they divorce?" Nick was intrigued, Liane looked all innocence, not the harlot or the home wrecker, somehow she didn't figure in this plot, but Liane slowly shook her head.

"No. She died when I was eighteen, and Armand was almost destroyed. We all were, I think. I think I was numb for almost a year."

"And he fell in love with you?" Now the story began to make sense.

Liane drifted back in memory, her eyes wearing a far-off

look and her mouth a gentle smile. "Not as quickly as all that. It took a year or two before we realized how much we cared. I was twenty-one when we finally admitted it to ourselves and each other and we got engaged."

"And got married and lived happily ever after." He liked the story better still. They were fairy-tale people after all. But again Liane shook her head.

"No. Just after our engagement was announced, Armand got transferred. To Vienna. And my father insisted that I finish my last year at Mills." She turned and smiled at Nick. "It was a very long year for us at the time, but we survived it. We wrote to each other every day, and as soon as I graduated he came back, and we were married, and off we went." She was smiling broadly now. "Vienna was a wonderful spot. We were very happy there, and then London after that. Marie-Ange and Elisabeth were born in those two posts respectively, and then we came back to the States."

"Your father must have been pleased." And then suddenly he remembered the error of what he had just said, remembering that her father had probably been dead for nearly ten years.

"No, my father was already gone. He died right after Elisabeth was born." She smiled gently at Nick then. "That seems a long time ago now."

"Do you go back to San Francisco often?"

"No. It's really not my home anymore. I've been gone for too long and I only have my uncle now. We've never been very close and . . ." Her voice was very gentle as she spoke. ". . . my home is with Armand."

"He's a very lucky man."

"Not always." She laughed. "Even fairy tales have their rocky spots. I'm as difficult as anyone else. He's a very good, very kind, wise man. I am fortunate to have known him for all these years. My father didn't think I'd get along as well with a younger man, and I think he was right. I lived alone with my father for too long."

"Is your husband a great deal like him?" He was still curious about them, even more so now after hearing her tale.

"No, not at all. But my father had prepared me well. I ran his home, I listened to the business problems he and my uncle had. I wouldn't have been satisfied with much less."

"Were you an only child?"

"Yes."

"So is my wife. But she had less responsibility than you, less exposure to the real world. She grew up expecting Christmas every day, and birthday parties, and debutante balls. It's fun, but it's not exactly the essence of real life."

"She's a very beautiful girl. It would be difficult for her not to be spoiled. Women who look like that often grow up expecting life to be something that it is not." But as she said the words he found himself wanting to ask her "And you? Why aren't you like that?" Liane was lovely too, but in a different way. In a gentler, quieter, more womanly way than his wife. Instead, he thought of something else.

"You know, it's funny our paths never crossed, with our fathers doing business with each other, and we aren't that far apart in age." And the elite from one end of the country to the other were a small group, as they both knew. Perhaps if she had gone to college in the East, he might have met her at some party or ball, but with her at Mills, and earlier he at Yale, their paths were never destined to cross, until now on the *Normandie*, on the high seas.

"My father was really a recluse for years. There were a lot of people I didn't meet, people my father knew or did business with. He never really recovered from my mother's death. It's a miracle I even met Armand and Odile, but I think he wanted me to meet them so I could show off my French." She still remembered Odile's report of their first meeting with Harrison. She thought of it again now and had to pull her attention back to Nick. "Where is Mrs. Burnham, by the way?" It was not impertinent to ask, and yet when she saw the look in his eyes, she regretted the question almost at once. There was something smoldering quietly there.

"She wanted to have a massage. Which is why I came

looking for you." Liane seemed surprised at his words and put her book down on the bench. "I was wondering if I could talk you into that tennis game we talked about yesterday. Does that appeal to you right now? There's no one on the courts. I was just there. John wanted to take a look at the dogs. Anyway, could I tear you away from your book for a quick game?"

She hesitated for an instant and glanced at her watch. "I have to meet Armand for lunch at noon. He promised that today he'd break away."

"That's fine. I'm meeting Hillary in the Grillroom at one."

"Then let's." She smiled at him. She hadn't had a male friend in years, not really since Armand. But it would be fun to have someone to play tennis with. "I'll hurry up and change and meet you there."

"Ten minutes?" He looked at his watch, a handsome piece of black enamel and gold from Cartier.

"Fine." They both rose and went up to the sun deck, where they lived, and met ten minutes later on the courts, she in a pleated tennis dress that exposed half of her slim thighs, and he in well-tailored white shorts and a tennis sweater over a shirt from Brooks Brothers. They played a relaxed, care-free game. He beat her twice, and she took him by surprise in the end, and beat him 6–2, with a whoop of victory and a handshake as he sailed across the net. Suddenly they both felt happy and free and young.

"You lied to me. You're very good." She congratulated him, still out of breath from the three quick games, but it had been fun.

"I'm not. But you're not bad yourself." It was just the out-let he had been longing for, and he felt better now. "Thanks. I needed something like that."

She looked up at his considerable height with a smile. "You must feel awfully cooped up here. No matter how large the ship is, it's still a confining space. I'm lazy enough not to mind, but I suppose it's different for you."

"Not really. I just get wound up sometimes. I have a lot

of things on my mind." She was reminded then of the contracts he had, both with Paris and Berlin, but she didn't mind as much now. He was a nice man, and there was something about him that suggested decency and integrity. Nick Burnham was a difficult man to dislike and she was growing comfortable with him. "Anyway, this helped a lot. Thank you again."

"Any time." She smiled. "Maybe this is the perfect antidote to all that food."

He grinned. "Then let's play again. Tomorrow at the same time?"

"All right." She glanced at her watch. "Now I really have to run, or I'll be late for Armand."

"Give him my best," he called out as she hurried back to the Trouville suite.

"I will. And enjoy your lunch." She waved and disappeared and he stood for a long time looking out over the rail, thinking back on the things she had said. He liked the story of how they had met. And Armand was really the perfect man for her. She seemed to know it too, which was nice. Unlike Hillary, who watched him approach at one o'clock in the Grill with a sense of impending doom. He was wearing his blazer and slacks again and she had changed into a peacock-blue silk dress and high-heeled blue kid shoes.

"Have a nice massage?" He signaled the waiter and they both ordered a Scotch.

"Very nice."

"Where did you say you get the massages?" He feigned innocence as he stirred his drink, his eyes boring into hers.

"Checking up on me, Nick?"

"I don't know, Hil. Do you think I should?"

"What difference does it make if I had a massage or not?" Her eyes drifted away from his, as though she were too bored to continue looking at him, but something inside her fluttered nervously. Now and then, dealing with Nick was truly like dealing with the man of steel.

"It makes a big difference to me if you tell me lies. And I

told you before, what you do here will become common knowledge on the ship. I get the feeling that you're spending a lot of time in second class and I want it to stop."

"Stupid snob. The average age of this group tallies up to Neanderthal man, for chrissake. At least downstairs there's a younger group, some people I can talk to. You forget, dear Nick, I'm not as old as you."

"Or as smart. Keep that in mind. It would be embarrassing to have to lock you in your cabin." His eyes were slowly beginning to blaze but she only laughed.

"Don't be an ass. All I'd have to do is ring for the maid. What do you want to do, tie me to the bed?"

"I get the feeling you've already taken care of that yourself. Who'd you meet on the ship, Hil? Some old friend from New York, or someone new?"

"No one at all. Just a bunch of young people traveling slightly less deluxe."

"Well, do me a favor and kiss them good-bye. Don't make a laughing stock of yourself, playing poor little rich girl visiting the plebes."

"That's not what they think."

"Don't bet on it. That's an old, old game. I used to do it on the ships myself when I was young. But I was in college then, and I didn't have a wife. I hate to bore you, Hil, but you aren't single anymore, and you don't belong downstairs on A deck, you belong up here. Life could be worse, you know."

"Not much." She was looking like a spoiled little girl again. "I'm bored to tears."

"So cry. We'll be in Paris in two days, you can survive up here till then." But she didn't answer him. She ordered another Scotch, ate only half a club sandwich for lunch, and afterward he walked around the shops with her, hoping to keep her mind off her new friends. But when he went to check on John at the pool after that, she disappeared. He sat in their cabin until she came back to dress, and when she walked in the door, he felt himself lose control in total, impotent rage, and he was shocked to find his hand pulled back to slap her face. Thankfully just then he saw Johnny peeking through the door of his room, and he rapidly regained control and lowered his hand. Time and time again she pushed him to the brink, but this was the first time he'd ever felt the need to strike at her. He motioned her inside their room. He could see that she had had a lot to drink, and suddenly he felt as though he had been slapped. There was a bite mark on her neck, and he dragged her to the mirror to show her, trembling with rage.

"How dare you come back to me like that, you little whore. How dare you!" He was sure that Johnny could hear his voice through the wall but he was beyond caring. She pulled free of him.

"What did you want me to do? Stay downstairs?"

"Maybe you should."

"Maybe I will."

"For God's sake, Hillary, what's happening to you? Don't you have any decency at all? Do you climb in and out of any bed you find?" This time it was she who raised her hand and slapped him.

"I told you before. I'll do anything I goddamn want. You don't own me, you son of a bitch. All you care about anyway is your bloody steel mill, your contracts, your goddamn dynasty that you'll leave to Johnny one day. And what do I get out of that? What do I care about your empire? I don't give a shit. Do you know that? Not about your empire and not about you." She fell silent then, knowing that she had said too much, and there were tears in Nick's eyes as he turned away. He said nothing at all to her. He went quietly out on their private deck, and she watched him for a long time, and then followed him outside. His back was turned as he leaned forward on the rail, and Hillary's voice was hoarse as she spoke to him.

"I'm sorry, Nick."

"Leave me alone." He sounded like a hurt little boy, and for a moment her heart ached, but in her eyes he was the greatest enemy she had. He wanted to keep her in chains, and she wanted to be free. He turned to face her then and there were tears in his eyes. "Go back inside."

"You're crying." She looked even more shocked.

"Yes, I am." He didn't seem to be ashamed, which shocked her still more. Men didn't cry. Not strong men. Not the men she knew. But Nick Burnham did. He was stronger than them all, and deep inside he grieved, not for her, but for himself, for the foolishness that had led him to marry her at all. "The game is over between us, Hil."

"Do you want a divorce?" She almost sounded pleased and she offered him no comfort at all.

But his eyes bore deep into hers. "No, I don't. And let me tell you right now, I never will. The only way you'll ever walk out of this marriage is alone. The day you agree to that, I'll divorce you on the spot. But until that day, you're married to me, for better or worse. Remember that. And from now on, I don't give a damn what you do."

"You mean leave Johnny if we get divorced?" She sounded shocked again.

"That's right."

"I'll never do that."

"Why not? You don't give a damn about him, any more than you do about me." It was a simple statement of fact and he was right, but she wouldn't admit that to him. Not now.

"I won't give him up." She sounded petulant again. Nick was always screwing up her life. Here he had tantalized her with talk of divorce, only to say that she would have to give up their son. "I wouldn't think of it."

"Why not?" He was goading her, and he noticed that she had had the decency to cover her neck with a scarf. All of a sudden he felt the urge to slap her again.

"What would people think if I gave him up?"

"Do you care?"

"Sure I care. They'd think I was a drunk or something."

"You almost are. And worse than that, you're a whore."

"If you call me names, you son of a bitch, you'll never get your son."

"Well, keep it in mind. You can have out anytime you want. But without him." She was about to say something vicious to him, but once again she was helpless in his hands. She knew that to divorce him, she would have to do so on grounds of adultery, and she would never be able to establish those grounds against him. Nick was faithful to her. She knew by the vehemence with which he took her now and then, he was a man burning with loneliness and desire. And she was a woman drowning in her own helpless rage. She would never get what she wanted out of him now. Never. She knew it as she went back inside. And why should she leave John with him? He was her son, after all, and in a few years he might be fun to have around. She liked young people. She would like him and his friends. She just didn't like little kids, that was all. She would never give him to Nick. Never. She'd never live it down. People would whisper behind her back for years. They would say that Nick had thrown her out. And she wouldn't tolerate that. When she left him, everyone would know that she had left *him*.

Nick stood alone on the deck for a long time, trying to calm his thoughts. He knew that a final turning point had come. It was the first time they had ever spoken seriously of divorce, even in a rage. But even on the ship, she couldn't stay out of other beds. He knew her for what she was now, and he would never open up to her again. And maybe in time she would tire of the game. Maybe she would run off and leave Johnny with him. He could give the child a happy life, whether he remarried or not. But that wasn't even worth thinking about now. He was married to Hillary, with all the agony that that meant. He stood staring at the sunset, thinking about his life, and his son, and then at last he went back inside to dress, and closed the door to the Deauville suite.

And it was then, and only then, that in an agony of embarrassment and pain, Liane could leave her deck chair on the private deck of the Trouville and go inside as well. They hadn't seen her when they had come out. She hadn't dared to move or speak. She didn't want them to know what she had heard, especially him. She felt deeply sorry for the man as she sat down in her own room. What a painful, lonely life he led. But what would he do now? What a lonely life that woman had condemned him to.

"My God, who died?" Armand walked in and kissed his wife. She had been sitting at her dressing table, staring at her feet.

"What? . . . oh . . . it's you." She tried to smile, but she had a heavy heart. Liane always cared about other people's private griefs.

"Were you expecting someone else?"

"No, of course not." She smiled up at him then, but he could see that something was wrong.

"What's the matter, my love?"

She looked up at him with stricken eyes. "I just happened on the most awful scene."

"Did someone get hurt?" He looked concerned.

"No. It was between Nick Burnham and his wife."

"Oh, dear. A domestic fight? How did you happen into that?"

"I was sitting in a deck chair outside, reading my book, and they didn't realize I was there. When they came out on their deck, I heard the whole thing. Apparently she's been sleeping with someone on the ship."

"I'm not surprised. But it's a bit his fault as well for not controlling his wife."

"How can you say such a thing?" She looked shocked. "What kind of woman is she to do a thing like that?"

"A little tramp, I suppose. But he's obviously let her get away with it before." Liane suspected that her husband was right.

"Nevertheless, the poor man, Armand . . . and he accused her of not caring about their little boy." There were tears in her eyes and Armand pulled her close.

"And now you want to adopt them both, and have them move in with us in France, is that it? Ah, Liane, sweet child, you have a soft heart. The world is full of people like that. They lead nightmarish, ugly lives."

"But he's a nice man. He doesn't deserve that."

"Probably not. Anyway, don't you feel too sorry for him. He can take care of himself, and you have other things to think about." Armand knew how women were, sometimes too much sympathy could create situations one could regret, and he wanted to protect Liane from that. She was still innocent in some ways, and he knew he had to protect her from herself. "What are you wearing to the gala tonight?"

"I don't know . . . I . . . oh, Armand, how can you talk about something like that?"

"What would you have me do? Offer to go over there and shoot his wife?"

"No." She laughed at him. "But still, the poor man . . . and that child . . ."

"Never mind that. They have each other, after all, and she may run off with someone else one of these days. It would probably be a blessing for them both. Now, don't get involved in the Burnham family fights, for all you know, by now they're making passionate love. Maybe he likes her like that."

"I doubt that."

"How do you know?" He gazed at his wife, wondering if there was more to this than met the eye, but he decided there was not.

"I played tennis with him today. He asked about us, and I could tell by the way he talked that he's not happy with her."

"At least that proves he's sane. But it's his problem, not ours. Now, I want you to forget about all that. Would you like a glass of champagne?" She hesitated for a moment and then decided that she would, and he returned a moment later with a glass for himself and another for her, and he kissed her tenderly on the cheek and the neck and the mouth and she put Nick Burnham and his wife out of her mind. Armand was right. There was nothing she could do. "Now, tell me what you're going to wear to the gala tonight." They would be sitting at the captain's table again, and tonight was the most important of all on the ship. The next day would be their last night, and the following day they would reach Le Havre.

"I thought maybe the red moiré."

"You'll look like a dream." And his eyes told her that he meant every word.

"Thank you." She sat down at her dressing table again, and watched him in the mirror as he began to undress. "Did you finish your work?"

"More or less." He was deliberately vague.

"What does that mean?"

"We'll see."

"You're coming to the gala tonight, aren't you?" For once she looked upset.

"Of course." He returned to where she sat and kissed her shoulder just at the base of her neck. "But, I may not be able to stay very late."

"You're going to work with Jacques after the gala?" She was suddenly tired of the trip, of not seeing Armand, of the people on board. She wanted to go home, or arrive in France.

"Jacques and I may have to work for a little while. We'll see how late it gets."

"Oh, Armand . . ." She looked crestfallen as he sat down on the bed.

"I know. I know. I feel as though I've hardly seen you during the trip. And I wanted this to be a second honeymoon for us, but I have such a mountain of work to do before we arrive. Liane, I promise you, I'm doing my best."

"I know. I don't mean to complain. I just thought that tonight . . ."

"So did I." But he hadn't realized how much Perrier had dragged along from his desk. Armand barely had time to breathe between their meetings every day, but he had to be prepared, whether it was hard on Liane or not. "Anyway, we'll see. Maybe I'll be too drunk after the gala to go back to work."

"You're inspiring me to devise a plot."

"Don't you dare!" He smiled down at his wife, and she went to run her bath.

And in the Deauville suite at exactly the same time, Hillary had just poured herself another Scotch. It had been a rough day, rougher than Nick knew, the guy in second class had almost broken her neck, he was so rough. He had insisted that he didn't know she was married, and when he got a good look at her wedding ring, he told her he was giving her a little "gift" to take back to Nick. Some gift, the bite on her neck had created a long-avoided scene. In a way, it was a relief, but she hadn't liked what Nick had said.

He stood looking at her now, a glazed look in his eyes. It was as though he had aged ten years in that one afternoon.

"Are you dining in first class tonight or not?" He no longer cared, but he wanted to know if he should give the captain an excuse.

"Yes, I thought I would."

"You don't have to, if you'd rather not." It was the dawn of a new day, and Hillary was more than a little shocked.

"Would you rather I didn't?" She was a little frightened by his new attitude, but there was no way to come back from the things she had said and she remembered the stricken way he had looked on the deck. There was nothing vulnerable about him now. He looked totally indifferent to her, and his eyes were icy cold.

"Suit yourself. But do us both a favor. If you dine at the captain's table, try to behave. If that's too big a strain, then take yourself to dinner somewhere else."

"Like in my room?" She would not be treated like a naughty child, not by him, or the moron downstairs. And she wasn't particularly anxious to go back there again. She had a feeling that that was getting a little out of hand. She would be safer upstairs in first class with Nick.

"I don't give a damn where you eat. But if you eat with me, you know the rules."

She said not a word, but walked into the bathroom and slammed the door.

Chapter 8

Tonight when Hillary came down the staircase in the Grande Salle à Manger, she didn't smile her sultry smile. Her eyes looked sulky and her face strained as Nick walked just behind her in white tie and tails. But she still made the same sensation she had before, this time in a white satin dress with long sleeves and a high neck, sewn with silver bugle beads and tiny white pearls, and when she reached the foot of the stairs and crossed the room, once again everyone stared, as the back of the dress was almost totally bare, revealing her creamy flesh in a large teardrop from the nape of her neck to a point just below her waist. But Nick didn't seem touched by the impression his wife created as he sat down across from Liane and smiled pleasantly. She was instantly aware that his eyes were different than they had been before, they seemed colder and somehow sad and she was reminded of what she had heard on the terrace that afternoon. But as she watched him she felt Armand watching her, and she turned to acknowledge him with her own eyes. He had admonished her before they came down that she shouldn't let it be seen that she was aware of what had passed between the two Burnhams on their private deck. She had told him that he didn't need to remind her to be discreet, but he had disagreed with her.

"Yes, I do. I know you too well. You have a tender heart for everyone you think is hurt. And you'll embarrass the poor man if he knows. It's bad enough to have been cuckolded by his wife." He still found the story shocking, although not difficult to believe, and he couldn't resist glancing at Hillary himself when she sat down. She was a remarkably beautiful girl, but she looked pure bitch. And the high neck of the dress covered what Liane had overheard described, the bruise on her neck left by her most recent lover. Perhaps that was why she had worn the dress, Liane thought to herself as she glanced at Armand.

His stare let her know he could sense what she was thinking and so she turned to the man on her left. He was a stern-looking German with a monocle in his eye, and countless ribbons on his chest, which was wide enough to rival Armand's. He was Count von Farbisch of Berlin, and Liane had to fight back an instant dislike for him. Armand had recognized him at once as the man Nick Burnham had been talking to on the second day of the trip, in the smoking room, and he wondered if they would acknowledge each other now, but he saw the count give a curt nod and Nick inclined his head. The captain introduced them all around, and with the exception of the Burnhams and the De Villierses and the captain himself, it was a different group than it had been before. And Liane realized once again how few people she had met on the trip.

"Isn't that right, Madame de Villiers?" Captain Thoreux had been asking her a question and she blushed. She just wasn't in the right mood tonight. Between the unhappiness she had heard between the Burnhams, and the unpleasant German on her left, who had been regaling everyone with propaganda stories about Hitler, she had had enough before the meal had begun, and she was almost sorry that she and Armand weren't dining alone in their cabin.

"I'm sorry, Captain, I didn't hear . . ."

"I was saying that our tennis courts are extremely fine. I understand that you and Mr. Burnham played this morning."

"We did." Nick smiled at her. It was an easy, open smile, with no suggestiveness to it. "And what's more, Madame de Villiers beat me. Six to two."

"Only after losing two games to you." She laughed, but her heart was not light tonight. Even less so when she saw the ugly look that suddenly crossed the eyes of Hillary Burnham.

"Did he really beat you?" Hillary's eyes glittered menacingly. "I'm surprised. He plays a very poor game." The diners at the captain's table were slightly taken aback at the remark and Liane entered the silence quickly.

"He plays far better than I." She felt Armand's eye on her. And her German neighbor was by then speaking to the American woman on his left, once again about the miracles Hitler had wrought. For a moment Liane began to wonder if she would survive dinner. There was an obvious strain to them all, which even the Chateau d'Yquem didn't cure, nor the Margaux, nor the champagne, nor the excellent food from caviar to soufflé. Somehow, tonight, the food and the wines were almost oppressive, and everyone seemed relieved when they moved on to the Grand Salon for the gala ball. It was meant to have the bright atmosphere of New Year's Eve, but for Liane it didn't.

"You shouldn't have made that remark to Burnham's wife." Armand reproached her gently as they danced.

"I'm sorry." Liane was contrite. "But she's such a hateful woman, Armand. And it was either that or throw my glass of wine into that German's face. Who in God's name is he? I thought if I heard one more word about Hitler, I'd throw up."

"I'm not sure. I suspect he's with the Reich. I saw him talking to Burnham in the *fumoir* earlier in the trip." His words silenced her, it reminded her again of what Armand had said before, that Nick probably did business with the Germans. And it still upset her. He seemed such a decent man. How could he provide anything to the Third Reich?

And if he was selling them steel, then they were obviously arming themselves again, which was a violation of the Versailles Treaty. Everyone knew the Germans had been arming themselves for years, but it made her sick to realize that a fellow American was helping them. There seemed to be too much to think about tonight, on all fronts, and it was almost a relief when Jacques Perrier appeared, discreetly, at eleven o'clock, and had a few quiet words with Armand. Moments later, he explained the situation to Liane. They had to go back to work for a little while. And she wasn't sorry when they excused themselves to the captain. She just wasn't in a festive mood, and she was happy to take off the red moiré gown she had put on only three hours before. It was a very handsome piece of work and she liked it, but now she cast it aside on a chair in her room as Armand left, and she settled into bed with a book. She had promised him that she would wait up, although he had said that she didn't have to. But even the book didn't hold her interest tonight. All she could think about were the mysterious Burnhams, Nick with his strange business alliances, and Hillary with her smoldering eyes and sullen mouth. She tried to concentrate on the book for half an hour, but at last she gave up and got out of bed and, pulling on a pair of slacks and a warm sweater, she went to sit on their deck, in the same chair she had been in when she had heard Hillary rant at Nick. She could faintly hear the music from the Grand Salon, and as she closed her eyes she could imagine people dancing. She was just as happy not to be there tonight. It would have been fun with Armand, on another night when she was in a better mood. But with him working, it would have been depressing to dance with the captain and the German and countless strangers.

But Liane wasn't the only one depressed that night. As Nick stood pondering his wife's latest antics, he looked far from cheerful. Hillary had rapidly recovered her spirits, dancing once with the captain, and once with the German count, and then Nick had seen her dancing with a handsome young Italian, who had already caused quite a stir on board the ship. He had brought a woman on the trip who wasn't his wife, and the two of them had caused a sensation, giving parties, reveling till all hours, and reportedly indulging in "multisexual activities" with any and all who were willing to join them in "secretly" held orgies in their cabin. They were just Hillary's speed, he thought bitterly to himself as he stirred his champagne with a gold swizzle stick he always carried on these occasions. The bubbles in the champagne always gave him a terrific headache the next day, and one of his German friends had given the swizzle stick to him years before, assuring him that he would never have a champagne hangover again, and he had been right.

It saddened Nick now to see what was happening to the Germans. They were slowly being overrun by fools like the count, and their country was being destroyed by Hitler. On the surface of course, Germany had never been in better shape, people had jobs, everything worked, the factories were booming, but there was a subtle poison beginning to run in their veins. He had sensed it for the last two years, and it troubled him more each time he visited Berlin or Munich or Hannover, and he suspected that he would see more of the same now. He had made arrangements with the count to meet him in Berlin in three weeks, to discuss their latest steel contracts. He had been doing business with this particular man now for over a year, but he had to admit, he couldn't stand him.

Like Liane, he found it impossible to concentrate on the chitchat tonight. Somehow it all seemed an unbearable burden, and he was tired of watching Hillary play her games. When he finished his champagne, he made his way quietly to the captain and explained that he had some work to do in his cabin, and that he didn't want to take his wife away from all the fun of the gala, but if the captain would be good enough to excuse him . . . Of course the captain said that he understood, although he joked that his ship was no longer a pleasure palace, but a large floating office for all these important men. He made reference to Armand having gone back to work.

"*Je regrette infiniment, M. Burnham* . . . that you are obliged to work tonight as well."

"So do I, Captain." They exchanged a pleasant smile, and Nick disappeared, relieved to put some distance between himself and the music. He had felt that if he had been forced to smile even for a moment longer, his face might explode. And he had no desire to see Hillary again until the morning.

When he reached the sun deck a few moments later, he sought out the chief steward immediately. He had made the decision earlier that evening. The purser showed no surprise at the request, he was accustomed to far more exotic requests than these, and Nick explained that he needed the additional studio room to use as an office for the rest of the trip. Now that they were approaching Le Havre, he had work to do. The purser assigned two stewards to Nick, and fifteen minutes later he was ensconced in the unused studio room adjoining his suite. He didn't even leave a note for his wife. He no longer owed her any explanations. He looked around the pleasantly decorated art deco room, usually occupied by secretaries or maids, or little children. But it suited him very well, and he felt suddenly more relaxed than he had during the entire trip. He walked outside onto the deck and looked across at the deck of the Trouville suite, and there he saw Liane in her deck chair, her head back, her eyes closed, and he wondered if she was sleeping. He stood gazing at her for a moment or two, and then, as though she sensed someone there, she opened her eyes and looked over at him. He was standing in a different part of the deck than he had been earlier that evening during the exchange with his wife. He hadn't been able to see her then, but he could now, and she looked up at him in surprise and sat up in her chair with a questioning look.

"You're not at the gala, Mr. Burnham?"

"Apparently not." He smiled across the rails at where she

sat. The two decks were adjoining. "I didn't mean to disturb you."

"You didn't. I was just enjoying the peaceful night."

"So was I. It's a blessed relief after all that chatter."

Her face relaxed in a smile. "It's a terrible strain sometimes, isn't it?"

"I thought that if I smiled one more time, my face would crack."

She laughed aloud. "So did I."

"But you must do a lot of that as an ambassador's wife. I think I would find it exhausting."

"Sometimes I do." For some reason it was easy to be honest with him. "Most of the time I enjoy it. My husband makes it very easy for me. He shares a lot of the burdens." Nick fell silent at her words, thinking of Hillary dancing with the Italian, and as she watched his face she felt that she had not been very tactful. "I'm sorry, I didn't mean to say . . ." But the added words only made matters worse, and Nick looked up at her with a sad, boyish grin.

"Don't apologize. I don't think the state of my marriage is much of a secret. There's very little we share, except our son, and a mutual distrust of each other."

"I'm sorry." Her voice was very soft in the warm night. "It must be difficult for you."

He sighed softly and looked up at the sky before looking back at her. "I guess it is . . . I don't know anymore, Liane. This is all I ever remember between us. It's been this way for a long time." It was the first time he had called her by her first name but she didn't mind it. "I suppose she takes more liberties now than she did at first. But she's fought against this marriage since the very beginning. My captive bride." He tried to smile but it was a feeble attempt. "It's a far cry from the romance you described to me between you and your husband."

"Marriage is never easy every day. We have our difficult moments too, but we share common goals, common loves and interests."

"And you're nothing like my wife." He looked her straight in the eye. And he suddenly realized that she must have heard them that afternoon. He wasn't sure how he knew, but he did. And she sensed that he knew. Had he asked her just then, she wouldn't have denied it. She sensed that this man needed a friend, and some open, honest talk. It was as though something within him were cracking wide open and he needed a hand to hold. She was willing to lend him hers for a time, and he felt that and was grateful to her. "My marriage is a joke, Liane. And the joke is on me. She's never been faithful to me right from the first. She has to prove that she doesn't belong to anyone, least of all me." It was rejection of the cruelest kind.

"Are you faithful to her?" Liane's voice was gentle in the night.

"I have been. I'm not sure why. Foolish, I suppose." And he felt the fool now, remembering the bite on her neck. And as he thought of it, something deep inside him began to stir. "I shouldn't tell you my problems, Liane. I must sound like a horse's ass, standing here, moaning about my wife. You know, the damnedest thing is that I'm not even sure I care. I saw her dancing with someone tonight, and I didn't feel a thing. I care about what people think, what they see, but I'm not really sure I care about her. I did once. But I think it's finally all gone." He stood looking out to sea, thinking of the years ahead. He would stay with her until Johnny grew up, he knew, but after that? He raised his eyes to Liane's again. "It makes me feel old sometimes, as though the good times are all gone, the happy moments to share, the ecstasy of being in love. I don't think I'll ever see that again." His voice was sad and soft and she left her chair and walked to where he stood.

"Don't say that. You have years and years ahead, you can't know what life has in store." Armand often said that and it was true, he had learned that after the death of Odile, after a year of despair, suddenly there had been Liane.

"You know what life has in store for me, my friend? It has

business deals and steel contracts and luncheons with important men. That's not much with which to warm the heart on a cold night."

Her voice was as soft as his. "You have your son."

Nick nodded, and she thought she saw tears in his eyes. "I do. Thank God for that. I would die without him." She was touched by his love for his son, but she also knew that it was unhealthy for a man his age to have only that. He needed a woman he could love and who could love him. He looked at her ruefully then. "I'm thirty-eight years old, and I feel like there's nothing left." It was a side of him she would never have known had they not talked that night. He seemed so confident, so sure of life, but she hadn't known about Hillary before, and her constant travels through other men's beds.

"Why don't you divorce her and try to get custody of the boy?" Indeed ships made for open talk between strangers.

"Do you really think I'd have a chance?" It was clear from the tone of his voice that he thought he did not.

"You might."

"In the States, where they believe in motherhood and apple pie? Besides, I'd have to prove what she is, and the scandal would destroy us all. I don't want Johnny to know about that."

"Eventually he'll know anyway, if that's what she is."

He nodded. In a way she was right. But he also knew that his chances of getting custody of Johnny were very slim. She had unlimited family money to back her up, and he didn't know of any man who had defeated his wife in court on a custody case. He could never win. "I think, my friend, that I have to make do with what I've got. At least for the next year, we'll have a change of scene. I'm going to have a lot to do over here."

"We all will." Liane stared out into the night and then back at him. "Looking out at this, it's hard to believe that there's a troubled world out there." She was curious about what she would find in France, if Armand was right that in a very short time there would be a war. "What will you do if the war comes, Nick? Go back to the States?"

"I guess I would. I might stay over here for a while, to finish my work, if I could. But I still don't believe we'll have to worry about that this year." He knew that the Germans were getting prepared, he could tell from the volume of his work, but he also knew that they weren't ready yet. "Hopefully we'll all get home in time. And America will probably never get into a war over there. At least that's what Roosevelt says."

"Armand says that Roosevelt doesn't mean what he says." She was being very honest with him. "He says he's been preparing the country for war for several years."

"I think he's just playing it safe. And it's good for the economy. It keeps people at work."

She spoke without accusation, but with truth. "That must also be good for you." And she was right. His steel contracts had boomed. But he leveled his eyes into hers.

"It's also good for you." He knew only too well how successful Crockett Shipping had been, particularly in recent years. And she knew exactly what he meant, but she shook her head.

"I don't feel a part of that anymore." Not since her uncle George had filled her father's shoes. Emotionally, she had severed her ties with that life a long time before.

"But you are a part of it, Liane." He remembered now that she had been her father's only heir, and he marveled at how little it showed, unlike Hillary, who flaunted her expensive dresses and her furs and her jewels. There was something very quiet about Liane. If one had not been aware of her maiden name, one would never have known who or what she was. "You have a responsibility too."

"To whom?" She looked troubled at his words.

"One day, if there is a war, your ships will carry troops. They'll go into battle, men will die."

"There's nothing we can do to stop that."

Nick smiled sadly at her. "Unfortunately, you're right. I think about it sometimes, about how people use our steel to build their war machines. But what can I do to change that? Not much. Nothing, in fact."

"But you trade with the Germans, don't you?"

He hesitated, but not for long. "I do. I'll be in Berlin in three weeks. But I also do business with Italy and Belgium and England and France. It's a big industry, Liane, and industries have no heart."

"Men do." She looked directly at him, as though she expected something more.

"It's not as simple as that."

"That's what Armand says."

"He's right."

She didn't answer him for a time, he had awoken something in her that she hadn't thought of in a long time, her responsibility to her father's shipping line. She put her dividends in the bank, put away the checks that came in, but she never thought anymore about where the ships went or what they did. It made her feel very helpless now. She couldn't begin to imagine questioning her uncle George. He would have been outraged at the thought, but if her father was still alive, she would have known more. "Did you ever meet my father, Nick?"

"No. We had someone else on the West Coast when he was alive. I was on Wall Street burning the midnight oil in those days."

"He was a very special man." It was easy for him to believe as he looked across the rail at Liane, and without thinking about it, he reached out and took her hand in his.

"You're very special too."

"No, I'm not." She left her hand in his, it was warm and powerful and strong, different from Armand's long, aristocratic fingers, lined by age since they had first held hers.

"You don't know how good you are, it's part of what's special about you. And you don't know how wise or how strong.

You helped me a lot tonight. I'm growing tired of it all, and standing here with you, suddenly life doesn't seem quite so bad."

"It's not. And it'll be better for you again one day."

"Why do you think that?" He was still holding her hand and she smiled at him. He was a beautiful man, in the flower of his finest years, and she hated to see him waste them with a wife like his, but she felt good things about this man.

"I believe in justice, that's all."

"Justice?" He looked amused.

"I think that difficult things happen in one's life in order to make one strong, but in the end decent people are rewarded with good people at their sides, and good things happen to them."

"You really believe that?" He seemed surprised.

"I do."

"I'm a little more cynical than that." So was Armand, and maybe most men were, but she still believed in things happening fairly in life, at least most of the time. It still didn't explain early deaths or children who were hurt or died, and yet most of the time she believed that life doled out the right rewards. Hillary would get hers. And Nick would too. "But I hope you're right, my friend." She liked what he had just said, it was precisely what she felt for him. They had become friends. "I hope we see you in Paris some time, if you and Armand aren't all swallowed up by diplomatic life."

"And you by your own steel deals." She smiled at him and finally withdrew her hand from his. "They say that things happen quickly on ships, friendships, romances, and that back on land everyone becomes normal again and forgets." She looked into his eyes and he slowly shook his head.

"I won't forget you. If you ever need a friend, call. Burnham Steel is in the Paris book. Over here we're called Burnham _Compagnie_." She liked the idea of knowing where he would be, and yet she couldn't imagine a call like that. Her life with Armand was very complete. Nick was far more likely to need them.

They stood quietly then for a time, looking out to sea, and at last Liane looked at her watch with a sigh and then at Nick. "My husband works too hard, I'm afraid. I was going to wait up for him, but I think I ought to get to bed. Tomorrow is the last day on the ship, and I'll have a lot of packing to do." They had brought so much, but there had been so many gala events, the theater, the captain's dinners, she had to dress for lunch and then again for tea every day. Even keeping to their rooms as much as they had, she had worn a great many clothes. It was easier for the men, spending every evening in white tie and tails. "It's funny, we've only been on the ship for ten nights, but it feels more like ten weeks."

He smiled. "It does to me too." But he was anxious to arrive now. He'd had enough. And he was glad that they only had one more day. And then he had a thought as he looked at Liane. "Can I interest you in another tennis match tomorrow?"

"I'd like that, unless Armand is free." And she was hoping that he would be. She liked Nick, but she was desperately hungry for some time with her husband.

"Of course. I'll look for you tomorrow morning, and you can let me know then."

"Thank you, Nick." She looked at him for a long time, and then gently touched his arm. "Everything will be all right, you know. You'll see."

He only smiled in answer and waved as she left. "Good night." She was an unusual woman, he thought to himself. He only wished he had met her ten or twelve years before, but he had been only twenty-six then. She was the kind of woman who understood older men, and he assumed that her father had been responsible for that. She would never have been interested in him. Nor would he. What he had wanted ten years before was excitement and flash, women who took his breath away and danced all night. He couldn't imagine Liane doing that. She was too solid, too sedate, too wise . . . and yet, he thought to himself, he would have liked to see her running barefoot through a garden in the middle of the night . . . or in a swimming pool, or with her hair loose on a beach . . . she filled him with a sense of quiet, happy beauty. And as he returned to his new studio room, adjoining the Deauville suite, he realized that for the first time in a long time, he felt peace.

Chapter 9

"Where were you last night?" Hillary eyed him through a haze of champagne from the night before, and she looked none too pleased as he entered their suite from the front door and poured himself a cup of coffee.

"In my room."

"And where's that?"

"Next door."

"That's cute. I saw that you moved your things."

"And cried all night, I suppose." They were words with a slight sting as he glanced at the ship's newspaper and buttered a croissant.

"I don't know why the hell you moved out."

"Oh, don't you?" He sounded strangely calm, and she glared at him from where she sat.

"Is this a new trend for us, separate rooms? Or is this just because you were angry at me last night?"

"Does it matter, Hil?" He looked up from the paper and set it down. "I think things will work out better like this. You looked as though you were having a good time last night. I didn't want to spoil your fun."

"Or your own? Are you playing tennis again today, Nick?" Her voice was all innocence at first, but he could see from the look in her eyes that there was more to come. "How's your little friend, the ambassador's wife?" She was pleased to see him bridle at this. "I assume that you've been playing more than tennis with her. A little shipboard romance perhaps?" Her voice oozed the evil spirit with which she thought, and pointed once again to her own guilt.

"That's more your style than mine."

"I'm not so sure."

"Then you don't know me very well. Or her. But I suppose you apply your standards to the rest of the world. Fortunately, they don't apply."

"Oh, dear Saint Nick. Is your little friend sweet and pure?" She laughed out loud and crossed the room. "I doubt that. She looks like a whore to me."

Nick stood up and there was menace in his eyes. "Don't speak that way about people you don't know. You're the only whore on this ship, from what I can see, and if that suits you, that's fine, but don't waste your time pointing a finger at anyone else. It doesn't apply to anyone but you, and just be damn glad that people all over this ship aren't calling you a whore."

"They wouldn't dare."

"At the rate you're going, one of these days they will."

"And wouldn't you love that." She stood watching him, baffled at what she saw in his eyes. Suddenly he didn't seem to care anymore. He wasn't angry, he wasn't sad, he was numb. And the only thing that had made him angry was what she had said about Liane.

"I'm not sure I care what people say about you anymore. I know the truth. What does it matter after that?"

"Have you forgotten that I'm your wife? What I do reflects on you."

"Is that some kind of a threat?"

"No, it's the truth."

"It hasn't stopped you before, and I doubt if it'll stop you now. Everyone in Boston and New York has had their eyes open about you for years. The only difference is that now I'm willing to face it too."

"And let me do what I want?" She looked stunned.

"As long as you're reasonably discreet. For you, that ought to be something new."

"You son of a bitch . . ." But as she rushed toward him, he grabbed her arm, and she was startled by the fierce grip. He was a powerful man, and he was no longer afraid to use his strength on her.

"Don't waste your time, Hil." It was all wasted on him now. Both her anger and her charm. And as they stood there in the dining room of their suite, she began to cry.

"You hate me, don't you?"

He stood looking down at her and shook his head, surprised at how little he felt for her now. Only a few days before there had still been hope. But yesterday she had ended it for him. For good, he thought. And it was just as well for him.

"No, I don't."

"But you don't give a damn, do you? You never did."

"That's not true." He sat down with a tired sigh. "I once cared very much." His voice grew soft. "I loved you very much. But you've fought me every inch of the way for years. And I guess, finally, you win. You don't want to be my wife, but you are. So we'll both have to live with that. I'm not willing to let you out, because of our son, but I can't force you to feel something you don't, I can't even keep you out of other men's beds, even on this ship. So, Hillary, the game's up. You wrote the rules, I'll play it your way. But don't expect me to care for you as I once did. I don't. I can't. You killed that for us both. It's what you wanted, and you've won." He stood up and walked to the door.

"Where are you going?" She looked suddenly afraid. She didn't want to be his wife with all the mature commitment that entailed, but she still needed him.

"Out." He smiled ruefully at her as he left. "I can't go very far. At least you'll know I'll be somewhere on the ship. I'm sure you'll be busy with your friends." He closed the door then and went back to his room. He felt better than he had in years. Half an hour later he went to find his son at the swimming pool, and they had a nice time, swimming together in the deep end for a while, and then he left him with some of his new friends and went to get dressed. He was thinking about Liane, and hoping that she was free for another tennis match. He wanted to tell her how much she had helped him the night before. But when he saw her, she was strolling happily with Armand on the promenade deck outside the Grill, their heads bent close, and she was laughing at something he had said. He didn't want to intrude, so instead he went to the gentleman's smoking room. He knew that anywhere else on the ship he might have run into his wife, so he spent the afternoon there, and eventually went back to his room. It seemed moments later when the dinner bell sounded in the hall. He put on his white tie and tails as he had each night and went back to the living room of their suite to meet his wife. She was wearing a black taffeta dress and carrying her silver fox. Even that didn't bother him anymore, it was as though overnight he had been freed from the agonies she had caused him for so long. The bite on her neck the day before had been the last straw.

"You look very nice."

"Thank you." Her eyes were distant and cold. "I'm surprised you came back."

"I don't know why. We dine together every night."

"We used to sleep together too." He didn't want to get into that now, so close to the open door to Johnny's room. "I gather that, according to your new rules, public appearances are all right, but private ones are not."

"That's about right." He sounded very cool as he went to kiss John good night. The boy looked up at him with a bright smile as he nuzzled his neck.

"You smell good, Dad."

"Thank you, sir. So do you." The child smelled of soap and shampoo and Nick wished that he could spend a little more time with him, but Hillary was standing in the doorway, anxious to interrupt.

"Ready to go?"

"Yes." Nick stood up and followed her out the door as Johnny went back to his games with his nurse, and in the Grande Salle à Manger, he and Hillary took their places at the table she had complained about before, but it didn't matter anymore. This was their last night.

There was an atmosphere of bittersweet joy and regret tonight, with people who had met clustered in friendly groups in the Grand Salon and couples walking along the deck. Even the music seemed sad and sweet as people danced, and Nick saw Armand and Liane, strolling peacefully on the deck. Again he wanted to say something to her, but the time didn't seem quite right.

"Are you sad to leave the ship?" Armand looked down at Liane with a gentle smile. She looked so pretty tonight, in a pale-blue organza dress with pale-blue-and-gold satin shoes and a matching bag. She was wearing aquamarines and diamonds set in gold at her ears, with a handsome necklace to match that had been her mother's, from the enormous cache of jewels bought by her father before she was born. "Have I told you tonight how lovely you look?"

"Thank you, my darling." She leaned up to kiss his cheek, "and yes, I am sad to leave the ship. But happy too. It's been a beautiful trip, but I'm ready to go home."

"Already?" He loved to tease. "Won't you stay in Paris with me for a while?"

"You know what I mean." She smiled in answer. "I'm anxious to get to Paris and set up house."

"And I know you will, with those speedy hands. A week from now it will look as though we've been there for twenty years. I don't know how you do it, Liane. The paintings go up, the curtains are hung, the table is set, and I see your touch in every room."

"Maybe I was just meant to be a diplomat's wife." They both knew it was true, and she grinned. "Or a gypsy. Sometimes I think it's the same thing."

"Please don't tell the Bureau Central that." They strolled

along some more, enjoying the warm night and talking over the days on the ship.

"I wish I had been able to spend more time with you on this trip. I've been almost sorry I brought Perrier along. He's too diligent about his work."

She smiled gently at her husband. "And so are you."

"Am I?" His eyes smiled. "Well, perhaps things will be better when we get to France." But at this she only laughed.

"What ever makes you think that?" She knew better and so did he.

"Because I want it to be. I want to spend more time with you."

"So do I." She sighed, but she didn't look unhappy. "But I understand."

"I know you do, but it doesn't seem right. Things were so different in Vienna years ago." They had had time for long walks after lunch, and quiet afternoons when he came back from his work. But that had been a long time ago. They were different now, and the world was different too.

"You weren't as important then, my love."

"I'm not very important now. Just overworked, and these are such troubled times." She nodded, suddenly thinking back to her talk the night before with Nick. She had mentioned it vaguely to Armand over breakfast, only that they had met on the "back porch," as it were, but Armand had been in a hurry to meet Jacques for a quick talk, and he hadn't really listened to her.

They stood quietly on the deck then, looking out to sea, in the direction of France, and Liane hoped that what they would find there would prove Armand wrong, at least to some degree. She didn't want there to be a war. She didn't want to see him devoured by his work. Like him, she wanted them to have more time together. It was a selfish reason to wish that there would be no war.

"Shall we go back, *chérie*?" She nodded and they went back to their suite and closed the door quietly, just as Nick turned the corner on the way to his new room. And he stood there for a moment, thinking of the night before, and the woman whose hand he had held for only a few minutes and who had told him that things were going to be different for him someday. He hoped it would be soon.

Chapter 10

$\mathcal{T}$he *Normandie* pulled into Le Havre at ten o'clock the next morning, just as the passengers were finishing breakfast. Their bags were packed, their staterooms ready to be emptied, the children dressed, the governesses prepared, and everyone was sorry to leave now. The romances that had been born on the ship seemed too poignant, the friendships too dear. But the frenzied activity on the quay proved that it was over. The captain was on the bridge, seeing that everything went smoothly, and for him another crossing was over. He had brought the *Normandie* safely back to France.

In the Trouville suite, Armand and Liane were ready to disembark and the girls were jumping up and down with excitement. They had watched the big ship glide into port from their private deck, and they had waved to John outside the Deauville suite, but now he waited with his mother and father. He was wearing a white linen Eton suit with a white shirt, knee socks, and saddle shoes, and his mother was staring out the window in a white silk dress and a large picture hat. Nick had already tipped all the stewards, and their trunks had left the suite. He knew that a car would be waiting for them on the dock, and they left the suite now and went downstairs to leave before the others. Their passports would be stamped on the quay by a special immigrations officer, and then they would be off.

"Ready, *chérie?*" Liane nodded yes and she followed Armand out, and they went downstairs with the girls behind them. She had worn the beige Chanel suit he liked, with the pink trim, and a pink silk blouse. She looked very pretty and fresh, and very much like an ambassador's wife as they prepared to leave the ship. She glanced behind her, at the girls in flowered organdy dresses and straw hats, their favorite dolls in their arms, and Mademoiselle, looking very official in a gray-striped uniform and her starched cap.

There was a small group of passengers who had been asked to gather in the Grand Salon for early disembarkation. The rest of the passengers would meet with immigrations and customs officers in the dining room, and leave the ship in an hour or so, in time to board the boat train from Le Havre to Paris. Liane noticed as they stood, waiting to be released, that the German she had met at the captain's table was waiting there too, and several other couples she hadn't met. In all, there weren't more than a dozen or so people, specially privileged, with diplomatic passports or important names. And as they waited, Armand's assistant, Jacques Perrier, joined them as well, the briefcase straining at his arm, his glasses in place, his face as mournful as ever. He was a constant reminder of unfinished work.

And it was then, as he and Armand conferred for a last moment before they left the ship, that Nick finally managed to come over for a moment to see her, to say good-bye to her and the girls, and nod to Armand.

"I wanted to say good-bye to you yesterday, but I didn't want to intrude. I saw you with your husband on the deck. . . ." His eyes seemed to touch her face, and she felt a strong urge to reach for his hand again, but this didn't seem the time or the place.

"I'm happy to see you now, Nick." She felt as though in leaving him, she was leaving the last familiar piece of terrain of her own country. And she felt homesick suddenly as they stood there and talked. "I hope that everything goes smoothly for you in Paris." She didn't glance at Hillary as she spoke, but he knew what she meant and he smiled.

"It will. Things are already better now." She wasn't sure what he meant and imagined that he was referring to some unexpected rapprochement with his wife. Perhaps he had forgiven her again, or she had promised to reform. Liane hoped so for his sake, but couldn't know that what he had meant was actually his new sense of freedom since the night they had talked. "I'd like to stay in touch."

"I'm sure that we'll see you in Paris. In a way, it's a small town."

Their eyes met and held for an endless moment, and she wasn't sure what she felt at all. Leaving him now was almost like losing a friend or a brother, and yet she scarcely knew him. It was the magic of the ship, weaving its spell, and she smiled at the thought.

"Take care of yourself . . . and John. . . ."

"I will . . . and you too. . . ."

"Liane! *On y va.*" Armand sounded hurried now. He was anxious to leave, and had been told that they could go. He came quickly to Liane's side, shook Burnham's hand with a broad smile, and a moment later they were on the dock, and their bags were being loaded into a small van, while Liane and Armand and the girls climbed into a large, comfortable Citroën, and Mademoiselle and Jacques Perrier got into the front seat with the chauffeur. And as the car pulled away, and the driver started the van's motor, Liane saw an enormous black Duesenberg pull up and Nick Burnham begin to instruct the chauffeur. She turned for a second glance and he waved, and she waved back, and then she turned back to hear what Armand was saying.

"Apparently there's a reception tonight at the Italian Embassy. I have to go, but if you want to, you can stay at the hotel. You'll have a lot to do, settling the girls." He glanced at his watch. The ride would take them about three hours.

"Does anyone know how long the furniture will take?" She was trying to turn her attention to the matters at hand, but she had the feeling of being haunted by Nick's face as he had waved. She wondered if she would ever see him again, and yet she had told him that they would. "Paris is a small town," she had said, but she suddenly wondered.

But Armand was entirely involved in the present. "The furniture will take six weeks. Meanwhile, we're at the Ritz." It was unusual even for an ambassador to stay there, but Liane had offered it as a treat from her income, and now and then he let her do that. It irked him that he couldn't make gestures like that, but he knew it meant nothing to her, and it was foolish not to use a little bit of her income. Her fortune was so large that a stay at the Ritz put no dent in it.

The girls chattered on through most of the trip and Liane was happy to be able to chat with Armand. She knew that the moment they arrived, he'd be off, and even tonight there was a diplomatic reception. She was almost sorry when she saw the Eiffel Tower pull into sight, and the Arc de Triomphe and the Place de la Concorde. Suddenly she wanted to turn the clock back and return to the luxurious womblike atmosphere of the ship. She wasn't sure she was ready to face Paris.

Three bellboys escorted them upstairs to the large suite of rooms they had reserved. Here there was one very large bedroom for the girls, an adjoining one for Mademoiselle, a living room, a bedroom for Armand and Liane, a dressing room, and a study. Armand looked around their bedroom at the mountain of trunks and smiled at Liane. "Not bad, my love."

But she looked sad as she sat down and smiled up at him. "I miss the ship. I wish we could go back. Isn't that silly?"

"No." He gently touched her face as she leaned against him. "Everyone feels like that at first. Ships are very special, and the *Normandie* is the most special of all."

"She is, isn't she?" They exchanged a warm smile for a moment, and regretfully, Armand pulled himself from her side.

"I'm afraid, my love, that the gentlemen to whom I report

are expecting to see me for a little while tonight, and afterward there's that reception. . . ." He looked at her apologetically. "Would you be happier here or do you want to go?"

"Honestly, I'd love to stay here and get settled."

"That's fine." He disappeared to run a bath for himself, and half an hour later he appeared in his dinner jacket, and his wife whistled as he walked into the room. "Don't you look handsome!" His eyes sparkled as he grinned at her. She had taken off her suit and was wearing a white satin dressing gown, and trunks were open all over the room. "The worst of it is that I'm going to have to pack up and move all over again in a few weeks." Liane sat down on the bed with a groan, and looked up at him. "Why did I bring all this?"

"Because you're my beautiful, elegant wife." He gave her a quick kiss. "And if I don't hurry up, they're going to send me someplace charming, like Singapore."

"I hear it's a nice post."

"Never mind!" He wagged a finger at her, stopped in the girls' room to kiss them good-bye, and went downstairs. The desk had already called to tell them that the Citroën was waiting for him, and he sprinted out of the lobby with a look of excitement in his eyes. Suddenly he felt alive again. He was home, in France. He didn't have to wait anymore to get the news secondhand. He was here, and soon he would know exactly just what was going on.

When Armand departed the Élysée that night, he was shocked at how calm his colleagues were. They seemed absolutely sure that the peace would last for a long while. Instead of terror, there was the feeling that Paris was enjoying a little boom. There was no doubt in their minds that Hitler represented a threat, but they felt equally certain that he would never cross the Maginot Line. This was not what Armand believed, and in a way, it wasn't what he had wanted to hear. He wanted to know that France was fully prepared for an all-out war, and that preparations for that possibility were being made, but none were. He had the impression that he had come to fight a fire in France, and instead of joining the ranks and rolling up his sleeves, he was being asked to admire the blaze. He felt confused as he slid back into the Citroën and directed the driver to the Rue de Varenne on the Left Bank. *"L'Ambassade d'Italie."*

And at the Italian Embassy he was even more aware of the same easy spirit he had felt in the hallowed halls of the Élysée. There was champagne, pretty women; talk of summer plans, diplomatic dinners, society balls. No one even mentioned the danger of war. And after two hours there, greeting scores of people he knew, he returned to Liane at the Ritz, and was grateful to sit down in a chair and share some soup and an omelet with her.

"I don't understand it. Everyone here is having a good time." It was not unlike what he had seen in April. "Is everyone blind?"

"Perhaps they're afraid to see."

"But how can they not?"

"How were things at the Élysée? Can you say?"

"Much the same. I expected serious briefings, and instead they're discussing agriculture and economics and are totally comfortable about the security of the Maginot Line. I wish I felt as secure."

"Aren't they afraid of Hitler at all?" Even Liane was shocked.

"To some extent. And they do think that eventually there will be a war between Hitler and the British, but they're still hoping for a miracle of divine intervention." He sighed and took off his dinner jacket. He looked exhausted and disappointed and suddenly older than he had in years, and he reminded Liane of a warrior ready to go into battle, with no battle to fight, and she felt suddenly sad for him. "I don't know, Liane. Maybe I see demons that aren't there. Perhaps I've been away from France for too long."

"It's not that. It's hard to know who's right. Maybe you

have greater foresight than they, or perhaps they've lived with the threat of war for so long that it no longer worries them so much, and they think it will never come."

"Time will tell."

She nodded quietly, and rolled away their tray. "Why don't you forget about it for tonight. You take it all too much to heart." She rubbed his neck gently, and a little while later he undressed and went to bed and fell into an uneasy sleep. But tonight Liane wasn't tired and she sat quietly alone in the living room of their suite. She still missed the ship, and wished that she could go out on the deck to look out at the peaceful sea. She felt far from home suddenly, although she knew Paris well from her frequent visits with Armand, but there was something different about it for her now. It didn't feel like home yet. They weren't living in a house yet, they were living in a hotel, she had no close friends here, and thinking of that reminded her suddenly of Nick. And she found herself wondering how the Burnhams' arrival had been. It seemed years since they had stood on the deck and talked, only two nights ago. She remembered Nick asking her to call anytime she needed a friend, but she knew that that wouldn't be appropriate here. It was harmless on the ship, but here as Armand's wife, she couldn't make friends with a man.

The suite was silent as she returned to their room, and Armand was snoring softly in the large double bed. Perhaps, despite his disappointment, the news had all gone well. If the situation in Paris was not as acute as he feared, maybe she would see more of him, and that thought appealed to her a great deal. Maybe they would have time for some walks in the Bois de Boulogne, or strolls in the gardens of the Tuileries . . . maybe they could even go shopping together . . . or take the girls for a boat ride. Cheered by the prospect, she got into bed and turned off the light.

Chapter II

$\mathcal{H}$illary walked into the house on the Avenue Foch with the chauffeur almost staggering behind her, carrying seven large dress boxes from Dior, Madame Grès, and Balenciaga, and several smaller packages as well. She had had a very pleasant day, and the evening would be more so, as Nick was still in Berlin.

"Just leave them over there." She tossed the words over her shoulder and then groaned at his blank expression as she pointed to a chair. "*Ici.*" He deposited the boxes as best he could on the chair in the long marble hall with its enormous crystal chandelier. It was a beautiful house and Nick had been enchanted when he saw it. But Hillary was less so. The water was never hot enough for her bath, there was no shower, she insisted that the house was full of mosquitoes, and she would rather have had an apartment at the Ritz. She thought the servants Nick's office had hired were unpleasant, they barely spoke English, and she had complained for days about the heat.

They had been in Paris for almost a month now and she had to admit that Paris this season was not entirely dull. Everyone was saying that the summer of '39 was the first good time since the summer before when Munich put a damper on everyone's spirits. But now costume balls and dinner parties abounded, almost with a vengeance, to keep everyone amused. The Comte Etienne de Beaumont had given a costume ball a few weeks before, with all the guests ordered to come as characters from the plays of Racine, and Maurice de Rothschild had actually worn his mother's famed diamonds on his turban and Cellini Renaissance jewels on his sash, to catch everyone's attention. Lady Mendl had given a garden party at Versailles for 750, with three elephants as objects of entertainment and conversation. And the best party of all had been that given by Louise Macy, who hired the famed Hotel Salé for the night, moving in priceless furnishings, and adding plumbing, a mobile kitchen, and several thousand candles. All of the guests were "ordered" to wear diadems and decorations, and amazingly they had. Hillary had arranged to borrow a tiara from Cartier, a spectacular confection of ten fourteen-carat emeralds, surrounded by clusters of very fine diamonds. She had hardly been bored in Paris, and yet she hadn't really enjoyed it, and now she had other plans for the rest of the summer. And with any luck at all, she and the friends she had run into from Boston would be in the South of France before Nick returned from Berlin. He had made her uneasy ever since they had arrived in France. The new demeanor he had adopted during the last of the crossing stayed with him. He was chilly and distant, always polite but not particularly interested in her doings. The only time he required her presence was for business dinners, or to entertain some industrialist's wife for tea. He made it clear what he expected of her, and she had found that she disliked his new attitude even more than his old one. In the days when he had been trying so desperately to please her, he had made her feel guilty, which had made her hate him. Now she felt as important in his life as a doorknob, and that made her even angrier. She had decided within a week of their arrival that she'd show him. He couldn't drag her out of the closet like a pair of old pumps everytime he needed her for a business dinner. She wasn't a dancing bear to be brought out for guests, and she was already sick of their life in Paris. In the week that he'd been gone, she had made her own plans.

She strolled into the paneled library with the depressing Aubusson tapestry on one wall and looked out into the garden. John was out there playing with his nurse and the puppy Nick had bought him, a small terrier that barked too much for Hillary's taste. Even now the barking and laughter assaulted her ears and annoyed her. She had a headache from the heat and her shopping, and she tossed her hat onto a chair, and peeled off her gloves as she walked toward the bar concealed in the boiserie, and then she almost jumped out of her skin as she heard a disembodied voice behind her.

"Good evening." She wheeled and saw Nick sitting at the enormous Louis XV desk in the corner. She hadn't even glanced in that direction as she came into the room. "Did you have a nice day?"

"What are you doing here?" She looked anything but happy to see him, but she had stopped before she reached the bar.

"I live here, or so I'm told." Although here, as on the ship, he had ensconced himself in his own room. But other than the insult it implied, Hillary didn't really mind that. What bothered her was that for years she had kept him at bay or in her bed, at her choosing, and now he had made the decision for her. But in truth, it wasn't a loss she regretted. She already had other plans. And now he was watching her from the desk, like a cat watching a mouse, and she wanted to slap him. "Aren't you going to have a drink? Don't let me interfere with your routine."

"I won't." She walked to the bar and poured herself a double Scotch. "How was Berlin?"

"Do you care?"

"Not really." They were remarkably honest with each other these days. In some ways it was a relief.

"How's Johnny?"

"Fine. I'm taking him to Cannes in a few days."

"Are you? May I ask with whom?"

"I met some friends while you were gone, from Boston, and I'm leaving for Cannes this weekend." Her eyes were defiant as she looked at him over her glass. If he wanted separate lives, he would have them, but he wouldn't stop her.

"May I ask for how long you plan to be there?"

"I don't know. It's too hot for me in Paris. I feel sick here."

"I'm sorry to hear that. But I'd like some idea of how long you plan to be gone." She scarcely recognized her husband in the tone of his voice. He had gotten immeasurably tougher in the past month, and she would almost suspect him of having a mistress, but she couldn't really believe he'd do that. He didn't have the balls, she would have said if he'd asked her, but he didn't, and she didn't volunteer. He sat now and waited for her answer as she tapped her foot and stared at her drink.

"A month. Maybe more. I'll come back in September," she decided as she answered.

"Have a lovely time." He smiled coolly. "But don't plan to take Johnny."

"May I ask why not?"

"Because I'd like to see him, and I have no desire to travel to Cannes every week to see you."

"That's good news at least. But you can't leave the child in the city."

"I'll take him away myself." She hesitated for a moment, about to answer him sharply, and then suddenly he could almost hear her thinking. She didn't really want to take the child and he knew it.

"All right. I'll leave him here." That had been an easy battle, Nick thought to himself, and he'd have to give some thought now to where he'd take Johnny. He had wanted to take some time off anyway that summer, and this would be the perfect excuse. Despite the atmosphere of power and aggression one sensed building in Berlin, he still felt confident that war wouldn't come too quickly and it would be nice to take Johnny somewhere in France, particularly if they were going to be alone.

"When did you say you were leaving?" Nick stood up at the desk and walked around it, and she glared at him, every ounce of her hatred showing. It was a marriage gone so sour, they could both taste it, and the taste was exceedingly bitter.

"In two days. Is that soon enough?"

"I just wondered. Will you join me here for dinner tonight?"

"I have other plans." He nodded and went out into the garden to see Johnny. The little boy squealed with delight as soon as he saw his father, and ran into his arms as Hillary watched from the window, and turned and walked out of the library and went upstairs.

As it turned out she left two days later then planned, but Nick scarcely saw her, he stayed late at the office every night, and he had to have dinner with some people from Chicago, and when he asked Hillary to join them, she refused.

She claimed that she was too busy packing for her trip, and Nick decided not to force her. He saw her the morning she left for Cannes, when a large limousine arrived to take her to the train. For a moment Nick wondered who she was going to Cannes with, and then he decided not to ask her any questions.

"Have a good time." She had asked him for two thousand dollars for the trip and he had given it to her the night before without question. She had barely said thank you to him.

"See you in September," she called out cheerily as she ran out the door in a red silk dress with white polka dots and a matching silk hat.

"You might call your son from time to time." She nodded and hurried out to the car. It was the first time he had seen her look happy in a long time, and as he went back inside to get ready to go to the office, he was sorry in a way that he insisted on maintaining their marriage. If she was that unhappy with him, they both deserved better. And as he straightened his tie and put his jacket on, he found himself thinking of Liane and wondering how she was. He hadn't seen the De Villierses at any of the dinners he'd gone to, but he imagined that they were more likely to stick to diplomatic receptions, and he hadn't been to any of those. He knew that the Polish Embassy was planning to give an elaborate dinner in a few weeks, and assumed they would go to that, but he would be careful not to attend that one. It was important that no one learn of his recent charity to Poland. It could only do them harm if it was discovered that they were arming themselves too. The diplomatic sources he had used to make his offer had been astounded by the minute prices he charged them. But it was the only way he knew to help them at the eleventh hour.

The Germans had stepped up all their contracts recently, and he felt an increasing desire lately to wind them up and get his business with Germany over. He felt uncomfortable every time he went there, and no matter how profitable the deals were, he couldn't bring himself to feel right about dealing with them anymore. It was impossible not to know what was coming. Liane had been right. The time to choose sides was coming close. In fact, for him, it had come already.

When he left for the office, he kissed Johnny good-bye, and was pleased that he didn't seem upset about his mother going away. He had already promised him a trip to Deauville, and they were going to ride horses along the beach there. They were both excited about the trip, planned for the first of August. They were going to be away together for at least two weeks.

"Have a good day, tiger, I'll see you later."

"Bye, Dad." He was playing with his bat and a ball, which he had stowed in one of his trunks. And Nick saw just as his limousine turned the corner of the Avenue Foch that the ball had just sailed right through one of the living room windows. He laughed to himself, remembering his saying to the doorman in New York that one of these days that would happen, and the chauffeur turned at the sound of his voice.

"*Oui, monsieur?*"

"I said 'That's baseball.' "

The chauffeur nodded with a blank stare and they drove to the office.

Chapter 12

On the thirty-first of July, Liane and Armand's things arrived from Washington, D.C., and within the week they moved into the house Armand had found for them in April. It was a pretty little place on the Place du Palais-Bourbon, in the Septième. And for the next ten days Liane sweated and slaved and opened boxes. She did almost everything herself, knowing exactly where she wanted each item placed, and she only asked the servants to wash dishes and dust tables. The rest she enjoyed doing herself. If nothing else it gave her something to do, now that she scarcely saw Armand. The dream of walks in the Bois de Boulogne and the Tuileries never happened. With or without a war, the Bureau Central had devoured him. He had lunch with his colleagues or at various embassies around town and he didn't come home until eight o'clock at night, if he didn't have an important business dinner. And if he did, she didn't see him until well after that.

This wasn't like their Washington life, when as the Ambassadress she was an integral part of his social life, entertaining, playing hostess, giving small dances and black-tie dinners, standing in receiving lines at his side. Here, more often than not, he went alone, and it was more the exception than the rule that he took her with him. Her entire life centered around the girls now, and when she finally saw Armand at night, he was almost too tired to talk to her. He would eat dinner and go to bed, exhausted, and he was invariably asleep within seconds of his head touching the pillow. It was a lonely life for her now, and she longed for their days in Washington or London or Vienna. This was a whole new life, and she didn't like it, and despite her efforts not to complain, he sensed it. She was like a little wilting flower in an untended garden, and it made him feel desperately guilty, but things were beginning to happen. France was coming awake to the danger of Hitler, and although they were still certain that they were safe in France, there was a certain heightened sense of protection and preparation. He felt alive again as he participated in endless meetings. It was a good time for him, but a rough time for her, and he knew it, but there was very little he could do about it. He didn't even have time to take her out for an occasional dinner.

"I miss you, you know." She smiled at him as he walked into the apartment one night to find her hanging a painting. As usual, she had created the effect of a home they had lived in for years and he was grateful to her. He came to kiss her now and helped her down from her perch, and he held her in his arms for a moment longer.

"I miss you, too, little one. I hope you know that."

"Sometimes I do." She sighed and set her hammer down on the desk, and then she looked up at him with a sad smile. "And sometimes I think you've forgotten I'm alive."

"I could never do that, little one. I'm just very busy." She knew that much already.

"Will we ever have a real life again?"

He nodded. "Hopefully soon. It's just that now there's such an increase in tension. We have to wait and see what happens . . . we must prepare. . . ."

There was such a bright light in his eyes as he spoke that her heart fell at his words. She felt that she had lost him to France, it was almost like losing him to another woman, only worse, because it was an opponent she couldn't fight. "What if there's a war, Armand? What then?"

"Then we'll see." Always the cautious diplomat, even with

her, but she wasn't asking about his homeland, she was asking him about her.

"I'll never see you then." She sounded tired and mournful and tonight she didn't feel like putting up a cheerful front for him.

"These are unusual times, Liane, surely you understand." He would be disappointed in her if she didn't, and she knew that. It was a heavy cross to bear. She had to be willing to make the same sacrifices as Armand, and sometimes that was too much to ask. If they'd just have a quiet night together, some time to talk, an evening when he wasn't too exhausted to make love . . . her eyes told their own tale.

"Never mind. Do you want something to eat?"

"I've eaten." She didn't tell him that she had waited for him. "How are the girls?"

"Fine. I promised them I'd take them for a picnic in Neuilly next week, when I've finished the house." It was lonely for them too. Once they were in school, they would make new friends. But for the moment all they had was their mother and their nurse.

"You're the only woman I know who can put a house together in a week." He smiled at her as he sat down in a chair in the living room, almost afraid to tell her that all he wanted was to go to bed and sleep.

"I'm just happy to be out of the hotel."

"So am I." He looked around at their familiar things, and it felt like home to him at last. But he hadn't really noticed much of anything in the last month. He was so busy at the office, that he could have come home to a shanty or a tent and it wouldn't have mattered to him, and Liane suspected that as she followed him to their bedroom.

"Would you like a cup of chamomile?" She smiled gently at him, and he reached out and kissed her hand as he sat down on their bed.

"You're too good to me, little one."

"I love you very much." And there had been so many times when he had been good to her too. It wasn't his fault that he was so busy now, and it couldn't go on forever. Sooner or later the problems would be resolved. She just prayed that they wouldn't erupt in a war.

She went to the kitchen to make him the promised cup of tea, and when she returned with a delicate porcelain tray and the Limoges cup she'd unpacked that afternoon, she set it down gently on the bed table with a smile. But when she turned to hand it to Armand, she saw that he was already asleep on his pillow, without the assistance of the chamomile.

Chapter 13

"Well, Tiger, what do you think?" Nick and John had ridden all the way down the beach side by side, and they stood now only moments after the sun had fallen into the sea. It had been a heavenly week in Deauville. "Ready for something to eat?"

"Yup." For the past hour he had pretended he was a cowboy on a ranch. He was enchanted with the tall, gentle white horse he was riding, and his father was astride a pretty chestnut mare. Johnny glanced over at his father then. "I wish we could eat hamburgers tonight, just like on a ranch."

Nick smiled at his son. "So do I." A hamburger and a milkshake would have tasted good, but they were a long way from any possibility of that. "Would you settle for a nice, juicy steak?" He knew that a steak *au poivre* was the closest they'd get, but at least it was something.

"Okay."

At Johnny's request they had talked to Hillary that day. She was having a nice time in Cannes and had been surprised by their call. Nick hadn't told the boy, but he had had to call four times just to find her in, and in the month that she'd been gone, the rumors had begun to filter back to him. The "group of friends" she was with in Cannes had been joined by a man named Philip Markham, whom Nick knew from New York. He was a playboy of the worst kind, had been married four times, and now his name was linked with that of Hillary Burnham. Nick didn't give a damn what she did, but he had told her to be discreet. Obviously discretion was beyond her. They went gambling in Monte Carlo every night, danced till all hours, and had given a raucous party at the Carlton, which had even made the Paris press. He had thought for a time about calling her and telling her to lay off, but he realized that it was already too late. He had no control over her, and whatever he said to her, she'd still do whatever she wanted anyway.

"It was nice talking to Mom today." It was as though the child had read his mind, and he looked over at him now as they guided their horses back to the barn.

"Do you miss her a lot, John?"

"Sometimes." And then he smiled loyally at his father. "But I'm having a real good time here with you."

"So am I."

"Do you think she'll be home soon?" The question cut to the quick. Despite Hillary's lack of interest in the child, Nick knew that Johnny loved them both. She had sent him a couple of presents from the South of France but she seldom called, and Nick tried to make it up to him, as he always had. But she was what she was, and he knew that one day his son would know the truth.

"I don't know when she'll be back, Son. Probably in a few weeks." Johnny nodded and didn't say anything more and they put away their horses and went back to their hotel.

As promised, that night, they ordered steak *au poivre*, and when they went back to their room, Nick read to him from his favorite book. They had spent every night like that. Nick hadn't even brought the nurse. He wanted the time they shared to be just for them, and he enjoyed having him to himself.

On the last day of their stay they took a final ride, and the sunset was even more beautiful than it had been before. They had played tennis that day, had a picnic on the beach, and then taken their daily ride. And as they sat watching the sunset now, Nick looked over at the boy with a warm smile.

"We're going to remember this for a long, long time, you and I." It was the best time they had ever shared, and he reached out to touch the child's hand, and they sat there like that for a long time, hand in hand, and John never noticed the tears in his father's eyes.

The day after they got back Nick had to go to Lyons for a few days, to talk to the owner of a textile mill. Four days after he got back from Lyons, he left again for what he hoped would be his last trip to Berlin. Johnny had asked if he could come along, but Nick had told him that he'd be back in a day or two. He sensed something very different in Berlin when he arrived, a kind of exhilaration that ran through everyone's veins, and that afternoon he understood why. It was the twenty-third of August, and Germany had just signed a mutual nonaggression pact with the Russians. The negotiations had been conducted in secret, but the results were big news. Germany's greatest potential enemy had just been rendered impotent. Nick knew instantly, as did everyone else, that their agreement would pose an enormous threat to France and the rest of Europe. And he was suddenly desperately anxious to get home to Paris and his son. Who knew how quickly there might be a reaction, and he would himself be trapped in Berlin. And as he hastened through his day he was secretly glad that he had done what he could for Poland.

He attended one meeting that afternoon, and took the next train back to Paris. As he saw the Eiffel Tower come into view, he felt enormous relief sweep over him. All he knew was that he wanted to be near Johnny. He rushed home to the Avenue Foch and put his arms around him as he sat at breakfast.

"You came back fast, Dad!"

"I missed you!"

"I missed you too."

The maid brought him a cup of coffee and he chatted with his son as he scanned the papers. He was anxious to see the reaction in Paris, but of course he had known what it would be. There was a general mobilization of the French army, the preparations for war were being made, and all available troops were being sent to the borders, to defend the Maginot Line.

"What's that, Dad?" Johnny was reading over his shoulder as he frowned. Nick explained to his son about the alliance between the Russians and the Germans and what it meant to France. The boy watched him with wide eyes. "You mean there's going to be a war?" He didn't look entirely displeased about it. He was young enough to find it intriguing, and he still loved anything that had to do with guns.

When Johnny went out to play, Nick walked into the library with a solemn face. He asked the operator for the Hotel Carlton in Cannes. It was time to bring back his wife, no matter how little she'd like that.

They paged her at the pool, and suggested he call back later. But Nick was insistent with the operator at the hotel. If she was anywhere in the hotel, he wanted her found, and at last they found her, in someone's room, he suspected, but he didn't give a damn. Whatever else she was, she was his son's mother, and he wanted her back in Paris, in case something drastic happened in France.

"Sorry to bother you, Hil."

"Is something wrong?" The thought instantly crossed her mind that something had happened to Johnny, and as she walked naked across Philip Markham's room, holding the phone, her face wore a nervous expression. She glanced guiltily at him over her shoulder and then turned away as she waited for Nick's answer.

"Have you read the papers yesterday or today?"

"You mean that thing about the Germans and the Russians?"

"Yes, that's exactly what I mean."

"Oh, for chrissake, Nick. I thought something had happened to Johnny." She almost sighed with relief as she sat down on a chair and Philip began to stroke her leg as she smiled at him.

"He's fine. But I want you to come home."

"You mean now?"

"Yes. That's exactly what I mean."

"Why? I was coming home next week anyway."

"That may not be soon enough."

"For what?" She thought he was being a nervous fool, and she laughed as she watched Philip make funny faces and make obscene gestures as he returned to their freshly rumpled bed.

"I think there's going to be a war. They're mobilizing the French army, and things are liable to explode any day."

"It won't happen as quick as that." She had been nervous about it before they left New York, but now she had other pursuits in Cannes and the possibility of war seemed very remote to her.

"I don't want to argue with you, Hillary. I'm telling you to come home. Now!" He raised his voice as he pounded the desk, and as he attempted to control his voice he realized that he was afraid, for her as well as their son. He had thought that a war in Europe was at least a year away. He had never intended to expose his family to danger over here, and now he was suddenly desperately sorry that they had come with him. "Hillary, please . . . I've just been in Berlin. I know what I'm saying. Trust me for once. I want you back here in Paris if anything happens."

"Don't be so nervous, for chrissake. I'll be home next week." And as she said it she accepted a glass of champagne from Philip.

"Do I have to come down there and get you myself?"

"Would you do that?" Her voice on the phone sounded surprised, and he nodded as he watched Johnny playing in the garden.

"Yes, I would."

"All right. I'll see what I can arrange. I'm giving a dinner party tonight for a few friends, and—"

"Never mind that. I'm telling you, damn it, get your ass on the next train to Paris."

"And I'm telling you that I'm giving a dinner party—" But he cut her off before she could finish her sentence.

"Look, if you won't listen to reason from me, damn you, tell that Markham bastard to bring you home. Come home with him if you want, but you have a child here and the country is about to go to war. Just get your goddamn ass back here!"

"Just what the hell do you mean?" Her voice trembled as she asked. It was the first time Nick had ever mentioned Philip, and she hadn't realized that he had known. The embarrassment of that only served to fan her fury.

"Hillary, I told you why I called. I have nothing else to say." His voice sounded tired on the phone.

"I want you to explain what you just said." She had set down the glass of champagne and was sitting up very straight on the bed next to Philip.

"I'm not going to explain a goddamn thing. You heard me. I'll expect to see you here in the next couple of days." And with that he hung up, and she sat staring at the empty phone.

"What was that all about?" Philip Markham was watching the look on her face, and he knew instantly. "Does he know about us?"

"Apparently." She stared at him.

"Was he angry?"

"Not at all, or not much anyway. He's just mad that I don't want to come home yet. He's convinced that the whole country is going to explode in the next few days." She took a sip of champagne and glanced at the man who had been her lover the past two months. He suited her very well. He was every bit as spoiled and decadent and hedonistic as she was.

"He may be right, you know. There was a lot of talk about it last night on the Croisette."

"Oh, the goddamn nervous French. Anyway, if there's a

war, I'm taking my ass home. And not to Paris. I mean Boston or New York."

"If you can get there, my friend. Does he want to go back now?"

"I don't know. He didn't say. He just wants me in Paris with our son."

"You know, you're probably safer here. Hell, if the Germans bomb anything, they'll be sure to hit Paris first."

"That's a comforting thought." His sarcasm didn't ease her fear. She looked pensive for a moment and held out her glass for more champagne. "Do you think I should go back?"

He leaned over and kissed the cleft between her breasts. "Eventually, pretty girl. But not just yet." He devoured one nipple gently with his lips, and as she leaned back against the bed she forgot everything that Nick had said to her on the phone. It was only later, as she lay on the beach outside the hotel, that she thought about it again, and some deep inner instinct told her that she should go home. She told Markham about it as they dressed for the dinner party they were giving, and he shrugged with a relaxed air. "I'll get you home in a few days. Not to worry, love."

"And after that?" She was combing her hair as she asked. It was the first time she had asked him that kind of question, and he looked at her now in surprise.

"Do we have to worry about that?"

"I'm not worried, I'm just asking. Will you stay in Paris with me for a while?" Her voice almost cooed as he watched her, but his face broke into a broad grin.

"Wouldn't Nick Burnham just love that!"

"I don't mean at the house, you ass. You can stay at the Ritz or the George Cinq. But you don't have to rush home yet." He lived off the income his mother gave him, and everyone knew he was a playboy. He made no secret of it, but he also made no secret of the fact that he was no longer looking to get permanently attached. Four ex-wives had cost him dearly, and he was no longer shopping for a fifth one. But for those purposes, Hillary was perfect. She was already married and she had long since told him that marriage didn't suit her, which made him all the more surprised by the worried look he saw in her eyes now.

"You haven't fallen in love with me, have you?" There was a devil-may-care attitude about him, and it was that that appealed to her so much. He wasn't a tame one she could have for the asking, like Nick. He made her sweat for it, and she liked that. He was the first man who had openly and lovingly called her a little bitch. "I'm a dangerous man for a woman to love, pretty girl. Ask any woman. Hell"—he laughed at his own joke—"ask any man." He had stolen plenty of wives from his cronies.

"I don't need to. I know what you are. And you're as rotten as I am."

"Good." He pulled her gently backward by her hair and kissed her mouth and then bit it. "Then maybe we deserve each other." He didn't want to admit it to her, but he was more taken with her than he had planned to be. He had thought in New York that it would be an amusing affair for the summer. She had almost openly invited him to meet her in France. But she had thought then that she couldn't have him, and it intrigued them both that having spent the summer with him she still wanted him now. "Maybe I will stay in Paris for a while." The idea of a month at the George V pleased him, and he wasn't really worried about a war. "Tell you what, I'll drive you up myself the first of next week. Will that do, or do you think Nick will come racing down here for you before that?"

"Not likely." She smiled. "He's too busy with Johnny, our son, and his business."

"Good. Then we'll go home when we're ready. I'll call the hotel tomorrow and see if I can get my usual suite."

She left him then to finish dressing for the party, and when she emerged from the dressing room they were sharing, he whistled loudly. She was wearing a red organza dress almost cut to her navel in front. It barely hung to her body by a thread, and he loved it. He loved it so much that with one evil look, and a leer, he tore it right off her body and threw her on the bed, pressing his body against hers, and taking her with such force that it left her panting and breathless, with no thought at all for the thousand-dollar creation from Dior that lay in shreds beside her.

Chapter 14

$\mathcal{T}$he weekend of August twenty-sixth, Nick and John went to the Gare de l'Est to watch the thousands of soldiers entraining. They were going to the northern frontier fortresses for the most part, and Johnny stood watching them in awe as they boarded. Nick had hesitated at first when the boy asked him if they could go to watch, but in the end he decided that history was happening around them, and Johnny should see it. There had been no news of Hillary since his call, but he assumed that she would be home at any moment. There was no point calling her again, he had certainly made his point the first time he called her.

And on this same Sunday afternoon at the Place du Palais-Bourbon, on the Left Bank, Liane and the girls waited for Armand to come home. He had had to work all through the weekend, but there was an aura of unexpected calm about him now. Everything was moving into action. In the streets, there were posters everywhere with the words APPEL IMMÉDIAT, calling men into the army. The girls had seen the signs everywhere on their way home from the park, and Liane had tried to keep them informed of what was going on. Their father no longer had time to. Elisabeth was still too young to understand very much, and she was desperately afraid of guns, but Marie-Ange was greatly intrigued with what was happening. There were other posters in the streets too, which she read aloud to her nurse and her sister, giving instructions in the event of a possible gas attack, and telling civilians about car headlights and house lamps during blackouts. The night before, Paris had been only partially illuminated.

And Liane had explained to them that the reason there were so many cars in the streets was that people were leaving Paris. They carried an odd assortment of belongings on their cars, sometimes with chairs and tables strapped to the hood, baby buggies, pots and pans. The evacuation had begun, and people were being asked not to hoard food, and, as much as possible, not to panic. When Liane took the girls to the Louvre museum, to distract them that afternoon, they discovered that it was closed, and a guard told them that many of the great treasures within were already being shipped to the provinces to be hidden. And everywhere in the streets, among men discussing the pact between Moscow and Berlin, one heard the phrase *"Nous sommes cocus"*— "We've been cuckolded." Armand had said it himself to Liane. She still couldn't believe what had happened.

"Do you think the Germans will attack us tomorrow?" Marie-Ange asked sweetly over breakfast a few days after the crisis had begun, and Liane shook her head sadly. They were all waiting for the same thing, even the children.

"I don't think so, sweetheart. We hope they never will."

"But I heard Daddy say—"

"You shouldn't listen to grown-ups' conversations." But as she said it she wondered why not. They were all listening to what other people said, in the hope of hearing something they hadn't known before. Everyone was hungry for information. "That's why the soldiers are all going off to the borders, to keep us safe." She felt that at least Marie-Ange should know what was going on, but she wanted her not to be frightened. But they all were, at the core. Despite the outward calm one saw everywhere, deep within, everyone was afraid, so much so that when the air raid siren sounded that Thursday, as it always did, it sounded for only an instant, for fear that the population would think they were being attacked. There had been an instant of tension as the siren began, the entire city seemed to stop breathing, and then breathed a sigh of relief when it stopped so quickly.

But on September first, they all held their breath again as the news reached them that Germany had attacked Poland. The year before, the same thing had happened when the Germans attacked Czechoslovakia, but after the Munich Accord, the world had been reassured. Czechoslovakia had been a sacrificial lamb, but there would not be others. But now, with the strength of their nonaggression pact with the Russians, the Germans felt that they had nothing to fear from the rest of Europe, and the march on Poland began with a vengeance. Armand came home at lunch with the news, and Liane sat down quietly as tears ran down her face.

"Those poor people. Can't we help them?"

"We're too far away, Liane. And so are the British." Eventually, of course we can help, but not right away. For the moment . . ." He couldn't finish the sentence.

And on the same afternoon, Nick sat in the library of his rented house on the Avenue Foch, staring out the window. He had just called Hillary in Cannes, only to be told that she had checked out of the Carlton. It had been a week since he had told her to come home, and she still hadn't. They had told him that she checked out that morning, and no, they did not know, monsieur, how she was returning to Paris. He hoped that it was by train and that she would be home quickly. He was sorrier than hell now that he had brought her and Johnny over. There was obviously going to be war in Europe.

The next day was a tense one for everyone, as all of Europe waited to hear news of what was happening in Poland. And Armand told Liane that night what he had heard through diplomatic channels. Warsaw was in flames and it was a slaughter, but the Polish were a valiant people and they would not give up. They would fight the Germans until there was nothing left. They were determined to die with honor.

That night, they darkened the lights, and respected the blackout as they had been told, and it was an eerie sensation as they sat in the darkened room, with the shades drawn. Neither of them could sleep, and Liane found that all she could think of was the people fighting against the Germans in Poland. She thought of women like herself, in their homes, with two daughters or were the women and children fighting for their lives too? It was a horrifying image.

But on the next day, September 3, there was a great deal more to think about than Poland. Armand didn't come home this time to tell her the news. She didn't see him until late that night. But long before that, she had heard it on the radio. The British ship *Athenia* had been sunk by a German U-boat west of the Hebrides. And the reaction was instant. Britain declared war on Germany at once, and France joined them, honoring the pledge to Poland. The years of surmisal and guesswork were over. Europe was at war. Liane sat in the living room, staring at the Paris sky, with tears in her eyes, and then she went into the girls' room and told them. They both began to cry at once, as did Mademoiselle, and the two women and two little girls sat together for a long time, crying. But Liane forced the girls to wash their faces after a time, and she went to make lunch for them all. It was important that they stay calm. Crying wouldn't help anything, she told them.

"And we have to do everything we can to help Papa."

"Will he go to be a soldier now?" Elisabeth had looked at her with enormous blue eyes and almost choked on her lunch as she stifled a sob, but Liane gently stroked her face as she shook her head.

"No, darling, Papa serves France in a different way."

"Besides, he's too old." Marie-Ange added matter-of-factly. Liane was surprised at the remark. She never thought of Armand as old, and she was surprised that her daughter was even aware of his age. He was so youthful and dynamic that his age seemed irrelevant to her, and Elisabeth was quick to his defense.

"Papa is *not* old!"

"He is too!" And before Liane could stop them the girls were fighting. In the end, she almost slapped them both, their nerves were all pulled taut, and after lunch she left them with Mademoiselle to play quietly in their room. She didn't want them in the garden. Who knew what would happen now. With France officially at war, there could have been anything from an air raid to a gas attack, and she wanted them in the house. She longed to talk to Armand, but she didn't dare disturb him.

"Daddy, does this mean we'll have to go back to New York?" Johnny was watching him with wide eyes. Nick had just told him the news, and the boy looked shocked. The idea of war was exciting, but his father had looked so grim when he told him the news that it didn't seem like fun now. "I don't want to go home yet." He liked it in France. And then, suddenly, real panic. "If we go home, can I take my puppy?"

"Of course you can." But he wasn't thinking about the dog as he sat in the child's room. He was thinking of the boy's mother. She had left Cannes two days before and she wasn't home yet. He left Johnny after a little while and went down to his study. He had come home from the office the moment he heard the news, to reassure his son, but now he wondered if he should go back. He called them and told them to call at home if they needed him. But he wanted to stay with John until they heard more news about what would happen. But there was little news to hear. Paris was strangely calm once war was declared. The exodus of the masses to the provinces continued, but on the whole Paris seemed very self-contained, and there was no panic.

And it was late on that afternoon of September 3, that Nick heard her. The front doorbell rang, there was a clatter of voices in the hall, and a moment later the library door swung open. It was Hillary, deeply tanned, her hair swinging loose, her eyes like enormous inlays of onyx and ivory in her face, and a straw hat, which matched her beige cotton sundress, swinging from her arm.

"For God's sake, Hil . . ." He had the same reaction one has when one recovers a lost child, the instant confusion as to whether to hug it or slap it.

"Hello, Nick." Her face looked strangely calm, and there was obviously not going to be a warm greeting. He noticed instantly a large diamond bracelet on her arm, totally out of keeping with what she was wearing, but he said nothing about what was obviously a very expensive gift from her new lover. "How've you been?" Her voice was bright. He watched her, feeling as though he were moving underwater.

"Do you realize that France and England declared war on Germany today?"

"So I hear." She seemed remarkably cool as she sat down on the couch and crossed one leg over the other.

"Where in hell have you been?" The conversation was surrealistic and disjointed.

"In Cannes."

"I mean for the last two days. I called and they said you'd checked out."

"I drove home with friends."

"Philip Markham?" It was crazy. France had gone to war, and he was questioning his wife about her lover.

"Are we going to start that again? I thought those days were over."

"That's not the point. This was no time to go careering around France, for chrissake."

"You told me to come back, so I did." Her eyes were openly hostile, and she hadn't yet asked for their son. As he watched her he realized that he had begun to hate her.

"You came back exactly ten days after I told you to come home at once."

"I had plans I couldn't walk out on."

"You have a son, and there's a war on."

"So I'm back. Now what?"

He sighed deeply. He had thought about it all day, and it

wasn't what he wanted, but he knew he had to do it. "I'm sending you both home, if we can get you home safely."

"I think that's a fine idea." For the first time since she'd entered the room, she smiled. Philip and she had discussed it before he got out of the car at the George V. He said he was taking her back to New York, whether Nick liked it or not. But Nick had just solved that problem. "When do we leave?"

"I'll have them research it at the office. It's not going to be easy now."

"You should have thought about that in June." She stood up nervously then and walked around the room, and then glanced at him over her shoulder. "I guess you were too busy doing business with the krauts to think of what danger you were putting us in. You realize, don't you, that you're part of all this. You're partly responsible for starting the war. Who knows how the Germans use the steel you sell them?" It was a horrifying thought and one that had been on Nick's mind for weeks now. The only consolation he had was that two days before, he had canceled all the rest of his German contracts. His company would take a loss of any size, he had announced, but he would no longer deal with Hitler's Reich. He was only sorry he hadn't done that before. And as he stood there staring at his wife, he remembered Liane's words on the ship . . . "The time to choose sides will come" . . . it had, and he had, but too late, he had to live now with the knowledge of what he had done, and how he may have indirectly helped them. It was small consolation that he had also helped to arm Britain and France and Poland. What hurt so much now was that he had also assisted the Germans. But more than that it hurt him that Hillary had driven the spear in even deeper into his side, and he looked at her now with open amazement.

"Why do you hate me so much, Hil?"

She appeared to think about it for a time and then shrugged. "I don't know. . . ." And then she looked at him sadly. "Maybe because you've always reminded me of what

I'm not. You wanted something that I never had to give." It was a truth he had only recently accepted. "You gave me too much. You stifled me from the first moment we met. You should have married some sweet little schoolteacher who would give you eight children."

"That wasn't what I had in mind. I loved you." He looked tired and sad. It was all over between them.

"But you don't anymore, do you?" It was a question she had to ask. She had to know. It was her final ticket to freedom.

Slowly he shook his head. "No, I don't. It's better for both of us like this."

She nodded. "Yes, it is." And then she took a deep breath and walked to the door. "I'll go see Johnny now. How soon do we leave?"

"As soon as I can arrange it."

"Are you coming with us, Nick?" She watched him as she asked, and regretfully he shook his head.

"I can't for a while. But I'll come home as soon as I can." She nodded and left the room, and he walked quietly to the window and stared out at the garden

Chapter 15

$\mathcal{O}$n the night of September 6, Armand and Liane shared a light dinner she warmed for him at midnight. All Armand wanted was some soup and a piece of bread. He was too exhausted to eat. He had had an endless day of frantic meetings. The news from Poland was worse than ever, though thankfully Warsaw had not yet fallen. According to reports, the situation was critical and the Poles were facing mass extermination. Liane watched Armand's face now and she saw the grief there, and the years, and the concern for his own country.

"Liane . . . there's something I want to tell you." She wondered what grim bit of news he would impart. It seemed as though that's all there was now.

"Yes?"

"The *Aquitania*, a British ship, docked in Southampton last night, and she will make one more trip back to the States, where they're going to convert her to carry troops. And when she sails"—he almost choked on the words—"I want you and the girls on her." She sat and listened to him in total silence, and he watched her. For a moment there was no reaction, and then slowly she shook her head.

She sat up very straight and looked him in the eye. "No, Armand, we're not going."

For an instant it was his turn to be startled into silence.

"Are you mad? France is at war. You must go back. I want to know that you and the girls are safe."

"On an English ship, with the Atlantic probably crawling with U-boats? They sank the *Athenia*, why not this ship?"

Armand shook his head. The horrors they were hearing out of Warsaw were too fresh in his mind. He would not allow his wife and girls to stay in France to fight the Germans.

"You must not argue with me." But he was too tired to say much more, and he met in Liane a resolve he had never anticipated.

"We are not going. The girls and I are staying here with you. We discussed it as soon as war was announced. There are other women and children here. Why should we go?"

"Because it's safer for you in the States. Roosevelt has insisted that he will not enter this war." That much wasn't news, and Liane heard it again with disgust.

"Have you no faith in France? It will not fall like Czechoslovakia or Poland."

"And if they drop bombs, which they surely will, do you want to be here with the girls, Liane?"

"Others lived through it in the last war." He was so tired he was almost ready to fall asleep at the table, and she was too determined to stay. He couldn't fight her. They talked about it again the next morning, the moment he awoke, but she was even more immovable then. She ignored almost everything he said, and as he prepared to leave for the office at seven thirty, she looked at him for a last time with her gentle smile. "I love you, Armand. My place is here with you. Don't ask me again. I won't go."

He watched her eyes for a long moment. "You're an extraordinary woman, Liane, but I knew that before. You still have the choice. You should get back to the States while you can."

"I have nothing there. My home is here with you."

There were tears in his eyes as he bent to kiss her good-bye. She had moved him more than she ever had before. She was as brave as any of them in Poland. "I love you."

"I love you too." She spoke in a whisper as she kissed him, and then he was gone. She knew that she wouldn't see him again until after midnight that night, and that he would return almost stumbling with exhaustion, but at least it was for a good cause now. The country was at war. And she was staying. She would always stand by him.

Chapter 16

"Are you ready to go?" Johnny nodded with big sad eyes, his puppy in his arms, and his nurse beside him. "Do you have your baseball bat in your trunk?" The child nodded again, the tears sliding down his face at last. And his father pulled him close. "I know, Son . . . I know . . . I'm going to miss you too . . . but it's only for a little while." He clenched his teeth and prayed that what he said was true. But he couldn't go back yet. He couldn't desert their interests in Europe.

"But I don't want to go home without you, Dad."

"It's just for a little while . . . I promise. . . ." He looked at Hillary over the child's head, and she was strangly quiet. Their bags were waiting in the hall. This time there was no second carload of trunks. They had been told that they could each bring two bags. The ship was loaded to the gills, and it was not going to be a luxurious journey, although the passenger list was sure to be impressive. Hundreds of wealthy American tourists had been trapped abroad and they had besieged their embassies in desperation to get home. All the British and French sailings scheduled for September had been canceled. The *Normandie* had reached New York on August 28, and had been cabled by her owners to remain in New York for safekeeping. The American ships had canceled their schedules as well, and Ambassador Kennedy in London was going mad, cabling frantically that there were an army of American tourists stranded abroad, and ships had to be sent for them. Accordingly, the *Washington, Manhattan,* and *President Roosevelt* were all on their way, but no one knew when, and the *Aquitania* was the only ship with a certain sailing date. And this would be her last journey before being pressed into military service.

The dangers of this last crossing were well-known to all, with terrifying tales of German U-boats on the high seas, but due to her structure, she was less vulnerable to underwater attack than most of the others. And she had made her last crossing by zigzagging handsomely across the Atlantic, at great speed and in total blackout. The trip back to the States was going to be an interesting journey.

The large black Duesenberg was waiting outside the house on the Avenue Foch and Hillary, Nick, Johnny, and the nurse somberly climbed in. They were driving to Calais, where Nick had rented a large yacht, which would take them to Dover. And he had a car waiting there to take them on to Southampton. The trip was not so much perilous as exhausting, and by the time they reached the dock on the day the ship sailed, Hillary, to her own surprise, was close to tears. She was suddenly terrified that the ship would be sunk at sea and she clung to Nick in a manner most unlike her when they read a warning before passengers boarded the ship. They were all told that they were making the crossing at their own risk, "on a belligerent ship and were subject to sinking without notice." It brought the point home in a way nothing else could and the three Burnhams held each other tight for a moment before Nick took them on board. He had been able to get them only one small airless cabin with three beds, a decent one for his wife, and a double bunk for Johnny and the nurse. At least, he noticed, they had their own bathroom.

He stayed with them until the last signal that he had to leave, and then he held Johnny tightly in his arms for an endless moment.

"Be a big boy, tiger, and take care of your mommy for

me. And do everything she tells you on the ship. It's very important."

"Oh, Daddy . . ." His voice trembled almost as much as Nick's. "Do you think we'll sink?"

"No, I don't. And I'm going to think good thoughts about you every day. And the minute you get home, Mommy is going to cable me."

"What about my puppy?" She was trembling under the bed. Johnny had hidden her to get her on the ship. They had been told no pets, but knowing the English's soft heart for dogs, he knew that nothing would happen once she was discovered. "What'll I do with my puppy if we sink?"

"You won't. Just hold on to her real tight and keep her in your life vest." It was a hideous thought, and he held on to Johnny's hand as he stood up to look at his wife. "Take care of yourself, Hil . . . and John. . . ." He glanced down at their son, who was crying openly as he looked up at his father.

"I will, Nick. Take care of yourself over here." And then, with a gulp, she hugged him. "Come back soon." In the last moments on board the hatred between them seemed to dispel. This was no time for that. The possibility that they might never see each other again occurred to all three of them, and the nurse was almost hysterical as she sat sobbing on her bunk. It was going to be quite a trip, Nick knew, as he left them. He only prayed that the *Aquitania* would make it safely.

And he stood alone on the deck, waving frantically to the ship, until he could see them no more, and then when it was too far for his son to see, he dropped his face into his hands and began to sob. A workman on the dock coughed softly as he walked past him, and he stopped to pat Nick's shoulder.

"She'll be all right, mate . . . she's a great ship, she is. . . . I came over with her from New York . . . moves like the wind, she does . . . the krauts won't be able to touch her." Nick nodded, grateful for the encouraging words, but he was unable to answer. He felt as though his very life and soul had set sail on the ship. He went inside the lounge for a drink of water, and saw the manifest posted on the wall. As though it would bring Johnny closer to him again, he looked at the list and saw them there. "Burnham, Mrs. Nicholas . . . Burnham, Master John . . ." The nurse was listed farther down, and then he felt his heart turn to ice as he read the name "Markham, Mr. Philip."

Chapter 17

*T*he normal number of passengers accommodated on the *Aquitania* was 3,230 with a crew of 972, but for this last voyage, as much furniture as possible had been removed, and extra beds put in. They were carrying an additional 400 people. The accommodations were more than cramped, and there were several families traveling like Hillary and Johnny, cramped into one room, when they normally have had two or three cabins or a suite. But this trip was entirely different. Dinner was served at four and five in the afternoon, and by nightfall everything was in total blackout. The passengers were urged to be in their rooms by then, so as to avoid accidents in the corridors. The windows were painted black all over the ship, and the passengers were requested to use the bathrooms without turning on the lights, a circumstance everyone seemed to get used to. There were a vast number of Americans on board, and English too, and the British appeared particularly calm, coming to dinner in black tie every night, as though nothing were amiss, as they discussed the war news.

As for the ship itself, what was left intact still had the aura of elegant Victorian drawing rooms, and it was an odd contrast to the notices on the walls, instructing passengers what to do in case of attack by a German U-boat.

By the second day out John had seemed to calm down, enough so that Hillary felt she could introduce him to Philip

Markham. She explained that he was an old friend from New York, and she had run into him on the ship, but as Hillary and Philip talked, Johnny watched them with open suspicion. And the next morning, when he saw them together on one of the promenade decks, he told his nurse, "I hate that man." She scolded him soundly, but he didn't care, and that night he said much the same to his mother. She slapped him soundly across the face, and he looked at her without a tear. "I don't care what you do to me. When I grow up, I'm going to live with my daddy."

"And don't you think I am too?" Her hands were still shaking but she tried to control her voice. The child was much too smart for his own good, and she was glad that he couldn't tell Nick. She wondered if he had seen them kissing. She had been in her own bed every night, though not by choice. There were three other men in Philip's cabin. "What do you mean you're going to live with your daddy? So am I."

"No, you're not. I'll bet you're going to live with *him.*" He refused to even say his name, or acknowledge Philip when they met.

"That's a stupid thing to say." But it was precisely what she and Philip had been discussing lately. She wasn't at all sold on Nick's idea that they had to stay married forever, and if she could get him to agree to a divorce when he got back, or if she could get grounds to sue him, she would, and marry Philip. "I don't want to hear you say that again." And she didn't. He scarcely spoke to his mother again on the trip. He stayed with his nurse, and spent most of the time playing with his puppy in the cabin. It was a long, tiresome journey for them all, following a zigzag course, and with the nightly blackouts. It took them longer than usual to reach New York, and when at last they did, Hillary hoped she never saw a ship again, and she had never been so grateful to be in New York in her life, although she stayed there for only a few days before taking Johnny up to Boston to stay with her mother.

"Why do I have to stay here? Aren't we going home?" Johnny didn't understand why he had to stay with his grand-mother.

"I am. And I'm going to get the apartment ready in New York." It had been closed for four months, and she claimed that she had a lot of work to do to get it ready. But two weeks later his grandmother registered him in a school in Boston. She said that it was just for a little while, so he wouldn't miss too much school while his mother was getting the apartment ready. But he overheard his grandmother talking after that. It had been her idea to put him in school. She had no idea when Hillary was going to come back for him, and she seemed to be stalling. Johnny knew why, though he kept silent. She was probably with that man . . . Mr. Markham. . . . He was going to write to his father about it and tell him, but something told him that that wouldn't be such a good idea. His dad might get too worried. It would be better to tell him when he saw him. And in the last letter he'd gotten from his dad, Nick told him that he would come home as soon as he could, probably right after Christmas. It seemed like a long time to Johnny, but Christmas was only two months away, his father reminded him in the letter.

It was a lonely life for Johnny with his grandmother. She was elderly and nervous. Johnny was just glad that she had let him bring his puppy with him.

It was a week after Nick had written the last letter to Johnny that he ran into Armand and Liane at a small dinner party given by the American consul. It was the first time Armand and Liane had been out in months, and everyone seemed to have aged considerably over the summer. Liane was wearing a very pretty long black satin dress, but she looked very tired. The strain was telling on them all, al-though on the surface Paris was very calm. But everyone was still grieving over the surrender of Warsaw a month before. The Poles had fought valiantly until the end, but the Soviets had attacked them from the east on the seventeenth of September, and on the twenty-eighth it was all over, despite all their efforts, including Nick's steel. Their sister city of the east had fallen.

"How have you been?" Nick found himself sitting next to Liane at dinner, with Armand at the other end of the table. And Nick thought Armand looked ten years older than he had on the ship in June. He had been working fifteen and eighteen hours a day and it showed. Armand looked like an old man now, and he had just turned fifty-seven.

"We're all right." Liane spoke very softly. "Armand has been burning the candle at both ends and in the middle." She saw the ravages too, but there was no help for that. He would push himself until he dropped, for the love of his country. It left her alone with the girls almost all the time, but she accepted that too. She had no choice now. And she was doing volunteer work for the Red Cross. There wasn't much she could do yet, but it was something. They were helping to ship vast numbers of German and Eastern European Jews out through France, and at least she knew she was helping to save some lives. They were going to South America and the United States, and Canada and Australia. "How's my friend John?" She smiled at Nick now.

"He's all right. I'm not entirely sure where he is though." Nick had expected him to be in New York, but the letter he had gotten from Johnny had said that he was with his grandmother in Boston, probably for a visit, to reassure her that he was all right.

But Liane looked confused. "Isn't he here with you?"

Nick shook his head. "They sailed on the *Aquitania* in September, on her last trip over. Actually, what I meant was that I thought he was in New York, but he appears to be in Boston with my mother-in-law."

"You sent him alone?" Liane looked shocked. It was the ship that Armand had tried to get her to sail on.

"No, his mother went too. I didn't want them over here anymore. I feel better knowing that they're in the States." Liane nodded. It made sense even though it hadn't been what she had wanted. She suspected however that Hillary Burnham had been only too happy to go. She had heard the rumors about Philip Markham. The international community in Paris was small and inbred and very loquacious. But Liane looked at Nick now, wondering how he was faring. He looked tired too, although not as much as Armand. She remembered their last conversation on the ship and wondered how his life had been since then. It seemed a thousand years ago since they had all come over, and it had only been four months since then.

"And how are you doing?"

"All right, I suppose." He lowered his voice to speak his mind. She always brought that out in him. She was that kind of woman. "I have to live with my mistakes and my misjudgments." She knew immediately what he meant, that he was referring to his German contracts.

"You're not the only one who misjudged them. Think of what they're saying in the States. Roosevelt is trying to get reelected next year on the basis that the Americans won't ever get involved in the war over here. It's madness."

"Willkie is saying the same thing. They might as well be on the same ticket."

"Who do you suppose will win?" Liane asked. It seemed odd to be speaking of the American elections while Europe was in blazes around them.

"Roosevelt will, of course."

"For a third term?"

"Do you doubt it?"

She smiled. "Not really." It was nice speaking of those things with him. A taste of sanity and home in the midst of the nightmare they were living.

The dinner party ended early and Armand took Liane home. He yawned all the way and patted his wife's hand in the back of the Citroën, with its government driver. "I see that Burnham was there tonight. I never got a chance to talk to him. How is he?"

"Fine." Their conversation had had none of the personal

flavor of their talks on the ship, but that was to be expected.

"I'm surprised he's still here."

"He says he's going home after Christmas. The boy and his wife went home on the *Aquitania*."

"Probably with Philip Markham."

"Did you know about that?" She looked at Armand in surprise, and then she grinned. He had never mentioned it to her, she had heard it on her own, from some of the Americans she knew in Paris. "Is there anything you don't know, Armand?"

"Hopefully not. Information is my business." He knew also about Burnham's secret deals with Poland but he didn't say so. And then Armand glanced quickly at the driver. But the man was to be trusted. He had top security clearance.

"Is it?" Liane looked surprised. That wouldn't have been how she would have described his work. But nowadays everything was changing.

And Armand drifted away rapidly from the subject. "It was nice seeing you all dressed up tonight, my love. Like the old days, when we lived in a peaceful world." She nodded slowly. She was still thinking about what he had said, but she didn't want to question him in the car. She had seen him glance at the driver. But she had been wondering about his activities for a while. He never told her anymore about what was going on at the office. He told her just the news that she read every day anyway in the paper. But he was much more secretive than he had been in the past. And more tired than she had ever known him. They hadn't made love since late August. And she suspected that tonight would be no different. He was already drifting off to sleep in the car before they reached the Place du Palais-Bourbon. She woke him up and they went upstairs, and while she was undressing, he did the same and reached the bed first, and was sound asleep when she got there.

Chapter 18

$\mathcal{O}$n the thirtieth of November, two days after Americans all over the United States had carved their turkeys, Soviet air and ground troops attacked Finland. As usual, Liane did not see Armand. She was starting to feel that their marriage was beginning to crumble along with Europe. For months she had felt that she could serve France by serving him, but more and more now he kept a distance from her that she had never felt before. He was distracted and silent, uninvolved with the girls; their sex life was at a total standstill. He gave all of his energies to France, and would allow her to give none of hers to him. He told her absolutely nothing now, and she no longer asked him what was new. She felt as though she were living alone with the girls, and they noticed it too, although, out of respect for Armand, she denied it to them.

"Papa is just very busy. You know that. It's the war." But she was beginning to wonder if it was just that, or if it was something more. There were constant secret meetings at all hours of the day and night, and once or twice he went away for the weekend, but could not tell her where or with whom. She wondered briefly if he was involved with a mistress, as well as the war, but she didn't really think that.

Whatever was happening in his life, it did not include her. She might as well have gone back to the States, for the little she saw of him. And she found herself wondering now and then how Nick Burnham was holding up without his son, living in the enormous house on the Avenue Foch, all alone.

In fact, he was even more lonely than Liane. At least she had her daughters. He had no one at all. He had heard not a single word from Hillary since he'd left her on board the *Aquitania* in September. His only letters had been from Johnny, and one from his mother-in-law. All he could gather from what she told him was that Hillary was terribly busy in New York, and for some vague, undisclosed reason, Johnny was going to continue staying with her. Nick knew exactly what Hillary was up to. It was either Philip Markham, or someone else, but she didn't want to be saddled with her child, any more than she had wanted to the past summer. It turned Nick's stomach to think of the boy alone with his grandmother in Boston, but for the moment nothing could be done. He had planned to stay in Paris until after Christmas, but by the end of the week he knew that he couldn't go back yet. He had made a commitment he had to live up to, to assist the French. Now he hoped to be back in New York by April, though he didn't tell Johnny that when he wrote to him, not wanting to get the child's hopes up until he was sure. He just said soon. He cabled his office in New York to buy the boy a mountain of Christmas presents and have them delivered to Boston. It wasn't much of a replacement for a father or a mother, but it was something; it was all he could do for the moment. And it was more than *he* had in Paris on Christmas Day.

He stood alone in the paneled library, where he had once stood watching Johnny play in the garden, and now there was no one and nothing. The trees were bare, the garden was pale gray, there was no sound in the house . . . no Christmas tree . . . no carols . . . no shining face exploding with glee, digging through an overstuffed Christmas stocking. There was only the sound of his own footsteps as he walked up the stairs to his bedroom, carrying the last bottle of brandy he had bought before the war, and praying for a few hours of oblivion, when he wouldn't be aching for his only son. But even the brandy didn't help, and he stopped after three stiff drinks. They were just enough to take the edge off and then he sat down to write Johnny a letter, telling him how much he missed him, and how next Christmas would be much better than this. Nick Burnham was grateful when at last night fell, and he drew the curtains, turned off the light, and went to sleep.

Chapter 19

*T*he next four or five months were characterized by a period of limbo, a time referred to as the "phony war" in France, when nothing seemed to happen. The French stood staunchly at the Maginot Line, prepared to defend their country but not being asked to. And in Paris life went on almost as normal. After the initial shock, there were very few changes, unlike London, where rationing was acute and uncomfortable, sirens shrieked, and air raid drills were common almost every night. But in Paris, life was very different from all that.

It created a kind of subterranean tension, coupled with a false sense of security that nothing would ever change. Armand went on with his constant secret meetings, and rather than being supportive, Liane was beginning to get annoyed. At least he could tell her something about what he was doing, she reasoned. He had always trusted her before, but it was clear that he didn't now. He went on with his mysterious war work, disappearing occasionally for a few days at a time. She would get a quiet call from his office, telling her only that Monsieur had gone out of town.

The lull that appeared to overtake Paris allowed Nick to continue his work. There was the feeling in the air that this could go on for quite a while. Nick almost left in April, as he had planned, but things were so peaceful in Paris that he decided to tie everything up himself and stay for just one more month. And it was that month that was decisive. Suddenly the cancer that had spread so quietly erupted all around them. On May tenth Hitler attacked the Lowlands—Belgium, the Netherlands, and Luxembourg—and on May fourteenth the Dutch surrendered, after which the Germans moved into northern France. Suddenly everyone was frenzied and alert as they hadn't been since the previous August and September. The lull was over, and terror reigned. It was obvious now that Hitler had only been biding his time before attacking the rest of Europe. Once again the British had been right. But when Liane attempted to discuss it with her husband, he said nothing more to her. He had his hands full with his secret work.

Amiens and Arras fell on May 21, and the Belgians surrendered officially a week later, on May 28. During this time the evacuation of Dunkirk had begun, on May 24, and had continued for eleven horrendous, frenzied days. The news in Paris was appalling, the loss of life beyond anyone's worst fears. And on June 4, when the evacuation ended, Churchill spoke to the House of Commons, promising to fight in France, in Britain, or on the seas, whatever the cost would be. ". . . we shall fight on the beaches, we shall fight on the landing grounds, we shall fight in the fields and in the streets, we shall fight in the hills; we shall never surrender!"

Six days later Italy entered the war. And on June 12, tragedy of tragedies in all eyes, Paris was declared an open city. The French had decided not to fight. On the fourteenth of June, Armand and Liane's eleventh anniversary, the Germans marched into Paris, and within hours the swastika flew from every major building in sight. From the Place du Palais-Bourbon Liane watched them, the ugly red flags flying in the breeze, as tears poured down her face. She hadn't seen Armand since the day before, and she was praying for his safety. But more than that, she was crying for France. The French had appealed for aid from her own country, but had been declined, and now Paris was in the hands of the Germans. It was enough to break anyone's heart.

Armand returned to the house for a moment that afternoon, on foot, by the back streets, to assure himself that Liane and the girls were not in danger. He told them to lower the drapes and keep the doors locked. The Germans would harm no one, but it was best not to catch their attention. He found her crying in their bedroom the moment he came in, and he took her in his arms. He was hurrying back to his office. They had destroyed truckloads of papers the day before, but there was still work to do before they turned the city over officially to the Germans, and now he told her that Premier Reynaud's cabinet would resign on the day after next. They had plans to flee south to Bordeaux, and Liane looked at him in sudden panic.

"Are you going with them?"

"Of course not. Do you think I'd leave you here alone?" His voice was tired and sharp and angry, and she didn't understand what he was saying.

"But don't you have to? Armand . . ."

"We'll discuss it later. Now, do as I tell you and stay indoors. Keep the girls quiet. Don't let the maids out. . . ." He left her with a flurry of last instructions and disappeared into the silent streets. Others like them were indoors, hiding. It appeared almost like a deserted city as the German troops made their way through the town. There was not even one café open. There was nothing. No people, no open shops, no French soldiers. Those who had chosen to flee had left days before, and those who had chosen to stay were hiding. But by that night, a few ventured to their balconies, waving small German flags, and as Liane saw them she felt sick to her stomach. They were traitors, pigs. She wanted to scream as she saw them, but instead she closed the curtains quietly and waited for Armand to return. For days she had wondered what they would do next. There was no escape now. They were in the hands of the Germans. She had known when she had decided to stay in Paris with Armand after war was declared that one day this might happen. But in her heart of hearts she had never believed it. Paris could not be taken. And it wasn't. It was given.

Armand did not return to the house until almost dawn two days later. He was strangely quiet, his face pale, and he said nothing to his wife as he laid on the bed with all his clothes on. He did not sleep, he did not speak, he just lay there. After two hours he got up and bathed and changed his clothes as Liane watched. It was obvious that he was going out, but to where? He no longer had an office to go to. It belonged to the Germans.

"Where are you going?"

"This is the day of Reynaud's resignation. I must be there."

"Do you have to leave?" He nodded. "And then what?"

He looked sadly at his wife. Finally he had to tell her something. For months now he had belonged to France and not Liane. It was like belonging to two women, and he didn't have the strength for both. It was almost as though he had betrayed Liane, with all her patience, all her trust, her love. He had to tell her. For too long now he had kept his secrets. "Reynaud leaves today for Bordeaux, Liane." The words had an ominous ring to them, but he had told her that much two nights before. And he had said he wasn't going. "Before he leaves, there will be an official surrender."

"And we will be ruled by the Germans."

"Indirectly. Maréchal Philippe Pétain will become our President, with the approval of the Germans. He is supported by Jean François Darlan and Pierre Laval, two fine naval men of France." It sounded like a party line and Liane stared at him.

"Armand, what are you saying? That Pétain will collaborate with the Germans?"

"For the benefit of France." She couldn't believe what he was saying. And where was he in all this mess? With Reynaud and the old world, or Pétain and his collusion with the Germans? She could hardly bring herself to ask him, but she had to.

"And you?" But suddenly she realized that he had already told her. The two nights before when he had told her that Reynaud was fleeing to Bordeaux, he had told her that he was staying. She almost felt sick as she remembered, and she sat down on the edge of their bed, her eyes huge in her face. "Armand, answer me." At first he said nothing, and then he sat down slowly beside her. Perhaps it was safe to tell her more than he had planned to. He had missed her for so long now. But it had been vital that he not involve her. "Armand?" The tears ran slowly from her eyes.

"I stay with Pétain." The words fell from him like rocks. but in sharing it with her, it took a burden off his shoulders. She only shook her head and cried as she listened, and then she looked at him, brokenhearted.

"I don't believe you."

"I have to."

"Why?" It was a single word of accusation as she cried uncontrollably beside him.

And then he spoke to her in a whisper. "I can serve France better this way."

"With Pétain? You're crazy!" She was shouting at him, but suddenly she saw something in his eyes and sat very still on the bed as she watched him. "What do you mean?" She lowered her voice, and he took her hands in his own.

"*Ma* Liane . . . what a good woman you have been . . . so brave and strong all this winter . . . stronger than I sometimes . . ." He sighed deeply and spoke so that only she could hear him. "Pétain trusts me. He knows me from the First World War. I fought well for him, and he believes I will again."

"Armand, what are you saying?" They were speaking in hushed whispers and she wasn't even sure why, except that suddenly she suspected that he was about to tell her what she had wondered about for months.

"I'm telling you that I will stay here in Paris and work for Pétain."

"Working for the Germans?" But it was not an accusation now. It was a question.

"So it will appear."

"And in truth?"

"I will be working for the others, in every way I can. There will be resistance from many quarters. The government may go to North Africa. I will stay in close touch with Reynaud, De Gaulle, the others."

"And if you're caught, they'll kill you." The tears barely staunched began again now. "For God's sake, what are you doing?"

"The only thing I can now. I'm too old to run to the hills with the others. And that isn't what I'm good at. I've been with the diplomatic service all my life. I know what I need to do to help them. I speak German—" He didn't finish the sentence, and suddenly she pulled him close to her and held him.

"Something will happen. . . . I couldn't bear it. . . ."

"Nothing will happen. I will be very cautious. I will be safe here." But from his words she sensed what he was going to say next and she didn't want to hear it. "But I want you and the girls to go back to the States now, as soon as we can get you out of France."

"I won't leave you."

"You have no choice. I shouldn't have let you stay in September. But I wanted you here with me—" His voice faltered and then he went on. He knew how hard the past nine months had been for her, and he was sorry he had kept her beside him. It had been selfish and he knew it. But now those days were over. "You will endanger my mission if you stay, Liane . . . and the girls . . . it will be too dangerous for them here now, with the Germans all over Paris. You have to go when I can arrange it." She hoped that he would not be able to arrange it quickly. It terrified her to think of leaving him in France, acting as a double agent, against the Germans and Pétain.

But despite her fears for him, when he left her again to go back to confer with Pétain and the Germans a little while later, she was relieved as she hadn't been in months. She had suspected that something was going on and the ignorance of what it was had almost killed her. She had even come to distrust him, to suspect him. And now she felt guilty about that. But she also felt something for him that she hadn't felt for a long, long time. A kind of passionate respect and affection. He had confided in her. He trusted her, and she believed in him as she had in the very beginning. As Paris fell, their marriage rose from the ashes, and she went to make breakfast for the girls with a lighter heart than she had felt in a very long time.

That afternoon, Pétain was installed as the official head of France. As Armand had foretold, Reynaud fled to Bordeaux. Brigadier General Charles de Gaulle went to London to discuss getting troops to North Africa, and Churchill vowed to assist the French Resistance in every way he could. De Gaulle broadcast a brief speech into France on June 18, begging those still faithful to France "to carry on the fight," and Liane listened to him avidly on a radio concealed in her dressing room, lest the house be invaded suddenly by the Germans. One could no longer be certain of one's safety, Armand had warned her since the fall of Paris. That night she recounted the speech to Armand. He told her then that he was researching a ship for her. It was imperative that he get her out of France quickly. To do it later would arouse suspicion among Pétain's men. Why would his wife want to leave? But if she left immediately after the fall of Paris, he could explain that Liane as an American disapproved of his loyalties and they had had a parting of the ways, and she wanted to go home.

Four days later Armand went to Compiègne, in the North of France, to watch Hitler, Goering, and Keitel, Chief of Hitler's Supreme Command, read the conditions of their occupation and officially become the masters of France. It was a ceremony that tore at his soul, and as the band played

"Deutschland, Deutschland über Alles," he thought he might faint, but he smiled valiantly through it all, and in his heart he prayed that one day the occupation would end. He would gladly have given his life at that moment to buy back France from the Germans. And when he returned to Liane that night, he looked worse than she had ever seen him. He was a man who had looked so youthful for so many years, but in the past months she had watched him grow old. And for the first time in many years, he turned to her that night in their bed and touched her with the gentleness and passion she remembered from long ago. They lay side by side afterward, thinking their own thoughts and dreams, as Armand tried to force from his mind what he'd seen that day. He had watched his country, his first love, being raped. Liane sat up on one elbow then and looked down at him, and she could see that there were tears trickling slowly from his eyes.

"Don't, my love . . ." She pulled him close to her. "It will all end one day soon." But she wished that he were in Bordeaux with the others, and not dancing on the tightrope he had committed himself to here in Paris.

He took a deep breath then and looked at her. "I have something to tell you, Liane." She wondered what more he could tell her now, and for an instant there was a flash of fear in her eyes. "I have found a ship for you and the girls. A freighter. She's still outside Toulon. I'm not sure they know about her yet, and she's not important enough for them to care. I received word through the underground. She has stayed off the coast, a good distance out. A fishing boat crossed her path a week ago and told her of the fall of France. And now she waits. She was going to head back to North Africa to serve the government, but there are still others like you here, and this may be the last chance to get out. I'm going to take you to Toulon myself. A fishing boat will take you out. It's dangerous, but it will be far more dangerous for you here."

"It will be much more dangerous for you, Armand." She sat up quietly in their bed and looked sadly down at the only man she had ever loved. "Why don't you go to North Africa to serve the government?"

He shook his head. "I can't. They have their work to do there. I have mine here." He smiled sadly. "You have yours as well. You must leave here, taking my secret with you, and our girls. And you must keep them safe until this madness ends. And then you can come to me again." He sighed and his mouth formed a bittersweet smile. "I may even retire then." But who knew when that would be?

"You should retire now."

"I'm not that old."

"You've given enough."

"I will give them my best now." She knew he would and could only pray that it would not cost him his life.

"Is there nothing less dangerous you can do for France?"

"Liane . . ." He pulled her into his arms. She knew her husband very well. It was much, much too late to change his mind. She was only glad that he had told her the truth before they left France. It would have killed her to believe him allied sincerely with Pétain. At least now she knew the truth. She would not be able to tell anyone, lest her indiscretion cost him his life, but at least she knew, and one day they would tell the girls, who were too young to understand anyway for now.

It took her a long time to gather up the courage to ask him what she least wanted to know. "How soon do we leave?"

For a moment he didn't answer her, and then he pulled her tighter still. "Tomorrow night." She gasped at his words, and in spite of her best efforts to be brave, her shoulders shook and she began to cry.

"Shhh . . . *mon ange* . . . *ça ne vaut pas la peine* . . . we will be together again soon." But God only knows when. They lay awake side by side for a long time that night, and Liane wished, as the sun came up, that the night would never end.

Chapter 20

They made their trip to Toulon by back roads in a borrowed car with their headlights off, and Armand's new official papers with them in the car. Liane wore a black dress and a black scarf. She had dressed the girls in slacks and shirts and sensible shoes. They each carried one small bag with their things. The rest they would have to leave in France. They spoke very little on the trip. The girls slept, and Liane glanced at Armand frequently, as though to drink in her last hours of him. She could scarcely believe that in a few hours she and the girls would be gone.

"This will be worse than my last year in school," she joked in a soft voice as the girls slept. And they both remembered the year they were engaged, when he was in Vienna and she at Mills College in Oakland. But this could go on for much longer than a year, as they both knew. No one knew for how long. Hitler had a firm grip on Europe's throat, and it would take time to loosen his grasp. But she knew that Armand would do all he could to make the end come soon. And there were scores of others just as devoted as he was. Even the children's nurse had astonished her. Liane had told her regretfully that she was taking the girls back to the States, and that they could not take her along. And she had been amazed to find Mademoiselle pleased. She told Liane bluntly that she would not work for one of the followers of Pétain, and then, in a passionate outburst, she admitted that she was going to leave them anyway, she was going to join the Resistance centered in the heart of France. It was a brave admission for her to make, but she trusted Liane, and the two women hugged and wept, and the girls cried when she left them earlier that day. It had been a long, painful day of good-byes, but the worst of all came on a creaking dock in Toulon as Armand handed the girls to the powerful men on the fishing boat. They clung to each other and cried, and then Liane held on to him for a last time, her eyes begging him, her voice beyond control.

"Armand, come with us. . . . Darling, please . . ." But he only shook his head, his body ramrod straight, and his arms as powerful as they had always been.

"I have a job to do here." He looked once more at the girls and then at her. "Remember what I told you. I will get letters to you, censored or not, in whatever way I can. And even when you hear not a single word, know that I am well . . . be confident, my love . . . be brave . . ." His voice began to crack and tears filled his eyes as well, but he looked down at her and smiled. "I love you with all my heart and soul, Liane." She choked on her own sobs and kissed him on the mouth and then gently he pushed her into the men's hands. "Godspeed, my love . . . *Au revoir, mes filles. . . .*" And without waiting a moment more the boat pulled out and left him there, waving in the night in his pin-striped suit, his mane of white hair blowing in the summer breeze. "*Au revoir . . .*" He whispered it again as the little fishing boat was swallowed up by the dark of night. "*Au revoir . . .*" And he prayed it was not adieu.

Chapter 21

As it turned out, it took them two days, not one, to meet the freighter, the *Deauville*. She had had to move farther out several days before to avoid detection, but the fishing boat from Toulon knew exactly where she was. They had been making this same trip all week, each time stopping on the way back to fish, so that they would have something to show for their absences if they were stopped. But the Germans were too busy enjoying France, and the Resistance had not gotten under way in full yet. There were cafés and girls and boulevards to catch their eyes on the shore. And all the while the *Deauville* sat, collecting passengers that had been arriving on board all week. She had left her cargo in North Africa, and she was traveling light, with the exception of the sixty passengers occupying the fifteen cabins on board, mostly Americans, and two French Jews, a dozen Englishmen who had been living in the South of France, and some Canadians. It was generally an amazing assortment of people, anxious to be out of France and relieved to be on the ship.

They huddled quietly on the deck all day, and sat in the overcrowded dining room at night with the crew, waiting for the ship to set sail. The captain had said that they would sail out quietly, late that night, though he was still expecting a woman and two little girls, the family of a French diplomat. And when Liane and the two girls boarded the ship, they discovered that they were the only females on board, but Liane was too numb and exhausted to care. The girls had cried for two days for their papa, and all three of them reeked of fish from the little fishing boat. Elisabeth had been sick the whole way, and all Liane could think about was Armand. It was a nightmarish beginning to their return to the States, but they had begun the journey now and they had to persevere. She owed it to Armand to keep the girls happy until they were all together again, but every time she thought of it, she had to fight back tears of her own. She almost fell into the arms of the crewmen on the *Deauville*, who half carried Liane and the girls to their room. Both the girls were sunburned and chilled, and Liane herself felt too exhausted to walk another foot. They closed the door and fell onto the bunks, and all three of them fell asleep. Liane didn't wake again until late that night when she felt the gentle pitching of the ship. She looked out the porthole into the night, and she realized that they had set sail. She wondered if a U-boat would catch them before they reached the States, but it was too late to turn back now, and Armand would never have let her anyway. They were going home. She went quietly back to her bunk, after tucking the girls in as they slept, and then went back to sleep until the dawn.

When she got up, she took a shower in the bathroom they shared with approximately fifteen men. There were four bathrooms for the use of the fifteen cabins on the ship, and the lines were long, but not yet at that hour of the day, and she returned to the cabin, feeling refreshed and hungry for the first time in three days.

"*Madame?*" There was a soft knock at the door and an unfamiliar voice, and she opened it to see a swarthy-looking sailor of the French merchant marine, holding out a steaming mug to her. "*Du café?*"

"*Merci.*" She took a careful sip of the steaming brew after she had sat down again, and was touched at the thoughtfulness. As the only woman on board, she was liable to earn courtesies that no one else would share. But that didn't seem quite fair to her. They were all in the same boat. She grinned to herself at the bad joke. And as much as she didn't want to leave France and Armand, she was grateful for the escape. She vowed to herself to do anything she could to help on the ship, but when she and the girls stepped into the dining room, she saw that everything was very much under control. Breakfast was being served in shifts to the passengers on board, and people were quick to eat and give up their seats. The atmosphere was one of camaraderie and helpfulness, and she was aware of no impertinent stares. A number of men spoke kindly to the girls. Most of them were Americans who, for one reason or another, hadn't been able to get home since the outbreak of the war. She discovered quickly that at least a dozen or so of the men were journalists, the two Canadians were doctors, and the rest were for the most part business-men who for whatever reason had held on in France until the end. There was much talk of Hitler now, and the fall of France, how easily Paris had opened up its doors . . . De Gaulle's recent speech . . . Churchill . . . The room was ablaze with interpretations of the news, bits of gossip were passed around, and then suddenly she saw a familiar form across the room. She couldn't believe it could be him. He was a tall blond man in sailor's garb that didn't seem to fit quite right, his shoulders were straining at the seams, and when she looked down, she saw that the pants were more than a little short. But when he turned to help himself to more coffee from the pot, their eyes met, almost as though he sensed her glance, and he stared at her in equal disbelief until his face broke into a broad smile, and he abandoned his chair at once and came to shake her hand and hug the girls.

"What the hell are you doing here?" Nick Burnham stared down at Liane with a broad grin and then glanced down at the pants he wore. "My luggage fell overboard when I ar-rived. Damn, it's good to see you all. Where's Armand?" He looked around and then realized the answer, as Liane's face fell.

Her voice was husky as she answered. "He stayed in France."

"Will he be going to North Africa?" He lowered his voice, but she only shook her head. She didn't have the heart to tell him that he was staying in Paris with Pétain.

She turned her eyes up to Nick's then and shook her head. "Isn't it amazing, Nick? A year ago we were all on the *Normandie*. And now look at us." She smiled at his pants, and they both looked sadly around the room. "France has fallen into German hands . . . we're all running for our lives . . . who would have believed . . ." And then she looked at Nick again. "I thought you left long ago."

"I wasn't that smart. Things were so quiet then, I decided to stick around for another month, and then all hell broke loose, and it was too late to get out. I could have gone back on the *Queen Mary* in March. But instead"—he grinned— "well, at least we'll get home. Not as elegantly as we arrived perhaps, but what the hell."

"What news do you have of John?"

"He's fine. I'm going home to rescue him. He's been with his grandmother since he left." Something unhappy crossed Nick's eyes, they all had such complicated lives, such painful histories they brought along. And then he gestured to three empty seats. "Why don't you three sit down and eat. I'll catch you later and we can talk."

"No tennis courts this time?" She grinned. It was so strange to see him here, and a relief too. Suddenly the sorrow of fleeing the war was reduced to an absurd adventure. And she could see the same thoughts in his eyes too.

"It's crazy, isn't it? Crazier yet to see you here." He had been fascinated during the entire day before to learn of how the others had heard of the ship, but somehow, remarkably, they had. It was indeed an interesting assortment on board. Crockett Shipping, via Liane, Burnham Steel, thanks to him, two Harvard professors who had finished a stint at Cambridge the month before and were anxious to get out . . . the tales went on and on. He went back to his seat to grab his coffee cup, and came back to Liane's table to chat for a moment before he moved on. They would have plenty of time to talk on the trip.

They had no idea how long it would take them to get to New York. It depended on how far they had to wander off course to avoid any dangers the captain feared. Nick had been told the captain's instincts were good—he was sure to keep them out of danger—and he passed the cheering information on to Liane, on the upper deck later on.

"So, old friend, how have you been?" The girls were playing with their dolls in the sun, and Liane sat propped against a ladder, while Nick leaned against a rail. "We seem to meet in the oddest spots. . . ."

His thoughts drifted back to the year before as he glanced out to sea and then back at Liane. "Do you realize that the name of my suite on the *Normandie* was the Deauville suite? It must have been prophetic." He shook his head.

"And do you remember how we talked about the war, as though it would never come?"

"Armand thought it would. I was the fool then." He shrugged. "And you told me that one of these days I'd have to make a choice about who I sold my contracts to. And you were right."

"You made the right choices in the end." It made her think of Armand again. How could she explain to anyone that he was now working for Pétain?

He looked intently at Liane then. "Doesn't all of that seem terribly unreal? I don't know . . . I feel like I've been on another planet for the past year."

She nodded, feeling the same way. "We've all been so engrossed in what's happening here."

"It's going to be very strange to go back, you know. They aren't going to want to hear about what we know, what we've seen."

"Do you think that's true?" That seemed shocking to her now. The war in Europe was so real. How could the United States go on ignoring that, yet she recognized that in the

States everyone felt that they were safe, Europe was so far away. She shook her head. "I suppose it is."

"Where are you and the girls going to live, Liane?"

It was a question she had debated at great length with Armand on the way to Toulon. He wanted her to go back to San Francisco—to her uncle George, but she was adamant about that. Washington felt more like home. "Back to Washington. We have friends there. The girls can go back to their old school." She was going to stay at the Shoreham hotel if she could get a room, and then she'd try to rent some sort of furnished house in Georgetown, where they could wait out the war. She wasn't even sure she was going to tell her uncle that she was back in the States at first but undoubtedly he would find out from her bank, and she knew that she owed it to him to tell him. But she had never felt close to the man, and she didn't want him pressing her to come home. The only home she had recognized for years was wherever she was living with Armand.

Liane glanced at Nick now, thinking of his life. There had been several questions she'd been wondering about. "You're going back to New York, to pick up the threads of your old life?" It was the only way she could think of to ask him about his wife. And he nodded slowly.

"I'm going to bring Johnny back from Boston." And then he looked at Liane with honest eyes. He had been honest with her before, and there was no reason not to be now. "I don't really know what Hillary's been up to since she left. I wrote to her, I cabled her a number of times. But ever since her cable in September, telling me that they had arrived safely in New York, I haven't heard a word. I suspect she's seen damn little of Johnny." The green eyes began to burn, and he wanted to tell her now that he had seen Philip Markham's name on the manifest of the *Aquitania*. He had told no one since it had happened.

"Does he sound all right in his letters?" She was asking about John and her eyes reached deep into Nick's as she did.

She was wondering all of the same things that he was. Most of all, why had Hillary left the boy in Boston?

"I think so. But he sounds lonely."

Liane smiled gently. "I'm sure he misses you very much." She had already seen a year before that he was a wonderful father.

"I miss him too." His eyes softened as he thought of his son. "I took him to Deauville before the war broke out, and we had such a good time. . . ." They both fell silent then. It seemed a thousand years ago, and it brought their minds back to the occupation of Paris. It was still difficult to believe that Paris was now in the hands of the Germans and it made Liane think of Armand and the difficult position he would be in. She was so frightened for him, and there was no one she could tell. No one. Not even Nick. He watched her face, and he assumed that he knew what she was thinking. It was inevitably about Armand. He touched her arm gently as she stared out to sea. "He'll be all right, Liane. He's a wise and capable man." She nodded and said nothing. The question was if he was wise enough to outsmart the Germans. "You know, when I put Johnny on that damn ship last year, I thought I was going to pass out on the dock, just thinking about them crossing with German U-boats in the waters. But they got on just fine, and God knows the waters were dangerous even then." He looked pointedly at Liane. "Even surrounded by Germans, Armand will be all right. He's been a diplomat all his life. It will serve him well now, no matter what." No matter what . . . Her mind echoed his words. . . . If he only knew. . . .

She looked sadly at Nick and tears began to fill her eyes. "I wanted to stay with him."

"I'm sure you did. But you were wiser to leave."

"I had no choice. Armand insisted. And he said that I couldn't endanger the girls—" Her voice choked and she couldn't go on. She turned away so he wouldn't see her cry, but suddenly she felt him holding her in a warm, brotherly hug, and she stood there on the deck, crying in his arms. It was not an unusual sight now, even among the men. They had all suffered losses and terrible separations in leaving Europe. And it suddenly didn't even seem strange to be crying in Nick's arms, this man whose path had crossed hers from time to time, and whom she scarcely knew, and yet they both felt they knew each other well. They had always met at peculiar times, in circumstances that allowed them both to be surprisingly open. Or maybe that was just the way he was. But she didn't think about it now. She just stood there, grateful for his warmth and compassion. He let her cry for a while and then he patted her back with a gentle hand.

"Come on, let's go inside and have a cup of coffee." There was a constantly available pot in the dining room, and it did a land-office business. There was nothing else to do on the ship except sit around and talk, or walk the decks, or sit in one's cabin while others slept or poured out their stories of the war. The ship wasn't set up for entertainment or distraction. And the few books that had been lined up on shelves in the dining hall had disappeared when the first passengers boarded. Even the zigzag course grew tedious very quickly, and it was difficult to escape one's own thoughts in the monotony of looking out at the empty horizon. The mind drifted back to recent weeks, to the events of the past month, to the people one had left. . . . Liane sat down in the dining room at an empty table and tried to stop her tears. As she blew her nose in a lace handkerchief the children had given her for her last birthday, she looked up at Nick with an attempt at a smile.

"I'm sorry."

"For what? For being human? For loving your husband? Don't be silly, Liane. When I put Johnny on the *Aquitania,* I stood on the dock as it pulled out, and cried like a baby." He still remembered the dockworker who had patted his shoulder and muttered a few comforting words. But nothing had really helped. He had never felt so bereft in his life. But

Liane was looking at him now and her face registered a question. He hadn't mentioned Hillary.

"But you told me that Hillary went with him." Suddenly she was confused. Had he sent the child alone? But she thought . . .

"Yeah." He decided to tell her now. "And with Philip Markham. Do you know who he is?" Nick's eyes grew hard as he stared into his coffee and then back at Liane. He spoke in a low voice and his hand shook slightly on his cup.

"I've heard the name." All over Paris for a while, linked to Hillary. But she didn't say that. "He's something of an international figure."

Nick smiled a bitter little smile. "An international playboy, to be exact. My wife has charming taste. They spent the summer in the South of France together."

"Did you know they would be on the ship together?"

Nick shook his head. "I saw his name on the manifest after they left that morning."

She couldn't resist asking the next question. Does it still bother you, Nick?" He should have been used to her indiscretions by now.

He looked into her face, at the softness of her skin, and wondered as he had before how two women could be so different. "My source of concern isn't because she's my wife. I'm past that. I never got a chance to tell you, but after we spoke on the *Normandie* that night, I don't think I ever felt the same way again. I think she'd pushed me too far. And I let her do what she wanted in Paris. But I care because of Johnny. If she continues carrying on like that, one of these days she's going to find someone who suits her, and she may get ideas into her head about leaving and taking Johnny. Up to now she's been content to live with me and fool around. I've gotten to the point where I can live with that." He fell silent for a moment and then told Liane the truth. "I'm scared . . . I'm so goddamn scared that I'd lose Johnny."

"You couldn't."

"I could. She's his mother. If we got divorced, she could do anything she damn well pleased. She could move to Timbuktu, and then what? I see him once a year for a two-week vacation?" It was a horrifying thought he had pondered often, particularly lately. He knew from Hillary's silence that things had changed in the last six months. Before, she had felt some obligation to report to him. But there had been not a word, not a line, not a sound since the first cable.

"I didn't think she was that interested in the boy." Liane looked worried for him.

"She's not. But she cares about what people think. And if she gives him up, people will say a lot of ugly things about her. She'd rather keep him and park him somewhere with his nurse while she goes off to play. She hardly ever called him last summer when she was in Cannes with Markham."

"What are you going to do about all that, Nick?"

He sighed deeply and finished the last of his coffee before he set his cup down and looked her in the eyes. "I'm going to go home and shorten her leash again. I'm going to remind her that she's married to me and that's the way it's going to stay. She'll hate me for it, but I don't give a damn. It's the only way I can keep my kid. And, damn it, that's what I'm going to do."

Liane felt bold as she listened to him. She was going to tell him what she thought. They were once again on a ship, suspended between two worlds, and all was fair. "You deserve a better woman than that, Nick. I don't know you very well, but I do know that much. You're a good man and you have a lot to give. And she's never going to give you a damn thing in return except heartache."

He nodded. She already had done much of that. But at least his heart was no longer involved. Only his son. And to him that was more important. "Thank you. That's a nice thing to say." They exchanged a smile over their empty coffee cups, and a group of the journalists on board wandered in for a round of coffee. One of them was carrying a half-full bottle of whiskey to add a little kick to the coffee. But neither of them accepted his offer of a nip. Nick was thinking over what Liane had said. "The trouble is that in order to get myself another woman, I'd have to give up my son, or at least living with him. And I'd never do that."

"It's a high price to pay."

"It is either way. And in ten years he'll be grown up and things will be different."

"How old will you be then?" she asked softly.

"Forty-nine."

"That's a long time to wait to be happy."

"How old was Armand when you married him?"

She smiled at the question. "Forty-six."

"I'll only be three years older. And maybe if I'm very lucky, I'll find someone like you." She blushed at his words and looked away, but he reached out and touched her hand. "Don't be embarrassed. It's true. You're a wonderful woman, Liane. I told you when I first met you that Armand was a lucky man, and I meant it." She brought her eyes back sadly to his.

"I gave him a hard time this year in Paris." She felt guilty about that, now that she knew what he'd been doing. "I didn't understand what pressures he was under. We hardly ever saw each other and . . ." Her eyes filled with tears again and she shook her head. But she had been haunted for days now by her anger at Armand over the past months. If she had only known . . . but how could she have?

"You must both have been under a tremendous strain."

"We were." She sighed. "And so were the girls. But Armand most of all. And now he won't even have us to lean on." Not that he really had in the past year. He had carried all the burdens alone. She looked at Nick with agony in her eyes. "If something happens to him . . ."

"Nothing will. He's too smart to take chances. He'll be all right. You just have to hang on." And he knew she would. She was that kind of woman.

They went back outside then and stood on the deck for a while, and then she went to find the girls. They were enjoying the trip, and acute boredom hadn't set in yet, although she suspected it would later.

They didn't see Nick again until that night, when he played guessing games with the girls in a sheltered corner of the deck. Most of the male passengers had stayed in the dining room to drink and talk, and Liane had thought it best to remove the girls. No one had got rowdy yet, but perhaps they would. Although no one spoke of it on the darkened ship, the tension was beginning to run high. There were inevitable fears that a German U-boat would strike, and the only way to live with the fears was by drinking. And the men did. A lot.

Liane sat with Nick and the girls, trying to keep their spirits up.

"Knock, knock, who's there? . . ." The jokes and stories and riddles went on forever, and the four of them laughed as they sat on the stairs. Eventually Liane put the girls to bed and went back outside for a walk. She had left their life vests at the foot of their beds, as the passengers had been instructed to do, and she didn't venture too far, but she needed to get out. The atmosphere in the tiny room was oppressive. The *Deauville* had been prepared to take on twenty passengers and no more, there were five double rooms and ten singles, and instead they were carrying sixty men, a woman, and two children, with a crew of twenty-one. With eighty-four people on board, the ship felt like it was about to burst at the seams, and the noise from the dining room grew more and more raucous as she stood on the deck with her eyes closed in the wind. She was chilly but she didn't care. It just felt good to be out.

"I thought you'd gone to bed." She turned as she heard Nick's familiar voice beside her, and she turned to look up at him with a smile. They were all getting used to being in the dark.

"I put the girls to bed, but I wasn't tired."

He nodded. "Is it hot in your room?"

"Stifling."

He smiled. "Mine's like an oven, and there are six men in it."

"Six?" She looked shocked.

"I have the deluxe suite, so-called on the *Deauville*. So they put five more beds in it. Cots actually. But I don't think anyone cares." They had all been lucky to get passage at all and they knew it. "But to tell you the truth, I'm not sleeping in my room."

She remembered the studio he'd switched to on the *Normandie* after his blowout with his wife. "You do that a lot, don't you?"

"Only on transatlantic crossings." He grinned and they both laughed. "This time, the captain showed me a perfect little spot. There's a secluded area under the bridge. And they put up a hammock for me. No one ever comes around, and I'm out of the wind, but if I peek around a little bit, I can see the stars . . . it's heaven." He looked pleased. Despite his enormous fortune in steel, he was an easy man to please. A hammock under the stars, borrowed clothes from a sailor when his luggage fell overboard. He was good-natured and easygoing and unpretentious. And in that way, he was much like Liane. Between the two of them they had two of the largest private fortunes in the United States, but to look at them one would never have known it. He was in his borrowed seaman's garb. She was wearing gray flannel slacks and an old sweater, her hair was loose in the wind, and she wore no jewelry save a narrow gold wedding band, and they both looked perfectly at ease as they were. The men on the ship had been startled to realize who Nick was, and had they known that Liane was Crockett Shipping, they would have been even more so. She had totally unassuming ways, as did Nick. It was part of their inner beauty. He looked down at Liane after a while. "Do you want me to bring you another cup of coffee or a drink?"

"I'm all right. I'll go to bed in a little while. The girls will stay up talking all night if I don't, and it's so hot down there, they can't sleep either."

"Do you want me to have another hammock rigged up in my little hideaway for them? There isn't enough room for two hammocks, but they could share one and then at least you'd have peace in the cabin." It was a sweet suggestion and she smiled at him.

"Then you won't get any sleep. They'll keep you up all night, telling jokes and asking questions."

"I'd love it." And she knew he would, but she thought it best to keep them with her.

And then, after a little while longer, she bade him good night. And as she returned to her cabin she thought how remarkable it was that they should meet again, crossing the Atlantic. Before she went to bed, she washed her hair again. She had already had to wash it three times since they'd arrived to get the smell of the fishing boat off her. What an experience that had been. She smiled to herself as she got undressed. It would be funny, if it weren't so tragic. But at least laughing at it now and then kept her from crying for Armand all the time. She was barely able to think about having left him without her eyes filling with tears, and she fought the thoughts off again now as she washed her hair in the tiny sink and dried it with a towel. She did everything in the dark, and she had forced the girls to stop talking when she came in. And she could hear now from the silence in their bunks that they were sleeping at last.

She had just gotten into her own bed, and pulled the sheet over her, when suddenly there was a terrifying, unfamiliar whooping sound, and she sat up in bed like a shot, trying to remember what the sound meant. Was it a fire alarm, an air raid, or were they sinking? With a speed and deftness she hadn't known she had, she leaped from her bed, grabbed their life vests, and shook the girls. "Come on, girls, come on . . . quickly. . . ." She pushed Elisabeth into her vest. The child was still half asleep, despite the noise. Then she grabbed Marie-Ange and helped her, and she had both girls halfway out the door in nightgowns, life vests, and shoes, and she struggled to pull her own life vest on over her night-gown. She hadn't even had time to find her own shoes in the dark, but it didn't matter, she crowded into the passage-way with the others, emerging from their cabins with startled looks. Most of them had still been awake, but a few of the men looked as sleepy as the girls did. There was an instant cacophony of voices and questions and a shout from the far end from someone who couldn't find his life vest. They pressed onto the deck almost as one mass, and there, in the distance, they saw the reason for the sirens. A ship of indeterminate size looked like a ball of fire on the horizon, and members of the crew moved among them now, explaining in rapid French that a troop ship out of Halifax had been hit by a U-boat two days before. The *Deauville* had just now gotten the message. There were men in a lifeboat with a transmitter too weak by now to have reached them at any greater distance. The ship had been burning for two days, and it had carried more than four thousand men bound for England.

Both the news that they heard and the sight of the burning ship were terrifying in the stillness of the summer night. There had been a gentle breeze before, but now there wasn't even that. It was as though they were moving toward hell, and all eyes were held riveted by the inferno ahead.

The captain came out on the bridge with a bullhorn in his hand, and spoke to them all in English. He knew that most of the passengers were Americans and he needed their immediate attention.

"If any of you have medical training . . . nursing . . . first aid, any experience at all, you are needed very badly. We do not know how many men from the *Queen Victoria* are still alive. . . . Will the two doctors on board please come forward . . . we will be taking on as many men as we can." There was a moment of silence. "We cannot radio to other ships for help, or the Germans in the area will identify our position." As this reality sank in, a total silence fell on them all. It was entirely possible that the Germans were still nearby, and the *Deauville* might be next. It was a terrifying thought, and the fire raging on the *Queen Victoria* was a clear illustration of what could happen to them.

"The burden of helping these men falls entirely to us. We need you all . . . now, those of you who have medical knowledge, please step forward." A half dozen men moved rapidly toward the captain, he nodded, spoke to them in quiet voices, and then picked up the bullhorn again. "Please, everyone, try to stay calm. We will need bandages . . . towels . . . sheets . . . any clean shirts you have . . . medicines. We are limited in what we can do, but we must do all that we can. We are going to come as close as we can to the ship, and we will pick up as many survivors as possible." Already, as the *Deauville* continued her approach, they could see one or two lifeboats in the distance, but there was no way of knowing how many lifeboats there were, or how many men were floating in the water. "We will use the dining hall as sick bay. I thank you now for your help. We have a long night ahead." He paused again. "May God be with us." Liane had a strong urge to say amen, and she looked at the girls, who stood beside her, their eyes filled with terror. She bent quickly to speak to them in the hubbub that ensued.

"Girls, I'm going to take you back to our cabin, and I want you to stay there. If anything happens, I will come to find you at once. If I don't come, go out into the hall, but don't go anywhere, unless one of the men takes you." If they were torpedoed and she couldn't get back to them, she knew that someone would take care of them. "But you must wait very quietly. You can leave the door open if you're afraid. Now, I'm going to take you back."

"We want to stay with you." Marie-Ange spoke in a frightened wail, speaking for herself and her already crying sister.

"You can't. I'm going to do what I can here." She had taken a first aid class when she was in Paris, although in the sudden panic now she found herself wondering how much she had absorbed. But two more hands could do no harm, so she hurried the girls back to their cabin, where she stripped her bed of both sheets, and took the top sheets off the girls' bunks. They could make do with their blankets, and in the heat of the room, they didn't even need those. But she knew that they might if later on they too had to take to their lifeboats. She pulled the blanket off her own, and tore open the room's small closet to look at their clothes. There were several of the girls' cotton shirts and she sacrificed two from each child to use as bandages for the survivors of the *Queen Victoria*. She grabbed several bars of soap, a small roll of bandages of her own, and a bottle of pain pills she had been given by her French dentist. Other than that, she had nothing else to contribute to the rescue. She dressed quickly and kissed the girls good-bye as she left the room, reminding them to sleep in their life vests tonight, and Elisabeth called after her with a sudden thought just as she was leaving.

"Where's Mr. Burnham?"

"I don't know," she called back and disappeared down the hall, praying that the girls would be safe. She hated to leave them but knew that they would be safer out of the confusion.

And when she reached the dining hall, she found every single adult on board gathered in the room, getting instructions from the chief officer, a wizened man with a gravelly voice, who was giving curt, well-organized orders. They were being assigned into teams of three, and as much as possible, each group was assigned someone who had some experience in first aid, so that even if the other two people had no expertise, there would be one member of the team capable of some real assistance. The two doctors on board were already organizing supplies, and one of them made a brief speech about handling burns. His explanations turned several stomachs, but there was no avoiding reality now. And it was then, as Liane handed over her sheets and supplies, that she saw Nick at the far end of the room. She held up an arm to signal him, and he approached her, just in time for the chief officer to assign them to the same team. He preferred to assign people who knew each other to work together, it would make it easier to work as a unit, he explained briefly, and then the captain reappeared to make another announcement to the crowded room.

"We think that many of the men died in the initial explosion; however, we believe that there are still many survivors. There are only four lifeboats afloat, but hundreds of men in the water. Please take your positions on deck for the stretcher teams. My men will bring the survivors on board. We need you to treat them where they are, or assist in bringing them in here. The doctors will tell you who of all of you they want working with them in here. And I want to thank those of you who've given up your rooms. We do not know yet if we'll have to use them, but it's possible we will." He looked grimly around the room with intense eyes, nodded, and left them. It would be another hour or more before they were close enough to pick up survivors, and now the assigned teams of three went on deck to watch and wait. Nick told Liane that more than half the men on board had given up their cabins and volunteered to sleep on the deck, so that the survivors could sleep indoors, and already crew members were hanging hammocks in the cabins to accommodate as many as possible. And he didn't tell her directly, but she gathered from what he said that he was among those who had given up his cabin. He was already sleeping outdoors anyway, and she sensed that it wouldn't have made any difference if he was not. He had been among the first to volunteer and now he appeared calm as they stood on deck, and he handed her a cup of coffee laced heavily with Scotch.

"I'd rather not . . ." She started to refuse but he was firm.

"Never mind. Drink it up. You'll need it before the night is out." It was already one o'clock in the morning and they had a long night ahead. He looked at her worriedly then. "Have you ever smelled burning flesh, Liane?" She shook her head and took a sip of the brew he had handed her. "Brace yourself. It's going to be rough." No one knew how many had survived the blaze. There was no way to tell. And even the men radioing weakly from one of the lifeboats couldn't tell them much. They had drifted far from the ship, and what they saw in the water around them were mostly bodies of the dead, they said. The *Deauville* had radioed back only once to let them know that they had heard their SOS. They didn't want to say more on the radio, for fear that the Germans were listening too. They gave no information about their position but as they approached, they flashed a single beam in Morse code to let the men in the lifeboat know that they were there, and a weak signal returned. "Thank God" the signal said, and Nick translated it for Liane as they waited tensely. They were not allowed to smoke while on deck, and the whiskey that had been passed around only seemed to heighten their senses. It seemed hours before they finally reached a huge mass of charred wood from the ship with a dozen or so men clinging to it, but they had been literally fried alive. There was another group of bodies after that, and then suddenly a shout from below as crew members from the *Deauville* carefully placed two men in a rubber raft that was hoisted carefully on board to the first waiting team. The two bodies were charred beyond belief and were rushed in to the doctors in the dining room. It had been turned into a surgery with lights ablaze behind the black-painted windows. The lights violated the blackout regulations on the ship, but it could not be helped in the emergency. Liane had stared at the two bodies in disbelief and fought not to retch as she watched, and instinctively she had clutched Nick's arm. He said nothing to her but she suddenly felt his hand in hers, and then a moment later she felt no revulsion and no fear as she and Nick and a Canadian journalist assisted three men onto the deck, two of them burned hideously, and the third had been lucky to get burns only on the face and hands, and both his legs were broken. Liane supported the third man's head as Nick and the Canadian put him on the stretcher and another team moved to help the other two.

"It was unbelievable . . . they got us fore and aft. . . ." The young man's eyes were wild and glazed, his face a mass of charred flesh, and Liane had to fight back tears as she listened to him and murmured softly.

"It's all right now . . . you're all right . . ." It was what she would have said to the girls if they'd been hurt, and she found herself holding him tenderly as the doctors worked over him. The next thing she knew, she was watching them in surgery and Nick was outside. And when one doctor was through, he asked her to stay as he applied salves to burns and tended wounds and amputated one hand. It was a night they knew they would never forget.

And at six o'clock the next morning, the doctors sat down for an instant and looked at someone's notes. There were 204 survivors of the *Queen Victoria* on board, and there was no further sign of life outside. Hundreds of charred bodies had floated past, and a lifeboat of walking wounded had come on board half an hour before with only minimal wounds. They had been taken to one of the vacated cabins that had been prepared. There were twelve and fourteen men to a cabin now, in hammocks hung side by side, on beds, and on sleeping rolls on floors. The dining room still looked like an infirmary, and everywhere was the smell of burned flesh. They had been covered with tar and oil as they came on board. Washing the wounds had been the worst of it, and that fell to Liane as the doctors observed her gentle hands, but now as she sat beside them, she knew that she could not do one more. Her entire body ached, her neck, her arms, her head, her back, and yet if they had brought one more in, she would have stood up again, as they all would. The passengers of the *Deauville* wandered slowly inside now. They had done what they could and done it well, and many of the survivors of the *Queen Victoria* would live because of what they'd done.

For many of the men who had formed teams on the deck, it was their first real taste of war. For the doctors, the work was not yet done, and already there had been volunteers to work in shifts who would nurse the survivors until they reached New York, but the worst was over. And silently, on deck, they watched the *Queen Victoria* sink at eight o'clock, belching horribly as she went, plumes of steam shooting into the sky, and the captain and crew scanned the sea for two hours afterward. There was not a single soul left, only the dead floating horribly amidst the gentle waves. Already nine of the survivors of the night before had died, reducing the survivors aboard to 195, all of them housed in the cabins the passengers had given up. The passengers would sleep now with the crew, in hammocks or on sleeping rolls, their luggage shoved under beds or out in the halls. The only exception in the midst of the chaos was to have been Liane and the girls, but she had insisted that their cabin be used too. And at 4:00 A.M. she had hastened briefly downstairs with one of the crew, to carry the girls to the quarters of the first mate. He would sleep in the captain's cabin for the remainder of the trip, and the two girls were to sleep in the first mate's narrow single bed.

"*Et vous, madame?*" The crew member had looked at her with awe, she had worked all night like Florence Nightingale, but she shrugged quickly.

"I can sleep on the floor." And then she had hurried back to the doctors in the dining room, the hands to hold, the wounds to clean, the limbs to set. The sounds of sheets being torn into bandages, of groaning men, became as monotonous as the sounds of the sea, hour after hour. But as the *Queen Victoria* sank, there was no sound on the deck. And moments later the captain spoke to them all on his bullhorn.

"*Je vous remercie tous* . . . I thank you all. . . . You have performed the impossible tonight . . . and if it seems that so few have lived, remember that nearly two hundred more would have died, without your help." They had learned that thirty-nine hundred men had died on the ship.

The passengers and crew worked in shifts, attempting to keep the survivors they had fought so hard to hold on to alive and stave off infections that would cost them limbs and lives. There were men so fever ridden that they were delirious but only two more had died, and many of the problems were under control. The doctors were ready to drop as the trip wore on, as was Liane, but they were still less than half-way there. They had lost more than a day in assisting the men from the Canadian ship, and their zigzag course cost them still more time, but the captain was even more cautious about encountering the Germans now as they made their way to the States.

It was only on the second day after the rescue that Liane was persuaded to go to the first mate's cabin, and there she fell into bed. The girls were somewhere on the ship, crew members had taken them in charge and she knew that they had spent much of their time on the bridge. But she could barely think of that now as she lay down on the narrow bed, and it felt as though she hadn't slept in years as she fell into a deep black pit and slept. And when she woke, the blackout was in force again and the ship was dark. She heard a soft scuffling sound somewhere in the room and sat up in the unfamiliar bed, wondering where she was, and then she heard a familiar voice.

"Are you okay?" It was Nick, and as he approached the bed she could just make out his face, from the moonlight that snuck in through the corners of the windows around the black paint. "You've been asleep for sixteen hours."

"My God." She shook her head trying to wake up. She was still wearing the same filthy clothes she had worn for two days, but he looked even worse. "How are the men?"

"Some of them are better."

"Have we lost any more?"

He shook his head. "Not yet. Hopefully we won't and they'll hang in until they get to shore. A few of them are walking around the ship." But he was more concerned now with her. She had been amazing in the makeshift operating room. He had seen her each time he had brought another man in. "Do you want something to eat? I brought you a sandwich and a bottle of wine." But the thought of food made her feel ill. She shook her head and sat up in the bed, patting it for him to sit down.

"I couldn't eat. What about you? Have you had any sleep?"

"Enough." She saw him smile, and she took a deep breath. What an incredible experience to live through.

"Where are the girls?"

"Asleep in my hammock upstairs on the deck. They're safe there and the officer on watch is keeping an eye on them. They're all wrapped up in blankets. I didn't want them coming down here to wake you." And then, "Come on, Liane, I want you to eat." They were all living on reduced rations now with more than three times as many people on board than before the rescue, but the cook was working miracles and everyone was still being fed. The coffee and whiskey were holding out, miraculously, and there was enough for all. He handed her the sandwich then and uncorked the half-full bottle of wine. He pulled a cup from the pocket of the borrowed jacket he wore and poured her some.

"Nick, I can't . . . I'd throw up."

"Drink it anyway. But eat the sandwich first." She took a tentative bite, and felt her stomach contract at the shock of food, but after an initial wave of nausea, she had to admit that it tasted good, as did the first sip of wine. She handed him the cup then and he took a sip too.

"I should get up and see what I can do to help."

"They've survived this long without you. They'll make it for another hour."

She smiled at him in the dark, their eyes were accustomed now to the lack of light. "What I wouldn't give for a hot bath!"

"And clean clothes." He smiled. "Mine are ready to get up and walk away." And then suddenly they both thought again of the *Normandie* the year before and they both began to laugh. They laughed until the tears streamed from their eyes. Here, in the first mate's cabin, in the dark, they were far from the nightmare reality of the men who had survived, and it was a relief to think of the absurdity of gala nights and dinners in white tie and tails. "Do you remember all the trunks we brought?" The two collapsed in mirth again; it was laughter born of tension and exhaustion and relief. In torn filthy clothes, on a ship carrying almost three hundred men, including the original passengers and the crew, the *Normandie* seemed like a ship of fools, with its kennel and promenades and deluxe suites and *fumoir* and Grand Salon. It had been a lovely ship, but it was a thing of the past, and here they were, sharing a bottle of wine on a narrow bed, wondering if a U-boat would torpedo them within the hour. They both sobered again eventually and Liane watched the shadows on Nick's face in the dark.

"Look at how our lives have changed. It's extraordinary, isn't it?"

"Soon the whole world will change. This is only the beginning. We just got involved in it earlier than most." His eyes looked deep into hers, and even in the darkness he could feel their pull, and without a second thought he spoke what was on his mind. Who knew, maybe in another hour they'd all be dead and he'd never have another chance. "You're beautiful, Liane. More beautiful than any woman I've ever known . . . beautiful inside and out. I was so proud of you last night."

"I think I was able to do it because I knew you were there. I felt your thoughts with me." Suddenly there was no other world but this, no life but theirs, alone in the tiny room, and he reached out and took her hand, and without saying another word he pulled her close, and they kissed, her lips as hungry as his. They clung to each other for a long time, and they kissed again with a desperation and a passion born of tasting death and still being alive.

"I love you, Liane . . . I love you. . . ." His mouth devoured her neck, her face, her lips, and another voice than hers seemed to answer him.

"I love you, Nick . . ." Her voice was soft and his words were a caress as their clothes seemed to fall away as they lay on the bed and their bodies meshed, other lives forgotten, other faces, other times . . . they were the only two survivors left of a forgotten time, and the only thing left to remember was this brief moment of passion as they made love and then, holding each other close, slept until the dawn.

Chapter 22

*N*ick and Liane woke up slowly in each other's arms with a bright sun peeking through the black paint, and he looked down at her with no regrets, watching her face to see the same peace mirrored there. He looked down at the long, graceful limbs, the big eyes, the tousled blond hair, and he smiled at her.

"I meant what I said to you last night. I love you, Liane."

"I love you too." She didn't understand how she could say the words. She loved Armand, yet she knew that in some way, she had loved this man for a long time. She had thought of him often during her lonely months of watching Armand drift away, and she had always felt some deep, inexplicable respect for Nick from the first. It was a different kind of love from the one she had known before, but she felt no regrets for what they had done. They had survived, together, alone, in a world no one else could know, and she belonged to him. Perhaps she never would again, but she knew that she did with all her heart and soul right now. "I don't know how to tell you what I feel . . ." She sought the words but she could see in his eyes that he understood.

"You don't have to. I know. And it isn't wrong. We need each other right now. Maybe we have for a long time."

"And when we go back?" She was groping to understand, but he shook his head, watching her eyes.

"We don't have to think about that now. Right now, we

216

live here. With these people on the ship. We've all survived. It's something to celebrate, to make us love each other more. We don't have to look further than that." And somehow she knew he was right. He kissed her gently on the mouth, and she let her hands wander up and down his back, his arms, his thighs. She knew that she wanted him again, and wondered if that was wrong or if it was only their way of confirming life. She asked him no more questions then as they made love again, and then regretfully she got up and began to wash in the room's tiny sink as he watched. It was as though they had been lovers for years, and there was no shame or modesty between them. They had watched death together only hours before, and now this was far more natural and something they shared. It was life. "I'll go check on the girls while you dress." He smiled at her, and felt happier than he had in years. Side by side, they had helped to save almost two hundred lives, and now they had a right to this . . . two more. "And then I'll see if I can find an empty shower somewhere. I'll meet you upstairs for a cup of coffee before we go back to work."

"Okay." She smiled openly at him, not the least embarrassed at having him see her like that. She kissed him once more before he left, and as thoughts of Armand threatened to make her question it all, she forced them from her mind. That would do her no good here. Later she and Nick would have to sort it all out. But not yet. They had not yet really survived, and they were less than halfway home. It was too soon for anything but living what they felt, day to day, hour by hour. For the first time in a long time she was grateful that she was alive.

She met him outside the galley with the girls. They looked as bedraggled as everyone else by now, but they seemed perfectly happy with Nick. They told her about the hours they had spent on the bridge, explained to her about the radio, and were apparently on first-name terms with the cook, who had brought out a small cake from God knew where and given it to the girls the day before. In remarkable fashion they had adjusted to this strange new life, and they didn't seem afraid. They told Liane about sleeping under the stars, and then they went back to the bridge again as Nick and Liane went slowly downstairs. They had shared a large steaming mug of coffee and a piece of toast, and she looked at him as they reached the first room filled with the men that had been saved. She touched Nick's hand before they went in and looked into the deep-green eyes.

"Do you suppose we've all gone mad?"

But he shook his head, and he didn't look crazy at all. "No. People are strange beasts, Liane. They adjust to almost anything. Strong people cannot be defeated." And he was not embarrassed to add, "You and I are very strong. I knew that the first day we met and I loved it about you then."

"How can you say a thing like that?" She spoke in whispers so no one would hear. "I've had everything I've wanted all my life. I've been comfortable, pampered, loved. I don't even know myself if I'm strong or not."

"Think back over what you've lived through in the last year. Doubt, fear, loneliness, the first months of a war. And I know even without having seen you then, that you didn't even waver once. And I put my son on a ship not knowing if it'd be sunk or not. I let him go because I knew that even with the risks, he would be safer at home, if he got home all right. I've lived through years of loneliness with my wife . . . and I've survived, and so have you. We survived what we went through the other night, and neither of us had ever seen anything like it before." He looked down at Liane. "We'll make it through the rest, my love." And then he added softly, "We have each other now." And then they walked into the room, and Liane almost had to hold her breath, the stench was so great, of sweat and bodies, and vomit and blood, and burns. But they worked on, side by side, for hours, and did everything the doctors told them to as they made their frequent rounds, and when they met with the other passengers to divide their rations on the deck, a kind of camaraderie and humorous toughness had been born. It did not make them immune to the tragedies they saw, but it let them put the sorrows aside and laugh at the little things. It gave Liane new patience with the girls when she saw them later on for a while, and it filled her with a fresh passion for Nick she had never known herself capable of. She had never been so in love with a man, and had never felt quite so strong and young. Her life with Armand had been part of a different world. She loved him, respected him, looked up to him, and yet she had found something different now, a man with whom she seemed to move with a powerful force, each one stronger from knowing that the other was at his side. It was not unlike what she had with Armand, and yet it was something more.

Liane and Nick shared a shift that night from nine o'clock until one, and then they went back to the room she was using. The girls were in Nick's hammock again, having begged him to let them sleep there, and now he and Liane fell into her bed, and made love as never before. They slept peacefully in each other's arms and then woke again, and made love, and then snuck into a shower together before the others got up, and went outside on deck to watch the dawn.

"This will sound crazy to you"—she looked at Nick with a smile—"but I've never been this happy before. It's almost sinful to say that with all the suffering on this ship . . . but that's how I feel."

He put an arm around her shoulders and held her close. "That's how I feel too." It was as though this was the life for which they had been born. And she no longer asked what would come next. She no longer wanted to know.

For the next six days they shared the same shifts, working with the ailing men, took their meals with the girls, and at night made love in her borrowed room. Their life fell into a comfortable routine and it came as a shock to both of them when the captain made a quiet announcement the next day that they would reach New York in two days. The journey so far had taken thirteen days. Now they looked at each other and said not a word. They moved as skillfully as they had before as they made their rounds, but when they went back to their room that night, Liane looked at him with big sad eyes. They both knew that the end was near, and it was important that the wounded men get home soon, and yet she wished that the crossing could go on, and she saw the same wish in his eyes as she looked at him. She sighed as she sat down in the familiar darkness of the room. It had become their home in the past week. And she didn't want to ask him now what they would do, but he heard her words without her saying them.

"I've thought about it a lot, Liane."

"So have I. And the answers don't come. Not the ones I want." She wanted to have met him before ever meeting Armand, but fate hadn't arranged things like that, and she had her life with Armand to think of now. She could not simply brush him away. Yet how could she forget Nick? She felt as though she was committed to him now. And what was more, she needed him. He had woven himself into the very fiber of her being. And now what to tell Armand? Or should she say anything at all? All their life together, she had been totally honest with him. She knew what she owed Armand, yet she couldn't bring herself to give up Nick. It was an impossible decision. Yet Nick seemed to have already made up his mind.

He looked soberly at Liane now and spoke in a calm voice. "I'm going to divorce Hillary. I should have done it years ago."

"And John? Will you be able to live with yourself if you leave him?"

"I don't think I have a choice."

"That's not what you thought when this ship set sail. You were determined to go home and get him back from his grandmother. Could you be really happy, Nick, only seeing him a few times a month, and knowing that he's being neglected by Hillary?" There was sorrow in her eyes as she asked, and she saw the same pain in his but he struggled to answer her.

"It's his life or mine. Ours." He smiled, but his eyes were sad.

"Is that a choice you can make?"

"What are you telling me?"

"What I know you feel deep inside. If you divorce your wife to be with me, a part of you will never forgive yourself. Every time you look at Elisabeth and Marie-Ange, you're going to think of John and what you gave up to be with me. I can't ask you to do that. And to tell you the truth, I'm not ready to make a decision myself. I don't know what to do. I've tried not to think about that for the last week. I've always been honest with Armand. And now suddenly I can't. When I think of telling him . . . or writing to him . . . or waiting until after the war to tell him . . . something inside me shouts, I cringe at what it would do to him, and the girls." She looked sadly at the man she had come to love on the ship. "He believes in me, Nick. I have never betrayed him before and I cannot do so now." Tears filled her eyes and she grew hoarse. "But I cannot leave you."

"I love you, Liane. With all my heart." Nick's voice was distraught.

"I love you too, if that's what you want to know." Her eyes never left his. "But I love Armand too. I believe in the vows we made eleven years ago. I never thought that I would be unfaithful to him. And the funny thing is that I don't feel I have been. I opened a door and there you were, and now you're someone I love. I want to be with you . . . but I don't know what to do about him. If I told him now, it might kill him, Nick. It might make him careless about himself in France. We are going back to peace. He stayed to fight a war. What right do I have to walk away? Is that what I promised to do eleven years ago? To get out when I'd had enough? It isn't fair."

"Life never is. And one of the things I've always loved about you is that you are. But there's no way to be fair about this. Whatever we do, someone gets hurt, we give something up, there's someone who'll lose . . . Johnny, or Armand, or you and I."

"That's an impossible choice to make." Her voice sounded strained. "It's like standing with a gun and deciding who to kill." He nodded and took her hand and they both sat lost in their own thoughts for a long time, and then, putting the others out of their heads, they made love again. They reached no resolution that night, or the next day, as they took their shifts and made their rounds, and when they went to bed they held each other tighter than before. It was their last night on the ship, and they both knew that nothing would ever be quite the same again. If they chose to make a life of it together, they would have to climb over the obstacles that lay ahead, causing themselves and other people pain, and if they chose to let each other go, there would be a sense of irreparable loss. Only tonight, for this one last night, could they love each other as before.

It was almost morning when they spoke of it again, and it was Liane who brought it up this time. She sat up in bed and touched his face, kissed his lips, and looked down at him as she would a child. She had been putting the moment off for hours, but it couldn't wait much longer now. They would leave the ship in a few hours, and some decision had to be made. But she had made hers, and by doing so, she had also made the decision for Nick.

"You know what we have to do, don't you?"

He looked up at her and for a long time neither spoke.

"You have to go back to your son. You would never be happy with us, without him."

"And if I fight for custody?"

"Would you win?"

He was as honest with her as she was with him. "Probably not. But I could try."

"And tear the child in half. You couldn't live with yourself, and you know it as well as I do. No more than I could live with myself if I left Armand. We're decent people, you and I. We have consciences and responsibilities, and other people we love. It's different for people who aren't like us, Nick. They can walk off and wave good-bye. We can't. I know you can't, and neither can I. If you didn't care about Johnny so much, you'd have left your wife years ago. But you didn't. And I can't let you do that now, for us." He nodded. And she sighed softly. "Besides, it's not that simple for me." Her voice dropped down to a whisper. "I still love Armand." Tears filled her eyes, and she looked away as Nick watched her.

"What will you do now, Liane?" He took her hand and stroked her arm, his eyes locked in hers. He almost wished that they could turn the ship around and start again, but he knew it couldn't be done. They had to move ahead, no matter how painful it was. "What happens to you?"

"I wait for the war to end."

"Alone?" He ached for her. She was a woman who needed a man, to give all the love she had to give, and there was so much love in him that he wanted to give her.

"Of course alone." She smiled.

"Do you suppose . . ." An idea crossed his mind. It had occurred to him before in the past few days, but he hadn't known how she would react. But almost as soon as she heard his opening words, she shook her head.

"I couldn't do that. If we let this go on for a long time, we would never be able to let go. It's only been less than two weeks and I can barely let go now." She could already feel her flesh and soul being torn from his and it was more than she could bear as she held on to his hand tightly. "In a year or two it would be worse, unbearable." She sighed as she looked at him. "I think, my friend, that the time has come for us to be strong, as strong as you say we are. We have no choice. We fell in love. We've had two weeks. A miracle . . . a lifetime in itself that I will remember all my life, but there can't be more, for either one of us." Her voice began to crack and tears slowly filled her eyes. "And when we leave the ship today, my love, we must look ahead, and never look back . . . except to remember how much we loved each other and to wish each other well. . . ."

There were tears in his eyes now too. "Could I call you from time to time?"

She shook her head no and then with a sob that flew from her like a small injured bird, she threw herself into his arms, and he held her that way for an hour, fighting back his own tears as he lay awash with hers. There was simply no other way to do what had to be done. The bond they'd formed had to be cut, and it would be as painful for them as it had been for the man they had watched in the dining room a week before, when the doctors had cut off his hand.

Chapter 23

They left each other in her room shortly after eight o'clock with a last kiss and eyes filled with pain. He sent the girls back down to her, and she helped them dress. The three of them looked like vagabonds now, as did everyone else on the ship, as they gathered on the deck. The captain told them that they would reach New York by noon. He had long since radioed ahead for help, ambulances to collect the wounded from the rescue at sea. Another three had died from infections of their burns, but the *Deauville* was returning victoriously with the surviving 190. There was a jubilant atmosphere on the deck as the ship moved ahead, and everyone spoke animatedly. The girls had made friends with all the original passengers aboard and the crew, and the walking wounded were on deck now too to watch the ship come in. Everyone was too excited to eat or drink, and one would have thought that they had been together for a year as they stood side by side at the rails, calling to each other by name. Only Nick and Liane seemed to stand slightly apart from it all. He wore a dazed look, and she hovered over the girls, and now and then their eyes met and held, and once when the girls went downstairs to get their dolls, he held her close for just an instant, and she left her hand in his. Neither could imagine how they would survive the rest of their lives, and yet they had no choice. As intransigently as the *Deauville* steamed ahead, so too were they being forced out of their dream and back to real life. The moments on the ship were about to end, and they had to go their separate ways, wondering if they would ever meet again. He wondered if one day, on another ship, he would run into Armand and Liane again. The war would be over, and the girls grown, and he would still be married to Hillary, for the sake of their son. For a second, but no more than that, he almost hated Johnny. But it wasn't the boy's fault, any more than it was Armand's. They wanted something they couldn't have, and now they had to face what they owed, to themselves as well as Armand and John. He knew Liane was right, but as they finally glimpsed the skyline of New York ahead, Nick knew that in all his life, he had never felt greater pain. He was barely able to keep his mind on his son. It was the only thing he had to cling to now. And yet for these last few moments all he wanted was to cling to Liane.

There were shouts of joy on the deck as the Statue of Liberty appeared, the sun glinting on her torch on a hot July day, and shortly after that, the tugboats came to the *Deauville*'s side and they sailed into the harbor of New York. Fireboats joined the procession they made and shot streams of water in the air, and when they reached the dock, the ambulances were lined up in rows to take the wounded off the ship. Immigration proceedings had been waived, and the *Deauville* tied up at the dock as cameras flashed and journalists attempted to interview anyone they could.

Liane seemed to know almost each survivor by name, and a camera went off in her face as she bent to kiss one man on the cheek. The rest of the passengers seemed almost reluctant to leave, and they hugged each other and exchanged home addresses, slapped each other on the back, and congratulated the captain and the crew for getting them across, and then at last, one by one, they took their bags and left the ship. Liane and Nick and the girls were almost the last to leave, and when they finally reached the dock, they looked at each other in disbelief.

"Well, we're home." Nick looked at Liane over the girls' heads, both of them were unable to rejoice, and all she wanted was to reach out to him.

"It doesn't feel like home yet." She still had to get the girls to Grand Central Station, to take the train to Washington, D.C.

"It will." He sounded calmer than he felt, and he insisted on hailing a cab for them, and accompanying them to the train, and suddenly, as they stepped inside, Liane began to laugh and Nick grinned. "We must look like a bunch of tramps." He looked down at the borrowed clothes he still wore, and it was the first time he could remember that he hadn't left a ship by limousine.

They bantered back and forth with the girls on the way to Grand Central, and they reached it all too quickly. They walked inside to the tracks after Liane bought their tickets. She had thought about staying at a hotel in New York, but it was just as well for them to get back. If she had stayed in town, the temptation would have been too great to see Nick. He put their few belongings in their compartment, and then stood for a moment looking down at Liane as she and the girls looked up at him.

"Good-bye, Uncle Nick. Come to see us soon." Elisabeth extended the invitation, echoed by Marie-Ange. They had abandoned "Mr. Burnham" long since on the ship.

"I will. And you take good care of your mother." Liane could hear his voice grow hoarse with emotion, and once again she had to fight back tears. But they came anyway as she hugged him and he held her close and whispered softly in her hair. "Take care of yourself, my friend." And then he backed away slowly, and with a last mute wave, he left them, and hurried on to the platform, brushing away the tears before the girls would see him again. He stood there waving, smiling broadly, as the three of them hung out the window, and then Liane forced the girls back inside as she blew him a kiss and he mouthed I love you, and he stood there for as long as she could see him, and with a terrible gulp of sorrow to stifle a sob, she pulled her head back inside.

She sat back on the maroon velvet banquette as the girls squabbled over the assorted knobs and lights and levers, and she closed her eyes for a moment, seeing Nick's face before her, and longing with every ounce of her soul to touch him, just once more . . . for an instant . . . She saw herself back in the first mate's cabin, in Nick's arms, and felt a pain of loss almost beyond bearing, and then unable to stifle her sobs a moment longer, she said something to the girls and walked out into the hall, closing the door behind her.

"May I help you, ma'am?" a tall, immaculate, white-coated Negro porter asked her, but she was unable to speak as she shook her head and the tears flowed. "Ma'am?" He was startled by the agony he saw but she only shook her head again.

"It's all right." But it wasn't. How could she tell him that in the last two weeks she had left her husband after the fall of Paris, and they had crossed the Atlantic on a freighter in defiance of German U-boats, watched a ship sink, and seen men lying dead in the water all around them, that she had nursed almost two hundred men suffering from wounds and burns . . . and fallen in love with a man she had just said good-bye to and may never see again . . . it defied words as she stood there, leaning against the window of the moving train with her heart breaking.

And in Grand Central Station, Nick walked slowly toward the exit, his head down, his eyes damp, looking as though his best friend had died in his arms that morning. He hailed a cab on the street and went home to find the apartment empty. Mrs. Burnham was in Cape Cod with friends, a new maid told him. And the train to Washington sped on.

Chapter 24

Liane and the girls checked into the Shoreham hotel at eight o'clock that night, and she felt as though she hadn't slept for days. They were exhausted and filthy and the girls were weepy. They had all been through too much in the last few weeks, and months before that, and now it was difficult to fathom that they were back in the United States. Everyone looked so happy and unconcerned and normal. There were none of the strained faces one had seen in Paris before the occupation, or the swastikas they had seen flying after the fall, there were no wounded as there had been on the ship. There was none of what had become familiar to them, and which was far from normal. And hour after hour, as Liane lay in bed in her hotel that night, she had to fight not to call Nick in New York, and reverse all the reasonable promises they'd made to each other based on their responsibilities to other people. Suddenly all she wanted was to be in his arms again. And in his bed in New York, Nick had to fight just as hard not to call her in Washington at the Shoreham.

The next morning, she sent a cable to Armand to tell him they had arrived safely. The story of the *Deauville* was all over the morning papers, including a photograph of her kissing the cheek of the young Canadian on the stretcher as he left the ship. And in the background she could see Nick, watching her with a look of sorrow as others smiled with tears running down their faces. She felt the same lead weight on her chest again as she stared at the photograph in the paper, and the girls found her suddenly very hard to get along with. So much had changed so quickly for all of them that the girls were whiny, Liane nervous. They had been through so much and suffered so many losses that the backlash from it all was taking its toll, and when she finally decided to call her uncle George in San Francisco, to tell him they were back in the States, Liane almost snapped at him. He made an endless series of tactless remarks about the fall of France, and how the French had literally given Paris to the Germans on a silver platter and deserved what they got as a result. And Liane had to fight not to scream at him.

"Well, thank God you're back. How long have you been here?"

"Since yesterday. We came back on a freighter."

There was a pregnant silence. "The *Deauville*?" It was in the San Francisco papers that morning too, but without the picture.

"Yes."

"What kind of crazy fool is your husband to put you on a ship like that? For God's sake, there must have been some other way to get you out of France. Were you part of that rescue at sea?"

"I was." Her voice sounded exhausted and defeated. She didn't want to have to defend Armand to him. She didn't want to think, because all she could think about was Nick. "We saved a hundred and ninety men."

"I read that. And there was only one woman on board, a nurse with two children."

Liane smiled. "Not a nurse exactly, Uncle George, just me, and the girls."

"For God's sake . . ." He spluttered on and asked her when she was coming back to San Francisco, and she said she wasn't. "What?"

"We came to Washington last night. I'm going to rent a house here."

"I won't have it." After what she had been through, fighting with him was too much.

"This was our home for five years, we have friends here, the girls like their school."

"That's ridiculous. Why didn't Armand send you to me?"

"Because I told him I wanted to stay here."

"Well, if you come to your senses, you're welcome here. A woman alone doesn't belong in a strange city. You could stay with me here at the house. It was your home before Washington ever was. What a lot of nonsense, Liane. I'm surprised you didn't try to go back to London or Vienna."

She was not amused by his remarks and spoke in a quiet voice. "I wanted to stay with Armand in Paris."

"At least he wasn't foolish enough to let you do that. And I imagine he won't be there long anyway. That fool De Gaulle is already headed for North Africa, and the rest of the government is scattered all over France, from what I hear. I'm surprised Armand is still in Paris. Did he retire?"

She spoke in a quiet voice. She was not going to tell him that Armand was with Pétain. "No, he didn't."

"Well, he'll be on the run like the others, then. You were smart to come home with the girls. How are they?" His voice softened as he asked, and Liane gave him the latest report and then let them speak to their great-uncle, but it was a relief when the conversation ended. She and her uncle had never had anything in common. He in no way resembled her father. He had always disapproved of the way she had lived with her father, sharing his life and his concerns, and being informed of world affairs. He thought it no way to bring up a girl, and disapproved of her as a young woman. "By far, too modern for my taste." He had made no secret of his disapproval. And he hadn't thought much of Armand when they had met. He thought him much too old for Liane and said so, and when she had married him and moved to Vienna, he had wished her luck and told her she'd need it. And in the ensuing years they had met seldom, and when they did, they found they disagreed on everything, above all, his policies for Crockett Shipping. But at least the firm had continued to flourish, and although she disagreed with him, she had no complaints on that score. Thanks to Uncle George, business was booming, and one day it would leave her all the more to will to the girls, and that pleased her. But not much else about Uncle George did. He was opinionated, overbearing, old-fashioned, and extremely dull.

She also called a real estate agent that morning, and arranged to see three furnished houses in Georgetown. She wanted something small and unpretentious, where she could wait out the war in peace with the girls, entertain a few friends from time to time, and lead a quiet life. Gone were the days of grandeur at the French Embassy and other places like it, but she knew she wouldn't miss it.

She rented the second house she saw and arranged to move in in a week. Then she hired a maid to live with them, a very pleasant elderly black woman who cooked and loved children. She shopped for the girls and herself and they began to look as they once had. She even bought them some new toys, since they had brought none with them. And she was grateful for every single moment of activity and all the arrangements for moving. It helped to distract her from thoughts of Nick, at least for a few minutes at a time, but there were times when she really thought she wouldn't survive it. She kept wondering what he was doing, if he had gone to Boston and gotten John back. Her mind kept drifting back to the ship and it was almost as though that had been the bulk of her lifetime. It was impossible to believe that it had been only thirteen days. Again and again, she had to remind herself that she should not be thinking of Nick, but of Armand.

She wrote to her husband and told him the address of the new house, and two weeks after they moved there, she got his first letter. It was brief, because he said that he was in a hurry when he wrote it, and half of what he had written had been blacked out by the censors. But at least she knew that he was busy and well, and he hoped that she and the girls were comfortable among their old friends. He asked her to give his best to Eleanor, and she knew that the President was also included in the greeting.

But all in all, for Liane and the girls it was a long, lonely summer. All of their friends were away from Washington, in Cape Cod and Maine and other places. The Roosevelts were, as always, in Campobello, and it was September before they saw a soul. But long before that, Liane thought she would lose her mind trying to entertain the girls, and keep her mind off Nick. Every day she hoped he'd call, or that she would find a letter despite the vow of silence they'd made. Instead, every few weeks she received one from Armand, in which he told her almost nothing, and most of the letter would be blacked out by the Nazi censors. She felt as though she and the girls were living in a vacuum, and often wondered for how long she could bear it.

And the world news only made her feel that she had left Europe to come to another planet. Three thousand miles away the war raged on, and here people bought their groceries, and drove their cars, and went to movies, while her husband existed amidst the Nazis in Paris, and the Germans continued to ravage Europe. And on the first page of a Washington paper, was carried the story that Tiffany and Co. in New York, the jewelers, had moved uptown to fifty-seventh street after thirty-four years in their old location. The new building was a marvel, with air conditioning, as they called it, which kept the store cool no matter what the temperature outside. With that item on page one, Liane wondered if the world had gone mad, or she had.

On the seventeenth of August, Hitler had declared a blockade of British waters, and Armand had phrased it in such a way in his letters, that the censors hadn't touched it. But Liane had heard the news by then anyway. And on August 20, she read in the papers, Churchill had made a deeply moving speech to the House of Commons. Three days later London was bombed and the blitz began, with the shelling of houses and streets and people night by night until Londoners spent more time in bomb shelters than their homes. And by the time Elisabeth and Marie-Ange went back to their old school, the English were attempting to get their children out of London. Houses were falling, with entire families killed every night. Several ships had already left Britain, sending children to Canada for the duration of the war.

And then finally, in mid-September, Eleanor called her, in her familiar, reedy voice, and Liane almost cried with relief, it was so good to hear her.

"I was so pleased to get your letter in Campobello, my dear. But what a ghastly crossing you had on the *Deauville*." They talked about it for a while, and it only fanned Liane's thoughts of Nick. And she sat alone in the garden for a long time after she hung up, thinking of him, and wondering how he was. She wondered how long she would feel that way, as though she were only half alive, as she pined for him. It had been two months since he had left her on the train in Grand Central Station and still he lived on in her heart. Every article she read, every thought, every letter, every day, seemed somehow to relate back to thoughts of him. It was a private hell she lived in, and she knew that his life had to be much the same. But she did not dare to call him to see how he was. They had promised not to call each other, and she knew she had to be strong. And she was, but she cried more easily than she had in the past, and the girls frequently found her testy. The benevolent maid they'd hired told them that it was because their father was away, and their mother would be happy again once he came home. And the girls agreed that they would all be happier when the war was over.

Liane had no social life in Washington at all. The people who had invited her so constantly when they were stationed there, no longer knew whether or not to invite her. She was a woman alone, which made it awkward for them, and they promised themselves they would invite her eventually, but as yet no one had. Except, finally, Eleanor, who asked her to a small family dinner in the last week of September. Liane felt relieved when she arrived at the White House in a cab, and saw the familiar portico. She longed for intelligent conversation with someone. And she wanted to hear all the war news from Eleanor. She enjoyed the dinner to no end until Franklin took her aside quietly after dessert and spoke frankly to her.

"I've heard about Armand, my dear. And I'm very, very sorry." For a moment her heart almost stopped. What had they heard that she didn't know? Had the Germans ravaged Paris after all? Was Armand dead? Was there a secret communiqué of which she was not aware? She grew deathly pale and the President touched her arm. "I understand now why you left him."

"But I didn't leave him . . . not in that sense. . . ." She looked at him, confused. "I left because Paris was occupied and he thought we'd be safer here. I would have stayed if he had let me."

The President's face went taut. "Do you realize that he's working with Pétain, in collaboration with the Germans?"

"I . . . yes . . . I knew that he was going to stay in Paris with—"

But Roosevelt cut her off. "Do you understand what that means, Liane? The man is a traitor to France." He said it like a death knell over Armand, and Liane felt tears sting her eyes. How could she defend him? She could not tell anyone what she knew, not even this man. She could do nothing to clear her husband's name. And she hadn't realized that news of it would reach the States. She looked helplessly at the President.

"France is occupied, Mr. President. These are not . . . normal times." But her voice faltered.

"Those faithful to France have fled. Some of them are in North Africa now. They're equally aware that the country is occupied, but they are not working for Pétain. Liane, you might as well be married to a Nazi. Can you accept that?"

"I'm married to a man I love, whom I have been married to for eleven years." And for whom she had just given up someone she cared for deeply.

"You are married to a traitor." And it was clear by the tone of his voice that she was now considered a traitor by association. As long as he had thought she had left Armand for good, then it was all right. But if she insisted on standing by Armand, then she was as guilty as he. It was written all over his face and in the way he said good night to her.

Eleanor did not call her again, and within a week word was all over Washington that Armand was a traitor to France, and working for Pétain and the Nazis. She was shocked at the gossip that she heard. Two or three troublemakers went out of their way to call and tell her. And she wasn't sure what she was more grief-stricken over, the gossip about Armand being a Nazi, or the news that on October 2, German U-boats sank the *Empress of Britain*, a British ship carrying a shipload of children to safety in Canada. She felt sick as she remembered the *Queen Victoria* and the bodies floating in the water a few months before, and now the bodies would be those of innocent children.

She felt as though she were living a nightmare underwater as she fought against her own depression over events, and her constant sense of loss. Somehow she managed to crawl from one day to the next, waiting for letters from Armand, and fending off phone calls from her uncle George, badgering her to move back to California. It had only taken him a few weeks to hear the gossip that was circulating like wildfire around Washington. There had even been a veiled slur in one of the gossip columns about the shipping heiress who now flew Hitler's flag over her Georgetown house.

"I always told you the man was a son of a bitch," George roared into the phone from San Francisco.

"You don't know what you're talking about, Uncle George."

"The hell I don't. You didn't tell me that was why he stayed in Paris."

"He is faithful to France." She was beginning to feel as

though she were repeating empty words. Only she and Armand knew the truth. And there was no one she could tell. She wondered if by now Nick had heard it too.

"My ass he's faithful to France, Liane. The man is a Nazi."

"He is not a Nazi. We're being occupied by the Germans." She sounded as tired as she felt and she was near tears.

"Thank God 'we' are not occupied by anyone. And don't you forget it. You're an American, Liane. And it's goddamn time you came back where you belong. You've been living in international communities for so long that you don't know who the hell you are."

"Yes, I do. I'm Armand's wife, and don't *you* forget that."

"Maybe one of these days you'll come to your senses. Did you read about those children killed when the British ship sank? Well, he's one of the people that killed them." It was a cruel thing to say and Liane's whole body went tense. She knew only too well what the sinking of a ship looked like.

"Don't you dare say that! Don't you *dare!*" She sat trembling and then without another word she hung up. The nightmare would never end. Not for a long, long time, and she knew it. And she had to remind herself every day of what Nick had said: "Strong people cannot be defeated." But as she lay in her bed and cried every night, she no longer believed him.

Chapter 25

After Nick had got to the apartment in New York, and had been told by the maid that Hillary was in Cape Cod and Johnny was still in Boston, with his face grimly set, he had taken his car out of the garage, where it had sat for a year, and had driven the bottle-green Cadillac directly to Gloucester. He knew exactly where she was, or he guessed, and a few careful phone calls confirmed it.

He did not call to tell her he was coming. He arrived, like an expected guest, on the enormous handsome old estate. He walked with determination up the front steps and rang the bell. It was a beautiful July night, and there was obviously a party in progress. A black-uniformed maid with a cap and lace apron appeared and smiled as she opened the door for him to enter. She was a little surprised at the grim set of his face, but he very pleasantly asked to see Mrs. Burnham, who he understood was a guest there. It was clear by then from his lack of formal attire that he wasn't planning to stay for dinner. He handed the maid his calling card, and she disappeared with it immediately and, returning a moment later, looking even more nervous than before, she asked him to come into the library with her, and there he found the formidable Mrs. Alexander Markham, Philip's mother. He had met her many years before, and knew her immediately as she glanced at him through a lorgnette, her hands littered with diamonds, and her long elegant frame in an ice-blue evening dress. Her hair was so white, it was almost the same color as the dress.

"Yes, young man, what do you want here?"

"How do you do, Mrs. Markham. It's been many years since we've met." He was wearing white linen slacks, an impeccable white silk shirt, his blazer, and a bow tie, and he very properly shook her hand and introduced himself. "I am Nicholas Burnham." Beneath the powder, she blanched slightly, but her eyes gave nothing away. "I believe my wife is here for the weekend. You've been very kind to have her." He smiled and their eyes met, each knowing exactly what was going on, but he was willing to play the game, for the old woman's benefit at least, if not Hillary's. "I've just returned from Europe at last, a little later than expected. She doesn't know I'm back, and I thought I'd drive up here and give her a little surprise." And to prove that he was not malicious, he added, "I'd like to drive her to Boston tonight so that we can pick up my son. I haven't seen him since I put them on the *Aquitania* in September." There was a moment of silence in the room as the old woman watched him.

"I don't believe your wife is here, Mr. Burnham." She sat down with the utmost grace and total composure, her rigid spine never touching the back of her chair and the lorgnette never flagging.

"I see. Then perhaps your cousin made a mistake. I called her before I came up." He knew how close the two women were. They had married brothers. "She mentioned that she saw Hillary here last weekend. Since she hasn't arrived home, I assume she's still here."

"I really don't know how—" But before she could finish her sentence, her son burst into the room.

"Mother, for God's sake, you don't have to—" He stopped but he was too late. He was going to tell her that there was no need for her to trouble herself with Nick Burnham. Nick turned where he stood and looked Philip full in the face.

"Hello, Markham." There was total silence among all three, and Nicholas proceeded. "I came to pick up Hillary."

"She's not here." He said it with pure derision in his voice as his eyes glittered.

"So your mother tells me."

But Hillary proved them both liars. She was the next one through the door to the library, in a gossamer-thin gold-and-white evening gown made of Indian sari fabric. And she was a vision to all eyes, with her dark hair swept up, her deep tan, and long dangling diamonds at her ears and on her neck. She stood still and stared at Nick. "Then it is you. I thought it was a bad joke." She made no move to approach him.

"A very bad joke, Hillary dear. Apparently you're not even here." She looked from Philip to his mother at Nick's words and then shrugged her shoulders.

"Thank you anyway. But it doesn't matter. Yes, I'm here. So what? The point is, why are you here?"

"To take you home. But first we're going to pick up Johnny. I haven't seen him in ten months, or had you forgotten?"

"No, I haven't forgotten." Her eyes began to blaze like the diamonds hanging from her earlobes.

"And how long has it been since you've seen him?" Nick's eyes burned into hers as he asked the question.

"I saw him last week." Her words gave away nothing.

"I'm very impressed. Now, go and pack your bags and we'll leave these nice people to their party." He spoke to her in a smooth, even tone, but it was clear that he was on the verge of exploding.

"You can't just yank her out of this house." Philip Markham stepped forward, and Nick stared at him evenly.

"She's my wife."

The elderly Mrs. Markham watched them all and said nothing. But Hillary was quick to speak up for herself.

"I'm not leaving."

"May I remind you that we're still married. Or have you filed for divorce in my absence?" He saw Hillary and Philip exchange a quick nervous glance. She hadn't, but had meant to, and Nick's sudden arrival would hamper their plans. They were practically ready to announce their engagement. Mrs. Markham was unhappy about it. She knew what Hillary was and she didn't like her. Not at all. And so she had told Philip. The girl was worse than any of the wives he had had, and she would cost him a fortune. "I asked you a question, Hillary." Nick pressed the point. "Have you filed for divorce?"

He heard the old familiar petulance in her voice. "No, I haven't. But I'm going to."

"That's interesting news. On what grounds?"

She glared at him. "Desertion. You said you'd come back at Christmas, and then in April."

"And all this time, poor love, you've been pining for me. Funny, I never got an answer to any of my letters or cables."

"I didn't think you could get mail—with the war on and all." Her voice faltered and he laughed.

"Well, I'm home, so now it doesn't matter. Get your things and we'll leave. I'm sure Mrs. Markham is very tired of us." He looked at the old woman and for the first time saw a smile.

"Actually, I'm quite amused. It's rather like an English drama. But more entertaining because it's real."

"Quite." Nick smiled pleasantly and turned to his wife. "For your information, although we can discuss it later, what has kept me in France all this time were matters of national defense. Major contracts that affect the economy of our country, and defense matters that involve us against the Germans, should they ever become a threat to us directly. You would have a very hard time convincing any court that you'd been deserted. I rather think they'd sympathize with the reasons for my staying so long."

She was furious at his words, and Markham didn't look pleased either. "I thought you were selling to the Germans. You were last year."

"I canceled all my contracts, at a considerable loss, but the President was very pleased when I told him." Not to mention his gift to Poland, which had pleased the President too. Checkmate, friends. Nick smiled at his audience. "So, desertion won't do, and adultery doesn't apply." He forced the image of Liane out of his head as he spoke, although thoughts of her hadn't left him for an instant since he had walked out of Grand Central Station. "I'm afraid that leaves us still married, with a son waiting to be picked up in Boston. Let's go, my friend, the party is over." The three of them stood there for a long moment, with Mrs. Markham watching and she decided to step in at last.

"Please go and get your things, Hillary dear. As the man says, the party is over." Hillary turned to her and then Philip, with a look of total frustration on her face, and then she turned to Nick.

"You can't do this, damn it. You can't disappear for almost a year and then expect to pick me up like a piece of furniture you left somewhere." She made a move as though to slap him and he caught her arm in midair.

He spoke in a clear, even voice. "Not here, Hillary. It's not pretty."

And with that she stormed out of the room, and returned twenty minutes later with two large bags and her maid and a French poodle. Philip had left the room instantly on her heels and Mrs. Markham had invited Nick to sit down and have a drink while they were gone. They both had double bourbons, while he apologized for keeping her from her guests.

"Not at all. Actually"—she smiled—"I've enjoyed it. And you're doing me a great favor. I've been very worried about Philip." They sat in silence again for a time, with their drinks, and she glanced at Nick again. She had decided that she liked him. He had one hell of a lot of balls, and she had to admire him for tackling that bitch he was married to. "Tell me, Nick . . . may I call you Nick?"

"Of course."

"How did you get saddled with that little baggage?"

"I fell madly in love with her when she was nineteen." He

sighed, thinking of Liane, and then looked back at Mrs. Markham. "She was very pretty at nineteen."

"She still is, but she's a dangerous woman. No," the old woman reconsidered with a shake of her head, "not a woman, a girl . . . she's a spoiled child." Her eyes met Nick's over their drinks. "She'll destroy my son if she gets him."

"I'm afraid she'll destroy mine." He spoke in a quiet voice and she nodded, as though she were satisfied about something.

"You won't let her. Just don't let her destroy you. You need a very different kind of woman." It was the oddest half hour he had spent in years, and he had to smile as he thought of Liane. She was indeed a very different woman. And he almost wanted to tell Mrs. Markham that he had found her . . . and lost her. . . .

And at that moment Hillary walked back into the room with her bags, the dog, the maid, and Philip. Nick politely thanked Mrs. Markham then for a lovely time, and Hillary said good-bye to her and her son, with another fulminating look of rage directed at her husband.

"Don't think this is for good. I just don't want to make a scene while they're having a party."

"That's a new touch. Very thoughtful of you." He shook hands with Mrs. Markham, nodded at her son, and took Hillary's arm as they walked to the door while a butler carried the luggage. Moments later it was stowed in the car, and Nick turned on the ignition and headed for Boston.

"You won't get away with this, you know." She was sitting at the extreme other side of the car, practically steaming as the dog panted in the heat, its nails painted the same color as Hillary's.

"And neither will you." The charming, well-modulated tone he had used at the Markhams' was no longer evident. "And the sooner you get it into your head, Hillary, the better for all of us." He pulled the car over to the side of the road once they had left the estate, and looked at her with eyes that told her he was not going to take any more non-sense from her. "We are married, we have a son, whom you neglect shamefully. But we are going to stay married. Period. And from now on, you are going to goddamn well behave, or I'm going to kick your ass for you in public."

"You're threatening me!" she shrieked.

But Nick roared, "You're goddamn well right I am! You've practically deserted our son for the last year, from what I hear, and you're never going to do that again. Do you understand me? You're going to stay home for a change and be a decent mother. And if you and Markham are madly in love, then terrific. Nine years from now, when Johnny is eighteen, you can do anything you goddamn well please. I'll give you a divorce. I'll even pay for your wedding. But in the meantime, my dear, this is it." He lowered his voice. "For the next nine years, like it or not, you are Mrs. Nicholas Burnham." It sounded like a death sentence to her and she began to cry.

When they reached Hillary's mother's house, Nick got out of the car without another glance at her, rang the doorbell, and rushed inside the minute the door was opened. Johnny was already in his room, in his pajamas, and he looked like the most forlorn little child Nick had ever seen, until he looked up and gave one wild whoop as he saw his father.

"Daddy! Daddy! . . . You're back! . . . You came back! Mommy said you were never coming back."

"She did what?" He looked at the child in horror.

"She said that you liked it better in Paris."

"And did you believe that?" He sat down on the bed as his mother-in-law watched from the hall, with tears streaming slowly down her face.

"Not really." The child spoke in a soft voice. "Not when I read your letters."

"I was so lonely there without you, tiger. I almost cried every night. Don't ever think that I'm happy anywhere without you, 'cause I'm not, and I'm never going to leave you again. Never!"

"You promise?" There were tears in Johnny's eyes too, and Nick's.

"I swear. Let's shake on it." They shook hands solemnly and Nick pulled Johnny into his arms again.

"Can I go home soon?"

"How soon can you get packed?"

Johnny's face was ablaze with joy. "You mean now? Back to our house in New York?"

"That's what I mean." He looked apologetically over his shoulder at his mother-in-law. "I'm sorry to do this to you, but I can't live another day without him."

"Or he without you," she said sadly. "We did our best but—" She began to cry in earnest and Nick put his arms around Hillary's mother.

"It's all right. I understand. Everything will be all right."

She smiled at him through her tears. "We were so worried about you. And when Paris fell, we were afraid you'd fall into the hands of the Germans." She sighed deeply and blew her nose. "When did you get back?"

"This morning. On the *Deauville*."

"The ship that made the rescue?" He nodded. "Oh, my God . . ." Johnny had overheard a few words and insisted that his father tell him all about it. Nick thought about telling him that he had seen the De Villiers girls on the ship, but he decided not to. He didn't want Hillary to know anything about it.

They left the house half an hour later, amid tears and good-byes and promises to call and write. But Johnny was so obviously ecstatic as he climbed into the car with the dog his father had given him in Paris, now full grown, that even the leave-taking wasn't overly sad. And his grandmother knew it was best for him to go home to his parents. The only further surprise was when he saw his mother in the car.

"What are you doing here, Mom? I thought you were in Gloucester."

"I was. Your father just picked me up."

"But you said you'd be there for three weeks . . ." He looked confused and Nick tried to change the subject. "Why didn't you come into the house to see Grandma?"

"I didn't want to leave the dog in the car, and she gets nervous in new houses." The explanation seemed to satisfy Johnny. Nick noticed that there hadn't been so much as a kiss between them.

The boy fell asleep long before they arrived in New York, where Nick carried him upstairs to his own bed, and tucked him in as an astonished maid looked on. They had actually come home again, all of them. That night Nick walked around the house, pulling dust covers off the furniture and looking around, getting accustomed to his home. Hillary found him sitting quietly in the den, staring out at the New York sky and the bright summer moon, his thoughts so far away that he didn't even hear her come in. And as she stared at the man who had almost literally kidnapped her from Philip Markham in Gloucester that night, she didn't have the energy left to be angry with him. She simply stood there and watched. He was a stranger to her. She could barely remember what it was like being married to him. It seemed a hundred years since they'd made love, and she knew that they never would again, not that she cared. But she was remembering what he had said to her in the car before they picked Johnny up. The next nine years, he'd said . . . nine . . . and as she thought the word aloud he turned around to look at her.

"What are you doing up?"

"It's too hot to sleep."

He nodded. He had so little left to say to her. And yet he knew that if he was with Liane, he could talk to her all night. "Johnny didn't wake up, did he?"

She shook her head. "He's all you care about, isn't he?"

He nodded. "But it didn't used to be that way. And in a lot of ways, I still care about you too." In the ways that affected their son, but that wasn't the same thing. They both knew that.

"Why do you want me to stay your wife?" She sat down on a chair in the dark and he looked at her.

"For him. He needs us both. And he will for a long time."

"Nine years." She echoed his words again.

"I won't give you a rough time, Hil. As long as you're decent to him." He wanted to ask her how she could have left him for almost the entire year. He ached to think of how lonely the child must have been. And to think of how lonely he himself had been in France, without Johnny.

"Don't you want something more than this for yourself, Nick?" He was a mystery to her, and she didn't want to be here with him. They both knew that. She didn't have to hide it from him anymore. She still couldn't believe he'd actually made her come back, but he was a powerful man, too powerful for her to fight. It was part of why she hated him sometimes.

He looked at her now, wondering who she was, just as she wondered about him. "Yes, I want something more for myself. But this isn't the time."

"Maybe you just haven't met the right girl." He didn't answer her, and for a moment she wondered—but that wouldn't be like Nick. She knew how faithful he'd been to her, not that it had ever meant much to her. In fact it annoyed her.

"Maybe not." He answered at last and stood up with a sigh. "Good night, Hil." He left her sitting in the darkened room alone, and went upstairs to the guest room, where he'd put his things. They would never again share a bedroom and hadn't since the night he'd moved out of their suite on the *Normandie* the year before. Those days were over.

He rented a house that summer in Marblehead, and took the month of August off so he could be with Johnny. Hillary came and went. He knew that she was with Philip Markham, but he didn't care. She was more discreet now than she'd been in the past, and once she saw that he wasn't going to stop her, she was less unpleasant when she was around. In a funny way, he sensed that Philip Markham was good for her. They were a great deal alike. And he wondered if Markham was responsible for calming her down.

Nick was happiest when he was alone with Johnny. He had longed for moments like these with his son, and during the long months in Paris he had thought of times such as this. And the days in Marblehead gave him a chance to think of Liane. He would take long walks on the beach, looking out to sea, remembering their trip, the rescue at sea, the hours they'd talked, the passionate lovemaking in the tiny cabin. It all seemed now like a distant dream, and each time he saw his son, he knew that she'd been right to set him free, yet they had both paid such a high price for their love. He thought often of calling her, to find out how she was, to tell her how much he loved her still and always would, and yet he knew that reaching out to touch her for even an instant would be cruel.

It was in the fall that he actually went so far as to pick up the phone, late one night in the apartment. Hillary was away for a few days, and Johnny was asleep, and he had been sitting in the living room for hours, thinking of the sound of Liane's voice, the feel of her skin. He knew that he'd never get over her. But perhaps by now, he told himself, she had got over him. And he put the phone down gently again, and went outside for a long walk. It was a cool, breezy September night, and the air felt good. He knew that the maids would hear Johnny if he woke up, and he was in no hurry to get home. He walked up and down the New York streets for hours, and then finally went back. He was still awake when Hillary came in at two in the morning, and he heard her bedroom door close. He remembered too well the days when something like that would have driven him mad, but it no longer did. He was going mad instead with loneliness for Liane.

Chapter 26

On November 11, 1940, the Vichy government was officially formed, with Pétain as its President, and Armand de Villiers in its highest ranks. His alleged perfidy to the old France was no longer a secret anymore. By then, Liane was accustomed to being shunned. She had long since become a pariah in Washington. She never expected the phone to ring, there were no invitations anywhere. On many days now she just sat at home, waiting for the girls to arrive from school. In many ways it reminded her of the days in Paris after war was declared and Armand was at the office fifteen hours a day. But then at least, no matter how late, she knew that eventually he would come home to her. Now God only knew when they would be together again. There were times when she wondered if she had been mad to tell Nick they couldn't go on. What harm would it have done? Who would have been hurt by it? Who would have known? But she would have, and perhaps eventually the girls, and one day Armand. She had done the right thing, but it tasted bitter in her soul as she thought of Nick. She had been tormented now for four months over thirteen bright days on a freighter, following a zigzag course from France to the States.

Armand's letters were infrequent and brief, brought out by members of the Resistance now, and left unsigned. They reached her through intricate, elaborate underground routes, eventually reaching London or some British port, and sent to the States on freighters or troop ships or whatever was coming across. There were odd gaps in the letters also at times, and she wondered always if the messengers had been killed or the troop ships sunk. There was no way to know. But what she did know, or sensed, was that Armand was in constant danger now. He was so high up in the ranks, that were his treason to Pétain and the Nazis known, he would have been killed at once.

> . . . We are very busy now, my love. We have been salvaging treasures as well as lives, spiriting pieces from the Louvre and having them disappear into barns and sheds and haystacks all over France before they can be shipped to Berlin. It may take us a lifetime to retrieve them again, covered with hay and goose manure, but it is one thing less for them to steal from us . . . even one tiny piece of history remaining ours is a victory for our side . . . that and the people who have managed to disappear, in order that their lives be saved. Knowing that we have done this, saved even one life, makes it bearable to be without your gentle touch, your love, your smile . . .

The letters tore at her heart now, and made her wonder again if what he was doing was worth the risk. One painting, one statue . . . one piece of history . . . and all of that perhaps in exchange for his life? Could he really think it worth the risk? And yet she sensed in his letters the same devoted passion he had always had for France. His country was truly his first love, above all else. He had served her well all over the world, and now he was saving her from those who would leave her bleeding and dead, squeezed dry and lying by the roadside.

Liane admired the principles behind Armand's work, and yet now as she began to see their daughters shunned by their friends, she once again questioned the wisdom of what he had done. Better to have gone to North Africa or London with De Gaulle, to fight there, to work with the Free French openly, than to remain in France to undermine the Nazis at every turn, but earn no glory at all, wearing the banner of Pétain. She knew that there was far more important work he did than saving the artwork of France, yet she also knew that just as he had been forced into secrecy in the year before Paris fell, now it was even more important that he share none of that with her, lest it risk other lives and his as well, so she had almost no way of knowing what agonies he really suffered, what risks he ran.

And at his desk in Paris, with the swastika spread across the wall, Armand would look out at the Paris sky, remembering Liane's touch, her face, the sunshine in her voice, the way she had looked at nineteen and twenty-one, and then he would force her from his head and go back to his work. He had grown deathly thin since she had left France, from overwork, from lack of sleep, from strain. He had developed a nervous tic in one eye, but other than that he always appeared steadfastly calm. He appeared to believe in the Vichy cause, and by November of 1940 he was carrying an important load of trust, placed on him by both sides. His only fear was the knowledge that time wasn't on his side. He had aged fifteen years in the last two, and the mirror didn't lie to him. He was approaching fifty-eight, and felt more like ninety-five. But if he could give his last days to France, and serve her well, he knew that he would die with honor on his side. And he felt sure that Liane knew it too. He hinted at that to her in letters once or twice—"*Si je meurs pour ma patrie, mon amour, je meurs en paix*"—If I die for my country, I die in peace. But the words made her hands tremble each time she read something like that. Losing Armand was not what she had in mind. But at other times there were anecdotes, or reports of funny things they'd done, an artistry of confusion committed by the comrades of the Resistance. She marveled now and then about the things the Resistance did, and the tales that Armand dared to tell. She marveled too that the Nazis rarely found them out. But "rarely" still made it a dangerous game. There were constant close calls, far more than she knew.

In November there was one that almost cost Armand his life. He was delivering a series of important papers he had copied in minute detail, carried taped to his chest, and he had been stopped by the police on his way out of town. He explained that he was going to visit an old friend, and had rapidly shown the documents, which proved him a henchman of Pétain. The German officers had hesitated for a time, and then waved him on. The papers had been delivered into the right hands, and he had returned that night, almost limp with fatigue, but he returned to the house he and Liane had shared, and he sat down slowly on the bed, aware of just how close he'd come, and that the next time might be his last. But even as he looked at her empty side of the bed, he had no doubts. He never had. "_Ça vaut la peine, Liane . . . ça vaut bien la peine . . . pour nous, pour la France,_" he said aloud. It's worth the pain . . . well worth the pain . . . for us . . . for France. . . .

But that was not a sentiment shared by Liane as the doorbell rang in the Georgetown house on a Friday afternoon. The girls had been due home from school half an hour before. And she had glanced at her watch several times. Marcie, the maid, had told her to calm down, but there was no calming her once she saw the girls. They had walked home alone, as they often did, but as they stood now on the front steps, their dresses in rags, with red paint in their hair and ravaged looks on their faces, Liane gasped and began to shake as she led them inside. Elisabeth was trembling from head to foot and hiccuping through her sobs, but Liane could see that there was more than grief to Marie-Ange's tears, there was also fury.

"My God . . . what happened?" She was about to lead them into the kitchen, where she was going to peel their clothes from their backs, but she stopped as though she had been slapped when she turned Marie-Ange around. There on her back, in a broad slash of red paint, was a swastika. And without a word she turned Elisabeth around too and saw another one there. And choking on her own sobs, she clutched them to her, their painted little bodies smearing red all over her, and the three of them stood in the kitchen like that as Marcie watched with tears pouring down her own withered black cheeks.

"Oh, my babies . . . what they done to ya?" She pulled them slowly free of Liane and began to take off their dresses, but the girls were crying harder now and Liane had to fight to regain control. She was crying not just for them, but for herself, and France, and Armand, and what the horrors there had done to them all. There was no turning back now. And she knew too that there was also no staying. She couldn't go on exposing the girls to that. They had to leave. They had no choice now.

Liane walked them quietly into their bathroom and ran a warm bath. Then she tenderly bathed both of them. Half an hour later they looked like the same little girls they had always been, but she knew they weren't, and would never be quite the same again. She threw away the ravaged dresses, her brow furrowed in anger and fear.

She brought them dinner in their room, and they sat and talked for a long time. Elisabeth looked at her as though her entire childhood had melted in one afternoon. At eight she knew more than most children at twice that age, she knew pain and loss and betrayal.

"They said Papa was a Nazi . . . Mrs. Muldock told Mrs. McQueen and she told Annie . . . but Papa isn't a Nazi! He's not! He's not!" And then, with a look of sorrow, she asked Marie-Ange and Liane, "What's a Nazi?"

Liane smiled for the first time that afternoon. "If you didn't know what a Nazi was, why were you so upset?"

"I think it means a robber, or a bad person, doesn't it?"

"Kind of. The Nazis are very bad Germans. They're on

the other side of the war from France and England, and they've killed a great many people." And she did not add, "and children."

"But Papa isn't German." To the pain in her eyes, she now added the obvious fact that she was completely baffled. "And Mr. Schulenberg at the meat market is German. Is he a Nazi?"

"No, that's different." Liane sighed. "He's Jewish."

"No, he isn't. He's German."

"He's both. Never mind. The Nazis don't like Jewish people either."

"Do they kill them?" Elisabeth looked shocked as her mother nodded. "Why?"

"That's very hard to explain. The Nazis are very bad people, Elisabeth. The Germans who came to Paris were Nazis. That's why Daddy wanted us to leave, so we'd be safe here." She had explained that to them before, but it had never really sunk in until this moment, until it touched them, having had red paint in their hair and swastikas on their backs. Now the war was theirs too. But now Elisabeth had an added worry.

"Will they kill Papa?" Liane had never seen her eyes so wide, and she wanted to tell them it could never happen, but should she? She squeezed her eyes shut and shook her head.

"Your papa won't let that happen." She only prayed that it was true, that he would outwit them for as long as he had to. But at tea, Marie-Ange knew more than Elisabeth, and tears slid slowly down her face again as she sat on her bed, still in a state of shock. She hadn't touched her dinner.

"I'm never going back to school . . . Never! I hate them."

Liane didn't know what to answer. They couldn't give up school for the duration of the war, but she couldn't let this happen again either.

"I'll talk to the headmistress on Monday."

"I don't care. I won't go back." They had bruised something deep within her soul, and Liane hated them too, for what they had done to her children.

"Do I have to go back, Mommy?" Elisabeth looked openly scared and they both tore at Liane's heart, each in her own way, each cut to the quick by something they didn't understand. How could she tell them that their father was not a Nazi, not what he seemed to be, a henchman of Pétain, but a double agent? One day, when it was all over, when it was too late, then she would be able to tell them. But what would it matter then? They needed to know now, and she couldn't tell them. "Do I have to, Mommy?" Elisabeth's eyes pleaded with her.

"I don't know. We'll see." She kept them close to her all weekend. The three of them were quiet and subdued, they took a long walk in the park, and Liane took the girls to the zoo, but neither of them was her usual self. It was as though the children had been beaten, which was exactly what she told the headmistress on Monday. The girls had stayed home, but Liane appeared at the school before nine o'clock, and when the headmistress, Mrs. Smith, reached her office, Liane was waiting. She described the condition the girls had come home in and what it had done to them, and she turned to her with an expression of grief. "How could you let something like that happen?"

"But I had no idea, of course . . ." She was instantly defensive.

"It happened here at the school. Marie-Ange said that seven little girls in her class did it, and they even did it to her younger sister. They took scissors and paint and they dragged them into a room. It's like hoodlums in the ghetto, for God's sake, only it's worse. The children are punishing each other for things that they don't understand, that have nothing to do with them, because of gossip that their parents circulate."

"Surely you can't expect us to control that?" The headmistress looked prim.

And Liane raised her voice. "I expect you to protect my daughters."

"Outwardly it may appear that your children were the victims of other children, Mrs. de Villiers, but the fact of the matter is that they are suffering because of your husband."

"What in hell do *you* know about my husband? He's in occupied France, risking his life every day, and you tell me that my children are suffering because of him? We lived through a year of Europe after the war was declared, we were there when Paris fell, we spent two days on a goddamn fishing boat sitting on a load of stinking fish in order to meet a freighter and come home, and then we spent two weeks dodging U-boats on the Atlantic, and we watched almost four thousand men die when a Canadian ship was torpedoed. So don't tell me about my husband or about the war, Mrs. Smith, because you don't know a goddamn thing about either one, sitting here in Georgetown."

"You're absolutely right." Mrs. Smith stood up, and Liane didn't like the look in her eye. Maybe she had gone too far, but she didn't give a damn. They had all had enough. Washington had been worse than Paris before or after the occupation, and she was sorry she had come home. They would have been better off living with the Germans in Paris with Armand. And if she could have, she'd have taken the next ship to him. But of course there was none, and she knew very well that Armand would never let her. They hadn't risked their lives to get back to the States just to turn around and go back again four months later. She felt half crazy with frustration.

And now the headmistress of the school was glaring at her with ill-concealed contempt and anger. "You're right. I don't know anything about the war, a 'goddamn thing,' as you put it. But I know children, and I know their parents. And parents talk, and children listen. And what they're saying is that your husband is with the Vichy government, that he's collaborating with the Germans. That's not a secret. It's been all over Washington for months. I heard it the first week the girls came back to school. I'm sorry to hear it. I liked your husband. But his children are paying for his political choices, and so are you. That's not my fault, it's not yours, but it's a fact. They're going to have to live with it. And if they can't, they'll have to go back to Paris and go to school with all the other little French and German children. But there's a war on, you know it, I know it, and so do the children. And your husband is on the wrong side of the war. It's as simple as that. I suspect that that's probably why you left him. There happens to be a rumor around too that you're getting divorced. At least that might help the children."

Liane's eyes blazed as she stood up to face the other woman. "Is that what people are saying?"

Mrs. Smith didn't flinch for a moment. "Yes, it is."

"Well, it's not true. I love my husband and I back him up one hundred percent in everything he does, including now—especially now. He needs us. And we need him. And the only reason we left Paris is because he wanted to be sure that we weren't killed." Liane began to cry, like her daughters three days before, out of frustration and hurt and anger.

"Mrs. de Villiers, I'm sorry for what you're going through. But I can only assume from what you say that your entire family is sympathetic to the Germans. And as such, you're going to pay a price for that—"

Liane interrupted her at once, she couldn't bear it a moment longer. "I *hate* Germans! *I hate them!*" She walked to the door and pulled it open. "And I hate you, for what you allowed to happen to my children."

"We didn't allow it to happen, Mrs. de Villiers. You did." Her voice was frigid. "And I'm sure that you and they will be much happier with another school. Good day, Mrs. de Villiers." Liane slammed the door to the office and walked out into the fall sunshine. When she reached home, the girls were anxious to know what had happened. Marie-Ange immediately came running down the stairs.

"Do I have to go back?"

"No! Now go to your room and leave me alone!" She walked into her bedroom and closed the door and sat down on her bed and cried. Why did it all have to be so goddamn difficult? And a little while later her daughters came in, not to pry, but to comfort their mother. She had got control of herself by then, but her eyes were still red from crying and she was angry at Armand as well as everyone else. He had placed them in an untenable position. She feared for him and she loved him, but she hated him too. Why in God's name couldn't he have come home with them? But it wasn't his home, she knew only too well. France was, and he had stayed there to defend the country he loved, but in a way she could explain to no one.

"Mommy? . . ." Elisabeth advanced slowly toward the bed and put her arms around her mother.

"Yes, love?"

"We love you." The declaration brought fresh tears to her eyes as she hugged them.

"I love you too." She looked at Marie-Ange then. "I'm sorry I shouted at you when I came home. I was just very angry."

"At us?" Her eldest child looked worried.

"No, at Mrs. Smith. She doesn't understand about Papa."

"Couldn't you explain it to her?" Elisabeth looked disappointed. She liked her school, even if no one invited her to their houses to play anymore. But she liked going to school, even if Marie-Ange didn't.

Liane shook her head. "No, I couldn't explain it, sweetheart. It's much too complicated to explain to anyone right now."

"So we don't have to go back?" Marie-Ange hammered the point home.

"No, you don't. I'll have to find you both a new school."

"In Washington?"

"I don't know." For the last half hour she had been asking herself the same question. "I'll have to think it out." The next weekend was Thanksgiving. But that afternoon was the last straw. She saw Elisabeth standing near the hall phone, crying. "What's the matter, love?" She suspected that she missed her friends, if she still had any.

"Nancy Adamson just called to tell me that Mrs. Smith told everyone we had been kicked out of school."

Liane was horrified. "She said that?" Elisabeth nodded. "But it's not true. I told her . . ." She rapidly reviewed the conversation in her head, and realized that Mrs. Smith had told her that the children would be happier somewhere else and she had agreed. She sighed and sat down on the floor beside her youngest child. "We agreed that you shouldn't go back. No one kicked you out."

"Are you sure?"

"I'm positive."

"Do they hate me?"

"Of course not!" But after what they had done to the girls on Friday, that was a tough one to prove to either child.

"Do they hate Papa?"

Liane considered her words. "No. They don't understand what he's doing."

"What *is* he doing?"

"Trying to save France so that we can all go back someday to live."

"Why?"

"Because that's what Papa does. All his life he has represented France in a lot of different countries. He takes care of France's interests. And that's what he's doing now. He's trying to take care of France so the Germans don't ruin it forever."

"Then why does everyone say he loves the Germans? Does he?" She was exhausted by the child's questions, but each one needed a thoughtful answer. What she said now would stay with the children for years, and she knew it. They would always remember what she said, and it would color their views about their father and themselves for a lifetime.

"No, Papa doesn't love the Germans."

"Does he hate them?"

"I don't think Papa hates anyone. But he hates what they're doing to Europe." Elisabeth nodded slowly. It was what she had needed to hear, and it made her father a good guy.

"Okay." She stood up then and went slowly upstairs to find her sister. And that night, Liane thought long and hard. She had to do something, and putting them in another Washington school wasn't a solution. She already knew the answer to her own questions, but she hated to do it. She decided to sleep on it one more night, but the next morning, she still had the same answer. She dialed the operator and asked her to place the call. She had waited until noon eastern time to call, which was nine o'clock for him in California. He came to the phone at once, his voice gruff.

"Liane? Is something wrong?"

"No, Uncle George, not really."

"You sound sick or tired or something." He was a canny old man. In truth, she was both, but she wouldn't admit it now. She was going home with her tail between her legs and that was bad enough.

"I'm all right." She decided to get right to the point. "Do you still want us to come out?"

"Of course!" He sounded pleased, and then, "You mean you've finally come to your senses?"

"I guess you could call it that. I want to change the girls' school, and I thought that as long as I was doing that, we might as well make a big change and come out to California." He sensed instantly that there were deeper reasons than that. She was far too stubborn to have given in unless she was almost beaten. And she was. More so than he knew.

They made arrangements, Liane all the while holding back tears of anger, but she was grateful that she had somewhere to go. Things could have been a lot worse. There were people all over Europe who were homeless. "Uncle George?"

"Yes, Liane?"

"Thank you for letting us come."

"Don't be ridiculous, Liane. This is your home too. It always has been."

"Thank you." He had made it easy for her and he hadn't mentioned Armand. She went to tell the girls.

Marie-Ange looked at her strangely then. "We're running away, aren't we, Mom?"

It was almost more than she could bear. She felt so drained that she couldn't stand one more question. "No, Marie-Ange"—she spoke to her daughter in a voice that surprised the child—"we're not running away any more than we were when we left Paris. We're doing the right thing, at the right time, in the best way we know how. It may not be what we like, but it's the smartest choice we've got, and that's why we're going to do it." And with that she told the girls to go out to play. She needed some time to herself. And she stood at her bedroom window, watching them. They had grown up a lot in the last four months, and so had she, more than some people grow up in an entire lifetime.

Chapter 27

$\mathcal{L}$iane and the girls had a quiet Thanksgiving dinner alone in Washington before they left. It was as though they were living in a town where they were strangers. No one called, no one dropped by, no one invited them to share their turkey dinner. Like millions of others in the nation, they went to church that morning, and came home to carve their turkey, but they might as well have been on a desert island when they did it.

And the next weekend they packed up the things they had bought when they arrived, and Liane put everything on a train to the West Coast. On Monday, they boarded the train, and for just a brief moment, as they sat down in their sleeper, Liane thought of Nick and when she had last seen him at Grand Central Station. It seemed a thousand years ago now, though it had been only four months. But they had been very long months for Liane and the girls. She felt relief as the train pulled slowly out of the station. None of them were sorry to leave Washington. It had been a mistake to come back. Armand had told her to go back to San Francisco, right from the first, but she couldn't have known then what they knew now, the price they would pay for his association with Pétain and the Vichy government.

The trip across the country was both monotonous and peaceful. The girls played and read, kept each other amused, and sometimes fought, which kept Liane busy. But much of the time she slept. She felt as though she were regaining her strength after almost five agonizing months of tension, not to mention the months of tension before that. In truth, life hadn't been normal for them for over a year. It never had been since they arrived in Paris nearly eighteen months before. And now suddenly she was able to relax and think of absolutely nothing. Only when they stopped in various stations and she read the papers was she reminded of the rest of the world, and their troubles. The British were being bombed day and night, and the streets were apparently filled with rubble. Children were still being evacuated whenever possible, and Churchill had ordered the RAF to bomb Berlin, which only redoubled Hitler's efforts to destroy London.

But all of that was hard to believe as they rolled through the snow-covered fields of Nebraska, and watched the Rockies appear in Colorado. And at last on Thursday morning, they awoke, within hours of San Francisco. They pulled into the city from the south, through the ugliest part of town, and Liane was surprised that it still looked so familiar. Very little had changed since she had come back for the last time after her father's death eight years before.

"Is this it?" Marie-Ange looked shocked. The children had never been to San Francisco. There had been no reason to bring them here. Her father was gone, and Uncle George had passed through the various cities where they had lived over the years.

"Yes." Liane smiled. "But it's much prettier than this. This isn't a very nice part of town."

"It sure isn't."

Uncle George and the chauffeur were waiting for them at the station, and they were escorted to his home in grand style, in a Lincoln Continental. It had just arrived from Detroit and the girls thought it a very luxurious car. She could tell that they were suddenly excited to be here. And George had brought them each a new doll, and when they reached the house on Broadway, Liane was touched to see the trouble he had gone to, to arrange rooms for the girls. They were filled with toys and games, and there were pictures of Walt Disney characters on the walls. And in Liane's old room, waiting for her, there was an enormous vase of flowers. Even though it was the first of December, the weather was balmy, the trees were still green, and there were flowers in the garden.

"The house looks wonderful, Uncle George." He had made some changes after her father's death, but on the whole the place had actually changed less than she had feared, and everything was well run and well staffed. He had settled down in his old age, abandoning the wild party days of his youth. He had done well by Crockett Shipping too. And in a funny way it was nice to come home. After the painful rejection they'd met in Washington for nearly five months, it was a blessed relief to be here, or so she thought until after dinner. The girls had gone to bed and she was sitting in the library, playing dominoes with George, as she often had with her father.

"Well, Liane. Have you come to your senses yet?"

"About what?" She pretended to concentrate on the game. She was stalling.

"You know what I'm talking about. I mean about that fool you married."

She raised her eyes to his, with a cold, hard look, which surprised him. "I'm not going to discuss that with you, Uncle George. I hope I make myself perfectly clear."

"Don't take that tone with me, girl. You made a mistake and you know it."

"I know nothing of the sort. I've been married for eleven and a half years and I love my husband very much."

"The man is practically a Nazi. And maybe 'practically' is being too kind. Could you really live with him again after knowing that?" She refused to answer. "For God's sake, he's almost six thousand miles away and you belong here. If you filed for divorce now, they would grant it to you under special circumstances. You could even go to Reno and have it over in six weeks. And then you and the girls could start a new life here where you belong."

"I don't belong here. I'm here because I have nowhere else to go while France is occupied. We belong with Armand, and that's where we'll be as soon as the war ends."

"I think you're crazy."

"Then let's not discuss it anymore, Uncle George. There are things about the situation that you don't know."

"Like what?"

"I'd rather not discuss it." As usual, her hands were tied. And she didn't thank Armand for that. But she was growing used to living in silence.

"That's crap and you know it. And there's plenty I do know. Like what drove you out of town on a rail—the girls were kicked out of school, no one invited you anywhere, you were a pariah." Her eyes looked sad as they met his. What he said was true. "At least you had the sense to come here, where you can have a normal, decent life."

"Not if you go around calling my husband a Nazi." Her voice was tired and sad. "If you do that, the same thing will happen here, and I can't pull up stakes every five months. If you talk like that, the girls will pay for it just like they did in Washington." She didn't ask him where he'd gotten his information, he had connections and associates everywhere, and it really didn't matter. What he said was true, but what she was saying now was also.

"What do you expect me to say? That he's a nice guy?"

"You don't have to say anything, if you don't like him. But if you do, mark my words, you'll cry, the way I did, when the girls come home with paint in their hair, and their dresses torn off their backs, with swastikas painted on them." There were tears in her eyes as she spoke, and he looked at her with fresh compassion.

"They did that to the girls?" She nodded. "Who?"

"Other children in school. Little girls from nice families. And the headmistress said she wouldn't be able to do anything to stop it."

"I'd have killed her."

"I would have liked to, but that wouldn't have solved the problem. As she put it, parents talk and children listen, and she happens to be right. So if you talk, Uncle George, so will everyone else, and the girls will end up paying for it." That she did by now seemed normal. He was pensive for a long moment after she had spoken and he nodded slowly.

"I understand. I don't like it, but I understand."

"Good."

He looked at her gently then. "I'm glad you called me."

"So am I." She smiled at him. They had never been close, but she was oddly grateful to be with him now. He was giving her shelter at a time when she desperately needed it. And here life seemed so civilized and so far away from the war, one could almost pretend that it wasn't happening. Almost. But not quite. But it seemed blissfully distant.

They chatted on for a little while then, on safer subjects, and at last they went upstairs to their respective rooms, and when Liane went to bed that night, she fell into her old bed and slept as she hadn't in years. "Like the dead," she told George the next morning. And after he left the house, she made several calls, but not to old friends. She hardly knew anyone here anymore, and he had already arranged a school for the girls. They were going to Miss Burke's and they were starting the following Monday. But there was something else Liane had in mind, and by late that afternoon, she had arranged it.

"You did what?" George asked in consternation.

"I said that I got a job. Is that so shocking?"

"I think so, yes. If you're anxious to do something, why don't you join the Metropolitan Club, or a women's auxiliary or something?"

"Because I want to do something useful. I'm going to work for the Red Cross."

"For money?"

"No."

"Thank God." That would have been too much for him. "I

don't know, Liane. You're a strange girl. Why would you want to work? And every day?"

"What do you think I should do? Sit here and count your ships going by?"

"They're not just my ships, they're yours too, and it wouldn't do you any harm. You look exhausted and you're too thin. Why don't you rest, or play golf or tennis or something?"

"I can do that on the weekends, with the girls."

"You're a nut, and if you don't watch out, in your old age you'll turn eccentric!" But he was secretly proud of her, as he told a friend at his club the next day. They were playing dominoes at the Pacific Union Club, and he was boasting about Liane over a Scotch and soda.

"She's a hell of a woman, Lou. Intelligent, quiet, poised, she's a lot like my brother in some ways, and smart as a whip. She's had a very rough time in Europe." He explained that she had been there during the fall of Paris, but heeding Liane's words, he refrained from saying that she'd been married to a man who turned out to be a Nazi.

"Is she married?" His friend looked at him with an interested eye. And George recognized it as an opening. He wanted to help Liane. He had been thinking about it for days, and he knew just how he wanted to do it.

"More or less. She's separated. And I think in a while she'll be going to Reno. She hasn't seen him in six months"— it was true, after all—"and she has no idea when she'll see him again." That was true too. And then the biggie. "I'd like to introduce her to your son."

"How old a woman is she?"

"She's thirty-three, and she has two lovely children."

"So does Lyman." George's friend won the game and sat back with a smile. "He's thirty-six, thirty-seven in June." And he was one of the best attorneys in town and handsome as hell, or so George thought. He was from an excellent family, had gone to Cal, was respectable, and lived in San Francisco. He was perfect for her, and if she didn't agree, there were plenty of others like him. "I'll see what I can do," Lou said.

"Maybe I'll arrange a little dinner." George spoke to his secretary the next day, and a few days later he made some calls, and that night he told Liane when she got home from the Red Cross. She liked her job and she was in good spirits, and she had gotten a letter from Armand that day, it had been forwarded to her from Washington the day they had left. He sounded well, and didn't appear to be in any immediate danger. For her, it was a constant worry.

"How was your day, Uncle George?" She kissed him on the forehead and sat down to have a drink with him. Life was so easy here that she almost felt guilty, particularly when she thought of Armand, precariously perched between the two hostile governments he served. She knew what a toll it was taking on him, and here she sat, in a splendid house, with a lovely view, surrounded by servants and a doting uncle.

"My day was pretty fair. How was yours?"

"Interesting. We're coordinating additional locations for some of the British children."

"That's a nice thing to do. How are the girls?"

"Thriving. They're upstairs doing their homework." And the best news for them was that in ten days they would have Christmas vacation.

"You know, I had a thought today. Would you mind helping me give a little dinner? You used to be awfully good at that, when you lived with your father." She smiled at the memory, and it brought thoughts of Armand back to mind—everything did—for she had done it for him too after Odile died, and for the eleven years they'd been married.

"Thank you, Uncle George. I enjoyed it."

"Would you mind helping me out? I've fallen a little behind with some of my entertaining."

"Not at all. Did you have something special in mind?"

"I thought a little dinner next week." He didn't tell her that everyone had already accepted. "How does that sound?

About eighteen people. And we could have a few musicians, and a little dancing in the library after dinner."

"Dancing? Isn't that rather elaborate for a 'little dinner'?"

"Don't you like to dance?"

"Of course." And then she smiled. She had forgotten what a gay blade George used to be, and apparently still was, although he was seventy-three years old, for he was spry for his age. She suddenly wondered if he had an ulterior motive, maybe some dowager he was wooing. "I'd be happy to help. Just tell me what you want me to do."

"I'll invite the guests, you handle the rest. Get yourself a pretty new dress, order some flowers. You'll know what to do." Of course she did, and on the night of the dinner party she came down to check everything out. The entire group of eighteen was being seated at the large oval Chippendale table. There were three large arrangements of white and yellow roses on the table, tall ivory tapers in the elaborate silver candelabra, and she had used one of the lace tablecloths that had been her mother's and that she had left behind when she left the house. She had hired musicians, just as her uncle wanted. They were already playing gentle strains in the enormous living room before the guests arrived. She looked around and decided everything looked all right, when she caught a glimpse of Marie-Ange and Elisabeth peeking over the banister.

"What are you two doing?"

"Can we watch?"

"For a little while." Their mother smiled and blew them a kiss. She was wearing a pale-blue satin evening dress she had bought at I. Magnin the day before and it was exactly the color of her eyes. Her hair was swept up and she felt more elegant than she had in years.

"You look like Cinderella!" Elisabeth whispered loudly from the stairs and Liane ran up to give her a kiss.

"Thank you, my love."

And then Uncle George came down, the guests began to arrive, and the party got under way. Liane thought that it went very smoothly. George had done the seating himself, since he knew all the guests, and Liane sat between two very pleasant men, a stockbroker named Thomas Mac-Kenzie, who was about forty years of age and was divorced with three sons, and an attorney named Lyman Lawson, whom she guessed to be about her own age, and who was also divorced and had two little girls. And as she watched her uncle watching her a little later, she suddenly understood. He was trying to introduce her to the bachelors around town. She was shocked at the thought. After all, she was a married woman.

It was a beautiful dinner, and the musicians were marvelous, but she was suddenly terrified about what George was trying to do, and very gingerly she brought it up at breakfast the next morning.

"Well, my dear, how did you enjoy last night?" He looked immensely pleased with himself, and she smiled at him over her coffee.

"Very much. It was a beautiful evening, Uncle George. Thank you."

"Not at all. I've been meaning to reciprocate a number of invitations for quite a while, but with no woman in the house . . ." He tried to look mournful but didn't succeed, and Liane laughed.

"I'm not sure I believe that." And then she looked quietly at him and decided to take the bull by the horns. "Uncle George, may I ask you a very rude question?"

"That depends how rude it is." He smiled at his niece. He was liking her better than he had in years. She had a lot of spunk, even if she had made a miserable choice of a husband. But that would be remedied soon enough. He knew she'd come to her senses. She was a sensible woman, and she had the girls to think of. "What did you want to ask?"

"You aren't trying to launch me with . . . er . . . ah . . . the single men around town, are you?"

He feigned innocence and looked amused. "Do you prefer

married ones, Liane?" Personally, he had always had a weakness for married women.

"No, Uncle George. I prefer my own husband." There was a sudden silence at the table.

"I don't think there's any harm in your knowing a few of the men around town. Do you?" But that was a loaded question.

"That depends on what they know of my marital status. Do they think I'm married or divorced?"

"I can't remember what I said." He cleared his throat and picked up his newspaper. But she very gently took it out of his hand and looked him in the eye.

"I'd like an answer. I think this is important."

"So do I." He looked her squarely in the eyes. "I think it's time you looked around and thought this thing through. That man is nearly six thousand miles away, doing God knows what, which we won't discuss, since you don't want to discuss it. But you know what I think about that. And I think there's a lot better out here for you."

"I don't agree with you." And as she said it she found herself thinking of Nick Burnham. She forced thoughts of him from her head and faced her uncle. "I'm a married woman, Uncle George. And I intend to stay that way. I also intend to remain faithful to my husband." Again her single indiscretion flashed into her mind and she pushed it from her. She couldn't allow herself to think of him anymore. Dreaming of Nick led nowhere.

"Whether you're faithful or not is entirely your affair. I just thought it might do you good to meet a few San Franciscans."

"And that was a very nice thought. But trying to break up my marriage isn't."

"You don't have a marriage, Liane." The force with which he said it took her by surprise.

"Yes, I do."

"But you shouldn't."

"You have no right to make that decision for me."

"I have every right to try to bring you to your senses. You're wasting your youth on an old fool who must be blind to what he's doing." Liane clamped her mouth shut and he went on. "And you're a damn fool if you don't do something about it."

"Thank you." She got up very quietly and left the room, feeling guilty and ungrateful. He had meant well, but he had no idea what he was doing. She would never betray Armand again. Never. She was not a debutante to be auditioning at dinner dances. And she felt suddenly foolish for having unwittingly played her uncle's game.

She felt even more so when Lyman Lawson called her that afternoon at the Red Cross. He invited her to dinner the following night, but she said that she was busy. He wasn't the only one who called, the stockbroker who had been sitting on her other side called her too, and she felt extremely uncomfortable about the impression her uncle was obviously creating, that she was a single woman. But if she told them that she was not, she would make a liar of her uncle. Matters got even worse when an item appeared in the paper a few days later about George Crockett's attractive niece from Washington, D.C., who was separated from her husband and had come back to San Francisco to live. The item even inferred that in the near future she would be making a six-week visit to Reno.

"Uncle George, how could you?" She stood in the library that night and waved the newspaper at him.

"I didn't tell them a thing!" He didn't even look embarrassed. He was convinced that he was right.

"You must have. And Lyman Lawson called me again this afternoon. What in hell can I tell these men?"

"That you'd like to have dinner with them sometime."

"But I wouldn't!"

"It would do you good."

"I am married. Married! M-a-r-r-i-e-d. Married. Don't you understand?"

"You know how I feel about it, Liane."

"And you know how I feel about it too. How exactly would you explain my cheating on my husband to my children? Do you expect them to simply forget that their father ever existed? Do you think I can?"

"I hope so in time."

It was a campaign she had no idea how to deal with. He brought people home at night, showed up with them for drinks, picked her up at the Red Cross for lunch with friends. By Christmas she felt as though she had met every single man in town, and not one of them understood that she was very seriously married. It was almost funny, except that it was driving her crazy. She sought refuge in her work and with the girls, and she dodged every single invitation.

"When are you going to get out of this house, Liane?" He roared it at her one night over their domino game and she threw up her hands with exasperation.

"Tomorrow, when I go to work."

"I mean at night."

"When the war ends and my husband comes back. Is that soon enough, or do you want me to move out now?" She was shouting at him and he was an old man and she felt very bad about it. "Please, Uncle George, for God's sake, leave me alone. This is a very difficult time for us all. Don't make it any harder for me. I know you mean well. But I don't want to go out with your friends' sons."

"You should be grateful they want to go out with you."

"Why should I? All I am to them is Crockett Shipping."

"Is that what's bothering you, Liane? They see more than that in you. You're a very pretty girl and damn bright."

"All right, all right. That's not the point. The point is that I'm married." And eventually the girls overheard them.

"Why does Uncle George want you to go out with other men?"

"Because he's crazy," she snapped as she dressed for work.

"He is?" Marie-Ange looked intrigued. "You mean senile?"

"No, I mean—damn it, you leave me alone too. For God's sake . . ." But the real problem was that she hadn't had a letter from Armand in two weeks and she was sick with worry that something had happened to him. But that wasn't a fear she could share with her daughters. "Look, Uncle George means well, and it's too complicated to explain. Just forget about it."

"Are you going to go out with other men?" She looked worried.

"Of course not, silly. I'm married to Papa." It seemed as though that was all she said these days.

"I think Mr. Burnham liked you when we came back on the ship. I saw him looking at you sometimes as though he thought you were very special." Out of the mouths of babes. Liane stopped what she was doing for a moment to look at her daughter.

"He's a very nice man, Marie-Ange. And I think he's special too. We're very good friends, but that's all. And he's married too."

"No, he isn't."

"Of course he is." Liane was already tired before she began her day, and she could hardly wait to leave the house as she pulled on her stockings. "You met his wife on the *Normandie* last year, and his son, John."

"I know. But it said in the newspaper yesterday that he was getting a divorce."

"It did?" Liane felt her heart stop. "Where?"

"In New York."

"I mean where in the paper." She had only read the front page, for news of the war, and she had been late for work.

"I don't know. It said that they were having a big fight, and he's suing her for divorce, and he wants to keep their son and she won't let him."

Liane was numb. The maid helped her locate the paper in the pantry. Marie-Ange had been right. There it was. An article on page three. Nicholas Burnham was allegedly pitted against his wife in an ardent dispute. She and Philip Markham had created a scandal in New York, and Nick was suing her for divorce, naming Markham as the co-respondent. And in addition he was demanding custody of his son, but there was no way of telling if he'd win.

When Liane got to the Red Cross office, she was tempted to call him. But as always in the past, she hung up the phone before she dialed. Even if he was getting divorced, she was not. Nothing had changed for her, including her feelings for Nick. And Armand.

Chapter 28

The week before Christmas Nick Burnham strode into his lawyer's office.

"Do you have an appointment to see Mr. Greer, sir?"

"No, I don't."

"I'm afraid he's with a client, and after that he's going to court."

"Then I'll wait."

"But I can't—" She began to give him the party line, but when he looked into her eyes, she almost took a step backward. He was a good-looking man, but he looked as though, with very little provocation, he would be willing to kill. She had never seen such total fury in any man. "May I tell him who you are?"

"Nicholas Burnham." She knew the name and disappeared instantly. And ten minutes later, when the client left, Nick was ushered in to see Ben Greer.

"Hello, Nick. How've you been?"

"I've been fine. More or less."

"Oh, boy." He took one look at Nick's face and knew that things were rough. There were circles under Nick's eyes, and his jaw was so tense that Greer could almost see him choking back rage. "Would you like a drink?"

"Do I look that bad?" Nick began to relax a little and sat back in the chair, producing a tired grin. "I guess things haven't been so hot after all."

"I guess not, or you wouldn't be here. What can I do to help?"

"Kill my wife." He said it as though it were a joke, but Ben Greer wasn't entirely sure. He'd seen that look on men's faces before, and at least once in his career, he'd ended up defending a man for murder instead of getting him a divorce. But Nick took a deep breath, sat back, and ran a hand through his hair. And then he looked sadly at Ben Greer. "You know, I've tried to make this thing work for ten years, but it just never has." It was no secret in New York, and Greer knew it too. "And when I came back from Europe in July, I tried to impress on her that I wanted to keep the ship afloat. By then it was"—he groped for the words—"a marriage of convenience at best, but I wanted to stay married for the sake of the child." Greer nodded. He'd heard the same tale ten thousand times before. "She was involved with Philip Markham by then. It had been going on for about a year. And I let her know, as best I could, that she could have free rein with him, but I wouldn't agree to a divorce. And do you know what the son of a bitch did yesterday?"

"I'm dying to hear."

But Nick didn't smile. "He put a gun to my son's head. When I came home from work, there he sat in my living room, cool as hell. And he pointed the gun at John and said that if I didn't let Hillary go, he'd kill my kid." Nick grew pale as he told the tale, and the attorney frowned. Things were desperate after all.

"Was the gun loaded, Nick?"

"No. But I didn't know that then. I agreed to the divorce, he put the gun down . . ." He thought back to the moment and clenched his teeth and his fists.

"And then what did you do?"

"I kicked his ass all over the room. He's got three broken ribs, a broken arm, and two chipped teeth. Hillary moved out last night and she tried to take Johnny with her. I told her that if she ever laid a hand on him again or showed up in my house, I'd kill her and Markham. And by God, I mean it."

"Well, you've got grounds for divorce." But that was hardly news. "Do you think you can prove adultery?"

"With ease."

"But what grounds do you have to win custody of the boy?"

"Do I need more than that? He pulled a gun on my child."

"The gun wasn't loaded. And Markham did that. Your wife didn't."

"But she was a party to it. She just sat there and let him do it."

"She probably knew it wasn't loaded. I'll admit, it was a cheap trick, but it's not grounds to get custody of the boy."

"Everything else is. She's a rotten mother, she doesn't give a damn about John, and she never did. She wanted an abortion before he was born, and she's never given him a second glance. When I was stuck in Europe after war was declared, she dumped him with her mother for ten months and almost never saw him until I got home. She's a rotten mother to him! Rotten, do you hear?" Nick was frantic, and he began to pace the room. He should never have listened to Liane. He should have left Hillary six months before and fought for custody of the child then. But he hadn't. And now he had lost her too. If he had been free, who knew what would have happened. It was a loss that he still felt, as he had for nearly half a year.

"Is she willing to give up custody of the child?"

Nick forced his thoughts back to Hillary again and shook his head. "She's afraid of what people will think if she gives him up. She's afraid they'll think she's a drunk and a whore, which she is, but she doesn't want to admit it to the whole town. She might as well, she's slept with them all, for chrissake." But not lately, he had to admit. She had been faithful to Markham, as she had never been to him.

"You're going to have a tough fight, Nick. Very tough. The divorce will be a snap, on these grounds, and she wants out, but custody cases are a bitch. The court almost always rules with the mother, unless she's a mental case locked up somewhere. Even if she's a drunk, as you put it, or a whore, most of the time that isn't enough. The courts believe that mothers should have the kids, not men."

"Not in this case."

"You may be right. But we have to prove that, and it's going to be an ugly fight. You'll have to pull out every ounce of dirt you can get. Do you really want to drag your son through that?"

"No. But if I have to, I will. And if you tell me I have no choice, then we'll start a smear campaign that won't quit. She's given me the ammunition over the years, and I'm going to use it all now. It's for Johnny's good in the long run."

Greer nodded. He enjoyed a tough case. "And if you're right and she doesn't really want the boy, she may give up."

"She might." But he didn't really think she would. "And in the meantime, I want a restraining order on Markham to keep him away from my son."

"Where's the boy now?"

"He's still at our apartment with me. I told the maid not to let Hillary back in for her things. I'll send them to Markham's place myself."

"She has a right to see the child."

"The hell she does. Not as long as she's consorting with a man who pulled a gun on him."

"That was to impress you, Nick." Greer's voice was painfully calm, but Nick was too wound up to hear him.

"Well, guess what? It did. Now, will you take the case?"

"I will. But I want to make something clear to you right now. I can't guarantee the outcome, Nick."

"I don't care. Give it the best shot you've got."

"Will you do what I say?"

"If it makes sense to me." He smiled, and Greer wagged a finger at him from across the desk. "All right, all right. How long do you think it'll take?"

"You can agree to let her go to Reno for the divorce. That way it would only take six weeks. But the custody matter could take a long time."

"How long? I don't want Johnny living with this thing over his head, or mine."

"Maybe a year."

"Shit. But if I win, she's out of his life for good?"

"Could be. You could also try to buy her off."

Nick shook his head. "That won't do. She's got a trust for six million dollars, and Markham's worth a small fortune too."

"So much for that. We'll have to win this one fair and square."

"And if you can't, cheat." Nick grinned, and Ben Greer did too.

"You tell me how and I will. Anyway, I'll get that restraining order for you today. I have to be in court in half an hour." He glanced at his watch. "And I want to meet with you to plan our campaign. How about next week?"

Nick looked disappointed. "Not before that?"

"You won't get to court on this for at least six months."

"All right. But, Ben"—he looked intently at his lawyer across the desk—"remember one thing."

"What's that?"

"I intend to win."

Chapter 29

Nick didn't see Hillary again for several days and when she came back to the apartment, he was waiting. She let herself in with her key when she thought he'd be at work, and tiptoed quietly upstairs. But Nick had suspected she'd do something like that and he hadn't gone to the office since she'd left. He'd taken all his calls at home, and kept Johnny home from school. He was in his room when Hillary opened the door, but Nick was right behind her.

"Get out of our house." She jumped a foot when she heard his voice behind her, and when she turned, she saw that he was rigid and pale and she was suddenly afraid that he would hit her.

"I've come for my son." She tried to look nonchalant but he saw that she was shaking. And then she turned to John. "Pack your bags. You're coming with me." The child looked immediately to his father.

"Johnny, please wait for me in the den. I want to speak to your mother."

"Pack your bags." Hillary's voice was shrill, and Nick crossed the room then and gently led the frightened child from the room.

"Daddy, is she going to take me?"

"No, she isn't, son. Everything's going to be all right. She's just upset. Now, wait for me downstairs. That's a good boy." He watched the boy scamper down the hall to the den, and then turned back and walked back into the child's bedroom, where Hillary was throwing clothes into a valise. "Don't waste your time, Hil. I'm going to call the police and they're going to throw you out on your ass. Or would you like to leave now and spare me the trouble?"

"You can't keep my child here. I'm taking him with me." She turned and there was fire in her eyes.

"You're a whore. You don't deserve to be his mother." She slapped her husband and he grabbed her arm. "Now, get out of my house. Go back to that son of a bitch who wants you. I don't."

Hillary glared at him in impotent rage. She knew she wasn't winning the battle. But she would. Come hell or high water, she was going to. "My son belongs with me."

"Not with a man who'd hold a gun to his head to get me to agree to a divorce. I assume you got the restraining orders." She nodded. Markham had been served with them the previous morning. "Good. Now, get out of this house before I call the cops."

"You can't take my son away from me, Nick." She was beginning to whine, and he had to fight himself not to hit her. Instead, he yanked open the door and waited for her to leave the room.

"You never wanted him before, and I don't see why that should change now."

"If I don't have him, my name will be ruined. . . ." She began to cry. Philip's mother was already giving them trouble. He had gone through most of his own fortune on his first four wives, and now he needed Mama to bail him out of his debts and eventually leave everything to him. He had told Hillary that she had to get the boy, or God only knew what his mother would think. She had to get him, no matter what, but she had told Philip this would happen. She knew Nick, and as she looked at him now she knew she was in for a world of trouble.

"Get out!"

"When can I see him?"

"After we go to court."

"When will that be?"

"Maybe next summer."

"Are you crazy? I can't see my child till then?"

It was not what Nick's lawyers had told him, but he didn't give a damn. He was not going to let this woman near Johnny. He still trembled when he thought of Markham putting the gun to the child's head, and she had peacefully sat there and let him. And maybe she had known that the gun wasn't loaded, but Johnny did not. He had been terrified, his face deathly pale, his breathing labored. Just thinking about it made Nick want to kill her.

"You don't deserve to ever see that child again, after what you've done."

"I haven't done shit!" she shouted at him. "Philip was just trying to scare you."

"Congratulations. I hope you'll be very happy. He's the perfect man for you, Hil. I'm just sorry you didn't meet him sooner." He grabbed her arm, pulled her out of Johnny's room, into the hall, and shoved her into the main hallway. "Now, get out of here before I kick you out the door." She looked at him strangely for a moment, his threat would have suited her plans. She was pregnant, and she wanted an abortion. But Philip had sworn to her that he'd find someone to do it in New Jersey. He didn't want a baby any more than she did, but just in case he couldn't find someone decent to do the abortion, he thought they should get married, and soon. Hence the gun. They had to get married before his mother got wind of the situation.

"If you threaten me, Nick, Philip will kill you."

"Let him try."

She glared at Nick then and walked slowly toward the front door. It was hard to believe this had once been her home. She felt nothing for it now. She never did. She had never felt anything of what she felt for Philip, for Nick. And when she reached the front door, she turned around and looked at him long and hard. "You'll never win this in court, Nick. Never. They'll give Johnny to me."

"Over my dead body."

"That"—she smiled sweetly at him before closing the door—"would be a pleasure."

And with that she was gone and he went to the library to find John, who was crying softly as he lay on the couch. Nick sat down next to him and gently stroked his head. "It's all right, son. It's all right."

Johnny turned to look up at his father. "I don't want to live with her and that man."

"I don't think you'll have to."

"Are you sure?"

"Almost. It's going to take some time, but we'll win. I'm going to go to court, and we'll fight a good fight." He bent down and kissed the child's hair. "And after Christmas vacation, my friend, you're going back to school, and everything will be just like it was before, except that it'll be just you and me around here, without Mommy."

"I thought that man was going to kill me."

Nick's jaw clenched again at the thought. "I would have killed him if he had." And then he forced himself to smile down at the boy. They had to get back to some kind of normal life, he knew. "Nothing like that will ever happen again."

"But what if they come back?"

"They can't."

"Why not?"

"It's too complicated to explain, but the court served him with some papers that say he can't come near you." And that afternoon, when Johnny was playing in his room, Nick made some new arrangements. He hired three bodyguards on loan from the New York police force to work a twenty-four-hour shift. There would be one of them with the boy at all times, in the apartment, in school, in the park. They were going to become Johnny's shadows.

The next day they were both relieved to read in the gossip

columns that Hillary, and Philip Markham, had left for Reno. Nick's lawyer had notified her at once that Nick would agree to the Reno divorce and that, as long as he didn't contest it, it would be legal. Hillary had lost no time. She was in a big hurry to get divorced and marry Philip Markham. And Nick was glad, it was Christmas Eve and he wanted to spend the evening peacefully with Johnny. They shared Christmas dinner quietly in their apartment, and on Christmas Day they went out to the park to play. Nick had bought Johnny a new bicycle, a new football, and a pair of skis. He tried the skis out on a little hill covered with snow as the bodyguard watched, grinning. Johnny was a cute kid, and Nick was a good father. He hoped he won his case. And in the meantime, nobody was going to lay a hand on Johnny.

Chapter 30

"Merry Christmas, Uncle George." Liane handed him a large package and he looked, surprised. They were sitting around the tree he had set up in the library downstairs. There hadn't been a Christmas tree in the house in years, but he wanted the girls to have a beautiful Christmas.

"You're not supposed to give me presents!" He looked embarrassed as he opened his gift, and seemed very pleased as he took out the dark blue and wine-colored silk dressing gown. And she had bought him navy blue suede slippers to go with it. She had teased him about the raggedy bathrobe he wore, and he always said that he'd had it for forty years and liked it. The girls gave him a new pocket watch, and they were as excited about it as he was. Liane had helped them pick it out at Shreve's, and they had also made him little gifts at school, ashtrays, and decorations for the tree, and pictures, and Elisabeth had made him an impression of her hand in clay. It was a Christmas that brought tears to his eyes, and Liane was pleased. He did so much for them that it was a good feeling to do something for him for a change.

They had Christmas dinner at home that afternoon, and then they all went for a drive to see the decorations around the city. But as they sat in the car, Liane found herself worrying about Armand and what kind of Christmas he was having in Paris. She suspected that it was grim, and knew how much he must have missed her and the girls. It was the first Christmas in eleven years that they had been apart, and she felt a dull ache in her chest to be without him.

Uncle George saw the look in her eyes as they got out at the St. Francis to have tea, and he was sorry too. He wanted her to forget him and meet someone else, but he knew that on Christmas it was inevitable that she think about her husband.

"Uncle George, look!" The girls distracted them both. They had discovered the enormous gingerbread house set up in the lobby. It was so large that the girls could have walked inside, and it was covered with thousands of tiny candies and tons of spun sugar. "Look at that!" Liane stood beside them with a smile, but her thoughts were far, far away. For days now, she had had a desperately worried feeling about Armand.

"Monsieur de Villiers?" He looked up from his desk. It was Christmas night, but there was no reason for him not to be working, and a few others had also come to the office. There had been an aura of tension in the office for weeks. The Resistance had stepped up their efforts so enormously in the past month that it was a struggle for Pétain's people to keep one step ahead of them. And the Germans did not find it amusing. In order to make their point, they had held their first public execution only two days before. Jacques Bonsergent had been shot for "an act of violence against an officer of the German Army," and a pall of depression had fallen over Paris. Even the softening of the midnight curfew after that, for one day on Christmas, had had no effect. The cafés were allowed to stay open until 2:30 A.M. that night, and all traffic had to cease by three. But after the shooting of Bonsergent, no one wanted to be out anyway, except the Germans.

It was bitter cold in Paris that year, and it suited Armand's mood. His hands were almost numb as he sat at his desk, thinking of Liane and his daughters.

"Monsieur, have you seen this?" His zealous young assistant handed him a sheet of paper with disdain. It was entitled "La Résistance" and dated December 15, 1940, and it claimed to be the first edition of the only bulletin of its kind, published by the National Committee of Public Safety, giving news "as it really was," as opposed to the propaganda being spread by the Occupied Forces. It spoke of the student demonstrations that had taken place in November, and the Faculté being shut down after that on November 12, and it reported the increased strength of the underground now. The little bulletin said that as of December, the Resistance had never been stronger. *"Soyez courageux, nos amis, nous vainquerons les salauds et les Bosches. La France survivra malgré tout . . . Vive de Gaulle!"* . . . Be brave, our friends, we will best the bastards and the Germans. France will survive in spite of it all . . . Long live De Gaulle! . . . Armand read it and was instantly sorry that he couldn't show it to Liane, and he didn't dare send it out in one of his letters, lest in some way it be traced back to him, and he couldn't afford to keep it on him. He handed it back to the young man, and wondered how Jacques Perrier had fared. He had gone to Mers-el-Kebir, in Algeria, the summer before, to be with De Gaulle. It was there that the French fleet had been seriously damaged, with the loss of more than a thousand lives. But Armand had heard several months earlier that Perrier was still alive, and he hoped he'd survive the war. But now his new assistant was looking down at him, expecting a reaction.

"Ça ne vaut pas grand-chose." It isn't worth much. "Don't worry about it."

"The little pigs. They call themselves the true press." Thank God for that, Armand thought silently, wondering why this young man was so fond of the Germans. He was ecstatic working for Armand, who was the official liaison now between Pétain's men and the German occupying forces in Paris. They were expected to report the collection of artifacts to be handed over to the Germans, the rounding up of Jews, and the discovery of any possible Resistance agents. It was a draining job and Armand looked ten years older than he had when Liane had left. But it was an ideal situation for him, giving him ample opportunity for reporting falsified facts, hiding the treasures he had spoken of to Liane, and assisting others in getting to the South of France, most often by shuffling and falsifying reports and papers. The young man who had handed him the newspaper was his greatest obstacle. He was much too interested in his job, like now, when he could have been home on Christmas with his family or his girl friend, but he was too busy trying to impress Armand.

"Don't you want to go home now, Marchand? It's getting late."

"I'll leave with you, monsieur." He smiled. He liked Armand. He was a great man for France, not like the other traitors who had gone to North Africa with De Gaulle. If he could have read Armand's mind at that moment and discovered the hatred there, he would have shuddered. But the years in the diplomatic service had served Armand well. He was ever charming and calm and efficient, and at times nothing less than brilliant. It was why Pétain had wanted him so much, and why the German High Command liked him, although they weren't always sure that they trusted him absolutely. In time, but not quite yet. The Pétain government was still too new, and they were only French, after all. But there was no doubt, Armand had been very useful to them.

"I may not leave for hours, André."

"It's all right, sir."

"Don't you want to spend at least some of Christmas at home?" They had been there all day, and the young man was driving him crazy.

"Christmas is much less important than this." And what had they done? Gone over endless lists of names of possible Jews, some only quarter Jewish, or half, and some allegedly being hidden in the suburbs. It was work that made Armand sick, but the younger man loved it. And Armand had skimmed over entire groups of names whenever he could, burning the lists quietly in the fireplace in his office.

At last, in desperation, Armand decided to go home. There was nothing left to do here, and he couldn't hide any longer from the fact that his house was silent and empty. He dropped André Marchand at his home in the Septième, and went on to the Place du Palais-Bourbon, aching, as he always did, for Liane and his daughters.

"Good night, girls." Liane kissed them in their beds in the house on Broadway. "Merry Christmas."

"Mommy?" Marie-Ange picked up her head after the light was out, and Liane stopped in the doorway.

"Yes?"

"How long has it been since you heard from Papa?" She felt the familiar mixture of worry and longing slice through her.

"A little while."

"Is he all right?"

"He's fine. And he misses you very much."

"Can I see his letters sometime?"

Liane hesitated and then nodded. There was much in them that she didn't want to share, but the child had a right to some contact with her father. And he had precious little time and paper to write very often to the girls, he saved most of his energy and thoughts for Liane. "All right."

"What does he say?"

"That he loves us, and he talks about the war, and things he sees."

Marie-Ange nodded and, in the light from the hallway, looked relieved. "No one at school here says that he's a Nazi."

"He's not." Liane sounded desperately sad.

"I know." And then after a pause, "Good night, Mommy. Merry Christmas." And with that Liane walked back across the room to kiss her again. She was almost eleven now and growing up very quickly.

"I love you very much." She swallowed to hold back tears. "And so does your papa."

Liane saw that her daughter's eyes were damp. "I hope the war is over soon. I miss him so much." She began to sob. "And I hated it—when—they called him—a Nazi—"

"Shh . . . darling . . . shh . . . we know the truth. That's all that matters."

Marie-Ange nodded and held her mother close and then she lay back on her pillow with a sigh. "I want him to come home."

"He will. We just have to pray that we can all be together again quickly. Now, go to sleep."

"Good night, Mommy."

"Good night, love." She closed the door softly and went to her own room. It was eight o'clock at night, already five o'clock in the morning in Paris. And Armand lay in his bed in the Place du Palais-Bourbon, in a deep, exhausted sleep, dreaming of his wife and daughters.

Chapter 31

*I*n December Roosevelt took a two-week vacation and went fishing in the Caribbean, and when he returned, it was with a revolutionary new idea, the Lend-Lease program for England. It was a system by which America could supply Britain with a large stream of munitions, free of charge, in exchange for which the United States got leases on naval bases from Newfoundland to South America, and the program allowed the United States to maintain neutrality and at the same time help the English. On the whole, America had changed her tune by the end of 1940. Everyone acknowledged at last that Hitler was a deadly threat to the survival of Europe, and admiration for the British had reached its height. They were a brave, noble people fighting for their lives. And Churchill's pleas from London did not fall on deaf ears: "Give us the tools and we will finish the job. . . ." And on January 6, Roosevelt spoke before Congress. With his Lend-Lease program he wanted to give the British the "tools," and a savage debate began that raged for two months. It was still raging when Hillary Burnham returned from Reno on February 8, a free woman.

She and Philip Markham had stayed at the Riverside Hotel for a little over six weeks, and like all the others, when she got her divorce, she threw the narrow gold wedding band Nick had given her into the Truckee River. The diamond ring he had given her along with it, she saved to sell when she got back to New York. But there were other things on her agenda first. She tried to see Johnny outside his school, but the bodyguard on duty wouldn't let her near him. Instead, she turned up at Nick's office without an appointment and forced her way in, despite his secretary's futile attempts to keep her out. She stood in the doorway in a new sable coat, wearing a new large pear-shaped diamond ring, which did not escape his notice.

"So, the great man is in. It's like trying to get in to see God." She looked very confident, and very vicious, and terribly pretty. But he was immune to her now. He looked up from his desk as though he were in no way surprised to see her.

"Hello, Hillary. What do you want?"

"In a word, my son."

"Try for something else. You'll have better luck."

"So I notice. Who's the goon who stands over him like a mother hen?"

Nick's eyes glittered unpleasantly. "I gather you tried to see him."

"That's right. He's my child too."

"Not anymore. You should have thought of that a long time ago."

"You can't wish me away, Nick, no matter how much you'd like to. I'm still Johnny's mother." But there was something very ruthless in his face as he got up and crossed the room.

"You don't give a damn about that child." But he was wrong. She did. She was getting married on the twelfth of March, and Mrs. Markham was already making comments about the scandalous legal proceedings between Hillary and Nick. She wanted Hillary to have custody so there would be no scandal. Philip and Hillary were creating enough of one by living together.

"I'm getting married in five weeks, and I want Johnny there."

"Why? So people won't talk? Go to hell."

"He belongs with me. Philip and I love him."

"That's strange." Nick leaned back against his desk. He didn't want to come any closer to her. It was as though she exuded poison. "I seem to recall that he's the man who held a gun to my child's head."

"Oh, for chrissake, stop talking about that."

"You came to see me. I didn't come to see you. If you don't like what I have to say, get out of my office."

"Not until you agree to let me see my son. And if you don't"—her eyes were just as vicious as his—"I'll get a court order and you'll have to." Philip had already taken her to see his attorneys, and she liked their style. They were a tough bunch of bastards.

"Is that right? Well, why don't you have your attorney call mine and they can discuss it. You can save the cab fare coming down here to see me."

"I can afford it."

"That's true." He smiled. "But your fiancé can't. I hear he's gone through his money and he's on an allowance from his mommy."

"You son of a bitch . . ." He had hit a nerve, and she walked to the door then and yanked it open. "You'll be hearing from my lawyers."

"Have a nice wedding." The door slammed, and he reached for the phone and called Ben Greer.

"I know you don't like it, Nick. But you have to let her see him. You have bodyguards for the boy, she can't do any harm."

"He doesn't want to see her."

"He's not old enough to make that decision."

"Says who?"

"The State of New York."

"Shit."

"I think you'd be smart to let her see him. She may lose interest after she sees him a couple of times, and that would look good for us in court. I really want you to think it over."

Nick did and he was still adamant when he met with Greer in the man's offices a few days later.

"You know, if you don't, she can get a court order and force you to let her see the boy."

"So she said."

"She happens to be right. By the way, who are her attorneys?"

"They must be Markham's men. Fulton and Matthews." Greer frowned at the names. "Do you know them?"

He nodded. "They're very tough, Nick. Very tough."

"Tougher than you?" Nick was smiling but he looked worried.

"I hope not."

"You *hope* not? That's some lousy answer. Can you beat them or not?"

"I can and I have, but they've beaten me a couple of times too. The fact is she's gotten herself the toughest bastards in town."

"She would. Now what?"

"You let her see the boy."

"It makes me sick."

"It'll make you just as sick if they force you."

"All right, all right." He had his secretary call Hillary that afternoon and suggest a visit on the following weekend. He expected her to say that she'd be away, but she agreed, and she appeared at the appointed hour at the apartment. Nick had instructed the bodyguard to call the police and have Markham arrested if he showed up with her. With the restraining orders still in force, that was fair play, but Markham was smart enough not to show up. Hillary came alone, looking demure in a navy-blue suit and a mink coat Nick had given her.

Nick stayed downstairs in his study, and the bodyguard was posted outside the child's room, and instructions had been given to leave his door open. It was not an easy visit by any means, and as she left, Hillary dabbed at her eyes and kissed Johnny.

"I'll see you soon, darling." And when she left, it was obvious that he was confused and torn by his mother's tears.

"Dad, she says she cries herself to sleep every night. She looked really sad. . . ." Johnny looked desperately unhappy as he showed his father the presents she'd brought him, a new baseball hat, some toy guns, a big stuffed bear he was much too old for, and a toy train. She had no idea what the boy liked so she had bought it all. And Nick had to restrain himself from further comment. It just upset the boy and he knew it. She was playing a game with him, and Nick thought it best not to confuse him any more than he already was. But the situation did not improve. She arrived every Sunday, laden with gifts, and sobbed in anguish in her son's room. Johnny was beginning to lose weight and look extremely nervous. And Nick reported it to his lawyer.

"Look, she's driving the kid nuts. He doesn't know what to think. She sits there and she cries, and she feeds him a lot of crap about crying herself to sleep every night." Nick ran a hand nervously through his hair. He had had an argument with the boy that morning when he'd called his mother a bitch. Johnny had defended her.

"I told you it was going to be rough, and it's going to get a lot worse before we're through. Fulton and Matthews are no fools, they're telling her exactly what to do. They've written the script and she's playing it to perfection."

"That's quite a little drama she's playing."

"Of course. What do you expect her to do?"

"She's capable of anything."

She continued the visits until the day of the wedding, and then she and Philip spent a three-week honeymoon in the Caribbean. And actually, she needed the rest. She hadn't felt quite herself since the abortion Philip had arranged in Reno, and the visits with Johnny were a hell of a strain. She was sick and tired of buying him gifts and waving a damp hankie.

"Look, damn it," she told Philip on the beach in St. Croix, "he's not an easy kid, and he's crazy about his father. What do you expect me to do next? I've bought out goddamn Schwarz. Now what?"

"Well, you'd better think of something. My mother says that if this scandal continues when we get back, she's cutting off my money."

"You're a grown man. Tell her to drop dead." The blush was off the rose, and the heat in the Caribbean was making her nervous. "What the hell do you expect me to do?"

"I don't know. What about your trust? That might be easier than trying to force Burnham to give up the kid."

"I can't touch my trust till I'm thirty-five. That's another six years." The income she got had helped a lot, but it was not enough for them to live the way they liked to. They needed Mrs. Markham's help to do that.

"Then we have to have the kid. Nick's a fool, if we go to court, he won't win."

"Tell *him* that." She sighed and looked up at the sun. "He's a stubborn man." As she knew only too well.

"He's a damn fool. Because he'll lose, and in the meantime my mother's going to drive me crazy." He stared out to sea, and Hillary got up and walked along the beach. It annoyed her now that Philip was so much under his mother's thumb. He hadn't seemed to be before, but he was now. When she came back and lay down next to Philip again, she sighed and closed her eyes in the bright sun. And the problem of Johnny was quickly pushed out of her head as her husband rolled over on top of her and began to pull the top of her bathing suit down.

"Philip, don't!" But she was laughing. He was an outrageous man, and she had liked that about him from the first.

"Why not? There's no one around for miles."

"What if someone comes along?" But his mouth silenced her words and a moment later the bathing suit was down, then off, tangled with his discarded trunks in the sand, as they lay on the beach and made love. And the last thing on either of their minds was Johnny.

Chapter 32

*I*t was the first of April when Hillary and Markham got back to New York and another week before Nick heard from her. It was unusually warm and Hillary said she wanted to take Johnny to the zoo. Her call dashed his hopes, because he had thought that maybe she wouldn't resume the visits when she got back, but here she was again. He sat in his office, looking annoyed as he spoke into the phone.

"Why the zoo?"

"Why not? He always liked it before." He did, but Nick felt better having her visit in the house, where he knew what was going on. And then he realized that if he refused, she'd probably tell the boy, and then he'd be the bad guy with his son.

"All right, all right." He'd send the bodyguard along, although he knew he had nothing to fear. She was biding her time until the court date, buying out F.A.O. Schwarz to impress their son. But it still made him feel better to have the guard along.

She showed up promptly at two o'clock on Saturday afternoon, in a bright red dress and a matching hat and white gloves, looking innocent and very pretty.

"Hi, sweetheart, how've you been?" She chirped at Johnny like a little bird, Nick thought to himself as they left. She had even had the forethought to wear flat shoes. He went back into his library after they left. He had some work to do. They were getting enormous contracts from Washington now, tied in with the new Lend-Lease program that had finally gone through in March. Nick had even gone to Washington twice to watch them lobby for the bill, and he was pleased with the results. It created an enormous new workload for him, but it tripled his income too. Burnham Steel was doing very well thanks to the war in Europe.

And he had almost gotten halfway through his stack of work when there was a pounding on his door and suddenly the bodyguard flew in, still breathless. He had run all the way home from the zoo. He looked at Nick with wild eyes now, his gun still in his hand.

"Mr. Burnham . . . Johnny's gone." The man's face was deathly pale, but Nick's was more so as he jumped up.

"What?"

"I don't know what happened . . . I don't understand . . . they were right there, next to me, and she wanted to show him something near the lion's cage, and suddenly they were running . . . and there were three men. They had a car parked on the grass. I ran like hell, but I was afraid to fire and hurt the boy. . . ." Suddenly there were tears in the man's eyes, he liked the boy and he liked Nick, and he had failed dismally. "Christ . . . I don't know what to say . . ." He looked bereft and Nick took the guard's shoulders in his own powerful hands and shook him like a little child.

"You let her take my son? You let her—" He was almost incoherent with rage, and he had to fight to hold himself back. He threw the man against the desk then, grabbed the phone to call the police, and then called Greer at home. His worst fear had come true. His child was gone, God only knew where. The police arrived in less than half an hour, and Greer just on their heels. "She kidnapped my son." He spoke in a trembling voice, and the bodyguard filled them in as Nick turned to Ben. "I want him found and I want her put in jail."

"You can't do that, Nick." Ben's eyes were sad but his voice was calm.

"The hell I can't. What about the Lindbergh law?"

"She's his mother, that's not the same thing."

"Markham isn't. He's behind all this. Goddamn—" Ben touched his shoulders with a quiet hand.

"They'll find the boy."

"And then what?" There were tears in Nick's eyes and his chin trembled like a child's. "I lose him in court? Goddamn it, isn't there any way I can keep my son?" And then he went upstairs and slammed the door to his own room, and he dropped his face into his hands and began to cry softly.

Chapter 33

$\mathcal{L}$iane read the newspapers in San Francisco the next day. JOHNNY BURNHAM GONE! the headline read, and just below, BURNHAM STEEL HEIR KID-NAPPED. She felt her heart leap in her chest as she read, and it was only as she read the paragraph beneath, as she held the paper with trembling hands, that she realized that Hillary had kidnapped him. She knew Nick must be beside himself and once again she thought of calling him. But what could she do now? Offer her condolences, her regrets? There was no point asking him how he was. She knew that from reading the newspaper. He must have been frantic, looking for Johnny.

She followed the news over the course of the next two months, and still Johnny had not been found, and the news was grim everywhere.

During this time, in a moment of madness, Hess, one of Hitler's chief commanders, had made a solo flight into Britain to try to get them to give up. Instead, he crashed, and was arrested on the spot, and Hitler declared him mad. But he wasn't as mad as all that. By the end of June it was apparent what he had tried to do. He had wanted the British to give up, so Hitler wouldn't open what the Germans called the Western Front. On June 22, Hitler invaded Russia, nullifying their mutual nonaggression pact and crossing their borders at all points, costing an incredible number of lives, much to everyone's horror. And within eleven days the Germans had occupied an area larger than France. The only good to come out of it was that on July 25, Roosevelt's right-hand man, Harry Hopkins, flew to Moscow to suggest a Lend-Lease program to the Russians. But they refused it and it became clear that the only good Hopkins had done was to arrange a conference between Churchill and Roosevelt on August 9, which took place in Argentia Bay, in Newfoundland, and the Atlantic Charter was born there. It was the first meeting between Churchill and Roosevelt, and each arrived on board ship, Churchill on the *Prince of Wales,* and Roosevelt on the *Augusta.* They moved back and forth between the two ships, both vessels in full wartime camouflage. Both men were extremely pleased with the results, and Britain was to receive further aid. And still Johnny Burnham had not been found by his father.

The court date had long since been postponed, and in the four months since Johnny had disappeared, Nick Burnham had lost thirty pounds. A fleet of investigators and bodyguards had combed the States, ventured into Canada, and looked everywhere. But the boy was simply nowhere. For once Hillary had really outsmarted him. He only hoped the child was safe. And then, miraculously, and out of nowhere, Nick got a call on August 18. A child who looked much like John had been spotted in South Carolina, near an antiquated, once-fashionable watering hole. He was with his parents though, and his mother was blond. Nick had chartered a plane and flown down himself with three bodyguards, and a dozen others met him there, and there they were—Johnny, Philip Markham, and Hillary, with dyed blond hair. They had rented a little antebellum house, and were living there with two black maids and an ancient butler. Markham had sworn to his mother that the scandal would end, and he thought it would, but the kidnapping had only made things worse. She was terrified now that her son would go to jail. It was she who was financing their secret lair until the fuss died down. But she wanted them to return the boy. And finally, in desperation and out of decency to Nick, it turned out that it was Mrs. Markham who had called him.

When Markham first heard the megaphones as the bodyguards surrounded the place, his first inclination was to run. But it was much too late. He was faced by two men with guns pointed at him.

"Oh, for chrissake . . ." He tried to bluff his way out. "Take the kid." The two men did, but Nick advanced on Philip with a murderous look in his eyes.

"If you ever come near us again, you son of a bitch, I'll kill you myself. Do you understand?" He grabbed his throat, and the armed guards watched as Hillary ran up to Nick and Philip and yanked hard on Nick's arms.

"For God's sake, let him go."

"God has nothing to do with this." And then he turned to Hillary and struck her hard across the face with the back of his hand. Philip grabbed him then and punched him in the jaw. There was a grinding sound in Nick's head and he lurched toward the ground, but he stood up again and punched Markham back as Hillary screamed.

"Stop . . . stop!" But Nick was already out of control and he grabbed Markham's head and slammed it into the ground, and then he stood up and left him there, bleeding profusely from a cut over his eye and groaning softly in the dirt. Hillary flew at Nick then and scratched his face, but he pushed her away from him and walked steadily toward his son.

"Come on, tiger. Let's go home." The jaw ached horribly but he felt no pain when he took Johnny's hand and walked him to a waiting car as the bodyguards covered them. But there was no fight here. There was only Hillary, and Markham, lying on the ground, and two black maids watching from the front porch of the little house. And Nick pulled his son close to him in the car, and then without shame he kissed the boy's face and let the tears come. It had been four months as close to hell as he had been, and he hoped to never come that close again.

"Oh, Dad." Johnny held him tight. He had just turned ten, and he looked as though he'd grown a foot. "I wanted to let you know that I was all right, but they wouldn't let me call you."

"Did they hurt you, son?" Nick wiped his eyes, but Johnny shook his head.

"No. They were all right. Mom said that Mr. Markham wanted to be my father now. But when his mother came to visit us, she said he had to give me back, or at least let you know that I was okay." And then suddenly Nick knew how he'd gotten the call. He vowed to thank her himself when they got back. "She said that she'd never give him any money, ever again, and that he'd probably wind up in jail." But Nick already knew that wasn't true. He wished it were. "She was always very nice to me, and asked how I was. But Mom says she's an old bitch." The guards and Nick smiled. Johnny had a lot to say on the way home, but all that Nick could glean was that the plan had got out of hand, and they'd had no idea what to do with him once they'd kidnapped him. "Will we still have to go to court against Mom?"

"As soon as we can." He looked crestfallen at that bit of news, but safe at home in his own bed that night, John held his father's hand and smiled. And Nick sat watching over him until he fell asleep, and then he walked slowly to his own room, wondering when it would all end.

But at least the next day in San Francisco Liane read the good news. JOHNNY BURNHAM FOUND. And a week after that the court date was set again. The trial was to begin on the first of October, and when it did, it was eclipsed in the news by the conferences in Moscow between Averell Harriman, Lord Beaverbrook, and Molotov, Stalin's foreign minister. They resulted in a signed protocol that the United States and Britain would send supplies to Russia, and Harriman had made a Lend-Lease agreement with the Soviets for up to a billion dollars worth of aid. Stalin had wanted the United States to enter the war, but on Roosevelt's instructions, Harriman had refused. Russia had to be satisfied with supplies and arms, and they were. And by the time the news of that had died down a little bit, Liane read that the Burnham–Markham trial in New York was in full swing.

Chapter 34

$\mathcal{H}$illary walked into court in a dark-gray suit, a white hat, her hair its natural color once again, in the company of both senior partners of the law firm representing her. And as she sat down in a chair between them, she looked extremely demure. And on his side of the court, Nick sat with Ben Greer, who had to remind him not to look so ferocious as he frowned in Hillary's direction.

The issue was set before the court—the matter of the custody of their ten-year-old son, John—and each side was given a chance to explain. Ben Greer depicted an image of Hillary as a woman who had never wanted a child, had rarely seen her son, went on extended trips without taking him along, and was allegedly promiscuous in the extreme while married to Nick Burnham.

Messrs. Fulton and Matthews, on the other hand, explained that she had a passion for her son, and had been rendered hysterical and distraught at her husband's refusal to let her take her child with her when she left him. Mr. Markham was depicted as a man who adored children and wished to assist his wife now in providing a home for Johnny. But, they continued—Nick Burnham was so consumed with jealousy and was such a violent man that he had threatened his wife and had done everything to undermine her relationship with the boy, all because he couldn't bear the fact that his wife had wanted to divorce him. The story went on and on. The issue of the kidnapping was one they handled with great care. Totally destroyed by the loss of her child, and helpless in the face of Nick's threats, Hillary had taken John, hoping to wait until they would all go to court. And then the matter had got out of hand. She was too afraid of Nick to return . . . she was afraid that Nick might hurt the child. . . . As Nick sat in court and listened to the yarn they spun, it was all he could do not to stand up and scream. And worse yet, he recognized how respectable a troop they were. Fulton and Matthews were the best, and although Ben Greer was good, Nick was beginning to fear that he was no match for them.

The trial was due to go on for two or three weeks, and Johnny himself was to be a key witness at the end. But in the third week of the trial he came down with the mumps, and the judge granted a continuance. The trial was due to resume on November 14. And in the end Nick and his attorney felt that the interruption did them good. It allowed them time to regroup and dig up additional witnesses, although Nick was disappointed at how few would testify. People didn't want to get involved. No one knew for sure . . . it had been a while . . . even Mrs. Markham wouldn't testify for him. She had done what she could in letting him know where the child was, the rest was up to him. In her eyes the damage had already been done. His name and theirs had been dragged through the papers for too long, and she didn't thank him any more than she thanked her son for that. Who got the boy now was of no importance to her, and she wished them all in hell. All that Nick could get was a handful of maids who had hated Hillary, but had never seen her actually neglect the child, they said. At the end of the second day back in court Nick threw up his hands when the Markhams left and he and Ben Greer went to confer.

"Jesus Christ, why is she doing this, Ben? She doesn't even want the child."

"She can't back down now. She's gone too far. Most court proceedings are that way. By the time you reach the end, no one wants to be there. But the machinery of justice is difficult to turn back."

In desperation the next day, he tried to buy her off, and for a brief moment he thought the battle was won. He saw the glimmer of interest in Markham's eye as they met in the halls of the court, but there was no interest in Hillary's eyes. And when Nick had walked away in despair, Philip grabbed her arm.

"Why the hell did you turn him down? How do you think we're going to live for the next few years? You can't get your hands on your trust, and you know what my mother said."

"I don't give a damn. I wouldn't take a dime from him."

"You fool." He grabbed her arm again and she shook him off.

"To hell with you both. I want my son."

"Why? You don't even like kids."

"He's mine." Like a fur coat or a jewel or a war trophy she didn't want but would reclaim. "Why should I give anything to Nick?"

"Take the money, for chrissake."

"I don't need the money." She stared at him in icy hauteur.

"Oh, yes, you do. We both need it."

"Your mother will come around." It was a possibility he was counting on too. But if she didn't, there was a struggle ahead he wasn't looking forward to. He might even have to go to work, something he didn't intend to do. And he knew Hillary never would. But she had thought of something that had escaped him. "Haven't you ever heard of child support?" She smiled sweetly up at him. "Nick is going to want to make sure Johnny has everything he wants. And so will we. *Voilà.*" She curtsied to him and he grinned.

"You're awfully smart for a pretty girl." He kissed her on the cheek and they walked back into court, and the battle raged on. The judge had estimated that they would be finished by Thanksgiving Day, and Nick tensed at the thought. What if he lost? What would he do? It was inconceivable to think of a life without his son. He dared not even think of that. And then suddenly they'd reached the end, and the attorneys were making their closing statements. Johnny had already taken the stand, but he sounded childlike and confused, torn between both his parents, a father he adored, and a mother who sobbed loudly in open court, and whom he clearly felt sorry for.

The judge had explained to all of them that normally he took a week or two to make up his mind, but given the tension that had already existed in both households for almost a year, the publicity in national press, the strain on the child, he was going to try to reach a decision more speedily this time. They would be notified when to convene again, and in the meantime everyone was to go home and wait. And when Nick left the courtroom that day, flashbulbs went off in his face, and as usual the press appeared. "What'd they say, Nick? . . . Where's the kid? . . . Who wins? . . . Do you think she'll kidnap him again? . . ." They were used to it by now, almost, and that day, when she left the court, Hillary stood on the front steps of the courthouse with Philip and gave them a charming smile. And as Nick climbed into his limousine he leaned back against the seat and closed his eyes. He'd gained back some of the weight he'd lost while Johnny was gone, but at forty, he felt twice his age.

He looked over at Greer, poring over some notes next to him, and he shook his head. "You know, sometimes I think this thing will never end."

"It will." Greer looked up at him. "It will."

"But how?"

"That we don't know. We have to wait for the judge to decide that."

Nick sighed. "Do you have any idea what it's like to have all that you hold most dear, in other people's hands?"

Greer slowly shook his head. "No, I don't. But I know what you're going through, and I'm sorry as hell." He looked at him for a moment not as an attorney, but a friend. "I hope to hell you win, Nick."

"So do I. And if I don't? Can I appeal?"

"You can. But it would take a long time. My advice to you would be to wait. Give her six months with the boy and she'll come running back to you with him. I've been watching her all this week, and she's everything you said she was. Tough, cold, shrewd. She doesn't care about him. You started something and she's going to get you back, where it hurts most."

"She has."

"But she won't. She'll give the boy back, mark my words. All she wants right now is to win. Publicly. So she looks like a good mother. America, motherhood, and apple pie, you know about that stuff."

Nick smiled for the first time in a week. "I didn't think she did. She's more interested in sable and Van Cleef."

Greer smiled too. "Not in court. She's a smart one, and her attorneys have been very good."

Nick looked at the man who had become his friend. "So have you." And then with a lump in his throat, "Win or lose, Ben, you've been great. I know you've done your best."

"That doesn't mean a damn unless we win."

"We have to."

Greer nodded, and both men fell silent as they watched the winter sky as the limousine glided swiftly uptown.

The next week was agony for them all as they waited for the call from the judge. Nick paced his room night and day, went to the office, ran home, tried to spend each spare moment with his son, and Greer felt like an expectant father. He had never cared so much about a case as he had come to care about this one in the past year. And in the Markham apartment, Hillary was as nervous as a cat. She wanted to go out and play, and for once Philip exerted some influence on her and insisted she stay home.

"How do you think it'll look if some gossip columnist sees you at El Morocco?"

"What am I supposed to be doing? Sitting here building a hobbyhorse for my son?"

"Don't be so smart. Sit tight. It's almost over." He didn't want to aggravate his mother. She was beginning to feel sorry for him, and one slip could spoil everything. He almost had to sit on Hillary, but she didn't go out. It made her very hard to live with, but Philip insisted. He played backgammon with her for hours, and bought her gallons of champagne to keep her happy, which only made him hope more ardently that his mother would relent soon. Hillary was an expensive woman to support, and his tastes weren't simple either. They had a great deal in common, as his mother pointed out whenever she could, in an unpleasant tone. Not that either of them cared. And once they had the Markham funds, or Johnny's child support, they would be happy again. Philip was just playing it safe, he told his wife as he carried her to their enormous bed. He had just pulled off her clothes and thrown them on the floor when they heard the phone ring.

It was the firm of Fulton and Matthews. Court was to convene at two. The judge had reached a decision at last.

"Hallelujah!" she told Philip with a grin as she stood naked beside the bed. "Tonight I'm free!" And not a word about Johnny was said as Philip pulled her roughly into bed and spread her legs with his own.

Chapter 35

The judge walked somberly into the courtroom, his robes flowing, his face set. The bailiff made the necessary announcement. All rose and then sat down again. And in his seat, Nicholas sat waiting with bated breath. Johnny was waiting at home for the news, Nick hadn't wanted to expose him to the tension here, and the corridors outside were already thick with reporters. Like vultures, they had sensed meat, and someone from the courthouse had tipped them off. The parties involved in the case had been barely able to fight their way in.

"Mr. Burnham," the judge began, "would you be good enough to approach the bench?" Nick looked at Ben, surprised, he had not been prepared for this, nor was Ben, it was a departure from the usual proceedings. And then the judge turned to Hillary and asked her to do the same.

They both got up and walked toward the bench and one could have heard the proverbial pin drop, and then the judge looked at them both. He was an old man with wise eyes, and he looked as though he had given the matter a great deal of thought. It had been a bitch of a case, and a tough decision to make, although to Nick the right solution to it all was clear.

"I would like to tell you both," the judge began, "that my heart aches for you both. And I have been given the ungrateful task of Solomon. Who does one give a child to? Does one cut him in half? In truth, in a situation like this, whatever one does injures the child. Divorce is a very ugly thing. And whatever decision I make, I hurt the child and I hurt one of you. It is a source of great sorrow to me that you couldn't work your problems out, for the sake of the child." He looked at them both and then went on. Nick could feel his palms sweating and his back was damp, and he could see by the way Hillary stood that she was nervous too. Neither of them had anticipated this speech and it only made matters worse. "In any case, you did not work your problems out. You are already divorced. Remarried, in your case"—he glanced at Hillary—"and because of that"—he glanced at Nick, who was in no way prepared for what came next—"I feel that the child will have a more stable home with you, Mrs. Markham. I award the child to you." He looked down at Hillary with a fatherly smile, he had been completely taken in. And suddenly Nick realized what had been said and he exploded into life, forgetting where he was.

He turned to the judge and almost screamed.

"But he held a gun to my son's head! That's the man you're giving him to!"

"I'm giving the child to your wife. And it was an empty gun, Mr. Burnham, as I recall. Your wife knew that. And . . . The voice droned on as Nick felt faint. He wondered if he was having a heart attack or only dying of grief. ". . . you will be able to visit the boy. You may submit a visitation schedule to the court, or arrange it among yourselves, as you prefer. You will turn the child over to Mrs. Markham by six o'clock today. And in light of your income, sir, the court has set the sum of two thousand dollars a month as child support, which we do not feel will be a hardship for you." Hillary had won all around and she beamed as she ran back and hugged Philip and both of her attorneys before the judge was through, and Nick stared at him and shook his head as the judge stood up and the bailiff called out "Court is adjourned!"

Nick turned on his heels then and rushed out of court, his

head bent low, with Ben Greer running right behind. They pushed their way through the crowd outside, refusing to say anything, and at last they almost fell into the limousine as a cameraman shot a last flash at the car, and Nick turned to stare at Ben.

"I don't believe what I just heard."

"Neither do I." But he did. Ben had heard it all before, but it was not the same for Nick, who sat stony-faced all the way home, wondering what he would tell his son. He had until six o'clock to pack Johnny's things, and send him away to a life he knew was wrong. And for an instant he thought of doing what Hillary had done. Kidnapping his son. But he couldn't stay hidden forever, and it would be too hard on the boy. He had to do what the court said, for now anyway.

Nick left the car and walked into the house like a man facing a guillotine. Ben walked slowly behind, not sure if he should leave or stay, and when he saw the child's face, he wished that he had left. There was more grief there than he ever wanted to see anywhere.

"Did we win?" Everything within the small boy strained and Nick shook his head.

"No, tiger. We lost." And without another word the boy began to cry, and Nick pulled him into his arms as Ben turned away, tears running down his face too, hating himself for what he hadn't been able to do. But all he could think of now were the child's sobs.

"I won't go, Dad. I won't!" He looked up at him defiantly. "I'll run away."

"No, you won't. You'll be a man and do what the court says, and we'll see each other every weekend."

"I don't want to see you on weekends. I want to see you every day."

"Well, we'll do the best we can. And Ben says we can try again. We can appeal. It'll take time, but we might win next time."

"No, we won't." The child was bereft. "And I don't want to live with them."

"There's nothing we can do right now. We have to wait a little while. Look, I'll call you every day. You can call me any time you want . . ." But his eyes were too full and his voice was shaking too. He simply held the boy next to him and wished that things had turned out differently. Life was so unfair. He loved the boy so much and he was all he had. But there was no point dwelling on that. He had to help the child, and it was difficult for them both. "Come on, tiger. Let's go pack."

"Now?" The child looked shocked. "When do I have to go?"

Nick swallowed hard. "At six o'clock. The judge thought we should get it over with right away. So that's the way it is, my friend." He held open the door, and Johnny stared at him. The boy looked as though he were in shock, but no more so than Nick. It had been the worst day of his life, and John's. And then, as he dragged his feet to the door, with tears running down his face, he looked up at Nick again.

"Will you call me every night?"

He nodded, fighting back tears with a tremulous smile. "I will."

"You swear?"

"I swear." He held up a hand and then Johnny threw himself into his arms again.

They got upstairs and as the maids watched they packed three bags full of toys and clothes. Nick wanted to do it himself. When he was finished, he stood up and looked around. "That ought to do. You can leave the rest here for when you come to stay."

"You think she'll let me do that?"

"Sure she will."

The doorbell rang at exactly six o'clock and Hillary stood outside. "May I come in?" She wore a sickly sweet smile and Nick hated her more than he ever had before. "Is Johnny packed?" She was putting salt in all the wounds, and he looked into her eyes. They were still beautiful and black, but there was no one there.

"You must be very proud of yourself."

"The judge was a wise man."

"He's an old fool." He only hoped that Ben was right and she'd tire of the child soon. Johnny came and stood beside him then and looked at his mother through his tears.

"Ready, love?"

He shook his head and clutched at Nick. And she looked into Nick's eyes.

"Is he packed?"

"Yes." He pointed to the bags in the hall. "And I want to discuss visitation with you."

"Of course." She was prepared to be magnanimous now. Nick could see him whenever he wanted. She'd made her point. The boy was hers. Let him say what he wanted about her past, it hadn't lost her custody of John. And even Philip's mother had called to congratulate them that afternoon. "I wanted to ask you something too."

"What?" He threw the word at her like a rock.

"Could we step inside?" He had never invited her to come in.

"Why?"

"I'd like to speak to you alone."

"There's no need for that."

"I think there is." Her eyes bore into Nick's, and he moved Johnny gently aside and strode into his library. She was quick to follow him in.

"I want him this weekend, if that's all right with you."

"I'll check and let you know. I'm not sure of our plans."

His hands itched to slap her face. "Call me tonight. The child's going to need time to adjust to all this. It'll do him good to come back here soon."

"How do I know you won't run off with him?"

"I won't do that to him." And she knew Nick well enough to know it was true. "What did you want to talk to me about?" His eyes were hard.

"My check."

"What check?"

"The child support. Since Johnny's coming with me now, I assume that begins today." He stared at her in disbelief, and then without a word he yanked open a drawer, dropped a checkbook on the desk, and bent to scrawl her name and his and the amount, and then handed it to her with a shaking hand.

"You make me sick."

"Thanks." She smiled at him and left the room and he followed her back to the front hall, where Johnny stood beside his bags. There was no avoiding it. The end had come. The war was lost. Nick gave him a powerful hug and rang for the elevator to take him down as Johnny cried. The bags were loaded one by one, and Hillary firmly took Johnny's hand. They stepped inside, and as the child bent his head and cried, the doors closed and they disappeared and Nick stood in the doorway, all alone, his head bent against the wall as he cried.

Chapter 36

Johnny moved in with his mother on the night of December 3. Liane read the results of the trial with grief for Nick three days later. She had feared it would come to that. It was rare for a father to win custody, yet like him, she had hoped and prayed. That morning, she folded the newspaper with an air of despair as her uncle looked at her.

"What's wrong?" He had never seen her look quite like that before, and it was a moment before she spoke. He wondered if something awful had happened in France, but he hadn't noticed it when he read the paper himself, and at last she spoke.

"Something rotten just happened to a friend of mine."

"Anyone I know?" She shook her head. He had probably read all about the trial, but she had never told him that she knew Nick Burnham. She felt a lead weight on her heart as she imagined him handing over the child. She stood up then. She had work to do. But all that day thoughts of him preyed on her mind, and this time when she picked up the phone, she didn't set it down again. She asked New York information for Burnham Steel, and when the operator dialed and the phone was answered at the other end, she asked for Nick. But they told her that he was away. She did not leave her name, and she wondered where he'd gone to lick his wounds.

She even wondered if in desperation he might call her, but he had no way of knowing she was on the West Coast. Their ties to each other had long since been cut, and it was just as well. She knew that she could never have gone on with the affair without tormenting herself about Armand, yet in Nick's case precisely what she had wanted to avoid had happened anyway. He had lost custody of his son. And now he had nothing at all. And then she smiled at herself, and realized how absurd she was. They hadn't seen each other in seventeen months and he'd been divorced for nearly a year. He probably had a charming lady friend by now, perhaps that was why he'd gotten divorced. But if he did, she hoped that the woman was kind and put balm on his wounds now, if one could. She knew how desperately he would feel the loss of his only child to a woman he hated.

"You look like someone died." George remarked on her mood again later that night. "I think you work too hard at that foolish Red Cross place." And it was Saturday too. He disapproved of that even more than her working there on weekdays.

"What we do isn't foolish, Uncle George."

"Then why do you look so depressed? You should be out having fun." It was an old refrain between them now.

She smiled at him. At least he's stopped trying to fix her up with his friends' sons. He had realized a year before that she wouldn't budge. All she lived for were the letters she got from Armand. They arrived dog-eared and limp, smuggled out through the Resistance in the South of France, and sometimes they were stalled for weeks before someone went to England or Spain, but eventually the letters reached her, and each time she would heave a sigh of relief and report to the girls that Papa was well. It still amazed George that she was so determined to hang in. There were plenty of women he knew who wouldn't have been as true. He had known some of them during the last war, he thought, smiling. But Liane was more like her father than like him. He admired it about the girl, although he thought her foolish too.

"You would have made a good nun, you know," he teased her that night.

"Maybe I missed my calling."

"It's never too late."

"I'm in training now." She always played dominoes with him and they bantered with each other night after night. It was hard to believe now that another Christmas was at hand, and she'd been in San Francisco for a year. It seemed as though the war had already gone on for a thousand years, actually more than two years in France, and Armand was still all right, she thanked God every night. He hinted now sometimes at the work he did, and she knew about André Marchand. But there was no sign anywhere that the war would end. The bombing in London still wore on, as the British carried on their brave fight, and although Germans were dying by the thousands behind Russian lines, they showed no sign of giving up the fight. And it all seemed very far from where she sat, until that same night, December 6, when she lay in bed, unable to sleep. She got up and walked around the silent house, thinking of Armand, and at last she wandered into the library and sat down at the desk. She liked writing to him late at night, it gave her more time to gather her thoughts, and she often did that. She hadn't slept well in months, and tonight she wrote for a long time, knowing that much of her letter to him would be blacked out. He could write to her through the underground, but she could not reach him by the same channels. Her letters had to reach him through the German censors in Paris. She tried to be aware of it as she wrote, and at last she yawned as she wrote the address, and stood looking out into the December night. And then, feeling better again, she went to bed.

But the next morning, she still had a troubled feeling as she rose. Her mind was filled with Armand, and she pored carefully over the paper as she always did, looking for reports of the war in Europe.

"Was that you I heard prowling around last night, Liane? Or was it a burglar?" He smiled at her over their breakfast on Sunday morning. He knew about her midnight forays now. The first time he had heard her, he had snuck out of his bedroom, holding a loaded handgun, and they had both screamed and jumped.

"It must have been a burglar, Uncle George."

"Did he get the Christmas presents?" Elisabeth bounded into the room. She was nine years old now, and the days of Santa Claus were over. She was far more concerned that a burglar might have made inroads in the enormous stack of presents gathering in an upstairs closet.

"I'll have to check." Liane smiled at her daughter as she went out to the garden with her sister. They were happy in San Francisco, and although they still missed their father, they had adjusted well, and the ugliness that had struck them in Washington had never happened here, thanks to George's caution in not referring to his niece's husband as a Nazi. Liane was grateful to him for that, and she left for her day at the Red Cross with a lighter step than she had the day before. She wondered how Nick was faring after the shock of losing custody of John, but she knew from her own sorrows that time had a way of softening life's blows. She was sure that it wouldn't be easy, but in time the agony would be less acute, just as it was now when she thought of him. He had stayed on her mind for a long time as she carried on her quiet life in San Francisco. She was often surprised at how near he seemed when she closed her eyes and remembered their crossing on the *Deauville*. But now he was beginning to seem like a distant dream. And sometimes at night, as she slept, her dreams of him would get confused with those of Armand, and she would awake not knowing where she was, or with whom, or how she had come there, until she looked out the window and saw the Golden Gate Bridge or heard the foghorns, and she would remember where she was, far from them all now. Nick was a part of the past, but a part she still cherished. He had given her something no one else ever had, and his words had stood her in good stead for the past year and a half. She had needed every ounce of the strength he had reassured her she had when they left each other. She needed it each time she waited three or four or five weeks for a letter from Armand, or read a news report that filled her with terror, or thought of Armand working with the Germans in Paris. She needed it every day, every hour, for herself, for the girls, even for Uncle George. And she needed it as she turned on the radio in her bedroom after returning from church with the children. She often listened to the radio, for the latest news, but as she did now she stood transfixed in the center of the room, unable to believe the words she was hearing. Six great battleships had been sunk or seriously damaged in Pearl Harbor, Hawaii, and the Air Corps was left with only sixteen serviceable bombers. The Japanese had made a surprise early-morning attack on Hawaii, leaving scores of dead and wounded, and there could be no doubt now, the United States had been pulled into the war with one swift, vicious gesture.

Her heart pounding, her face pale, Liane raced downstairs to find her uncle, and she saw him standing in the den, listening to the news himself, with tears streaming down his cheeks. For the first time in his life his homeland, the country he held so dear, had been invaded. Liane went soundlessly to him, and they clung together, listening to President Roosevelt's words a few moments later. There was no question about it. America was at war now. It remained only to be confirmed by the Senate the next morning, and three days later, on December 11, Germany and Italy declared war, and Congress passed a joint resolution accepting a state of war for the United States. For Americans, a new day had dawned, and a sad one. The entire country was still in turmoil over the attack on Pearl Harbor, yet everyone wondered if the Japanese would be even bolder, attacking major cities on the mainland. Suddenly nothing was certain or safe.

Chapter 37

On the morning of December 7 all was panic in New York too, but the terrors were not quite as acute as they were on the West Coast. Hawaii was a little remote, although the realization that America's shores had been attacked brought everyone to a screeching halt that morning. And Roosevelt's announcement to the nation, declaring war, was almost a relief. The United States could roll up its sleeves and fight back. The Americans' only hope was that the Japanese wouldn't get to them first, and attack the rest of the country as they had Pearl Harbor.

Nick didn't hear the news until an hour or so after it had happened. When Hillary had picked Johnny up, he had taken his car out late that night and begun driving, and by the next morning he awoke at the side of the road, deep into Massachusetts. He hadn't known where he was going and he hadn't cared. He just wanted to drive until he could go no farther. He called her the next day and spoke to Johnny, but when he inquired about the weekend, he was told that they had other plans. They were going to Palm Beach for a few days to visit Mrs. Markham, and he could imagine why, to kiss the old woman's ass for more money, not that they needed it now. All it meant to him was that he wouldn't see Johnny for another week. And having heard that, he called his office and told them he was taking a week off. Everyone knew why and he offered no explanation. He wouldn't have been able to keep his mind on his work anyway, and it was a relief to be out in the country. Although he ached for his son, he felt better after a few days of fresh air. He called Johnny every night as he had promised, and drove from one small town to the next, staying in quaint inns, eating simple meals, and getting up to go for long walks along wooded roads and beside frozen lakes. The countryside seemed to restore him, and on the day Pearl Harbor was bombed he stayed out until lunchtime, and then came back for a hearty meal at the little inn where he was staying. He had a bowl of soup, drank a tankard of ale, and ate a thick slice of cheesecake, and then absentmindedly cocked an ear as someone turned on a radio at the other end of the dining hall, sure that nothing much could be happening on a Sunday. At first he couldn't make out what they were saying, and then suddenly he listened to what was being said on the broadcast and like millions of others all over the country, he froze in shock. And then, without saying a word, he stood up and went to his room to pack. He wasn't sure what he would do there, but he knew he had to return to New York at once. His New England idyll was over. And after he paid his bill, he called Hillary's apartment and left a message for Johnny, to tell him he was on his way back and would see him that night. To hell with her goddamn visiting schedule. And with that he grabbed his bags and ran out of the inn. It took him four and a half hours to drive back to New York, and he didn't even stop at his apartment to change, he went directly to his office on Wall Street, and sat there in the Sunday silence in the clothes he had worn in the woods in Massachusetts. He knew what he was going to do now, and he had had to come here, to find peace, to be sure of what he was doing.

All the way home he had listened to the news on the radio. Air Force spotters were watching the entire West Coast, but no planes had been sighted. There were no further attacks after Pearl Harbor.

He dialed the private number himself, after making some notes on his desk, and they kept him waiting for a while, but the President came on surprisingly quickly. Everyone of any importance at all in the country would be calling Roosevelt now. But as the President of Burnham Steel, he also knew that he would have top priority.

As he sat at his desk, with the phone cradled beneath his ear, he made several hasty notes. And as he sat there in rugged clothes, on this Sunday evening, he felt in command again. He had been beaten for the first time in his life, but he wasn't beaten forever. One day he'd get Johnny back, and right now maybe it was just as well that he was with Hillary after all. He had a lot on his mind, and a lot of things were going to change now with the country at war. For a while he wasn't going to have a spare minute. He looked up seriously then as the President came on the line, and Nick told him why he had called him. It was a brief but satisfactory conversation, and Nick got everything he wanted. Now all that remained was to lock his office and see John. After he called Brett Williams.

Brett Williams was his right-hand man, and had run the United States operation for him during the year Nick was in Europe. And five minutes later Nick had him on the phone at home. Brett had expected to hear from him all afternoon, and wasn't surprised to hear from him now. They both knew what was coming. It would mean a boom for them, but it was still frightening.

"Well, Nick, what do you think?" There was no greeting, no welcome back, no mention of the disastrous attempt to win custody of Johnny. The two men knew each other well. Brett Williams had begun working at Burnham Steel in the days of Nick's father, and he had been invaluable to Nick since he took over.

"I think we're going to have one hell of a lot of work. And I think a number of other things too. I just called Roosevelt."

"You and every little old lady in Kansas."

Nick grinned. Williams was an intriguing man. He had grown up on a farm in Nebraska, earned a scholarship to

Harvard, and had been a Rhodes scholar at Cambridge. He had come a long way from the fields of Nebraska. "I made some notes. Peggy will type them up for you tomorrow. But I want to ask you a few pertinent questions now."

"Shoot."

He hesitated for a moment, wondering if he'd be willing to do it. It was a lot to ask. But Williams didn't let him down. He never had before, and Nick knew he wouldn't now. But it was good to hear it from Williams himself. He wasn't really surprised at what Nick asked, as Roosevelt hadn't been when Nick had called him. It was the only thing Nick could do, given who, and what, he was. And all three of them knew that. What Nick wondered now was if Johnny would understand too.

Chapter 38

*N*ick picked Johnny up at Hillary's apartment on Friday. He had wound everything up in the office before he left and he had the whole weekend free for his son. The boy was ecstatic to see him. Hillary watched them from the doorway with pursed lips and her greeting to Nick was cool, as was his to her.

"Hello, Hillary. I'll bring him back on Sunday at seven."

"I think five would be better." There was a brief lightning bolt of tension between them, and Nick decided not to argue with her in front of the child. He had been through enough, and Nick didn't want to spoil their visit.

"Fine."

"Where will you be?"

"At my apartment."

"Have him call me tomorrow. I want to know he's all right." Her words grated on Nick's nerves, but he nodded and they left and he questioned Johnny intensely in the car, but although the boy would have preferred living with his father, he had to admit that his mother was being decent to him. And Mrs. Markham Sr. had been very nice to him in Palm Beach. She had given him a lot of presents and took him on walks with her, and Johnny liked her. He admitted that he wasn't seeing too much of his mother and Philip. They were out most of the time, and he had the impression that Philip didn't care much for kids.

"They're okay, I guess. But it's not like living with you, Dad." He grinned broadly as he walked back into his old room and threw himself on the bed.

"Welcome home, son." Nick watched him with a happy smile, and the ache of the past nine days began to dull. "It sure is good to have you back."

"It sure is good to be here." They had a quiet dinner together that night, and Nick tucked him into bed. He had a lot to talk to him about that weekend, but it could wait. They spent Saturday skating in Central Park, and went out for a movie and a hamburger. It seemed very different from their old life, and it lacked the ease of an everyday existence, but Nick was just glad to be with John. And on Sunday he told him what he'd been putting off all weekend. They had talked several times about Pearl Harbor, and what it meant for the United States, but it was only on Sunday afternoon that Nick told him he was reenlisting.

"You are?" The child looked shocked. "You mean you're going to go fight the Japs?" He had heard that at school and Nick wasn't sure he liked the way he said it, but he nodded.

"I don't know where I'll be sent, John. I could be sent anywhere." The boy thought it over carefully and then he raised sad eyes to his father's.

"That means you'll be going away again, like when you were in Paris." He didn't remind his father that he had promised never to leave him again, but Nick saw the reproach in his eyes. No matter that the whole world was upside down and Hawaii had been bombed, he felt guilty suddenly for reenlisting. It had been that that he had wanted to check out with Williams. As the head of a major industry in the country, he could have gotten a deferral. But he didn't want that, he wanted to go and fight for his country. He no longer had his son with him, and he needed to get away from it all. From Hillary, and the courts and the agony of an appeal, and even from the reproaches in his son's eyes because he had been unable to keep him. He had realized that he needed to make some radical changes as he walked through the woods in Massachusetts, and when he had heard the news of Pearl Harbor, he had known instantly what he had to do. His call to Roosevelt had been to inform him and expedite his reenlistment. And his call to Brett had been to ask the man to run Burnham Steel in his absence. Brett was the only man he would have left it to. As long as he was willing, Nick was going. "How soon will you leave, Dad?"

Johnny seemed like a little grown-up as he asked. He had seen a lot in the last few months, and he had grown up a great deal.

"I don't know, Johnny. Probably not for quite a while, but it all depends on where they decide to send me." Johnny digested his father's words and nodded, but it threw a pall on the rest of their afternoon, and Nick was doubly glad that he hadn't told him sooner.

Even Hillary noticed how subdued the boy was when Nick brought him home. She looked at Johnny, then at Nick, and was quick to ask. "What happened?"

"I told him that I've reenlisted."

"In the Marines?" Hillary looked startled as he nodded. "But you already served."

"Our country's at war, or hadn't you heard?"

"But you don't have to serve. You're exempt."

Nick noticed their son listening to their words with interest. "I have a responsibility to my country."

"Do you want me to start singing 'The Star-Spangled Banner'?"

"Good night, John." He ignored her and kissed their son good-bye. "I'll call you tomorrow." He was reporting to Quantico, Virginia, on Tuesday, and after that he would be busy for a week or two. He had stayed in the reserves for a long time, so he didn't have to retrain, and he was going in with the same rank he'd had when he left, as a major.

And that night as Nick went back to the apartment, he wondered what Hillary would tell Johnny, that he didn't have to go to war? That he was being a fool? Then what would the boy think? That he was being abandoned. He felt suddenly tired again as he tried to sort it all out in his head, and went back to the apartment to go through some papers. He had a lot to do before Tuesday.

Chapter 39

*W*hen Nick reported to the base at Quantico on Tuesday morning, he was amazed at how many men were reporting back to duty. There were one or two faces he knew from the reserves, and legions of young boys signing up as enlisted men. And he was surprised too at how comfortable he felt to be back in uniform. He walked smartly down the hall, and a nervous young boy snapped to attention and addressed him as Colonel.

"That's General, sir!" Nick roared and the boy almost peed in his pants as Nick tried not to laugh.

"Yes, sir! General!" The brand-new private disappeared and Nick grinned as he turned a corner and ran into an old friend who had seen what he'd just done.

"You should be ashamed of yourself. Those kids are just as patriotic as you are. Probably more so. What are you doing, trying to get out of a tough week at the office?" The man who addressed him was an attorney he'd gone to Yale with, and served with in the reserves years later.

"What happened to you, Jack? Did they disbar you?"

"Hell, yes, why else would I be here?" The two men laughed and wandered down the hall. They had to pick up their orders. "I have to admit to you, though, by last night I decided I was nuts."

"I could have told you that at Yale." And then he glanced at his friend. "Any guess as to where they'll send us?"

"Tokyo. To the Imperial Hotel."

"Sounds nice." Nick grinned. It was strange being back in the military, but he didn't dislike it. He had talked to Johnny the night before too, and he thought the boy finally understood what he was doing. He had actually sounded proud of him and it took a huge burden off Nick's shoulders to hear him like that.

They saluted the officer who handed them their orders and she smiled. They were the best-looking pair she'd seen all week, and although Jack Ames wore a wedding band on his left hand, she noticed that Major Burnham didn't.

"Do we get to open these now, Lieutenant? Or do we wait?"

"Suit yourselves, just so you report for duty on time."

She smiled and Jack opened his first, with a nervous grin. "And the winner is . . . shit. San Diego. What about you, Nick?"

He opened the envelope and glanced at the single sheet of paper. "San Francisco."

"And then on to Tokyo, right, cutie pie?" Jack pinched the girl's cheek.

"That's Lieutenant to you."

They walked back into the hall, and Nick was lost in thought.

"What's the matter, don't you like San Francisco?"

"I like it fine."

"Then what's the matter?"

"My orders say I've got to be there by next Tuesday."

"So? You had other plans? Maybe it's not too late to change your mind."

"It's not that. I'll have to leave by day after tomorrow. I told my boy . . ." He stood lost in thought, and Jack understood. He had a wife and three daughters to contend with. He patted Nick on the shoulder and left him to his own thoughts, and that night Nick called Johnny at Hillary's place. There was no easy way to break the news. He already knew that he was to leave by train on Thursday night, and he would be given a twenty-four-hour leave before that. It wasn't long enough to say good-bye to his son, but it was all they had. He spoke to Hillary first and explained the situation to her, and for once she was decent and agreed to let him see the boy the following night, and on Thursday, for as long as he could. And then she put Johnny on the phone. She told Nick that she'd let him break the news himself.

"Hi, Dad."

"Major Dad, if you please." He tried to keep his tone light, but his mind was already on their good-bye. It wouldn't be an easy one for either of them, and he was terrified that the child would feel abandoned. But he knew that he was doing what he had to do. "How're you doing, tiger?"

"I'm okay." But he sounded sad again. He hadn't fully recovered yet from the news Nick had given him only two days before, and there was worse to come.

"How about spending tomorrow night with me?"

"Can I do that?" Excitement filled his voice. "You think Mom'll let me go?"

"I already asked and she agreed."

"Wow! That's great!"

"I'll pick you up at five o'clock. You can spend the night at my place, and you can figure out where you want to eat."

"You mean you already have leave?"

"Sure. I'm an important man."

His son laughed. "It must be easy being a marine."

Nick groaned. "I wouldn't say that." It was a distant memory but he still remembered boot camp eighteen years before. "Anyway, I'll see you tomorrow night. Five o'clock." He hung up and wandered slowly away from the phone. It was going to be rough saying good-bye to him, but no worse than what had happened to them only weeks before. He thought back to the trial, and then pushed it from his head. He couldn't bear the memory of the night Hillary had picked Johnny up. Not that this was going to be much easier, and he wasn't wrong.

He told Johnny over dinner the next night, and the child

simply sat and stared at him. He didn't cry, he didn't balk, he didn't say a single word. He just looked at him, and the way he did almost broke Nick's heart.

"Come on, tiger. It's not that bad."

"You promised you'd never leave me again. You promised, Dad." It wasn't a whine, just a small sad voice.

"But, Johnny, we're at war."

"Mom says you don't have to go."

He took a deep breath. "She's right. If I wanted to, I could hide behind my desk, but it wouldn't be right. Would you be proud of me if I did that? In a few months your friends' fathers will be going off to war. How would you feel then?"

"Glad that you were here with me." At least he was honest, but Nick shook his head.

"Eventually you'd be ashamed. Is that really what you want me to do?"

"I don't know." He stared into his plate for a long time. And then finally he looked up at him. "I just wish you wouldn't go."

"I wish the Japanese hadn't attacked Pearl Harbor, John. But they did. And now it's our turn to go and fight. They've been fighting in Europe for a long, long time."

"But you used to say we'd never go to war."

"I was wrong, son. Dead wrong. And now I'm going to do what I have to do. I'm going to miss you like crazy, every day and every night, but you and I both must believe that I did the right thing."

Tears seeped slowly into his son's eyes. He wasn't convinced. "What if you don't come back?"

His voice was gruff. "I will." He started to add "I swear," but he had sworn before, and lately they hadn't done so well with things he'd sworn about. "Just know that, son. Know that I'll come back and I will." He told him about San Francisco then, and eventually he paid the check and they went home. It felt strange to Nick to be back in uniform again, but for the last few days uniforms had begun to spring up everywhere. And as they left the restaurant, with their arms around each other, he wondered if one day his son would be proud, or if he'd never give a damn, feeling only that he'd been betrayed again and again, by a mother who didn't care, a judge who didn't understand, and a father who'd run off to play soldier. His heart was heavy as he tucked Johnny in that night, and the next day was worse. They took a long walk in the park, and watched the ice skaters swirling on the Wollman rink, but there were other things on their minds, and time moved too fast for both of them. He took him back to Hillary's at four, and she opened the door and looked at her son. He looked as though someone had just died, and she watched as Nick said good-bye.

"Take good care, son. I'll call from San Francisco whenever I can." He knelt beside the crying child. "You take care of yourself now, you hear? I'll be back. You know I will." But Johnny only flung his arms around his father's neck.

"Don't go . . . don't go . . . you'll get killed."

"I won't." Nick had to fight back tears too, and Hillary turned away. For once their pain had touched her too. Nick squeezed the boy tight once more and then stood up. "Go on in now, son." But he only stood there as Nick left, watching as he turned once more to wave good-bye, and then he was gone, running down the street to hail a cab, a tall blond man in uniform, with deep-green eyes swimming in tears.

He picked up his bags at his apartment then, and said good-bye to the maid. She cried too, and he hugged her once before he left, shook hands with Mike at the front door downstairs, and then he was off to catch his train, and as he took his seat with the other men, he was reminded of the last train he'd seen, the one carrying Liane to Washington as he'd stood on the platform and watched her go. How different their lives were now, or his at least. He hoped that for her nothing had changed, that Armand had survived the war thus far. And he knew now what they'd been through when she had left Toulon, the wrenching good-byes. All he could think of on the way west was his son, and his face as he'd looked up at his father and cried. He called him midway on the trip, but the boy was out and he'd had to board the train again quickly. He'd call him again from San Francisco when he arrived, but when he did, he never got to a phone at the right time. He was swamped with orders, assignments, and adjustments to the no-longer-familiar military regime. It was a relief when at last he got to his own room. The Marines had taken over several small hotels on Market Street, they had no more accommodations to house their men and it was the best they could do. And when Nick closed the door at last on Tuesday night, it was difficult to believe that he'd only been back in the military for a week. It seemed as though he'd been back for years, and he was already sick of it. But there was a war to fight. He hoped they'd ship him out soon. There was nothing for him in this town. There was a sea of uniforms everywhere. And all he wanted was a quiet place to sleep. He lay in the dark on the narrow bed in his hotel, and he was just drifting off to sleep when he heard a knock at the door. He muttered an expletive as he tripped on his way out of bed and stubbed his toe, and yanked the door open to see a nervous private standing there with a clipboard.

"Major Burnham?"

"Yes?"

"I'm sorry to disturb you but I was told to let everyone know . . ." At the very least Nick expected news of an enemy attack as he tensed to hear what the boy had to say. "There's a gathering tonight, given by the Red Cross. It's for all the new senior officers here. And because of Christmas and all . . ." Nick leaned against the doorway in his shorts and groaned.

"You woke me up for that? I've just come nearly three thousand miles and I haven't had a decent night's sleep in five days, and you banged on my door to invite me to a tea party given by the Red Cross?" He tried to glower, but he could only laugh. "Oh, for chrissake . . ."

"I'm sorry, sir . . . the CO's office thought—"

"Is the CO going to a tea party at the Red Cross?"

"It isn't a tea party, sir, it's cocktails."

"How nice." The absurdity of it all was too much for him, he sagged in the doorway and laughed until he cried. "What kind of cocktails? Kool-Aid and gin?"

"No, sir, I mean—I don't know, sir. It's just that the people here have been very nice to us, to the Marines, I mean, and the CO wants everyone to show up . . . to show our appreciation for—"

"For what?"

"I don't know, sir."

"Good. Then you can borrow my uniform and you go."

"I'll end up in the brig for impersonating an officer, sir." The private had been standing ramrod straight since the recital began.

"Is this an order, Private, or an invitation?"

"Both, I think. An invitation from the Red Cross, and—"

Nick cut in. "An order from the CO. Christ. What time is this shindig?"

"Eighteen hundred hours, sir." Nick glanced at his watch. It was almost that now.

"Shit. Well, there goes my nap. And thanks." He started to close the door, and then suddenly pulled it open again. "Where is this thing anyway?"

"It's posted on the bulletin board downstairs."

"Sir." Nick was amused. Fortunately his sense of humor hadn't left him yet. The private blushed.

"I'm sorry, sir."

"Where are you from?"

"New Orleans."

"How do you like it here?"

"I don't know, sir. I haven't been out yet."

"How long have you been here?"

"Two weeks. I was in boot camp in Mississippi before that."

"That must have been fun." They exchanged a smile of camaraderie. "Anyway, Private, since you won't agree to wear my uniform tonight, I'd better get my ass in gear and get dressed." Nick was one of the lucky few with a shower adjoining his room. He cleaned up from his trip, put on his dress uniform, and twenty minutes later he was downstairs, looking at the bulletin board. The address was clearly marked. Mrs. Fordham MacKenzie, on Jackson Street. He had no idea how to get there. He hadn't been in San Francisco in years, and he decided to call a cab. Three other officers had received the same "invitation" as he, and they shared the ride and stepped out in front of an impressive home with an iron gate and formal gardens. One of the officers whistled softly in his teeth as Nick paid the cab, and they stepped up to the iron gate to ring the bell. A butler led the way and Nick found himself wondering how many of these soirees Mrs. MacKenzie gave. The war had brought a host of new men to town. It was kind of her to throw her home open to the servicemen. Christmas was only two days away.

He had given Johnny his gifts before he left, but it certainly would be a lonely Christmas for them both. Nothing was the same this year. And now he was nearly three thousand miles away on the West Coast, walking down some strange woman's hall into a living room filled with uniforms and women in cocktail clothes as waiters passed trays of champagne. It was all a bit like a strange dream as he looked out at the Golden Gate, and then as his eyes strayed back he saw her there, standing quietly in a corner, holding a glass, speaking to a woman in a dark-red dress. And as he looked at her she turned her head, and their eyes met, as time stopped for him and the room spun for her. And slowly he walked toward her and she heard the voice she had remembered only in dreams for a year and a half. The voice was a caress and the crowds around them seemed to disappear as he spoke a single word. "Liane . . ." She looked up at him, her eyes filled with disbelief and amazement as he smiled slowly at her.

Chapter 40

"*I*s that really you?" Nick looked deep into Liane's eyes, and at the expression on his face, the woman in the red dress who'd been talking to Liane disappeared quietly. Liane smiled at him, not sure what to say.

"I'm not sure."

"I'm dreaming this." She smiled in answer. "Aren't I?"

"Could be, Major. How have you been?" Her smile was warm but there was no invitation in her words. "It's been a long time."

"What are you doing here?" He couldn't take his eyes off her face.

"I live here now. We've been here since last year." He searched her eyes for all the things he ached to know, but there was nothing written there. They were as big and beautiful as before, but they were veiled now. She had seen pain and loss and it showed, and he wondered instantly about Armand, but when he looked, the plain gold band was still in place.

"I thought you were in Washington."

"That didn't work out." Her eyes met his, but she didn't say more, and then slowly he saw the old, familiar smile. He had dreamed of it for almost two years. He had seen that smile as she had lain in his arms. "It's good to see you, Nick."

"Is it?" He wasn't so sure. She looked uncertain, almost frightened.

"Of course it is. How long have you been in town?"

"Just today. And what the hell are you doing here?" This didn't seem her kind of place, a cocktail party to meet military men. If she was wearing her wedding band, she couldn't be on the hunt, and that wasn't her style. Not the girl he'd left on the train in New York seventeen months before, unless everything had changed. Maybe her solitude had got to her.

"I work for the Red Cross. This is a command performance for us."

He bent low and whispered in her ear. "It is for me too."

She laughed at that, and then something gentle touched her face. She hadn't wanted to ask him at first, but she decided to now. "How's John?"

Nick took a quick breath and looked her. "He's fine. I don't know if you read about the trial out here, but Hillary and I got divorced about a year ago, and I fought her for custody and lost a few weeks ago. That was pretty rough on him." And he glanced at his uniform. "And so was this."

"It must have been rough on you too." Her voice was smooth as silk, and she couldn't take her eyes from his, but she also knew that she had to keep the walls up. She could never let them down again. Especially not for him. She had done that once, and she was still fighting to keep that door closed. "And yes, I did read about the trial." She spoke in the gentle voice he loved. "My heart ached for you."

He nodded and took a sip of his drink. "The judge thought Johnny would be better off with her, since she's married now. And you know what that bastard did?" His face went taut as he told her about Markham and the gun. "I was going to file an appeal, but then Pearl Harbor was hit. I'll try again when I go back, by then she may be ready to give him up. My lawyer thinks she just wanted to get back at me."

"For what?" Liane looked stunned. Had he told her about them?

"I guess for never loving me, crazy as that sounds. In her eyes, I kept her a prisoner for all those years."

Liane remembered instantly the incident on the ship, as did he. "You were far more the prisoner than she."

He nodded. "Well, that's all over now, for whatever it was worth. I got Johnny out of it, so I can't complain. Now all I have to do is get him back."

"You will." Her voice was quiet and strong. She was remembering his own words to her: "Strong people cannot be defeated."

"I hope you're right." He finished his champagne and looked at her. She was even prettier than she'd been before, but there was something quieter about her now, and more severe. The rigors she forced on herself had taken their toll, and yet her face was as lovely as it had always been, her eyes seemed even more blue, and her hair was wound into a smooth bun. She looked very chic, he decided, and smiled at his own thoughts. "Where are you living here?"

"With my uncle George."

"And the girls?"

"They're fine." And then, with lowered eyes, "They still remember you." And with that two more men in uniform suddenly joined the group, and a woman from the Red Cross, and a little while later Liane left. She didn't see Nick to say good-bye and she decided it was just as well. She drove home in the car she had borrowed from George and walked slowly inside. It had been strange to see Nick again. It opened wounds she'd hoped had healed. But there was nothing she could do about that. She had always wondered if they would meet again one day, and they had. Everything had changed for him since they had last met, but nothing had changed for her. Armand was still struggling to survive in France, and she was waiting for him here.

"Did you have a good time?" George was waiting for her when she got back.

"Very nice, thanks." But she didn't look as though she had as she took off her coat.

"It sure doesn't look like you did."

She smiled. "I met an old friend. From New York."

"Really, who?"

"Nick Burnham." She wasn't sure why she had told her uncle that, but it was something to say.

"Is he any relation to Burnham Steel?"

"He is. As a matter of fact, he *is* Burnham Steel."

"Well, I'll be damned. I knew his father about thirty years ago. Fine man. A little crazy, now and then, but we all were in those days. What's the boy like?" Liane smiled at his choice of words.

"Nice. And a little crazy too. He's just reenlisted in the Marines, as a major, he got here earlier today."

"You'll have to have him over some night before he ships out." And then suddenly George had an idea. "How about tomorrow?"

"Uncle George, I really don't know. . . ."

"It's Christmas, Liane. The man's alone. Do you have any idea what that's like in a strange town? Be decent to the man, for God's sake."

"I don't even know how to get in touch with him." And she wouldn't if she could, but she didn't tell that to him.

"Call the Marines. They'll know where he is."

"I really don't think—"

"All right. All right. Never mind." And then he muttered to himself, "If the man has any sense, he'll call you."

And the man had a great deal of sense. He had gone back to his hotel, and sat in his room for a long time, staring down at Market Street and thinking of Liane, and the strange quirk of fate that had brought them back together again. If the little private from New Orleans hadn't knocked on his door that night . . . He grabbed a telephone book off the desk and began looking for George Crockett, and found the address on Broadway with ease, and then he sat staring at it. She lived there, at that phone number, in that house. He made a note of it, and the next morning he called, but she had already left for the Red Cross, and an obliging maid gave him the number there. He dialed the number once and she answered the line.

"You're already at work at this hour, Liane? You work too hard."

"That's what my uncle says." But her hand trembled at the sound of his voice. She wished he hadn't called her, but maybe her uncle was right. Maybe inviting him to dinner was the decent thing. And maybe by exposing herself to him as a friend, the old dreams would fade at last.

"What are you doing for lunch today?"

"I have to do an errand for Uncle George." It was a lie, but she didn't want to be alone with him.

"Can it wait?"

"I'm afraid not." He was puzzled by the tone of her voice, but maybe there were other people around. The walls were up, as they had been for almost two years, he reminded himself. There was no reason to pull them down because he had breezed into town, and he hadn't asked about Armand the night before. He knew how she felt about all that, but he had accepted that before. He just wanted to see her again.

"What about lunch on Friday?"

"I really can't, Nick." And then she took a deep breath as she sat at her desk. "What about tonight? Dinner at my uncle's house? It's Christmas Eve, and we thought—"

"That's very nice. I'd like that very much." He didn't want to give her a chance to change her mind. She gave him the address and he didn't tell her he'd already written it down. "What time?"

"Seven o'clock?"

"Great. I'll be there." He hung up with a victorious grin and gave a whoop as he left the phone. He didn't feel forty anymore. He felt fifteen again. And happier than he'd been in seventeen months, or maybe ever.

Chapter 41

Nick arrived promptly at seven o'clock at the Broadway house, looking very dapper in his uniform, his arms laden with Christmas gifts for the girls. He had realized quickly what life in San Francisco was going to be like for him. There was virtually nothing for him to do. He had been assigned a desk and put in charge of some unimportant supplies, but basically, like the others, he was biding time until he shipped out, which gave him plenty of time to wander around and see friends. Now that he had found Liane and the girls, he was glad for the free time.

The butler led him down the long, stately hall and into the library, where the family had already gathered around the tree. It was their second Christmas with Uncle George, and the stockings, which they knew he would fill, were hung over the fireplace. The girls momentarily forgot about the stockings as they opened Nick's gifts eagerly, as George and Liane looked on. He had bought them beautiful toys. Each little girl hugged him warmly, and then he handed a package to George, which was obviously a book for the senior of the clan, and then he turned to Liane and handed a small box to her. He realized then that it was the first gift he'd ever given her. During their thirteen days on the ship there had been no time when he could have given anything to her, and from there they had gone straight to the train. He had thought about it often at first, with regret, that he'd never been able to give her anything, except his heart. But he would have liked to have known that she'd had something to remember him by. Little did he know that the memories he had left instead were far more durable than any gift, and she carried them deep inside her still.

"You shouldn't have." She smiled, the small box still wrapped in her hand.

"I wanted to. Go on, open it. It won't bite." George watched them with an interested eye. He had the feeling that they knew each other better than he'd realized, and perhaps better than they wanted him to know. And he watched Liane's eyes, as did Nick, as she opened the box, which held a single gold circlet for her arm, unbroken, without a catch, just a wide gold band. She slipped it over her arm now, but Nick reached out for it and spoke in a husky voice for no ears but hers. "Read what's inside." She took it off again, and there was a single word. "Deauville." And then she put it back on and looked at him, not sure if she should accept the gift, but she didn't have the heart to give it back to him.

"It's beautiful. You really shouldn't have, Nick . . ."

"Why not?" He tried to make light of what he felt, and said in a voice only she could hear, "I wanted to do that a long time ago; consider it a retroactive gift." And then Uncle George opened his book, and exclaimed with delight. It was one he'd been anxious to read, and he shook Nick's hand. George regaled them all with tales of Nick's father, and how they'd met, and an outrageous caper they'd embarked on once, which had almost got them both arrested in New York. "Thank heavens he knew all the cops." They had been speeding up Park Avenue and drinking champagne with two less-than-respectable women in the car, and he laughed at the memory, feeling young again, as Liane poured Nick a drink and another for herself. She sipped it as she watched him talk to Uncle George and felt the bracelet on her arm. She felt the weight of the gold almost as much as the single word written inside. "Deauville." She had to fight back the memories again as she sipped her drink, and force herself to listen to what was being said.

"You made a crossing together once, didn't you?"

"Twice, in fact." Nick smiled at her and she caught his eye. She hadn't told George that Nick had been on the *Deauville*.

"Both times on the *Normandie*?" He looked confused and Nick shook his head. It was too late to lie and they had nothing to hide. Anymore.

"Once on the *Normandie*, in thirty-nine. And last year on the *Deauville* when we both came back. I'm afraid I stayed over there a little too long, and got caught. I had a hell of a time getting out. I sent my son back on the *Aquitania* when the war broke out, but I didn't leave Paris until after the fall." It sounded innocent enough, and when George glanced at Liane, he saw nothing there.

"That must have been quite a trip, with the rescue at sea."

"It was." His face sobered as he remembered the men that had been brought on board. "We worked like dogs to keep them alive. Liane was absolutely extraordinary. She worked in the surgery all night, and made rounds for days after that."

"Everyone pitched in and did more than their share," Liane was quick to interject.

"That's not true." Nick looked her in the eye. "You did more than anyone aboard, and a lot of those men wouldn't have lived if it weren't for you." She didn't answer and her uncle smiled.

"She's got a lot of guts, my niece. Sometimes not as much sense as I would like"—he smiled gently at her—"but more guts than most men I know." The two men looked at her and she blushed at their words.

"Enough of that. What about you, Nick? When are you shipping out?" It sounded as though she were anxious for that, and in a way she was, not to send him into danger overseas, but to get herself out of a danger she still sensed when he was nearby.

"God only knows. They assigned me to a desk yesterday, which could mean anything. Six months, six weeks, six days. The orders come from Washington, and we just have to sit here and wait."

"You could do worse, young man. It's a pleasant town."

"Better than that." He smiled at his host, and then glanced casually at Liane. They had heard nothing from the girls since they'd opened their gifts. They were entranced with them, and he only wished that Johnny could be here too. The butler announced dinner then, and they went into the enormous dining room. As they walked, George told Nick the history of various portraits on the walls.

"Liane lived here as a girl, you know. It was her father's house then." And as George said the words, Nick remembered one of the first times they'd talked on the *Normandie*, when she had told him about her father, and Armand, and Odile, and even about her uncle George.

"It's a lovely house."

"I like to watch my ships pass by." He looked at the bay and then at Nick, with an embarrassed smile. "I suppose I'm old enough to admit that now. In my younger days, I might have pretended not to be proud of who I was." He looked pointedly at Nick, and then turned their talk to steel. He knew a great deal about what Nick did and he was impressed at his having taken on the business so young, and from what he knew, Nick had done a fine job. "Who have you left in charge while you're gone?"

"Brett Williams. He was one of my father's men, and he ran things for me in the States while I was in France." He thought for a moment and then shook his head. "Lord, that seems a hundred years ago. Who would have thought we'd be in the war by now?"

"I always did. Roosevelt did too. He's been getting us ready for years, not that he'd admit it publicly." Liane and Nick exchanged a smile, remembering their crossing on the *Normandie*, when so many had insisted that there wouldn't be a war.

"I'm afraid I wasn't as prescient as you. I think I refused to see the handwriting on the wall."

"Most people did, you weren't alone. But I have to say that I didn't expect the Japanese to come right down our throats." Already watch points had been set up all along the coast, there were blackouts at night, and California waited to see if they would strike again. "You're lucky to be young enough to fight. I was too old for the first one too. But you'll set things to right again."

"I hope so, sir." The two men exchanged a smile and Liane looked away. Her uncle never softened that way toward Armand, but then again he thought that Armand was in collaboration with the Germans. It hurt her not to be able to defend him, and Nick still didn't know about his liaison with Pétain. Somehow that bit of ugly news had never reached him. She dreaded the day that he would hear, and wondered if he ever would. Perhaps it would be after the war and then it wouldn't matter anymore.

The meal was a very pleasant one, and Nick left them early to go back to his hotel. George was an elderly man, no matter how spry he was, and Nick didn't want to overstay. He thought that Liane looked tired too when he left. She thanked him for the bracelet and the girls kissed him before he left, in thanks for the gifts. As he stood up he looked into Liane's eyes.

"I hope it's a better Christmas for all of us next year."

"I hope so too. And . . . thank you, Nick."

"Take care of yourself. I'll give you a call, and maybe we can have lunch sometime."

"That would be nice." But she didn't sound overly enthused and after he left, she put the girls to bed and came down for a few more minutes with Uncle George. He was extremely impressed by Nick, and curious as to why she'd never mentioned him before.

"I don't know him that well. We've only met once or twice, on the ships, and at a couple of parties in France."

"Does he know Armand?"

"Of course. He was traveling with his wife when we met too."

"But he's divorced now, isn't he?" And then suddenly he remembered the scandal in the newspapers all year. He rarely read that kind of thing, but that had caught even his eye. "I know, it was some kind of a shocking thing. She ran off with someone and they fought over the child." He frowned. "Where's the boy now?"

"His mother won custody of him last month. I suspect that may be why he enlisted again."

Her uncle nodded and lit a cigar. "Good man."

And then she bid him good night, and left her uncle there with his own thoughts, and returned to her room with her own. She carefully took off the bracelet that he'd given her, and looked at it for a long time, and then she put it down resolutely and tried to forget it. But even as she lay in the dark, she knew where it was and knew what was written inside. Deauville. The single word that cast a thousand forbidden images into her mind.

Chapter 42

Nick called to thank her the next day, and to wish a Merry Christmas to all of them. Liane was determined to keep the conversation formal and brief, but she felt a tug at her heart when she heard his voice. She suspected that he was desperately lonely without his son, and spending Christmas so far from home. And she couldn't resist saying something more to him.

"Did you call Johnny today, Nick?"

"I did." But his voice sagged on the words. Her guess had been correct. It was a rough day for him. "He cried like a little kid. It broke my heart. And his mother is leaving tomorrow for two weeks in Palm Beach without him." He sighed. "Nothing has changed. And there isn't a damn thing I can do about it now."

"Maybe when you go back . . ." She echoed his own thoughts.

"I'll do something about it then. My lawyer said I'd have to wait a while anyway for an appeal. And at least I know he's safe with them. Markham is a complete fool, but all he's interested in is the good life. He won't do the boy any harm." It wasn't what he had said before, but he had no choice now. He knew Hillary wouldn't shower love on him, but she would keep an eye on him. It was like leaving him with strangers for the duration of the war. "Brett Williams is going to keep an eye on things for me too. And if things get totally out of hand, he'll take control. That was about the best I could do before I left."

She listened, aching for him, she knew how much he loved the child. It was half of why she had let him go. "Is that why you signed up, Nick?"

"More or less. I needed to get out. And there was a war to fight. It's almost a relief after the last year."

"Well, don't get crazy when they ship you out." She almost thought he should have stayed home to watch over John himself, and at times he thought so too, but he was glad he'd signed up, especially since he had found her.

"I'm not gone yet." He smiled as he stood in the hall of his hotel, leaning against the wall. And then he decided to take a step. "I don't suppose I could see you today, Liane?"

There was a moment's pause. "I really ought to be here with the girls and . . ." Her voice drifted off. She didn't know what to say to him. She wanted him to know that for her nothing had changed in the last year and a half. Her feelings were the same. Both for him, and Armand. And her decision to end the affair hadn't altered.

"I understand." But again she heard the loneliness in his voice and she felt torn. A warning bell went off somewhere in her head, but she didn't heed it this time. What harm could it do? It was Christmas, after all.

"Maybe if you'd like to come by this afternoon . . ." The girls would be there, and her uncle.

"I'd like that very much."

"Around four?"

He held the phone tight. "Thanks, Liane. I appreciate it."

"Don't say that. You're an old friend."

There was a silence and then at last he spoke. "Is that what I am?"

"Yes." Her voice was soft, but firm.

"That's good to know."

He arrived promptly at four, and the girls were happy to see him when he arrived, and George was surprised.

"I didn't know we'd meet again so soon."

"I think your niece felt sorry for me, a poor sailor in a strange town." Uncle George guffawed and Nick sat down and played with the girls, and after a while Liane suggested that they go for a walk in the Presidio. George said that he'd stay home and wait for them, he wanted to read his new book. He smiled at Nick. And the others got their coats and went out as the girls pranced ahead, Marie-Ange on suddenly long, coltish legs, and Elisabeth charging along behind.

"They're growing up to be beautiful girls. How old are they now?"

"Elisabeth is nine, and Marie-Ange is eleven. And John is what? Almost eleven now?"

Nick nodded. "Time moves too fast, doesn't it?"

"Sometimes." But she was thinking of Armand, and Nick realized it at once and turned to her.

"How is he? Still in France?"

She nodded. "Yes."

"I thought he'd be in North Africa by now."

And then she looked at Nick and stopped their walk. There was no point pretending to him. She really couldn't bear it anymore. "Armand is with Pétain." Nick looked at her, but he did not seem stunned.

"You know, I got that feeling when we were on the ship. I don't know why, but I did. How does that affect you, Liane?" He knew it didn't affect her feelings, or she would have said so before.

"It's difficult to explain. But it's been hard on the girls." She told him about Washington then and the swastikas, and he winced.

"How awful for them . . . and you. . . ." He searched her eyes and found a new sadness there.

"That's why we came west. It's been easier, thanks to Uncle George."

"Does he know about Armand?"

"He knew before we came out." She sighed softly and they walked on, to keep up with the girls. It had been a relief to tell Nick, they had always been able to speak to each other openly before, and there was no reason for that to change now. After all, they were still friends. "He doesn't approve, of course, and he thinks I'm mad." And then she told him about his matchmaking during her first weeks in town, and they both laughed. "He's a dear old man. I never used to like him much, but he's mellowed a lot."

Nick laughed. "Haven't we all."

"He's been awfully good to us."

"I'm glad. I worried about you a lot. Somehow I always assumed that you were in Washington. When did you leave?"

"Right after Thanksgiving last year."

He nodded and then he looked at her. "There's more to it, isn't there?"

"To what?" She didn't quite follow his train of thought.

"To Armand being with Pétain."

She stopped walking again and looked at him with surprised eyes. How did he know? Was it something she said? But she nodded. She trusted him. It was the first time she had admitted that to anyone. To do so would have been to jeopardize Armand, yet she knew that the secret was safe with Nick. "Yes."

"That must make it even worse for you. Do you get news of him?"

"As often as he can. He runs a great risk if he says too much. I get most of his letters through the underground."

"They've been damn good in France." She nodded, and they walked on in silence for a while. It brought her closer to him to be able to be honest about Armand. He was truly her friend, and she looked at him after a time with a grateful smile. "Thank you for letting me tell you that. There are times when I thought I'd go mad. Everyone thinks—or they did in Washington. . . ."

"He's not that kind of man." He could never imagine Armand working sincerely for Pétain, even as little as he knew the man, he knew that. He just hoped that the Germans weren't as smart.

She felt as though she owed him a further explanation now. He'd been decent to her, and she'd never told him then. "That was why—I couldn't, Nick. Not with what he's doing there. He doesn't deserve that."

"I know. I understood." His eyes were gentle on hers. "It's all right, Liane. You did the right thing. And I know how hard it was."

"No, you don't." She shook her head, and he saw that she was wearing the bracelet he'd given her the night before. It pleased him to see it there, the gold glinting in the winter sunlight.

"It was just as hard for me. I must have picked up the phone to call you a hundred times."

"So did I." She smiled and looked at her daughters in the distance. "It seems a long time ago, doesn't it?" Her eyes drifted back to his then and he shook his head.

"No. It seems like yesterday."

And in a way it did to her too. He hadn't changed, and neither had she, although the world around them had. Almost too much so.

And then he played tag with the girls, and she joined them as they laughed and ran, and at last they went back to the house with pink cheeks and sparkling eyes, and George was pleased to see them, filling the old house with life. It truly felt like Christmas to him now, and to the others too. They invited Nick to stay for Christmas dinner with them, and when he left that night, they were all old friends, and Liane saw him to the door. He stood there for a moment and smiled at her.

"Maybe you're right. Maybe it is different now. I like you even better than I did before. We've both grown up a lot."

She laughed. "Maybe you have, Nick. I think I've just grown old."

"Tell that to someone else." He laughed and waved as he went out to the waiting cab. "Good night, and thanks. Merry Christmas!" he called back as the cab drove off, and Liane went back inside with a happy smile. Too happy, she decided, as she looked in the mirror. But she couldn't change the sparkle in her eyes, from the relief she felt when she went to bed. It had been good to unburden herself to him.

Chapter 43

Nick turned up in Liane's office at the Red Cross a few days after Christmas. He had had some errands to do around town, and he had the afternoon off. He strode into the office and half a dozen women stopped their work to stare. In his uniform, he was more handsome than ever. Liane laughed.

"You're going to start a riot in here if you don't watch out."

"It's good PR for you. How about lunch? And don't tell me you can't, or you have to do errands for your poor old uncle George, because I won't believe a word of it. How about the Mark Hopkins for lunch, old friend?" She hesitated, but he grabbed her coat and hat and handed them to her. "Come on." He was impossible to resist.

"Don't you have anything else to do, like fight a war?"

"Not yet. There's still time for lunch, thank God, and George says you never go out. It won't hurt your reputation to eat lunch in broad daylight. We can sit at separate tables if you want."

"All right, all right. I'm convinced." She was in a light-hearted mood and so was he; it was almost like the old days on the *Normandie*, when they'd had their tennis match. They sat at a good table and enjoyed the view. Nick told her funny stories about the men on the base and in his hotel, and for the first time in years she felt alive again. He was easy to be with, funny and smart, and he took her totally by surprise when he asked her what she was doing on New Year's Eve.

"Wait. Don't tell me. Let me guess. You're staying home with Uncle George and the girls."

"Right!" She grinned. "First prize goes to you."

"Well, you get the booby prize. Why not let me take you out? I'm safe. And if I misbehave, you can call the MPs and have me removed."

"What did you have in mind?"

"You mean I have a chance?"

"Not a bit. I just want to know what I'm going to miss."

"Oh, for chrissake." He grinned at her. "Come on, Liane. It would do you good. You can't lock yourself up in that house all the time."

"Yes, I can. And I'm happy there."

"It's not good for you. How old are you now?" He tried to count back. "Thirty-three?"

"I'm thirty-four."

"Oh, in that case . . . I had no idea you were so old. Well, I'm forty now. And I'm old enough to know what's good for you. And I think you should go out."

"You sound just like Uncle George." She was unconvinced but amused.

"Now, wait a minute. Forty is one thing, but I'm not that old!"

"Neither is he, in his heart. You know he used to be quite a rake in his day."

Nick smiled. "I can still see it in his eyes. Now, don't change the subject on me. What about New Year's Eve?"

"First it's lunch, and then it's New Year's Eve. You know, you could be quite a rake too, if you tried. Maybe even if you didn't."

"It's not my style." He looked at her seriously. "I meant a quiet evening between two old friends who've had a tough time and understand the rules. We deserve that much. Otherwise, what do I do? Sit in my lousy hotel, and you stay home? We could go to the Fairmont for dinner or something like that."

"I suppose we could." She looked at him, but she still wasn't sure. "Would I be safe?" It was a straight question and he looked her in the eye.

"As safe as you want to be. I'll be honest with you, I still love you, I always have since the first time we met, and I probably always will. But I'll never do anything to hurt you. I understand how you feel about Armand, and I respect that. I know what the boundaries are. This isn't the *Deauville*, or even the *Normandie*. This is real life."

She spoke softly as she looked at him. "That was real too."

He took her hand gently in his. "I know it was. But I always knew what you wanted to do after that, and I respected that. I'm free now, Liane, but you're not, and that's all right. I just enjoy being with you. There was more to us than just—" He didn't know how to say the words and she understood.

"I know that." She sighed and sat back in her chair with a smile. "It's funny that our paths should cross again, isn't it?"

"I guess you could call it that. I'm glad they did. I never really thought I'd see you again, except if I went to Washington sometime and ran into you on the street. Or maybe in Paris ten years from now, with Armand. . . ." And then he regretted saying his name, she looked pained again. "Liane, he made a choice, a difficult one, and you've stood by. You can't do more than that. Staying home, holding your breath, killing yourself, won't make it any easier for him. You have to go on with your life."

"I'm trying to. That's why I took the job with the Red Cross."

"I figured that. But you have to do more than that."

"I suppose I do." He made a lot of sense, and if she went out at all, she'd like it to be with him. He understood. And who knew how long he'd be around? He could be shipped out any day now. "All right, my friend, I would be honored to usher in nineteen forty-two with you."

"Thank you, ma'am."

He paid the check and took her back to work, and the afternoon seemed to fly by. She was happy to get home to see George and the girls. Her uncle noticed the look on her face and didn't say a word. And that night, she casually mentioned to him that she was going out for dinner with Nick on New Year's Eve.

"That's nice." He knew her well by now, he dared not say more, but he hoped that there was something afoot with "the Burnham boy." He buried his nose in his book, and she went upstairs to talk to the girls, and at dinner that night, not another word was said about Nick.

Liane didn't mention him again until she came downstairs on New Year's Eve, in a dress she'd bought four years before in France, but it was still beautiful and so was she. George looked her over with a happy grin as she waited for Nick, and whistled softly though his teeth as she laughed.

"Not bad . . . not bad at all!"

"Thank you, sir."

The dress had long sleeves and a high neck, it was black wool and reached to the floor, but it had tiny jet-black bugle beads sewn all over the top and a tiny cap to match, and it sat on her blond hair, swept up in a simple knot, and on her ears she wore tiny diamond clips. The outfit was simple and elegant and ladylike, and perfect for Liane. Nick thought the same when he arrived. He stood in the entrance hall for a moment and stared at her. And then he whistled, echoing George. It was the first time in years that she'd felt like a lady admired by men and it felt good. Nick said hello to George and Liane kissed him good night.

"Don't come back soon, it would be a shame to waste that dress. Go show it off."

"I'll do my best to keep her out." Nick winked broadly and all three of them laughed. The girls had already gone to bed. There was a festive feeling to the night as they left the house in the car Nick had borrowed. "I'm afraid I don't look half as elegant as you in my uniform, Liane."

"Want to trade?"

He laughed at her and they reached the Fairmont in high spirits. Nick had reserved a table in the Venetian Room, and they went inside, where he ordered champagne, and they toasted each other and a better year to come before Nick ordered them steaks, preceded by shrimp and caviar. It was a far cry from the exotic goodies of the *Normandie*, but it was a fine meal and they were both relaxed. They danced several times after dessert, and Nick felt happier than he had in a long time and so did Liane.

"You're easy to be with, you know. You always were." It was one of the first things he had noticed about her, in his days of misery with Hillary. He mentioned her now, and Liane smiled.

"You're well out of that, you know."

"Oh, God, yes! I knew it then. But you know why I stayed." It was because of John. "Anyway, those are old times, and this is almost a new year." He glanced at his watch. "Are you making any resolutions this year, Liane?"

"Not a one." She looked content as she smiled at him. "And you?"

"Yeah, I think I will."

"What?"

"Not to get killed." He looked her in the eye and she looked back at him. It brought home the point that at any moment he would be going to war, and that the casual dinners were only for a little while, and it suddenly made her stop and think, about him, about Armand, about the others around them going to war. The room was filled with uniforms. Overnight San Francisco had become a military town.

"Nick . . ." For an instant she wasn't sure what to say.

"Never mind, it was a dumb thing to say."

"No, it wasn't. Just see that you live up to it."

"I will. I still have to get Johnny back." It was something to look forward to when he got back. "And in the meantime, would you like to dance?"

"Yes, sir." They circled the floor to the tune of "The Lady's in Love with You," and it seemed only moments later when the horns sounded and there was confetti everywhere in the air, and suddenly the lights were dim, people kissed, the music played, and they found themselves standing in the middle of the floor, looking at each other, their arms around each other, and he pressed her close just as she turned her face up to his and their lips met, and as they kissed, the rest of the room disappeared and they were on the *Deauville* again . . . lost in each other's arms . . . until at last they came up for air, and Liane didn't pull away.

"Happy New Year, Nick."

"Happy New Year, Liane."

And then they kissed again. They hadn't drunk enough champagne to blame it on that, and they stayed on the floor and danced for a long time, until at last he took her home and they stood outside her uncle's house as Nick looked down at her.

"I owe you an apology, Liane. I didn't play by the rules tonight." But the truth was for the last two years he would have given his right arm to have what he had just had tonight. "I'm sorry, I didn't mean—" But she put up a hand and touched his mouth with her fingertips.

"Nick, don't . . . it's all right. . . ." Something he had said had touched a place in her heart, about making a resolution not to be killed. And suddenly she knew that they had to take the moments while they could. They had learned once before that the moments might not come again. And they had been given this second chance as a gift. She couldn't turn it back now. She no longer wanted to. She only wanted him.

He kissed her fingertips and then her eyes, her lips. "I love you so much."

"I love you too." She pulled away and smiled at him. "We don't have a right to waste that now. We did what we had to before, and we will again . . . but right now—" He pulled her close to him with a fierceness that took her by surprise.

"I'll love you all my life. Do you know that?" She nodded.

"And when you tell me to go away again, I will. I do understand what has to be."

"I know you do." She touched his face as he held her close. "Then we don't have to talk about it again." She pulled gently away from him then and opened the door with her key. He kissed her good night, and she watched him drive away. There was no stopping the tides now, and neither of them wanted to. They had held them back for almost two years, and they couldn't now . . . couldn't . . . and she had no regrets. She walked quietly upstairs and took off her dress and went to bed, and tonight there were no dreams of anyone. There was a strange weightless feeling of peace and light and joy as she slept on dreamlessly until morning.

Chapter 44

On New Year's Day Nick stopped by the house to see her, and they sat in the library for a long time, chatting by the fire. No mention was made of what had happened the night before. It was as though they had always been together and she had expected to see him. Even the girls didn't look surprised when they came in from the garden and saw him sitting there.

"Hi, Uncle Nick." Elisabeth threw her arms around his neck and cast her mother a guilty smile. "Do we still have to call him Mr. Burnham?"

"That's not up to me." She smiled at them both. It was nice seeing him with the girls. It had been so long since they'd had a man around, aside from Uncle George, and she knew that he did them good.

"Well, Uncle Nick?" Elisabeth turned to him now. "Can we?"

"I don't see why not." He stroked the silky blond hair so much like her mother's. "Actually I'm flattered." Marie-Ange followed suit and then they ran out into the garden again to play and Uncle George came downstairs.

"I just finished my book. It was excellent." He smiled at his benefactor. "I'd be happy to lend it to you, if you have time to read."

"Thanks very much." As usual, within moments, the men began discussing the war news. The world was still shocked at the Japanese sinking the British battleships the *Prince of Wales* and the *Repulse*, off the coast of Malaya four days after Pearl Harbor. The loss of life on both ships had been shocking, and the *Prince of Wales* had sunk with her admiral. She had been the battleship that Churchill had been on in Argentia Bay, when he met Roosevelt to sign the Atlantic Charter. "I don't suppose you know what ship you'll be assigned to yet?"

"No, sir, but I should know soon." George nodded and looked at Liane then.

"You looked very pretty last night, my dear. I hope you two had a good time."

"Very pleasant." And then they mentioned how many military men they'd seen at the hotel. In three and a half weeks since Pearl Harbor had been hit, it seemed as though the entire country had signed up, and all the young men they knew were being drafted. "Actually, you know, I'm surprised they sent me here. From the gossip, the United States is a lot more interested in wiping out the Germans before they level the Japanese." In the days immediately after Pearl Harbor, the Germans had launched an enormous submarine offensive in the Atlantic, and ships were being sunk within frightening close range of the eastern seaboard. The main ports of New York, Boston, and Norfolk were now being protected with mines and nets and coastal convoys, and everyone wondered just how close the Germans would dare to come. There were blackouts every night in both the east and west coastal areas.

"It looks like we're getting it from both sides." George stared into the fire with worried eyes. His homeland had never been threatened directly before and it was a shock to him. He looked at Nick and shook his head. "I just wish I were young enough to join you."

"I don't." Liane looked at her uncle. "Someone has to stay here with us, or hadn't you thought of that?" He smiled and patted her hand.

"That, my dear, is my only consolation." He left them then and went back upstairs to read the afternoon paper in the study next to his room, and Nick and Liane were left alone. He looked at her for a long moment and took her hand in his.

"I had a wonderful time last night, Liane."

"So did I." Her eyes met his without wavering. Even in the clear light of day, she had no regrets over kissing him the night before. He had drifted back into her life like a ship on an unknown course, and perhaps for a time they could sail on together. Not for long though, she knew; eventually he would ship out. Perhaps that was their destiny, she had thought to herself that morning, to meet now and then in the course of their lifetimes, and to give each other the strength they needed to go on. He had done that for her now as he had once before. She felt calmer this morning than she had in more than a year, and there seemed to be an aura of peace all about them.

"No regrets?"

She smiled at him. "Not yet." And then she explained what she had been thinking.

"It's funny but I thought almost the same thing on the way home last night. Maybe this is all we'll ever have, but maybe it's enough." Their eyes met and held, and then he asked her about an idea he had had that morning. "Do you suppose you could get away for a few days, Liane?"

"What did you have in mind?"

His voice was very gentle. "I was thinking of a few days in Carmel. What do you think?"

She smiled peacefully at him, amazed at her own reaction. But she was taking something for herself that she wanted very badly and had for a long time. She knew deep in her soul that she would never do it again. But just this once . . . this once more . . . "I think it would be lovely. Can you get away?" She forced herself not to think of Armand. That would come later.

"As long as I leave the number where I am. I have a three-day leave coming next weekend. Is there any place special you'd like to go?"

"I haven't been to Carmel in years . . ." She thought about it for a moment. "What about the Pine Inn?"

"Done. Can you leave on Friday morning?" And then he frowned. "What about the girls? Will they be upset?"

She thought about it for a moment and then shook her head. "I'll tell them it's something for the Red Cross."

He grinned, feeling like a mischievous boy kidnapping a virgin from her parents. "A likely story. Just watch out when they start telling *you* stories like that a few years from now."

She smiled happily at Nick. "I'll kill them." He laughed then, and they chatted on for a while, and then wandered out to the garden to see the girls. He left later, before dinner, despite their invitation; he had to dine with his commanding officer. And then she walked him to the front door and he looked at her as they said good-bye. They were alone in the cavernous marble hall, and he bent to kiss her gently, uttering the words "Don't forget how much I love you."

During the weekend and for the rest of the week, he had a hard time getting free, but he called on Thursday night to confirm their plans. Uncle George had purposely not asked for him, and Liane hadn't mentioned him once. "Is everything set for tomorrow?"

"It is here. What about you?" She had told them that she was going to a three-day Red Cross seminar in Carmel, and everyone seemed to believe her.

"Everything's fine." And then he laughed. "You know, I'm as nervous as a kid."

And suddenly she giggled. "So am I."

"Maybe we're crazy to do this. Maybe it was just a ship-board romance after all, and we're nuts to try it again." It was a very honest thing to say, but they had that kind of ease between them, even now, after all this time and only a few kisses to remind them of the past.

"We could flood the room and pretend that we're sinking."

"I don't think that's very funny."

"Sorry. Bad joke." But they both laughed anyway. They laughed a lot together, something he hadn't done in a long time and neither had she, and it did them both a world of good.

She left the house with a light step the next morning and a smile she could barely conceal. She was grateful that the girls had gone back to school three days before and didn't see her leave the house just before noon, and Uncle George was at the office. She took a cab to Nick's hotel, where he was nervously pacing up and down on the street, smoking a cigarette.

"You look like your wife is having a baby." She grinned as he paid the cab.

"I suddenly got panicked that you wouldn't show."

"Would you rather I didn't?" But in answer to her question, he took her in his arms and kissed her full on the mouth. They stood there like that for a long time, and two passing marines hooted and whistled.

"What do you think?" She smiled in answer. She was glad she had come. She had felt the same nervousness as he in the cab, and almost turned back once. What if they got in an accident and George and the girls found out? What if . . . but she had come and she was glad. He put her bag in the trunk of his borrowed car and they took off for Carmel, singing and laughing like two children.

It was a beautiful drive down the coast and the weather was lovely even though it was cool. They stopped at a roadside restaurant for lunch, and they reached Carmel at four o'clock, in time for a walk on the beach before it got dark. They left their bags in their room at the Pine Inn, and walked the two short blocks to the beach, stuffing their shoes in the pockets of their coats, and running through the sand, he barefoot, and she in silk stockings. The air felt wonderful on their faces, and at last, when they stopped far down the beach and sat down, they were breathless and happy and laughing. Everything looked so peaceful here, as though all were right with the world and always would be.

"It's hard to believe there's a war going on, isn't it?" Nick sat staring out to sea, thinking of the battleships defending their country halfway around the world. Carmel was totally untouched by the hubbub of uniforms they had seen in San Francisco. It was a sleepy little town, and it slept on, and Liane hoped it would never awaken. And she had a constant sense of gathering moments to remember later.

"It feels good to get away. My work at the Red Cross is beginning to depress me." She sighed and looked at him. He was surprised. He thought she liked it.

"How come?"

"I don't feel as though I'm doing enough. Organizing officers' teas and making lists isn't my style. It's been something to do for the last year. But I'd much rather be doing something useful." She sighed and he smiled, remembering how hard she had worked to save the men on the *Deauville*.

"I remember. What do you have in mind?"

"I don't know yet. I've been thinking. Maybe some hospital work."

He reached for her hand. "Florence Nightingale." And then he kissed her, and they lay side by side on the beach until it got dark and then they walked slowly back to their hotel. And Liane realized for the first time that they were about to spend a civilized weekend together, like ordinary people. On the ship, they had existed in the stuffy darkness of the first mate's cabin during the nightly blackouts, and suddenly here they were with a pretty little room and a shower, and she felt shy with him as they walked into the room, and they both glanced at the bathroom. It was like being newlyweds and she giggled.

"Do you want to shower first or shall I?"

"After you. You probably take longer than I do anyway."

She loaded her arms with her toiletries and what she was

going to wear, and closed the door, and half an hour later she emerged fully dressed, with her hair done in a smooth knot, and he whistled. "That's quite a feat in a room that size." She laughed. She had juggled all her things and her dress had almost fallen in the tub, but one would never have known it to look at her.

"You're next." And he was right. It took him less time, and when he came out, he was only wearing a towel. He had forgotten to take a fresh uniform in with him.

"There must be an easier way than this." He grinned, and she laughed.

"It's strange, isn't it? It was much easier on the ship, and God knows why in those conditions." But they both knew why. It was all familiar then, after the first time, they could have existed in half the space, and now everything was different. He looked at her gently from the bathroom door and he walked slowly toward her.

"It's been an awful long time, Liane . . . too long . . ." He stood very still and she reached her arms up around his neck and kissed him.

And very gently he pulled her toward him. There were no words needed for what they felt, as suddenly where they were, or where they had been for the last year and a half, no longer mattered. Their bodies seemed to surge together as her clothes seemed to melt away beneath his hands and his towel fell and he gently picked her up and carried her to the bed, and he devoured her with his lips and his hands, and she lay breathless with pleasure. It was hours before they lay side by side again, drowsy with contentment. He rolled over on one elbow to look down at Liane. She was more beautiful than ever.

"Hello, my love."

She smiled up at him with sleepy eyes. "I've missed you, Nick . . . even more than I remembered." She kissed his shoulder and his chest, and ran a finger lazily down his arm. It was even better between them than it had been before. Added to passion was something warm and easy and familiar.

At last at ten o'clock they got up and Nick strolled around the room, comfortable without his clothes, it felt as though they had always lived together. He looked over his shoulder with a smile as he fished a pack of Camels out of his jacket. "Well, I guess we blew dinner. Are you starving?"

She laughed and shook her head. She hadn't thought about food since the first time he had kissed her. "Maybe they'll let us forage around in the kitchen." But they were surprised, when they got dressed and went downstairs, to find that the dining room was still open, and they took a quiet table in a corner and enjoyed a candlelight supper of champagne and smoked salmon. For dessert Nick had apple pie à la mode, which wasn't in keeping with the rest, and she teased him about it.

"The military is giving me bad habits." But she shared it with him, and they laughed, and eventually went back to their room. There was a bright moon overhead, and the room was quiet and cozy. And almost before they closed the door he pulled her back to their bed and they made love again, and Liane drifted off to sleep at last in his arms with a happy smile on her face as Nick lay awake for a long time and watched her.

Chapter 45

The next morning, they woke up and ordered breakfast in their room. They sat naked on the bed and nibbled off each other's trays of croissants and Danish pastries, while Liane drank English breakfast tea and Nick drank black coffee. And as she looked up at him with a smile he grinned.

"Nice, isn't it, Liane?"

"Nice isn't the word for it." It was very different from her old life with Armand, it was different from anything she'd ever known before, yet at the same time it felt as though she had always lived it. Almost instinctively she had known what they would eat for breakfast, and she knew he drank his coffee black. She even knew just how hot he liked his shower. And as she sat in the bath afterward while he shaved, he whistled and she sang and then they sang a duet together.

He grinned when they were through and turned to her with a towel wrapped around his middle. "Not bad, eh? Maybe we should audition for a radio show."

"Sure. Why not?" She smiled. They both got dressed and went for a long walk on the beach, and then they strolled past some of the shops and art galleries. He bought her a little walrus carved out of wood, and she bought him a small gold sea gull on a gold chain.

"Will they let you wear that on your dog tags, to remind you of Carmel?"

"Let them try and stop me." They were silly trinkets but they each wanted something to remind them of Carmel in the months to come. And then she bought little presents for the girls and Uncle George, and they went back to their hotel to snuggle cozily in the big bed until they went downstairs for another late dinner.

On Sunday they stayed in bed until after noon, and Liane hated to get up. She knew that they'd have to go home soon and she didn't want their idyll to end. She sat in the bathtub with a distant look in her eyes, staring at the soap in her hand. Nick read her mind as he watched her. He touched her head gently and she looked up and smiled.

"Don't look so sad, love. We'll come back."

"Do you think we could?" But who knew when he'd ship out. It could be any day. But he read her mind again.

"We will. I promise."

They checked out of the hotel an hour later, after they made love "just one more time," and Liane giggled afterward as she wagged a finger at him.

"You know, you're giving me bad habits and I think this is habit-forming."

"I know it is. I had withdrawal for seventeen months last time."

"So did I." She looked at him sadly. "I used to dream about you at night. The night I ran into you at Mrs. Mac-Kenzie's I heard your voice and I thought I'd finally lost my mind."

"That's how I felt when I looked across the room and saw you. That used to happen to me all the time in New York, I'd look down a street and there you were, walking away, with the same blond hair, and I'd fly down the street to see and it was never you. A lot of women on the street must have thought I was crazy. And I was . . ." His eyes reached deep into hers. "I was crazy for a long, long time, Liane." She nodded.

"We're still crazy now." They had stolen three days, and they both knew that what they had was something they couldn't keep. It was only borrowed.

"I'm not sorry. Are you?"

She shook her head. "I thought of Armand yesterday . . . and what it must be like for him in Paris . . . and yet, somehow, I knew that what we were doing wouldn't change anything for him. I'll still be here for him when the war is over." Nick knew it too, and he didn't resent it. It was something about her that he had always accepted . . . almost always. . . . He also knew that Europe was having a terrible winter, but he assumed that she knew it too. And there was no point talking about that. There was nothing she could do for Armand, and he knew how much she worried.

They drove slowly back by the coast road again, and got home at eight o'clock, after stopping for a quick dinner just before they reached San Francisco. She hadn't called home all weekend and she hoped the girls were all right, and she noticed that Nick hadn't called Johnny either. It was as though just for those three days they belonged to each other in another world, and no one else and no other world had ever existed. They talked about the children in the last half hour of the trip and Nick sighed.

"I know he'll be all right. But I worry so damn much about him." And then he turned to Liane. "I want to ask you something . . . something special. . . ." Her heart raced, she knew suddenly it would be important.

"Sure. What?"

"If something happens to me . . . when I'm gone . . . will you promise me that you'll go see him?"

For a moment Liane was shocked into silence. "Do you suppose Hillary would let me?"

"She never knew about us. There's no reason why she wouldn't. And she's remarried now." He sighed again. "If I could, I'd leave him with you, then I'd know he'd be in good hands forever." Liane nodded slowly.

"Yes, I'll go to see him. I'll stay in touch with him over

the years." She smiled gently. "Like a guardian angel." But then she touched Nick's hand. "But nothing's going to happen to you, Nick."

"You never know." He looked at her in the darkness as they pulled up in front of her uncle's house. "I meant what I asked you."

"And I meant what I said. If that happens, I'll go to see him." But it was something she couldn't bear to think about.

They got out of the car, and he put her bag in the front hall. There was no one around. The girls were already in bed and she hoped that they wouldn't see him, but he hadn't wanted her to take a cab from his hotel so he had brought her home. She turned to him then just outside the door and they kissed for a long time.

"I'll call you in the morning."

"I love you, Nick."

"I love you, Liane." He kissed her again and then he left, and she went upstairs to her bedroom.

Chapter 46

𝒜rmand sat in his office, blowing on his hands to warm them. It had been a ghastly few weeks, with rare snow and ice on the streets of Paris, and all the houses held the cold. He couldn't even remember the last time he'd been warm, and his hands were so cold now he could barely write, even after rubbing them together for several minutes. As a liaison between Pétain and the Germans, he had moved his offices the month before, and he was now in the Hotel Majestic with the *Verwaltungsstab*, the German administrative offices of the High Command. Their corresponding military arm was the *Kommandostab*, under the command of Staff Colonel Speidel. Unfortunately, he had had to take André Marchand with him, and the young assistant was so excited to be in the same building as the Germans now that he always appeared rigid with zealous devotion, and it was becoming increasingly difficult for Armand to conceal his hatred for him.

And Armand's responsibilities these days were even more extensive than before. The Germans had finally come to trust him. He spent many hours with their Propaganda *Abteilung*, in order to help impress on the French what a blessing had befallen them in the guise of the Germans. And he had frequent meetings with Staff Colonel Speidel, and General Barkhausen to discuss what they referred to as "War Booty Services." It was here that Armand was secretly able to wreak havoc and sidetrack a lot of the treasures earmarked for Berlin. They simply disappeared and the Resistance was blamed, and no one seemed more irate than Armand. And as yet, no one suspected. And he also had frequent meetings with Dr. Michel, of the German Ministry of State Economy, to discuss the current state of the French economy, the controlling of prices, chemical industries, paper manufacture, labor problems, credit, insurance, coal, electric power, and assorted other minor areas.

Most of the big hotels had been taken over by the German High Command. General von Stutnitz, the Military Commander of Gross-Paris, was at the Crillon, Von Speidel and the others at the Majestic. The *Verwaltungsstab* were conveniently located near Armand's home in the Palais-Bourbon, and Oberkriegsverwaltungsrat Kruger, in charge of the city's budget, was at the Hotel de Ville. And General von Briesen, commander of the city of Paris itself, was at the Hotel Meurice, although eventually General Schaumburg took his place, and remained at the Meurice because he found it so enchanting.

And throughout the city posters in French issued terrifying warnings regarding information passed, acts of sabotage, violence, strikes, incitement to riot, or even the hoarding of articles for daily use, which were all punishable "with the utmost severity," by a War Tribunal. And inevitably there were frequent violations, mostly by members of the Resistance, who, the Germans immediately informed the public, were "communist students" and who were shot publicly to teach everyone a lesson. Public executions in Paris were almost commonplace by 1942, and the atmosphere in the city was subdued and depressing. Only in the hidden Resistance meetings around Occupied France was the atmosphere one of excitement and tension. But everywhere else the cities and the towns and the countrysides seemed blanketed in silent oppression. And not only were the Germans out to get them, but the elements appeared to be too. All that winter, people had been dying like flies from the cold and the shortages of food. As Armand looked around him he saw a dying nation. And the Germans had long ceased pretending that the "unoccupied South" would go untouched. They had moved in there too, and now all of France was swallowed up. "But not for long," De Gaulle still promised on his broadcasts from the BBC in London. And the most amazing man of all was a man called Moulin, who was almost single-handedly responsible for spurring on the Resistance. Without anyone understanding how he managed, he made constant trips to London to the organization of Resistance fighters waiting there and then would manage to infiltrate back into France again, to give everyone hope and new spirit.

Armand had only dared to meet with him once or twice. For him it was much too risky, and most of the time he dealt with him indirectly, particularly after the famous Edict of July 15 of the year before, when the Germans cracked down on art treasures all over France, demanding that any item valued at more than one hundred thousand francs be reported at once by their custodians or owners. It was these records that Armand was so busy destroying and misplacing in the winter of 1941 and the early months of 1942, and he knew that single-handedly he was already responsible for salvaging millions of dollars worth of treasures for France, in spite of the Germans. But more important than that, he was attempting to save lives, and that was becoming more and more dangerous for him. And for the last few weeks he had been sick from the desolate cold that attacked Paris. But he said nothing of it in the letter that Liane received the day after she got back from Carmel. All she could glean from it was that his work was going well. Yet she heard something else in his letter. Something she had never heard before. A kind of despair that almost reached desperation. She sensed through the things he didn't say that France was not faring well at the hands of the Germans, worse than anyone knew. And she stood at the window for a long time, looking out at the Golden Gate Bridge, after she had read the letter.

"Liane? Is something wrong?" Her uncle had not yet left

for work, and he had been watching her from the doorway. Her whole body seemed to sag and her head was down, and when she turned toward him, he saw that she was crying. But she shook her head and smiled through her tears.

"No. Nothing new. I had a letter from Armand." It had been smuggled out by Moulin during his most recent trip to London, but she couldn't tell her uncle that. Even he couldn't know about Armand's ties to the Resistance. Armand had told her to tell no one. And she hadn't, except Nick. But she trusted him completely.

"Did something happen?"

"I don't know. He just sounds so sad . . . it's all so depressing."

"War isn't a nice thing." The words were trite but true.

"He almost sounds ill." She knew her husband well. And her uncle refrained from saying he didn't wonder a traitor would be ill at the destruction of his country.

"He'll be all right. He's probably just lonely for you and the girls." She nodded, suddenly feeling the first spear of guilt slice through her.

"I suppose he is."

"How was your seminar in Carmel?"

Her eyes lit up in spite of herself. "It was lovely."

He asked her no further questions and they both left for work. She told Nick about the letter from Armand that afternoon when he picked her up at the Red Cross office. But he could only think of one thing, and his eyes searched hers in sudden panic. "Have you changed your mind about us?"

She looked at him for a long time and then shook her head. "No, I haven't. It's as though I have two separate lives now. My old one with Armand, and now this with you." He nodded, relieved, and she sighed. "But I feel terrible for him."

"Does he seem to be in any particular danger?"

"Not more than usual, I think. I didn't get any sense of that in his letter. Just a sense of terrible depression, mostly for France." She looked up at Nick. "I think he cares about that more than he cares about himself, or about us. His country means everything to him."

Nick spoke softly. "I admire him." And then he took her home, and joined the family for dinner. After dinner, he played dominoes with Liane and Uncle George, and then he went back to his hotel, and she found herself wondering when they would be together again, as they had been in Carmel. Women were not allowed in his hotel, and she wouldn't have wanted to go there anyway. But the next weekend, he solved the problem for them by suggesting that they reserve a room at the Fairmont. There was one problem that they didn't have, and others did. Neither of them was short of funds. But they had enough other problems. She, worrying about Armand in France, and he worrying about Johnny.

She listened that weekend, when he called his son, and she watched him with her girls, and she knew how much he missed the boy. He had a wonderful ease with children. And after they took the girls home, they went to dinner, and then back to the room they had rented at the Fairmont. The girls had been invited to spend the night with a friend, and she had told Uncle George another story he hadn't questioned.

"Do you think he suspects about us, Nick?" She smiled up at him as they lay on the bed in their room and drank champagne and ate peanuts. This time they didn't go to the Venetian Room. They wanted to be alone. Nick looked amused at her question.

"Probably. He's no fool. And he's probably done plenty of this in his day." She knew that herself, but she wondered.

"He hasn't said a thing."

"He knows you too well for that."

"Do you think he minds?"

"Do you?" Nick smiled gently and she shook her head.

"No, he wishes I'd divorce Armand and marry you, I suspect."

"So do I—I mean I suspect the same thing." He was quick to clarify when he saw the look in her eyes. She was desperately afraid that she was being unfair to Nick. She was a married woman, after all, and could offer him no part in her future. "Anyway, don't worry about it. As long as the vice squad doesn't show up, or the press, we'll be fine." She laughed at the idea. They were registered in the hotel as Major and Mrs. Nicholas Burnham.

They drifted on like that for quite a while with dinners and long walks in the afternoon, and stolen weekends at the Fairmont. They managed another quick hop to Carmel after a few weeks, but in February things began to get tense for Nick. Singapore fell to the Japanese, and Japanese land forces had taken Java, Borneo, the Dutch East Indies, and several islands in the South Pacific. The Japanese were so pleased with themselves that General Nagumo had retired north to Japan. And Nick expected to be shipped out at any moment. He somehow assumed every week he would hear, but still he didn't. U.S. aircraft carriers were making hit-and-run raids on the Gilbert and Marshall islands south of Japan, battering successfully at Japanese positions, but the main strongholds could not be won from the Japanese.

One day in March he looked at her in dismay, and after his second Scotch, he astounded her by slamming a fist onto the table. He had been nervous for weeks, waiting to be shipped out.

"Goddamn it, Liane, I should be over there too. Why the hell am I sitting on my ass in San Francisco?" Her feelings weren't hurt by his outburst, she understood and spoke to him in a soothing tone, but it didn't seem to help.

"Wait, Nick. They're biding their time."

"And I'm spending the war sitting around in hotel rooms." His look was one of pure accusation, and this time he got to her.

"That is your choice, Nick, it is not an obligation."

"I know . . . I know . . . I'm sorry . . . I'm just sitting here going goddamm nuts. I enlisted three months ago, for chrissake, and Johnny is in New York with Hillary, tugging at me by saying he misses me. I made him a big speech about going to war, and now all I do is sit here, having one long party." The anxiety in his voice touched her and she tried to calm him down. She had her own guilts about Armand, and there were times when she questioned herself too. But she couldn't leave Nick now, and she didn't want to. They were going to stay together until he left, and then they both knew that it would be over.

She snapped at him now and then, particularly once after she'd gotten a letter from Armand. He mentioned that he was having attacks of rheumatism in his legs from the cold, and the same day, Nick had complained to her that they had danced so much the night before that his back hurt, and she had suddenly turned on him in a rage.

"Then don't dance so much, for God's sake!"

He was surprised at the look on her face. He had never seen her like that before. "I didn't see *you* walk off the floor until two o'clock in the morning." But as he said the words she burst into tears, and as he cradled her in his arms he discovered the problem as she sobbed and told him about Armand's letter.

"I think he's sick, Nick . . . he's almost fifty-nine years old . . . and it's freezing cold over there. . . ." She sobbed in Nick's arms and he held her.

"It's all right, love . . . it's all right. . . ." He always understood. There was nothing she couldn't tell him.

"And sometimes I feel so guilty."

"So do I. But we knew that right from the beginning. It doesn't change anything for him." Liane wrote to him just as often, and she was helpless to help him.

"What if the Germans kill him?"

Nick sighed and thought about it, not sure what he could say to reassure her. There was very definitely a risk that the Germans would kill him. "That's a chance he took when he stayed there. I think he thinks it's worth it." He had a strong sense of Armand's passion for his country. Judging from things Liane had said, he sensed that it had almost become an obsession. "Liane, you just have to trust that he'll survive. There's nothing else you can do."

"I know." And then she thought of the night before, when they'd gone dancing. "But it's as though our life here is like one long party." She was echoing his words and they looked at each other long and hard.

"Do you want it to stop?" He held his breath.

"No."

"Neither do I." But in April he picked her up at the Red Cross one afternoon and he was strangely silent.

"Is something wrong, Nick?"

He looked at her sadly. He felt none of the excitement he had expected to feel. He felt loss and desolation. "The party's over."

There was a strange tingling in her spine. "What do you mean?"

"I'm leaving San Francisco tomorrow." She caught her breath and looked at him, and suddenly she was crying in his arms. They had both known it would come, but now they weren't ready.

"Oh, Nick . . ." And then fear struck her again. "Where are you going?"

"San Diego. For two days. And then we ship out. I'm not sure where. I'll be on an aircraft carrier, the *Lady Lex*." He tried to smile. "Actually, she's the *Lexington*. We're going somewhere in the Pacific." She had just returned for some repairs, Liane had read in the papers. And now as they drove home to her uncle's house, neither of them spoke. They were grim-faced and silent and Uncle George knew at once when he saw them.

"Shipping out, son?"

"Yes, sir. I'll be leaving here tomorrow for San Diego." George nodded and watched Liane, and it was a quiet dinner that night. Even the girls seldom broke the silence, and when he said good-bye to them that night, they cried, almost as much as they had when they had left their father.

He was more real to them now than Armand. They hadn't seen him in two years, and Nick had been in their midst almost constantly for the past four months. His loss would be felt by all, especially Liane, who kissed him tenderly in the doorway. She had promised to take the train to San Diego the next day, and they would have a little time together before he shipped out. He had to be on the ship the day before she sailed. That gave them one day and one night in San Diego together.

"I'll call you at the hotel in San Diego tomorrow night, if I can. Otherwise I'll get to you the next morning." She nodded again, with tears in her eyes.

"I miss you already."

He smiled. "So do I." Neither of them had been prepared for the pain they felt now. "I love you."

She waved as he drove away, and went back into the house, and when she got to her room, she lay on the bed and sobbed. She wasn't ready to give him up . . . not again . . . not now . . . not ever. . . .

Chapter 47

$\mathcal{L}$iane's train reached San Diego at eleven o'clock the next night, and she didn't reach the hotel until midnight. She knew that it was too late for Nick to call, and she waited breathlessly by the phone the next day, until finally he called just after noon. She had been awake and tense since seven o'clock that morning.

"I'm sorry, love. I couldn't call. I've got meetings and briefings and God knows what else."

She panicked at his words. "Can I see you?" She glanced out at the Pacific as she spoke, trying to imagine where he was. Her room had a view of the base and the port in the distance.

"I can't see you until tonight. And Liane . . ." He hated to do it, but he knew he had to tell her. "That'll be it. I have to report to the base at six o'clock tomorrow morning."

"When do you sail?" Her heart was pounding in her ears.

"I don't know. All I know is that I have to be on the ship at six o'clock tomorrow morning. I assume we sail the next day. But they won't tell us." That was standard military procedure, because of the war. "Look, I've got to go. I'll see you tonight. As soon as I can."

"I'll be here." She spent the day in her room, terrified that he would come early and she would miss him. And at ten minutes to six there was a knock on her door. It was Nick and she flew into his arms, crying and laughing and desperately happy to see him. For these few moments they could pretend that he would never leave.

"God, you look so good to me, love."

"So do you." But they were both exhausted from the strain of the past two days. It was a time she knew she would never forget. It was worse than when she had left Paris.

They talked frantically for half an hour, and then he took her in his arms and took her to bed, and after that, things seemed to slow down. They never left the room to go to dinner that night, and they never slept. They lay there and they talked and made love. And Liane trembled as she saw the sun come up. She knew that their last night was over.

At five thirty he got out of bed, and he looked at her soberly as she watched him. "Babe . . . I've got to go. . . ."

"I know." She sat up, wanting to pull him to her, wanting to turn the clock back.

And then he asked her something he had wanted to ask her for two days. "Will you write to me, or would you rather not?" They had agreed four months before that when he left it would be over.

"I'll write." She smiled sadly. She was already writing to Armand, and now she had lost two men to the war, for the time being at least. She didn't know what she would do when he came back. For weeks she had been asking herself that question. Things were different than they had been on the *Deauville*, she and Nick had had four months, not thirteen days, and she couldn't give him up so easily now. Once or twice she had thought of leaving Armand after the war, but she didn't think she could. Nor could she give up Nick Burnham.

"I'll write to you too. But it may take forever for you to get my letters."

"I'll be waiting."

He didn't shower before he put on his clothes. He didn't want to waste a single minute of their time together, he could shower on the ship, he had a lifetime to do that. And all he had now were a few moments left with Liane. "Remember what I said about Johnny." He had given her Hillary's address, but she had insisted again that she wouldn't need it. He'd come back to see to Johnny himself, and he had answered "Just in case." She had taken it to make him feel better.

Their last moments ticked by like the last seconds before a bomb explodes, and in the end they stood in her room and he held her tight. "I'm going to leave you here."

Panic struck her again. "Can't I take you back to the base?"

He shook his head. "It'll just make it harder." She nodded, tears already flooding her face, and he kissed her one last time and looked into her eyes. "I'll be back."

"I know." And neither of them asked the other what would happen then. It was too late to think of that. All they had was the present, and whatever fate dealt them later. "Nick . . . take care. . . ." She grabbed at him once as he left the room, and he held her again, and then with a last wave he ran down the stairs, and she went back into their room and closed the door, and she sat, feeling as though the last bit of life had been drained out of her. She was still sitting in the room two hours later, thinking of him, when she happened to glance out the window, and the whole Pacific Ocean seemed to have disappeared and in its place was an enormous ship, moving slowly out to sea. Her heart pounded as she watched. It was an aircraft carrier, and she knew as she watched that it was the *Lexington* and Nick was on it. She flung open the window of her room as though that would bring her a little closer, and she watched until it had left the harbor. And then she turned slowly and packed her bag, and two hours later she was back on the train, sitting silent and still as she returned to San Francisco.

Chapter 48

When Liane got back to San Francisco, she let herself into the house, and climbed slowly up the stairs to her room. It was late and the house was dark, and she jumped as though a bomb had exploded near her when she heard a voice. It was Uncle George. He was sitting quietly in her room, in the dark, waiting for her.

"Is something wrong? . . . The girls?"

"They're fine." He looked at her searchingly as she turned on the light. She looked ravaged. "Are you all right, Liane?"

"I'm fine." But she began to cry as she said it, and she turned away so he wouldn't see. "Really . . . I'm all right. . . ."

"No, you're not. And it's nothing to be ashamed of. I didn't expect you to be. That's why I'm here."

And then, like a little child, she flew into his arms. "Oh, Uncle George . . ."

"I know . . . I know . . . he'll be back . . ." But so would Armand. And all the way home on the train she had thought about both men. She was torn between the two now. And then her uncle poured her a glass of brandy. He had brought a bottle and two glasses to her room, and she smiled at him through her tears.

"What did I ever do to deserve a nice uncle like you?"

"You're a good woman, Liane." He said it without a smile.

"And you deserve a good man. And God willing, you'll have one."

She took a sip of the brandy and sat down with a nervous smile. "The trouble is, Uncle George, I have two of them." But he didn't answer. He left her a little while after that, and she went to bed, and in the morning she felt a little better.

She had a letter from Armand that day and he sounded a little better too. He seemed cheered by "recent events," as he told her, but he didn't say what they were. And the weather had warmed up and his legs weren't as painful.

In the next few days the news from London was cheering too. The British had received their first shipment of United States food, averting a drastic food shortage in London.

And on April 18, everyone read in the American press of the Doolittle raid on Tokyo, led by Lt. Colonel James H. Doolittle, the aeronautical scientist and pilot. He had modified sixteen B-25 bombers, and the team had headed for Japan, knowing full well that they couldn't return, with the intention of landing in unoccupied China, after they bombed Tokyo. And all but one of the planes made it, with the result of an enormous improvement in morale among the troops. Revenge had been served. Tokyo had been bombed. It was a thank-you for Pearl Harbor.

But the good cheer over the Doolittle raid was short-lived. By the night of May 4, everyone was talking of the battle of the Coral Sea, and Liane lay awake through the night, praying for Nick. The battle raged on for two days, under the direction of General MacArthur, who had wisely stayed behind in New Guinea, at Port Moresby. And by May 6 they knew the worst. The *Lexington* had sunk. Miraculously only 216 men had died. Another 2,735 had been saved and taken on board the *Lady Lex*'s sister ship, the *Yorktown*. But what Liane did not know was whether Nick was among the 216, or the others. As she sat frozen in her room day after day, listening to the radio she'd brought upstairs, she remembered the ghastly scenes in the Atlantic when the *Queen*

Victoria had sunk. And now she prayed that Nick would be among the survivors. She took her meals in her room on trays, and they returned to the kitchen, barely touched, as her uncle sat in the library, listening to the news there. But it would be weeks, if not longer, before they would have word of Nick. Unbeknownst to Liane, George had someone in his office call Brett Williams in New York, but he knew nothing either.

And also on May 6, the broadcaster told the nation that General Jonathan Wainwright had been forced to surrender Corregidor to the Japanese. General Wainwright and his men were taken prisoner. Things were not going well in the Pacific.

"Liane." George stood in the doorway of her bedroom on the morning of May 8, two days after the *Lexington* had sunk. "I want you to come downstairs for breakfast."

She stared at him lifelessly from her bed. "I'm not hungry."

"I don't care. The girls are afraid you're sick." She stared at him then for a long time, and silently nodded. And when she came down at last, she was weak from the days in bed, listening to the radio with the shades drawn. The girls watched her now as though they were frightened of her, and she made an effort to see them off to school, and then she went back to her room and turned the radio on again. But there was nothing more. The battle of the Coral Sea was over.

"Liane." He had followed her to her room again and she turned to look at her uncle with empty eyes. "You can't do this to yourself."

"I'll be all right."

"I know you will. And what you're doing isn't helping him." He sat down on the edge of the bed. "They've had no news in New York. If he'd been killed, they would have got a telegram. I'm sure he lived through it." She nodded, fighting back tears again. It was just too much worrying about both of them. And that day, she had had another letter from

Armand. Thirty thousand Jews had been taken out of their homes in Paris. It was one of the letters Moulin had gotten out, and like many of the others, it crossed the Atlantic on the *Gripsholm*.

The Jews in Paris had been locked in a stadium for eight days without water or food or toilets. Many people, including women and children, had died. The world was going mad. From one end of the globe to the other, people were dying and killing each other. Suddenly she knew what she had to do. She pulled a dress from her closet and threw it on the bed. She looked better than she had in days.

"Where are you going?"

"To my office." And she didn't tell him why. She bathed and dressed, and an hour later she had turned in her resignation, not from the Red Cross, but that chapter. And by that afternoon she had signed up at the naval hospital in Oakland. She was assigned to the care of men in a surgical ward. It was the most difficult work of all, but when she returned to the house on Broadway at eight o'clock that night, she felt better than she had in months. It was what she should have done long before, and always meant to do. She told her uncle that night after dinner.

"That's a terrible job, Liane. Are you sure that's what you want to do?"

"Absolutely." There was no doubt in her voice and he could see from her face that she had pulled herself back together. They talked of the Jews in Paris and he shook his head. Nothing was the same anymore. Absolutely nothing. Nothing was safe. Nothing was sacred. U-boats cruised American coasts, Jews were driven from their homes all over Europe, the Japanese were killing Americans in the South Pacific. Even the beautiful *Normandie* had burned three months before in New York harbor as workmen raced against the clock to turn her into a troop ship. And in London, bombs fell day and night, killing women and children.

For the next month Liane worked like a fiend in the naval hospital in Oakland, three times a week. She left the house at eight o'clock in the morning and came home at five or six at night and sometimes even seven, exhausted, smelling of surgical solution and disinfectant, her uniforms often covered with dried blood, her face pale, but her eyes alive. She was doing the only thing she could to help and it was better than sitting in an office. And a month after the battle of the Coral Sea, she was rewarded with a letter from Nick. He was alive! She sat on the front steps and cried as she read it.

Chapter 49

$\mathcal{O}$n the fourth of June, the battle of Midway began, and by the following day it was over. The Japanese had lost four out of five of their aircraft carriers, and the Americans rejoiced. It was the biggest victory by far for us. And Liane knew that Nick was safe. He was on the *Enterprise* by now, out of the storm of the battle. And although Liane trembled each time she heard the news, a regular stream of letters kept her informed that Nick was alive and well. She wrote to him almost every day, and as often as she could she wrote to Armand.

Her husband's most recent letters seemed to indicate a heightened sense of tension in Paris. More young Communists had been shot, more Jews had been rounded up, and in his frequent meetings with the *Kommandostab*, it was becoming increasingly clear that they were cracking down on Paris. The Resistance in the villages was reaching an alarming strength, and it was important to them that they keep a tight rein on the capital to keep it as an example. As such, the Germans were turning increasingly to Armand now, expecting him to account for artwork that couldn't be found, people who had disappeared, and people in Pétain's flanks who allegedly had Communist leanings. They needed someone to turn to each time there was a problem that couldn't be blamed on the Germans, and Armand was invariably it.

He provided a comfortable buffer for Maréchal Pétain, but it left him perennially tense and exhausted.

And as he sat in his office in the Hotel Majestic on a warm June day, André Marchand walked in and dumped a fresh stack of papers on his desk.

"What are these?"

"Reports on the people arrested last night. The High Command wants to know if there's anyone important here, masquerading as peasants." Marchand liked nothing better than turning his countrymen over to the Germans, and Armand was only sorry they didn't draft him and send him to Russia. If he wanted to be a German so badly, let him.

"Thank you. I'll take a look when I have time."

"The High Command wants them back by tonight." He looked Armand in the eye.

"Fine. I'll see to it." He wondered lately if Marchand had been assigned to him to make sure that he was faithful to Pétain and the Germans. But that was a ridiculous thought. Marchand was a child, a man of no importance. They couldn't possibly use him as a watchdog. Armand smiled to himself. He was so tired, he was seeing dangers everywhere now. The night before he even thought he was being followed. He turned to the reports on his desk then, adjusting the glasses he now wore to read. It was just as well that he got it done anyway. He was meeting with Moulin tonight, before the man went back to London.

At six o'clock he left the Hotel Majestic, and went home to the Place du Palais-Bourbon, as he always did, although tonight he had left earlier than usual. He went into the kitchen, which now showed months of disuse. It didn't look like the same house where Liane had once lived with the children. The copper pots had turned dark, the stove no longer worked, and he kept almost nothing in the icebox. There was a thick coat of dust everywhere. And he really didn't care. He used it as a place to sleep. But tonight he sliced some cold sausage that he had bought, and munched on an apple. He made a few notes to himself before he drove out to Neuilly. And he looked around carefully as he started the car, but no one was watching.

He made the short drive without a problem. He had a special emblem on his car now, which told the German soldiers posted in the street that he worked with the government. And he parked the car two blocks from the house where he was going. He knocked twice, and then rang the bell. He was let in by an old woman who nodded and closed the door, and then walked him into the kitchen, where he descended a stairway to her basement. And there, together, they shoved aside a pile of old boxes to reveal the trap door to the tunnel that had been made. He crawled through it, as he had before, into the next house, where three men were waiting. One was a man with short gray hair, in workman's pants, a cap, and a black sweater. It was Moulin. He held out a hand to Armand as the other two watched. They had come with him from Toulon this time. These two were new, but Moulin was familiar.

"Hello, my friend."

"It's good to see you." Armand smiled. He only wished that he knew the man better. He was doing great things for France. He was already a hero of the Resistance.

"It's good to see you too." Moulin glanced at his watch. He didn't want to waste time. He had half an hour before he was to return to Toulon, he had already completed his work in Paris. And that night, he would sneak back across the channel to London. "I have a proposition to make to you, De Villiers." Armand was surprised when he heard Moulin's proposal. "How would you like to come to London?"

"But why?" Nothing he did could be of use there. He was important where he was. "To what purpose?"

"A good one. To save your life. We have reason to believe that they suspect you." Armand nodded. He showed no fear.

"Why do you think that?"

"Some reports we intercepted from the Germans." Two

guards of the High Command had been killed the week before, and they had been carrying the commanding officer's briefcase, which had disappeared into the hands of the Resistance. Von Speidel had been livid.

"Was that you last week?" Armand inquired quietly.

"Yes. There were papers that lead us to think . . . we're not sure . . . but we don't want to wait until it's too late. You should go now."

"When?"

"Tonight. With me."

"But I can't. . . ." He looked frightened, he still had half a dozen important projects. There was a Rodin piece he wanted to spirit into Provence, a Jewish woman and her son hiding in a basement, a priceless Renoir lying hidden beneath a building. "It's too soon. I need time."

"They may not give it to you."

"But are you sure?"

Moulin shook his head. "Not yet. There is nothing definite. But your name was mentioned in two reports. They are watching."

"But you got those reports, Speidel didn't."

"We don't know who had seen them before that. Therein lies the danger." Armand nodded, and then he looked hard at Moulin again.

"What if I stay?"

"Is it worth it?"

"For the moment, yes."

"Can you finish what you're doing quickly?"

Armand nodded slowly. "I can try."

"Then do it. I'll be back in two weeks. You'll come then?"

Armand nodded, but there was something tentative in his face, which Moulin recognized at once. There were others like him; those who couldn't bear to give up the fight—beyond reason.

"Don't be a fool, De Villiers. You will serve France better if you stay alive. You can do a great deal from London."

"I want to stay in France."

"You can come back. We'll give you new identity cards and put you in the mountains."

"I'd like that."

"All right." Moulin stood up and the two men shook hands, then Moulin swiftly crossed the room and left. He exited by the same route that Armand had come, and a moment later Armand followed. He knew that they would be gone when he reached the street. Moulin always disappeared like the wind. But not tonight. As Armand walked to his car there was a sudden movement near him, and then suddenly armed soldiers leaped out from their hiding places with guns blazing. They didn't get a clear view of him, but in the distance there were three men running. Armand pressed himself quickly against a wall and the soldiers flew past him. There were more shots in the night, and Armand disappeared into a garden, where he hid, and he began to feel a dull throbbing in his leg, and when he touched it, it was damp with blood. He had been wounded.

He waited until there were no more sounds, and he made his way carefully out of the garden, praying that Moulin had fled, as he always did. Armand returned to the house where they had met, and the people there took him in and bandaged his leg. At midnight he went home, but his whole body was trembling, and he wished desperately that he still had some brandy. And as he sat and gazed at the rough bandage they had made, he realized how grave a problem it was for him. He could not go to the office the next day with a limp. And it was much too warm for him to convince anyone that he was suffering from rheumatism again. He practiced walking across his living room without a limp, wincing terribly with each step from the pain. There was no way he could do it, and yet he had to. He practiced again and again as the sweat poured down his face, and at last he mastered it. And with a horrible groan he climbed into his bed, but he was too exhausted to sleep. And he turned on a small light and took out a notebook. He hadn't written to Liane in over a week, and he needed her tonight. Suddenly he longed for her gentleness and her comfort, and as he wrote he did something he never had before. He poured out his heart and his soul and his anguish for France, and he told her just how grim it all was. And at the end of the letter he told her that he had been wounded.

It is nothing serious, my little love. It is a small price to pay in this fearsome battle. Others have suffered so much more than I. It grieves me that I have so little left to give. Even this small piece of flesh is not enough. . . .

And then he told her of Moulin's suggestion that he go to London, and that possibly in a few weeks he would be there, before coming back to France with new papers.

He said something tonight about putting me in the mountains. Perhaps then I shall truly join the fight. They are doing remarkable things there, troubling the Germans at every step . . . it would be a heavenly change from the damp walls of my office.

He folded his letter four or five times and placed it under the innersole of his shoe, lest something happen to him during the night, and the next day he dropped it behind a planter on the Rue du Bac. It was a drop he used often, although he preferred giving his letters to Moulin when he could. But he knew that the letters dropped here had reached Liane too. And this one did as well.

As Liane read it two weeks later tears streamed down her face. He was blind to what he was doing and she knew it. She read the lines where he told her that he had been wounded and she felt sick. If they were coming that close, and Moulin wanted him in London, it was almost too late. And he didn't see it. She felt desperation creep up within her like bile. She wanted to shake him, to show him what he wasn't seeing. Was he so blind that a portrait, a statue, a stranger, were all more important than her and Marie-Ange and Elisabeth? She sat there crying for half an hour, and then she did something she hadn't done for a long time. She went to church, and as she sat there and prayed, she knew what was wrong. It was what she had done with Nick. She had turned her values upside down. She had turned her back on her husband, and he had felt it. It was so clear to her now that it was almost as though she had heard voices or seen a vision. And as she returned to the house on Broadway, she sat for a long time, looking out at the Golden Gate Bridge. She had written to Nick every day, but she had only written to Armand once or twice a week. He must have felt the distance between them. And it was clear to her now what she had to do. She had known it all along, but she hadn't wanted to do it.

It took her hours to write the single page. She sat and stared at the paper and thought that she could never do it. It was more painful than leaving him at Grand Central Station or in the hotel room in San Diego. It was more painful than anything she had ever done. It was like cutting off her right arm. But as the Bible said, "If thine eye offend thee, pluck it out." And it felt as though that were what she was doing. She told Nick now that she knew that what they had done was wrong, and that she had led him to believe that there was hope for the future, when there wasn't. Armand needed her now. He needed her full support, full attention, full belief. He needed all she had to give. And to do it right, she could no longer betray him. She told Nick that she loved him with her whole soul, but it was a love that neither of them had a right to. She wished him well with all her heart, and she would pray for him each day of the war, but she could no longer write to him. She told him also that if anything happened, she would honor her promise and stay in touch with Johnny.

"But that won't happen, my darling . . . I know you'll come home. And I only wish . . ." She could not write the words.

You know what I wish. But our dreams were not borrowed, but stolen. I must return now to where I belong, in heart, in soul, in mind, to my husband. And remember always, my darling, how much I have loved you. Go with God. He will protect you.

With a sob wrenching at her throat, she signed the letter, and walked outside to mail it. She stood at the mailbox for a long time, her hand trembling, her heart breaking, but with a force of will she didn't know she had, she opened the mailbox and dropped in the letter. And she knew that it would find him.

Chapter 50

When Armand returned to his office the morning after the incident in Neuilly, his face was pale, and his palms damp with perspiration, but he did not limp as he walked to his desk, and he sat down at his desk as always. Marchand came to give him a stack of reports to read, forms to fill out, and assorted messages from the local generals.

"Will there be anything else?"

"No, thank you, Marchand." His face was drawn but his voice was normal. And for the next week he went on with his work, working at a furious speed. The priceless Renoir disappeared from under the building. The Rodin was hidden. The Jewish woman with her child was concealed in a basement in a farmhouse near Lyon, and there were countless other projects he saw to at full speed. He knew he had precious little time. And day by day the leg grew worse. It was badly infected but he had none of the things he needed to care for it. Each day he had to force himself to walk as though nothing were wrong with him. It took more strength than he had ever drawn on before, and he was gaunt now. He finally looked his age, and many years older.

And as he worked furiously every day, he stayed in the office long after the nightly blackout. And he was so anxious to complete his job that he took longer and longer to burn his notes, and it was difficult now to create a reason for making a fire. He often told Marchand, as he rubbed his hands and smiled, that his old bones needed warmth. Marchand only shrugged and went back to his work at his own desk.

There were only four days left until his next meeting with Moulin and he knew that he had to hurry. He left his office after ten o'clock one night, and when he went home, he had the feeling that someone had been in the apartment. He didn't remember leaving the chair quite so far from his desk. But he was too tired to care and the wound in his leg throbbed all the way to his hip now. He would have to have it looked at in London. He looked around the apartment that night, and out at the Place du Palais-Bourbon after he'd turned out the lights, and a piece of his heart ached to know that soon he would be leaving Paris. But he had left her before, and he would return again, and she would be free the next time he saw her.

"Bonsoir, ma belle." He smiled at his city and thought of his wife as he went to bed. In the morning he would write to Liane . . . or maybe the next day . . . he didn't have time now. But his leg pained him so badly that he awoke the next morning before dawn, and after he lay in bed in vain, he decided to get up and sit at his desk to write to her. He felt the now-familiar chill of his fever as he pulled a sheet of paper toward him.

> There is very little to tell since I wrote to you last. My life has been a frenzy of work, my darling.

And then suddenly he realized something and he smiled.

> I'm afraid that I've become a shocking husband. Two weeks ago I missed our thirteenth anniversary. But perhaps due to the extraordinary circumstances, you will forgive me. May our next thirteen be easy and peaceful. And may we be together soon.

And then he went on to talk about his work.

I'm afraid the leg isn't doing well. I regret now that I
told you about it, for fear that you will worry. It's nothing, I'm sure, but I walk on it every day and that doesn't
help. I suppose I've become an old man, but an old man
who still loves his country . . . *à la mort et à tout jamais* . . . to the death and forever, and at all costs, no
matter how dear. I would gladly give the leg, and my
heart, for this land I love so much. She lies pinned to
the ground now, raped by the Germans, but soon she
will be free, and we will nurse her back to health. You
will be at my side again then, Liane, and we will all be
happy. And in the meantime I am glad to know that you
are safe with your uncle, it is a better life for you and
the girls. I have never regretted sending you back to
the States. You will never know what it has been like to
watch France strangle at the hands of the Germans . . .
their hands at her throat, leering as they watch her
choke. It breaks my heart to be leaving soon with Moulin, but the only thing that cheers me is the knowledge
that I will come back shortly, only to fight harder.

It never occurred to him to stay in England, or to return to
Liane. He thought only of France, even as he signed the
letter.

Remember to give the girls my love, and keep a great
deal of the same for you. I love you very, very dearly,
mon amour . . . almost as much as I love France—

He smiled as he wrote

—perhaps even more, but I dare not let myself think of
that now, or I shall forget that I am an old man, and
run to where you are. Godspeed to you and Marie-Ange
and Elisabeth, and my warmest thanks and regards to
your uncle. Your loving husband, Armand.

He signed it with a flourish, as he always did, and on his
way to the office he left it in the usual location. He had

thought briefly of saving it until he left with Moulin, but he decided not to. He knew how anxious she was for letters and how much she worried. He could hear it in the questions she wrote, which still reached him through the censors.

And as he looked up at the calendar above his desk on the opposite wall from the portraits of Pétain and Hitler, he realized that his meeting with Moulin was only three days away. He was frowning as he was deciding what to do next when André Marchand walked into his office with a smile, and an officer of the Reich on each side of him, but neither of them was smiling.

"Monsieur de Villiers?"

"Yes, Marchand?" He didn't recall an appointment with the Germans this morning, but they were always calling him to the Hotel de Ville or the Meurice or the Crillon unexpectedly. He sat where he was and waited. "Am I expected somewhere?"

"Indeed you are, sir." Marchand's smile grew broader. "The gentlemen of the High Command wish to see you this morning."

"Very well." He stood up and picked up his hat. Even in these times he always wore a striped suit and a vest and a homburg, as he had during his years in the diplomatic service. He followed the soldiers outside to the car that had been sent for him. He always went in style, not that he cared. It still turned his stomach to realize what people, whispering "traitor," thought as he drove by.

But today Armand was not ushered in to the usual office. He was led into the office of the military command, and wondered what ugly new project they had for him now. No matter. He smiled to himself. He wouldn't have time to complete it. In three days he was leaving.

"De Villiers?" The German accent in French grated on his nerves as always, but he was concentrating on walking into the office without limping. He was in no way prepared for what came next. Three officers of the SS stood waiting for him. He had been discovered. A collection of evidence was laid out before him, including half-burned scraps of paper he had burned only the day before, and as he looked into the commanding officer's eyes, he knew. He had been betrayed by André Marchand.

"I don't understand . . . these are not—"

"Silence!" the officer roared. "Silence! I will speak and you will listen! You are a French pig, like all of the others, and when we finish with you today, you will squeal just like all the filthy pigs!" But they wanted no information from him at all, they wanted nothing. They wanted only to tell him what they knew, to prove to him the superior mind of the Germans. And when the commanding officer had finished his recital, which was pathetically incomplete, much to Armand's relief—they still knew almost nothing, he thanked God—he was led from the room by the SS. It was only then that he felt a tingle in his spine, that the leg dragged, that he thought of Liane, and Moulin, and he felt a creeping desperation. Before that the adrenaline hadn't been flowing too fast in his veins, but now it flowed faster and his mind whirled, and he reminded himself again and again that it had been worth it. That it was worth giving his life for his country . . . *pour la France* . . . he said it over to himself again and again and again as they tied him to a post in the courtyard outside the office of the High Command. As they shot him he shouted a single word, "Liane!" and the word echoed as he slumped, having died for his country.

Chapter 51

On June 28, 1942, eight German agents were caught by the FBI on Long Island. They had been delivered there by German U-boats, which served to remind everyone how closely the German's hugged the eastern seaboard. Already, since the beginning of 1942, the Germans had sunk 681 ships in the Atlantic, and had lost almost no ships of their own.

"And that is why we've interned the Japanese." Liane's uncle admonished her over breakfast in San Francisco. Only days before she had told him that she thought it was cruel and unnecessary. Their own gardener and his family were interned in one of the camps, and the treatment they were getting was worse than cruel. They had limited food, almost no medical supplies, and lived in quarters that wouldn't decently house animals. "I don't give a damn. If we didn't, the Japanese would be sending agents over here like the Germans, and they'd be getting lost in the crowd just like those eight tried to."

"I don't agree with you, Uncle George."

"Can you say that with Nick over there fighting the Japs?"

"I can. The people in the camps are Americans."

"Nobody knows if they're loyal and we can't afford to take the chance." It was something they had disagreed on before. He wisely decided to change the subject. "Are you working at the hospital today?" She was a full nurse's aide now and had stepped up her schedule from three times a week to five.

"Yes."

"You work too hard." His eyes softened and she smiled. She had been working every moment that she could since she had sent Nick the letter. As had happened after their days on the *Deauville,* she was haunted by thoughts of him again now. But now coupled with her own sense of loss was a sense of terror that her abandoning him would cause him to be careless. She only hoped that his love for his son would remind him to be careful. And she knew she had had no choice. Her first and only duty was still to her husband. She had closed her eyes to it for a time, but that time was over.

"What are you doing today, Uncle George?" She pushed Nick gently from her head as she did a thousand times a day. She had to live with the guilt now, and the fear that perhaps some vague intuition of what she had done had harmed Armand. She had to make up for it now and she was writing to him again every day, although she knew that the letters reached him in clumps, when the censors got around to going over them.

"I'm having lunch with Lou Lawson at my club." His face clouded over then and his voice was husky when he spoke again. "His boy, Lyman, was killed at Midway." Liane looked up. Lyman Lawson had been the attorney her uncle had tried to fix her up with when she'd first arrived in San Francisco.

"I'm sorry to hear that."

"So was I. Lou's taking it very hard. Lyman was his only child."

It reminded her again that Nick was there. But she couldn't allow herself to think of it or she would go mad. Nick was in the Pacific, fighting the Japanese, Armand in France, dealing with the Germans. Her heart was torn from one side of the world to the other. "I have to go to work." It was the only place she got away from it and even there, especially there, the war was ever present. Every day they brought wounded boys back on the troop ships, with their own horrible tales to tell of war in the Pacific. But at least she could help them, she could soothe brows, put compresses on, feed them, hold them, touch them.

"Don't work yourself too hard, Liane."

As she left the house he bemoaned the fact that she wasn't like the other girls, or damn few of them. Most of them spent their time arranging dinner parties for the officers. But no, Liane had to empty bedpans and scrub floors and watch men vomit when they came out of surgery. But as always, he had to admire her for it.

It was two weeks later when she came back to find Armand's letter. He complained of the leg again, and she was worried. And he said something about going to London with Moulin, and now she knew that there was trouble. And for an instant her heart soared . . . if he got out . . . but her hopes died with his next words. "It breaks my heart to be leaving soon with Moulin, but the only thing that cheers me is the knowledge that I will come back shortly, only to fight harder." It was all he thought about now, and she was almost angry as she read through the letter. He was fifty-nine years old. Why couldn't he let them fight the war and come home to her? Why? . . . à la mort et à tout jamais, she read . . . France was his whole life. There had been a time when there had been more than that, much more. And as she sat staring at his letter, she realized that nothing had ever been the same for them again since the moment they'd stepped off the *Normandie*. There had been those agonizing months before the war when he worked himself to the bone, and the tension of the months between September and the fall of Paris when she hadn't known what he was doing. And then she and the girls had left France, leaving Armand to fight his single-handed battle against the Germans, while pretending to collaborate with them. It was almost more than she could bear as she read the letter again and put it down. She was dead tired. She had spent the whole day nursing a boy who had lost his arms in the battle of the Coral Sea. He had been on the *Lexington* with Nick, but he was only a private and hadn't known him.

When she came down to dinner that night, George thought she looked especially tired. She had looked bleak and exhausted for weeks, and he suspected that there was something she wasn't telling him.

"Have you heard from Nick?" In the past she had told him when she got a letter. But she hadn't for a while. She shook her head now.

"I had a letter from Armand this morning. He sounds tired, and his leg is still troubling him." She wanted to tell him the truth then, about Armand, but she'd wait until he was in England.

"What about Nick?" He pressed her again and she flared up at him.

"Armand is my husband, not Nick."

But the old man was tired that night too. He was quick to answer. "You didn't remember that all this spring, did you?" He could have bitten out his tongue, particularly when he saw the stricken look on her face.

She answered him in a barely audible voice. "I should have."

"Liane, I'm sorry . . . I didn't mean—"

She looked at him bleakly. "You're quite right. I was very wrong. It was unfair to Armand and to Nick." And then she sighed. "I wrote to Nick a few weeks ago. We won't be writing to each other anymore."

"But why? The poor man . . ." He was aghast at her news.

"I have no right to, Uncle George, that's why. I'm a married woman."

"But he knew that."

She nodded. "I'm the only one who seems to have forgotten it. I've repaired the damage now, as best I could."

"But what about him?" He was incensed. "What do you think that'll do to him, while he's out there fighting a war?"

Tears stung her eyes. "I can't help that. I have an obligation to my husband."

He wanted to slam his fist into the table, but he didn't dare. The look on her face was one of total desolation. "Liane . . ." But he didn't know what to say. There was nothing he could say to her. And he knew that she was as stubborn as he was.

She left the table and went to work, she seemed to work longer and longer hours every day. And it was a week after she had received the letter from Armand that she came home to find a letter from London, with unfamiliar handwriting. She couldn't imagine who it was and she opened it as she walked slowly up the stairs. Her whole body ached. She had spent the entire day comforting the boy who'd lost his arms. He had a raging fever and there was still a possibility that they might lose him.

And then suddenly she stopped and her eyes froze on the words. *"Chère Madame . . ."* It began like a perfectly normal letter, but after that, the letter went mad.

> I regret to tell you that your husband died shortly after noon yesterday, in the service of his country. He died nobly, a hero's death, having saved hundreds of lives, and many of the treasures of France. His name will be engraved on our hearts and the heart of France, and may your children be proud of their father. We grieve for you in your loss. Your loss is ours. But the greatest loss of all is to his country.

The letter was signed by Moulin and Liane sank slowly onto the top step as she read it again and again but the words did not change. *"Chère Madame . . . I regret to tell you . . . I regret to tell you . . ."* But he lied. The greatest loss of all was not to his country. She crumpled the letter into a ball and threw it across the hall and she began to pound the floor as she cried. He was dead . . . he was dead . . . and he was a fool to have stayed there . . . to fight the Germans . . . to . . . She didn't even hear her uncle calling her name. She heard nothing as she lay on the floor and screamed. He was dead. And Nick would die too. They would all die. And for what? For whom? She looked at her uncle with unseeing eyes as she screamed, "I hate them! . . . I hate them! . . . I HATE THEM!!!"

Chapter 52

$\mathcal{S}$he told the girls that night and they cried when they heard the news, and they talked for a long time when she put them to bed. She had regained her composure, though she was deathly pale. She was so relieved to be able to tell them the truth now. The girls were startled to hear that their father was a double agent, appearing to work for Pétain, and actually working for the Resistance.

"He must have been very brave." Elisabeth looked at her mother sadly.

"He was."

"Why didn't you tell us before?" Marie-Ange was quick to ask.

"Because it would have been dangerous for him."

"Didn't anyone know?"

"Only the people he worked for in the Resistance."

Marie-Ange nodded wisely. "Will we ever go back to France now?"

"One day." But it was a question she herself hadn't yet answered. They had no home anymore, no place to return to after the war, no one to wait for. And she had no husband.

"I didn't like it very much," Elisabeth confessed.

"It was a hard time. Especially for Papa."

The girls nodded and she put them to bed at last. It had been a long night for them all. But she knew that she wouldn't sleep and she didn't want to go to bed. It was strange to realize that he had been dead for three weeks and she hadn't known. She had read his last letter after he had died, and she hadn't even known it. And all he had spoken of was his love for France . . . and for them . . . but for France above all. Perhaps to him it was worth it. But she felt an odd mixture of anger and despair as she walked into the library and sat down. Uncle George was still up, and worried about her.

"Would you like a drink?"

"No, thank you." She leaned back and closed her eyes.

"I'm sorry, Liane." His voice was gentle. He felt so helpless as he watched her. As helpless as she had felt that day as she tended to the boy who'd lost his arms. "Is there anything I can do?"

She opened her eyes slowly. She felt paralyzed and numb. "Not really. It's all over now. We just have to learn to live with it." He nodded, and in spite of himself he thought of Nick, and wondered if she would write to him now.

"How did it happen?" He hadn't dared to ask her before, but she seemed calmer now.

She looked him straight in the eye. "The Germans shot him."

"But why?" He didn't dare add "Wasn't he one of them?"

"Because, Uncle George, Armand was a double agent, working for the Resistance."

He opened his eyes wide and stared at her. "He *what*?"

"He appeared to work for Pétain as a liaison with the Germans, but he'd been feeding information to the Resistance all along. He was the highest-ranking official double agent they had in France. That's why they shot him." There was no pride in her voice, only sorrow.

"Oh, Liane . . ." The things that he had said about Armand came to mind instantly. "But why didn't you tell me?"

"I couldn't tell anyone. *I* wasn't even supposed to know, and for a long time I didn't. He told me just before we left France." She stood up and walked to the window and stared out at the bridge for a long time. "But someone must have known." She turned back to look at her uncle. "The Germans shot him three days before he was to leave for England." She had pieced that much together from his letter and Moulin's. And her uncle came to her now and took her in his arms.

"I'm so very, very sorry."

"Why?" She looked at him strangely. "Because now you know he was on our side? Would you care as much if you still thought he worked for the Germans?" Her eyes were sad and empty.

"I don't know . . ." And then he wondered about something. "Did Nick know?"

"Yes."

He nodded. "What are you going to do now, Liane?" He meant about Nick and she understood him.

"Nothing."

"But surely—" She shook her head.

"That wouldn't be fair to him. He's a human being, not a yo-yo. A few weeks ago I told him it was over, but now that Armand is dead we can dance on his grave? He was my husband, Uncle George. My husband. And I loved him." And then she turned away and her shoulders began to shake, and he came to her, sensing her grief in his very soul. She collapsed in his arms then, sobbing almost as she had on the stairs when she'd first read Moulin's letter. "Oh, Uncle George . . . I killed him . . . he knew . . . he must have . . . about Nick. . . ."

"Liane, stop that!" He held her shoulders firmly with his hands and shook her gently. "You didn't kill him. That's absurd. The man did a very brave thing for his country, but it didn't just happen. He made a choice a long time ago. He knew the risks. He weighed all the dangers and in his own mind it must have been worth it. That had nothing to do with you. A man makes those kinds of decisions for himself, regardless of other people, even the woman he loves. And I think a hell of a lot more of him now than I did before. But the point is that whether you and Nick fell in love or not, the man did what he felt he had to do. You couldn't have stopped him, you couldn't have changed his mind, and you didn't kill him." The wisdom of his words slowly got through to her and she eventually stopped crying.

"Do you think that's true?"

"I know it."

"But what if he suspected? If he heard some change in the tone of my letters—"

"He probably wouldn't have noticed if you'd stopped writing entirely. A man who makes a decision like that, Liane, does it with his entire mind and soul and body. It's rotten luck that he got found out, it's worse than that, it's a tragedy for you and the girls and his country. But you had nothing to do with any of that, and neither did Nick. Don't do that to yourself, Liane. You have to accept it." She told him then about Armand's last letter and the things that he had said, and she admitted that there were even times when she had wondered if he cared about her, or only his country. George nodded and listened to her late into the night until her head began to nod, and at last she fell asleep on the couch, and he brought a blanket from his room and covered her where she sat. She was totally drained and exhausted.

And when she awoke the next morning, she was surprised at where she was, and touched when she saw the blanket. She remembered talking to him until she drifted off, and she had had visions of Nick and Armand, walking arm in arm and stopping to talk to a man she didn't know. She shuddered to think about it now. She sensed that the man was Moulin. And she didn't want to think about Armand. Even if she never saw him again, she wanted Nick to live. He had a life to live and a son to come home to. And then she walked to the window and looked out at the bay.

"And what about us?" she whispered to the memory of Armand. "What about the girls?" She had no answers to her questions as she went upstairs to wake them.

Chapter 53

*I*n July, when Liane received the letter from Moulin, Nick was in the Fiji Islands with Task Force 61, doing a rehearsal for an assault on Guadalcanal. The Japanese had built an airstrip there, and Rear Admiral Fletcher had three carrier groups organizing to take it. And the *Enterprise*, the *Wasp*, and the *Saratoga* were preparing for battle. When the *Lexington* had sunk in the battle of the Coral Sea, Nick had been transferred temporarily onto the *Yorktown*, but within weeks he was moved to the *Enterprise*, to help coordinate marine and naval troops. He was one of the few marines of his rank aboard who was not a pilot. After the Coral Sea, he had been made a Lieutenant Colonel.

On August 6, 1942, the *Enterprise* entered the area of the Solomon Islands and the next day the Marines hit the beaches, and within days the airfield had been claimed and renamed Henderson Field but the battle around Guadalcanal raged on, and the Japanese maintained a strong grip on all but the airfield. The Marines paid a terrible price in the ensuing weeks, but the *Enterprise* held her own, even though she was badly damaged. Nick had been aboard whe_ she took some of her worst blows, and he was ordered stay with her when she went to Hawaii for repairs in e_ September.

Inwardly he raged to have to stay on the aircraft carr_

she went to Hawaii. He wanted to stay on Guadalcanal with the troops, but he was badly needed aboard the crippled carrier. And in Hawaii he cooled his heels at Hickam Base, aching to go back as he listened to the news. The battle at Guadalcanal was taking a tremendous toll and marines were dying on the beaches. But in the five months since he'd left San Francisco, he had seen nothing but action in the Coral Sea, at Midway, and then Guadalcanal, with scarcely a breather between them. It helped him keep his mind off Liane. This was why he had enlisted—to fight for his country. When Liane's letter had reached him, he had been stunned by what she said. The paroxysms of guilt had apparently only struck her after he left and there had been nothing he could do or say. He had begun a dozen answers to her letter and discarded them all. She had made a choice once again, and once again he had no choice but to respect it. And now he had the war to keep his mind off his pain, but every night in his bunk, he would lie awake for hours, thinking of their days in San Francisco. And it was worse once he reached Hawaii. He had nothing to do but sit on the beach and wait for the *Enterprise* to be battle ready again. He wrote long letters to his son, and felt as useless as he had in San Francisco. It was a beautiful summer in Hawaii, but the battles in the South Pacific raged on and he was anxious to get back. To help pass the time, he volunteered at the hospital for a while, and would talk to the men and joke with the nurses. He always seemed a good-humored, pleasant man to the nurses, but he asked none of them out.

"Maybe he doesn't like girls," one of them joked. But they all laughed. He didn't look that type either.

"Maybe he's married," another suggested. She had talked to him for a long time the day before, and she had had the feeling there was a woman on his mind, but he had said very little. It had just been the way he had said "we" that made her realize he hadn't been alone on the mainland before he'd, and she sensed a deep pain somewhere in his soul. A pain no one could touch and no one could heal. Because he wouldn't let anyone near him.

The women talked about him a lot on the base. He was unusually attractive and strangely open about some things. He talked about his son a great deal, a little boy named John, who was eleven. Everyone knew about Johnny.

"Do you know who he is?" a nurse's aide whispered to a nurse one day. "I mean in real life." She was from the hills of Kentucky but she had heard of Burnham Steel. She had put it together from something he had said. And she'd asked around and an officer had told her that she was right. "He's Burnham Steel." The nurse looked skeptical and then shrugged.

"So what? He's still in this war like the rest of us, and his ship sank underneath him." The nurse's aide nodded, but she was longing for a date. She made herself obvious whenever she saw him in the wards, but he talked to her no differently than he did to the others.

"Christ, you can't get near the guy," she complained to a friend.

"Maybe there's someone waiting for him at home." Not that that stopped the others.

It was not unlike the things they said about Liane at the hospital in Oakland.

"You got a boyfriend in the war?" a boy with a gut full of shrapnel asked her one day. They had operated on him three times, and still hadn't removed all the fragments.

"A husband." She smiled.

"The one who was in the Coral Sea?" She had talked to him about that when he first came in, and he knew that she knew a lot about the battle. But a strange look came into her eyes as he asked.

"No. He was in France."

"What's he doing there?" The boy looked confused. It didn't tally up with the rest of what he knew, or what she had said.

"He was fighting the Germans. He was French."

"Oh." The boy looked surprised.

"Where is he now?"

"They killed him."

There was a long silence as he watched her. She was folding a blanket over his legs and she had a gentle touch. But he liked her because she was so pretty. "I'm sorry."

She turned to him with a sad smile. "So am I."

"You got kids?"

"Two little girls."

"Are they as pretty as their mother?" He grinned.

"Much prettier," she answered with a smile, and moved to the next bed. She worked for hours in the wards, smiling, emptying bed pans, holding hands, holding heads while the men threw up. But she rarely told them much about herself. There was nothing to tell. Her life was over.

It was September when her uncle finally asked her out to dinner. It was time for her to stop mourning. But she shook her head. "I don't think so, Uncle George. I have to be at work early tomorrow, and . . ." She didn't want to make excuses. She didn't want to go out. There was nothing she wanted to do, except go to work, and come home at night to be with the girls, and then go to bed.

"It would do you good to get a change of scene. You can't just run back and forth to that hospital every day."

"Why not?" She looked at him with a look that said "Don't touch me."

"Because you're not an old woman, Liane. You may want to act like one, but you're not."

"I'm a widow. It's the same thing."

"The hell it is." She was beginning to remind him of his brother when Liane's mother had died at her birth. But that was crazy. She was thirty-five years old. And she couldn't bury herself with her husband. "Do you know what you look like these days? You're rail thin, your eyes are sunken into your head, your clothes are falling off your back." She laughed at the description and shook her head.

"You sure paint a pretty picture."

"Take a look in the mirror sometime."

"I do my best not to."

"See what I mean. Damn it, girl, stop waving that black flag. You're alive. It's a damn shame he's not, but there are a lot of women in the same shoes as you these days, but they're not sitting around with long faces, acting like they're dead."

"Oh, no?" Her voice had a strange icy ring. "What are they doing, Uncle George? Going to parties?" That's what she had done before. Before Armand had died. And it had been wrong. And she wouldn't do it again. Armand had died. And men were dying all over the world. And she was doing all she could for the ones who lived through it.

"You could go to dinner once in a while. Would that be so bad?"

"I don't want to."

And then he decided to brave the taboo subject again. "Have you heard from Nick?"

"No." The walls went up and froze over.

"Have you written to him?"

"No. And I'm not going to. You've asked me before, now don't ask me again."

"Why not? You could at least tell him Armand died."

"Why?" Fury began to creep into her voice. "What good would it do? I've sent the man away twice. I'm not going to hurt him again."

"Twice?" He looked startled and Liane looked annoyed at herself. But what difference did it make now if he knew.

"The same thing happened when we came over on the *Deauville* together after Paris fell. We fell in love, and I ended it because of Armand."

"I didn't know." She was a strange closemouthed woman in many ways and he marveled at her. So they had had an affair before. He had suspected it, but never been sure of it. "That must have made it much worse for you both when he left here."

She looked into her uncle's eyes. "It did. I can't go through that again, Uncle George, or do it to him. Too much has happened. It's better left like this."

"But you wouldn't have to put him through it again." He didn't want to add that she was free now.

"I don't know if I could live with the guilt of what we did. I still think Armand knew. And even if he didn't, it was wrong. You can't build a life on two mistakes. So if I write to him now, what good would it do? He'd get his hopes up again and maybe I couldn't live up to what he will expect when he comes home. I just can't put him through that for a third time."

"But he must have known how you felt, Liane."

"He did. He always said that he would play by my rules. And my rules were that I was going back to my husband. Some rules." She looked disgusted at herself. She had tormented herself for months. "I don't want to talk about it anymore." She looked away into a forgotten time when there had been two men she loved, and now there were none, or none that she would see again.

"I think you're wrong, Liane. I think Nick knows you better than you know yourself. He could help you through it."

"He'll find someone else. And he has Johnny to come home to."

"And you?" He worried about her a great deal. One of these days she was going to crack from the strain she put herself under.

"I'm happy as I am."

"I don't believe that and neither do you."

"I don't deserve anything else, Uncle George!"

"When are you going to come down off that cross?"

"When I've paid my dues."

"And you don't think you have?" She shook her head. "You've lost a husband you think you betrayed, but you stuck by him till the end. You even gave up a man you loved, and you kept Armand's secret for all those years even though I badgered you to death, and you were practically run out of

Washington, tarred and feathered. Don't you think that's enough? And now you spend your every living breath comforting those men in that surgical ward every day. What else do you want, a hair shirt? Sackcloth and ashes?"

She smiled. "I don't know, Uncle George. Maybe I'll feel better about the world again when the war is over."

"We all will, Liane. These are damn hard times for us all. It's ugly to think about Jews being dragged out of their homes and put in camps, and children being killed in London, and Nazis shooting men like Armand, and ships being sunk, and . . . you could go on forever. But you still have to wake up in the morning with a smile and look out the window and thank God you're alive, and hold a hand out to the people you love." He held a hand out to her and she took it and kissed his fingers.

"I love you, Uncle George." She looked like a girl and he touched the silky blond hair.

"I love you too, Liane. And to tell you the truth, I love that boy. I'd like to see you with him one day. It would be good for you and the girls, and I'm not going to live forever."

"Yes, you will." She smiled again. "You'd better."

"No, I won't. Think about what I said. You owe it to yourself. And to him." But she didn't heed his words, she just went back to the hospital in Oakland every day, killing herself in the wards, and then she'd come home to give whatever she had left to him and her daughters.

And on October 15, the *Enterprise* headed back toward Guadalcanal, with Nick aboard, aching to reenter the battle. The two months in Hawaii had almost driven him crazy.

The *Enterprise* reached Guadalcanal on October 23, and she joined the *Hornet*, with Rear Admiral Thomas Kinkaid in charge now. There were four Japanese aircraft carriers in the area, and they were still attempting to reclaim what was by then Henderson Field, and the Americans were holding their ground.

On October 26, Admiral Halsey, the Naval Commander-in-Chief in the South Pacific, ordered them to attack the Japanese and they did. It was a horrendous fight and the Japanese were stronger than the American troops. They set the *Hornet* ablaze and crippled her until she sank, with thousands of men killed. But despite brutal blows, the *Enterprise* survived. She continued the fight, much to everyone's delight, and in the States everyone sat glued to their radios, listening to the news. And George found Liane sitting there, listening to it too, with a look of terror in her eyes.

"You think he's over there, don't you?"

"I don't know." But her eyes said that she knew it.

He nodded his head grimly. "So do I."

Chapter 54

On the morning of October 27, the *Hornet* was still ablaze and sinking slowly, and the *Enterprise* had taken a series of ferocious hits, but she was still in action. Lieutenant Colonel Burnham was on the bridge watching the crew man the guns when the Japanese hit them with full force; a 550-pound bomb hit their flight deck and passed through the port side, spraying fragments in all directions. And suddenly there were fires everywhere and men were lying all over the deck, either dead or wounded.

"Jesus Christ, did you see that bomb!" The man standing next to him was gaping in disbelief, and Nick ran for the stairs in one leap.

"Never mind that, we're on fire. Get the hoses." Troops from all over the ship were trying to fight the blaze while others manned the guns and continued to spray the Japanese as dive bombers zoomed toward them, dropping bombs. One Japanese pilot crashed on the deck, setting off a ferocious explosion. And then suddenly, as Nick stood holding the hose, he saw two men crawling toward him, and he dragged them out of the fire one by one, spraying water on their clothes to put out the fires that were devouring their flesh. And as he looked down into the face of the second one, there was suddenly an enormous explosion behind him. He had a sensation of sunlight and lightness in his limbs as he flew through the air, watching pieces of bodies. He had the oddest feeling that he was suddenly weightless . . . and as he thought of Liane he knew he was smiling.

Chapter 55

The men continued to pour in from the battle of Guadalcanal all through November. Many of them had been kept at Hickam for a few days first, others had come straight through to Oakland. There were no longer facilities to care for them anywhere else. They had to be kept on ships until they returned to the States, and many of them died on the way. Liane watched them come in day by day, their bodies torn limb from limb, with hideous wounds and burns. And she heard the story of the 550-pound bomb over and over and over.

It was grim work watching them come in, and as she assisted the stretchers coming from the ships, she was once again reminded of the *Deauville*, but this was much worse than anything she'd ever seen then. The men were returning in pieces.

And once she had thought that someone was talking about Nick. The man had been half delirious and he was talking about his buddy who'd been killed beside him on the deck, but when she asked him about it later, the man's name had been Nick Freed. And he wasn't the Nick she knew. And the man died in her arms two days later.

It was the night of Thanksgiving when her uncle finally turned to her, unable to stand it any longer. "Why don't we call the War Office and find out?"

She shook her head. "If something happens to him, we'll

read about it in the papers." It would be worse to know where he was, she would be tempted to write to him and she was determined not to. And if he was wounded, sooner or later she'd know it. And if the head of Burnham Steel had been killed, the papers all over the country would carry items about it. "Let it go, Uncle George. He's all right."

"You don't know that."

"No, I don't." But she had her hands full enough with the men that she knew weren't. She was working twelve-hour shifts now, right alongside the nurses.

"They ought to give you a goddamn medal when this bloody war is over."

She bent and kissed his cheek, smiling, and then she stood up and looked at her watch. "I have to go, Uncle George."

"Now? Where?" They had just finished Thanksgiving dinner and the girls had gone to bed a little while before. It was nine o'clock at night and she hadn't gone out in months.

"We're shorthanded at the base, and I said I'd go back."

"I don't want you driving out there alone."

"I'm a big girl, Uncle George." She patted his arm.

"You're crazy." Crazier than he knew, crazy with fear and longing and aching. Crazy from wondering if Nick was dead. Day after day she listened to the tales, wondering if the dead man beside the man she tended had been Nick, or if he'd even been there at all. There was a constant look of anguish in her eyes. And on Monday morning George Crockett took matters into his own hands and for the second time in a year he called Brett Williams.

"Look, I've got to know."

"So do we." Brett Williams wondered at the old man. He knew who he was or he wouldn't have taken the call. But he wondered why he wanted to know. Maybe he had been a close friend of old man Burnham's. "We haven't heard a thing."

"But you can find out, for chrissake. Call the White House, the State Department, the Pentagon, someone."

"We have. It's such a mess over there that they have very

inaccurate records. Men have drowned, gone down with the *Hornet*, they're in hospitals all over the place. They say it'll be another month or two before they know much more."

"Well, I can't wait that long," the old man growled.

"Why not?" Brett Williams had had enough and they were shouting at each other. For a month now he'd been a nervous wreck not knowing where the hell Nick was. And Johnny had called him too, almost every day. And there was nothing to say to the boy, or this old man on the West Coast. Hillary had even called. She was actually worried that Johnny would lose his father. She was ready to give his son back now. "If we're sitting here, chewing our nails, goddamn it, so can you."

"My niece can't. She'll worry herself to death if we don't find out where he is."

"Your niece?" Brett looked blank. "Who in hell is she?"

"Liane Crockett, that's who." She hadn't been that in thirteen years, but in the heat of the moment he forgot that.

"But—" And then slowly he understood. "I didn't realize before he left. . . . He didn't say anything to me. . . ." He wondered if the old man was telling the truth, and yet knew he had to be. Otherwise, why would he be calling?

"Why the hell should he tell you? Anyway, she was married at the time, but she's a widow now—" He faltered, wondering why he was telling this man, but it was a relief to tell someone. It was killing him to watch Liane dying behind her walls. "Look, we've got to find him." And then he grabbed a notepad and a pen. "Who have you called?" Williams reeled off a list of names. He was beginning to like the old man. He had guts and he obviously cared about his niece, and Nick Burnham. He began trying to think who they could call that they hadn't, and the old man made a number of invaluable suggestions. "Will you do it, or shall I?" He knew full well that it didn't matter. Burnham Steel and Crockett Shipping were equally important.

"Let me give it another try, and I'll call you back."

And two days later Brett did. He didn't have much. Bu

he had something. "He was on the *Enterprise* when she was hit, Mr. Crockett. And apparently he was wounded pretty badly. We don't know much more than that except that he was shipped to Hawaii. And they just found out this morning that he was at Hickam."

"Is he still there?" The old man's hand shook on the phone. They had found him . . . but was he still alive? And how badly had he been wounded?

"They shipped him out last week on the USS *Solace*. It's virtually been turned into a hospital ship, and it's heading for San Francisco. But, Mr. Crockett . . ." He hated to dampen his hopes, but they all had to be realistic, even the unknown niece, maybe most especially she. He didn't realize that she knew nothing of her uncle's inquiry. George had wanted to wait till he had concrete news. "We have no idea at all what condition he's in. He was critical when he got to Hickam and we don't know how he was when he left, and apparently on those ships . . . a lot of them don't make it."

"I know." George Crockett closed his eyes. "We'll just have to pray." He was wondering if he should wait, or if he should tell Liane. But maybe she'd find herself looking into his face at that damn hospital. He opened his eyes then. "How did you find out?"

Brett Williams smiled. "I called the President again and told him you had to know."

"He's a good man." He grinned. "I voted for him in the last election."

Brett Williams smiled. "So did I." But it was a moment of relief in a sobering time.

"Do you know when the ship is scheduled to dock?"

"They weren't sure. Tomorrow or the day after."

"I'll keep an eye on it from here, and as soon as I know something, I'll call you." He hung up and called the Navy after that. The *Solace* was due to come in at roughly six o'clock the next morning. It gave him a lot to think about that afternoon before he saw Liane again. And when she came home at ten o'clock that night, she was pale and exhausted.

He watched her eat a sandwich and drink a cup of tea, and he thought of telling her then, but he just couldn't. What if Nick had died on the ship? And then he thought about it some more. What if he hadn't?

She was still awake when he knocked on her bedroom door an hour later. "Liane? Are you up?"

"Yes, Uncle George. Is something wrong? Don't you feel well?" She was wearing a pale-blue nightgown and she looked very worried.

"No, no, I'm fine, dear. Sit down." He waved her to a chair and sat down on the bed, and she felt an instant chill run through her. She had the feeling that he was going to tell her something she didn't want to know. Her last shred of hope died as she watched him. "I have something I want to say to you, Liane. I don't know if you'll be angry or not." He took a breath and went on. "I called Brett Williams a few days ago."

"Who's that?" And then suddenly she remembered, and she felt her whole body grow stiff. "Yes?" It was like falling down a dark hole and dying as she waited.

"Nick was in Guadalcanal." He tried to tell her quickly. "He was wounded . . . pretty badly, they think. But he was alive at the last report."

"When was that?" She spoke in a whisper.

"Over a week ago."

"Where is he?"

Her uncle watched her eyes as he spoke. She was in pain, but she was alive again. "On a ship coming to San Francisco."

She began to cry softly and he went to her and touched her shoulder.

"Liane . . . he may not make it on the ship. You've seen enough of that to know." She nodded, and looked up at him.

"Do you know which ship he's on?"

He nodded. "The *Solace*. They're coming in at six o'clock tomorrow morning, in Oakland." She sat very still as she closed her eyes and thought. Six o'clock . . . six o'clock . . .

in seven hours it would be all over . . . she would know. . . . She looked up at her uncle again. "We'll find out as soon as they arrive."

"No." Her voice was strong as she shook her head. "No. I want to go down there myself."

"You may not even find him."

"If he's there, I will."

"But, Liane . . ." What if he was dead? He didn't want her to face that alone. And then he had a thought. "I'll go with you." She kissed his cheek softly.

"I want to go alone. I have to." And then she smiled at the memory of Nick's words so long ago. "I'm a strong woman, Uncle George."

"I know that." He smiled through damp eyes. "But that may be too much for you." She shook her head, and a little while later he left the room. And all that night she sat in the dark and watched the clock, and at four thirty she showered and got dressed. She wore a warm coat, and when she left the house at five o'clock, there was a thick fog swirling around her.

Chapter 56

$\mathcal{A}$t five fifteen Liane was on the Bay Bridge and there was not a single car ahead of or behind her. Only two lone trucks in the distance. And the fog lay on the bay and on the bridge overhead. And when she reached the naval base, it was thick on the water. There were ambulances lined up to take the men off the ship, and teams of medics, blowing on their hands to keep them warm. They knew that the ship was already under the Golden Gate Bridge. It wouldn't be much longer. And then she saw a familiar face from the hospital where she worked, a young naval doctor.

"They've got you working down here now, Liane? I think you work harder than I do."

"No. I came to see . . . to find . . ." He saw the look in her eyes and nodded. She was not on duty here. He understood instantly why she stood shivering in the chill morning.

"Do you know where he was?"

"Guadalcanal." And they had seen the results for months, streams of wounded and dead and maimed.

"Do you know how badly he was wounded?" She shook her head and he touched her arm, and then he spoke softly. "We'll patch him up." She nodded, unable to say more, and then she wandered away to watch for the ship. But in the thick fog it was impossible to see anything. And then slowly, in the distance, a light appeared, and a horn sounded, and she noticed a group of women on the dock, waiting tensely. And she looked into the fog again as slowly the lights appeared, and then suddenly the *Solace* came out of the fog, like a vision. Her entire side was painted white with a red cross on it. And Liane stood in the cold, holding her breath. It seemed to take them hours to tie up, and the medics were getting ready. Men moved forward with stretchers and at last she tied up at the dock, and suddenly all was action.

The worst cases were brought off first and suddenly the ambulance sirens screeched into action. It seemed ironic to Liane as she watched. The wounded had drifted across the Pacific for days, and now they were being rushed to a hospital with a siren. But for some, even a moment lost could make the difference between life and death, and knowing that she had no choice, she moved forward and tried to see faces, but some had been blown off, or were hidden, or were so badly burned, they were beyond recognition. Her stomach began to churn as she moved along the dock, waiting, watching. This was different from her hospital work. She was looking for Nick, and each man she looked at counted, each time she braced herself for the worst. And then the young doctor called out to her.

"What's his name?"

She shouted back. "Burnham . . . Nick Burnham!"

"We'll find him." She nodded her thanks and he moved among the injured men, and she moved among others but Nick was nowhere in sight, and then slowly the walking wounded began to come up, and there were shrieks from the small group of women. And men limped forward with tears streaming down their cheeks, and suddenly in the fog she heard a roar, and as they looked up at the decks from the dock, they saw thousands of men hanging there, bandaged and crippled and wounded and maimed, but saluting their homeland with a mighty cheer. And an answering cheer went up from the dock as Liane cried for them and for Nick, and for herself . . . and Armand . . . There were so many who would never come home again. And she wondered now if Nick would be among them. Perhaps the information Uncle George had got was wrong . . . maybe he had died after all . . . or wasn't on the ship . . . or had died in transit. It was an unbearable wait as slowly the men streamed off. It was after seven thirty, and the fog was lifting slowly, and still they came and she hadn't found Nick. Many of the other women had left, and the young doctor still moved as quickly as he could among the stretcher cases as the ambulances traveled back and forth to the hospital. She knew that that morning the surgery would be blazing.

"Nothing yet?" The young doctor stopped next to her for only a moment, and she shook her head. "That may be a good sign. He may walk off yet." Or not at all, she thought to herself. She was chilled to the bone, and numb inside. And then she saw him. He was moving slowly through a group of men, and there were others in front of him. His head was bent, and his hair was long, but she knew him at once, even in the sea of men around him. And she saw as he approached that he was on crutches.

She stood deathly still as she watched, wondering suddenly if she should have come. If it was wrong. If by now he wouldn't want to see her. And as her eyes bore through the crowd he turned to say something to a man on his right, and then he stopped where he was, as he saw her. He moved not at all, nor did she. They just stood there, with the crowd moving steadily past them. And then, as though there were no turning back, she moved slowly toward him, through the men as they jostled her to get home. They were moving more quickly now, and there were still shouts and cheers, and for a moment she lost him, but he was still standing where he had been when the crowd parted again and she began to run, and laugh through her tears, but he bent his head and he began to cry too and he was turning his head from side to side, as though to say no, as though he didn't want to see her. Her steps slowed and she saw, his left leg was gone, and then she ran toward him on the dock, shouting his name. "Nick! Nick!" She flew on and he looked up, with a thousand years in his eyes that hadn't been there before, and then with a sudden lunge he grabbed the crutches and moved toward her and they stood there on the dock as he crushed her to him. They were much the same as they had been before, and very different. A thousand years had passed, and men had died all around them, and the fog lifted slowly over their heads. Nick was home at last and Liane was his now. He had been right long before. Strong people cannot be defeated.

DANIELLE STEEL

☐ CHANGES	11181-1	$4.95
☐ CROSSINGS	11585-X	4.95
☐ FAMILY ALBUM	12434-4	4.95
☐ FULL CIRCLE	12689-4	4.95
☐ LOVE: Poems	15377-8	4.50
☐ LOVING	14657-7	4.95
☐ NOW AND FOREVER	11743-7	4.95
☐ ONCE IN A LIFETIME	16649-7	4.95
☐ PALOMINO	16753-1	4.95
☐ PASSION'S PROMISE	12926-5	4.95
☐ A PERFECT STRANGER	16872-4	4.95
☐ THE PROMISE	17079-6	4.95
☐ REMEMBRANCE	17370-1	4.95
☐ THE RING	17392-2	4.95
☐ SEASON OF PASSION	17704-9	4.95
☐ SECRETS	17648-4	4.95
☐ SUMMER'S END	18405-3	4.95
☐ THURSTON HOUSE	18532-7	4.95
☐ TO LOVE AGAIN	18656-0	4.95
☐ WANDERLUST	19361-3	4.95

At your local bookstore or use this handy coupon for ordering:

DELL READERS SERVICE, DEPT. DDS
P.O. Box 5057, Des Plaines, IL 60017-5057

Please send me the above title(s). I am enclosing $_____ (Please add $1.50 per order to cover shipping and handling.) Send check or money order — no cash or C.O.D.s please.

Ms./Mrs./Mr._____

Address_____

City/State_____ Zip_____

DDS—11/87

Prices and availability subject to change without notice. Please allow four to six weeks for delivery.
This offer expires 5/88

Special Offer
Buy a Dell Book
For only 50¢.

Now you can have Dell's Readers
Service Listing filled with hundreds
of titles. Plus, take advantage of our
unique and exciting bonus book offer
which gives you the opportunity to
purchase a Dell book for *only 50¢*.
Here's how!

Just order any five books at the
regular price. Then choose any other
single book listed (up to $5.95 value)
for just 50¢. Use the coupon below
to send for Dell's Readers Service
Listing of titles today!

DELL READERS SERVICE LISTING
P.O. Box 1045, South Holland, IL. 60473

Ms./Mrs./Mr. _____

Address _____

City/State_____ Zip _____

DFCA - 11/87